Boyd County Public Library

D0330757

e and

CLONING
CHRIST

CLONING
CHRIST

A Challenge
Of
Science and Faith

By

Peter Senese

With

Robert Geis

★

★ ★ ★

★

Orion Publishing & Media, Inc.

Books By Peter Senese

War On Wall Street
Tax Magic
*Raw Energy**
*In Their Own Words**

Books By Robert Geis

Personal Existence after Death
*The Street**

* *2003 Forthcoming*

F
SEN
02-24-03 lug 25.95 c.1

Author's Note

As scientists unlock the mysteries of the human body, genomic researchers continue to provide a significant impact on society's medical wellness. Expected advances in the field of genetic research will clearly provide greater opportunity to combat degenerative, harmful diseases and, very possibly, eliminate dangerous genetic strains. Without question, genetic treatment developed to fight disease is modern medicine's new frontier, one with endless possibilities and responsibilities.

The challenges we face in accepting the discoveries of science and relating them to our own individual theological beliefs has challenged mankind since our creation. However, with our growing ability to understand the science of genetics, we now face a challenge so immense it prods the very nature of creation: the use of genetic cloning to enhance our individual lives.

In writing *Cloning Christ*, Robert Geis and I have attempted to challenge you to think through the many issues genetic science posses on various perspectives of *faith*, while providing you with an entertaining theological thriller based upon very real possibilities.

PETER SENESE

To All First Responders,
Your Courage Exemplifies What Is Right In This World.

This book is a work of fiction. The authors have created the names, places, characters, and incidents or have fictionalized them for the purpose of telling a fiction story. Any resemblance to actual persons, living or dead, business establishments, events, public opinions, or locations is coincidental.

Cloning Christ. Copyright (C) by Peter Senese with Robert Geis. All rights reserved. No part of this book may be used or reproduced in any manner whatsoever without written permission except in the case of brief quotations embodied in critical articles and reviews without the permission of Orion Publishing & Media.

Orion Publishing & Media, New York, New York

Copyright © Orion Publishing & Media 2002

All rights reserved

Senese, Peter, 1965 -

Geis, Robert, 1959 -

Cloning Christ/ Created by Peter Senese

Cloning Christ / Peter Senese with Robert Geis - 1st edition

0-9710826-4-2

www.cloningchrist.com

Jacket Design: The genetic sequence appearing on the novel's jacket was specifically designed not to coincide with accepted genetic sequence codes. After all, does anyone know if God has a genetic sequence code? Jacket concept and design by Scott Schiendler.

Acknowledgements

There are many individuals who have been
influential in the creation of this work.
In no particular order, we would like to share
our appreciation to the following:
My dear son Tyler, you are my world.
Kara, loving faith is endless.
Barbara, Peter, John, James, Maria, Ida,
and *John A.,* as always, thank you.
Anna Lea, Brian, and Michael,
In Friendship.
Ron, Joel, Frank and Ed: Thank you,
L.L. N., Celedonio, and our dear Marty,
formative influences before a word of this
book was written.
Scott, many thanks for so many things.
Brad,
your sense of drama and the literary art is hard to match.

Prologue

A light breeze captured Helen Baum's long blonde hair and play-fully lifted it in a manner any observant eye would be pleased to see, and this was true of those unpitying eyes gazing at her as she entered the crowded café in Jerusalem's Armenian quarter.

Her emerald green eyes innocently sparkled in search of her eclectic group of colleagues whom she had befriended at the university.

"Helen, over here," eagerly waved Ahmed.

Moments later she joined the seated group of diverse, good-natured young adults.

A handsome waiter came over to the table and asked her what she would like to drink.

Without warning, a fiery ball of hatred exploded from with-in the everyday student hangout, its brutal force annihilating almost everyone inside.

Helen's body was catapulted through a large, shattered win-dow and onto the debris filled city street. Mangled, the right side of her face cruelly slammed the hardened pavement, instantly fractur-ing her skull. As blood oozed out of her mouth, nose and ears, the light began to fade.

Darkness began to cover her.

Her eyes flickering, she saw the devastation of the latest ter-rorist attack. Again one that made no sense, for these were students of every religious belief eating and drinking together and somehow searching for peace.

Her lungs struggled for air as she tried to fight off the mounting darkness, a fight she was quickly losing. Her eyes sud-denly closed forever.

Another day in the Holy Land.

Chapter I

The sweltering Jerusalem heat emitted by the sun's glaring rays had little bearing on his lean frame. Internally, his heart pounded faster as nervous energy swooned through his taut body, causing his senses to intensify. Hot dust-laden dry air filled his lungs while determined brown eyes carefully roamed the Holy Land's war torn limestone hilltop. Apprehension covered him, but it would not prevent him from re-entering the recently discovered ancient cave nearby.

Introspectively, his fears were a blessing, if there was such a thing as divine disquietude, since anxiety acted as a catalyst that provoked him to expand his world.

He was lured to the unknown waiting for him somewhere in the man-made tomb that he discovered in the altered hillside the way a moth is attracted to light. Uncertainties were a common part of his world, not in the normal sense of human life, but for that which based itself on sustainable chaos. Without question, chaos was the common thread that ran deep through his veins, connecting the physical with the metaphysical.

Around him, his makeshift crew of two graduate students, both with a passionate interest in archeology, unknowingly prepared for another extraordinary day of field excavation the way they had the previous day. Though he went about his business in a mundane manner, Max sensed this day would be anything but ordinary. This silent premonition caused beads of sweat to freely cascade down his brow and cover his entire body in saltine moisture.

Motionless eyes stayed riveted on the small cave entrance as his tense muscles contracted heavily. For the first time in over a decade a dark shroud of apprehension he could not fend off was hazily draping his conscience, pulling him back into a past he tried desperately to forget.

Let it go! Stop it! Don't do this to yourself!

A bead of sweat pooled at the cleave of his upper lip until it fell onto his sun swollen bottom lip. The salty droplet was as tasteless as the brutal environment from where he stood.

Closing his eyes in an attempt to gain his composure, an image of a white moth climbing to a brilliant unidentified light captured his imagination.

1

The image was a familiar one.

Higher the moth flew - ecstatically flickering its wings towards eternal grace, and then it suddenly disappeared into silent, unforgiving darkness.

Death.

"Max, you seem preoccupied," said Lynn Johnson, one of Doctor Max Train's graduate students from Syracuse University who was visiting Jerusalem with the middle-aged Professor.

Max slowly opened his eyes but stayed motionless.

"Max?"

"Huh?"

"Are you all right?"

Turning toward the student, "I was just thinking about today's tasks," he replied, recovering from the painful nostalgia he momentarily reflected on. Rapid sonorous beats of turmoil and uncertainty pulsed in his head to near unimaginable proportions as the potential ramifications perpending if what he expected to discover was to come true overtook him.

Max looked back into the high afternoon sun and visualized the white moth dancing and climbing higher towards its own unknown. The further the moth ascended, the more tumultuous the pounding in his head became. Where the moth was ascending to, Max had no idea. Neither did he know why he was enraptured with the cave waiting in front of him, regardless of what may be waiting inside.

"We sure have a lot to do," said Lynn, not aware of Max's introspection.

Train stared into the foothills, saying nothing back.

"Max?"

"Max?" she repeated louder.

"I think we're getting close," he voiced underneath his breath before directing his brown eyes on her. "We'd better get started," he continued as he ran his fingers through his wavy brown hair. "You're right, we do have a lot to do."

"I'm going to get our gear," she nodded before turning to walk back to the old, beaten down green Ford pick-up truck located fifty meters from where they stood.

Max quickly gazed at her as she left before turning his attention to the cave's diminutive entranceway. His thoughts raced back to the mounting internal struggle rising within him. These intimate spiritual conflicts manifested themselves ever since he decided to move ahead and allow his mind to imagine endless possibilities. So overwhelming and limitless were his surfacing thoughts that it precluded him from sharing this possible discovery. It was clearly unnerving him. Still, there was something more powerful than fear that provided him with the resolve to continue his quest.

Breathing heavily, Train took notice of the historic, reveled landscape surrounding him.

For man, at least for Western civilization, all that was good and bad about human nature originated from action and reaction in the place many diverse followers of dogma called the Holy Land. It was here, in this desert landscape, that many faithful believers throughout the world held the greatest event in man's history occurred. For most of these individuals, this historical site possessed great spiritual significance and meaning, but Max Train knew how to keep a cautious distance from anything accepting of a higher element.

Fate's purpose brutally devoured his faith, leaving only skeptic eyes of brown for sight. There was no understanding, only deep emotional and spiritual scars.

Looking to his right, Max saw in the distance a sandstone wall built nearly eighteen hundred years ago by the Romans. It encompassed the perimeter of King David's city venerated by hundreds of millions of faithful followers. A domed edifice was visible from where he stood, close to the Mount of Olives. As the faithful foreign visitors made their way down the fabled Souk El-Dabbagha the expansive ringing from the bell tower of the century old Lutheran Church of the Redeemer in Jerusalem's Christian Quarter signaled the Holy Land survived yet another fleeting hour where believers of all faiths came together. Yet which very same believers had waged war on one another for thousands of years — a trait unfortunately not lost today.

Located in the epicenter of this town was the Basilica of the Holy Sepulchre. First constructed in the fourth century by the Emperor Constantine at the urging of his mother, Helen, whom the son was to one-day name *nobillisima femina*, it was now revered by all who *believed*. 'Midst battles, fires and earthquakes the shrine stood through time rebuilt and fortified as the memorial of the site where Jesus Christ was sent to his death, only to rise, the faithful held, three days later.

Subconsciously, Max glared down at his wedding ring and

with his right index finger gently touched the weathered golden band. His body immediately tensed.

Max Train was once a devout *believer*, but that was a long time ago.

As a young man his intrigue with unknowns led him into the world of science, where pragmatism and rationale overshadowed dogmatic grails. But Max was a rare breed: a brilliant biochemist by training and a leader in the field of gene research who never swayed from his faith in God's existence or the Holy Scriptures.

But things were different now.

The end of this month marked the twelfth year anniversary in which his world changed forever.

While working late one night on a new genetic coding technique he was developing in his laboratory at Syracuse University, someone broke into the home where Max's wife and autistic young daughter slept. The savage brutality of his family's murder made no sense to anyone. Not to the police, not to any friends or family members, not to the press, and especially not to Max.

Till this day the savage murders went unsolved despite every conceivable effort by law enforcement officials to determine who was behind the hideous crimes.

In the early years of the investigation, and after very little tangible progress, the local authorities, embarrassed by the lack of an arrest, needed a scapegoat.

Max Train became that person.

Max was considered the primary suspect for the murder of his own wife and daughter. He woke every day knowing the two people he loved more than life itself were gone and that he was still the police's main suspect. The fact Max had witnesses stating he was with them at the Syracuse labs the entire night of the murders didn't matter. The time of death could not be accurately specified, which made Max's alibi suspicious.

The catalyst perpetuating his living hell, outside of the obvious death of his family, could be clearly attributed to the salivating press which had made the local police look foolish, and so Max Train became the local law enforcement officials' temporary solution to their embarrassment.

It did not matter to the police, and for that matter, most of his colleagues at the University that Max was suffering through this hellacious ordeal – a living undiluted hell that placed guilt on his head regardless of his presumed innocence. The truth was Max Train was an innocent victim. He did not kill or orchestrate the murder of his family, but at the time of the murders there were no other suspects that made any sense to the police.

Nine years ago the arrest came. So too did the cameras and the press. A sensationalized trial that perversely entertained the public ensued. Max was found innocent, but the pain of his loss had no bearing on the victory of his innocence. Yet in and despite his innocence, public perception never extended a gentle hand. For Max, perception received was reality lived: someone unknown had killed his family.

The reason why, over a decade later, was still not known to him.

Perhaps the ugliness that continued to show was due to the law enforcement officials' discard of the idea that a burglary had gone wrong, due in part to the savage body wounds sustained by Max's wife and daughter. A theft did in fact occur in the young couple's home that night, but with little material possessions missing, the notion of the burglary being the primary criminal intent was less than plausible.

It was commonly asked by the entire central New York community why would a burglar have any reason to physically mutilate the bodies of a mother and daughter sleeping at home? No, whoever did this, the police held, had cruel intentions.

Ironically, the law enforcement community, to this day, had one lead that made sense: Max Train - a tried man judged innocent - still the scorn of the local police.

Luckily for Max, double jeopardy was not fair game.

Max's innocence did not matter to the general public, whose opinions were manipulated by a zealot-like press eager to sensationalize the unfortunate tragedy, while attempting to mock the legal system which Train and his high priced legal team allegedly manipulated.

For the blue-collar community, the perception was Max bought his innocence.

For the public at large, this was intolerable—they let it be known.

Max Train was a headliner. He was "copy" – and he was ostracized without any credible evidence or material fact.

The fact he was proven innocent did not matter. As much as society was forgiving, Max never publicly claimed accountability for his family's deaths, and the continual harsh suspicions he felt from his neighbors was near relentless.

The fact that after supper on the evening of the murders Max decided to go to his laboratory to continue his genetic research project did not matter. Nor did it matter his wife and child were seen out publicly at a local grocery store two hours after he arrived at his lab, where he stayed until 6:00 a.m. before returning home to find the bludgeoning which prevented the police from formally charging him.

Unfortunately for Max, the shadows of doubt were already cast. Like most issues about which reporters wrote to fuel circulation sales, without any major public retractions, guilt and condemnation even for the innocent were cast in stone.

The faculty leadership at Syracuse University, for the most part, wanted the tenured Doctor Train to take an extended sabbatical during his living nightmare. However, faced with Max's innocence, they were hard pressed to force his early retirement.

Over the passing years Max's resiliency and immunity to public opinion increased, and though the rumors periodically sprouted that the police were about to re-open the cold-case file of the mysterious murders of his family members, nothing ever came of it, and nothing ever would. He already had his trial.

The lack of true closure, where cold voids of darkness only the innocent could feel, eroded away at his spirit. Similar to those who suffered devastating losses or pain, Max could not come close to understanding why his God — the same God of Abraham — the God of Isaac — the God of Jacob — and the Father of Jesus — would have permitted something forged from the bowels of Hell to be directed at his wife and daughter, not to mention himself. Tidal waves of betrayal continually pounded away at his believing, faithful soul until the forces of its brutality and rage swept away any resemblance for connectivity to his faith and belief in a Higher Being.

Periodically, Max heard condescending words laced with disgust aimed at him. Their words did not matter to him, for the deep spiritual wounds and brutal psychological scars left on a once innocent, cerebral man had left its cruel effects, which included a substantial emotionless, subconscious wall. In many ways, he became a skeleton of the man he once was: now faithless and ascetic but for two interest: science and history.

Love? It would have been easier to knock down a granite

wall than for Max to show his heart again.

The sun's brilliant rays assaulted his straining eyes as he picked up a small pick and wearily approached the cave.

In itself, this cave was a new discovery barely visible to the common eye.

The previous day a small earthquake in the environs of Calvary, the crucifixion and burial site of Jesus Christ, shifted the limestone mountainside five hundred meters west of the town's walls, and out of nowhere a cave's tiny entranceway appeared. By chance, Train and his graduate students were in the immediate area at the time and discovered the opening. Aware the war-savaged Holy Land was looking for any antagonistic reason to break the short-lived peace, Max, with the students' aid, intentionally concealed the cave after first exploring the cave's accessible chamber.

What he discovered was highly unusual: a man-made tomb apparently hidden from time now revealed by nature's intent. Surreptitious field research indicated that an initial earthquake covered the hidden tomb, and a second earthquake, now these two thousand years later, unveiled it.

Removing the stones he placed in front of the cave's mouth, Max entered the stark, low-hanging cave illuminated with dull portable lights. Focusing on a small crevice no wider than eight inches and located forty feet from the entranceway, he approached the small corridor blocking a subterranean passageway.

An unexpected hollow breeze swept by. Max knew there was only one conclusion where the cool wind came from: behind the blocked entranceway to the second chamber – the same chamber he intended to enter today.

Removing a flashlight from his side, he walked over to the chamber. *What is in there?*

The cave's fragile slate rooftop could easily crumble on him if he were not careful. A miscalculation and he would instantly bury himself and anyone else inside the chamber.

These physical dangers were not the only concerns on Max's mind.

The *whoosh* of rushing air colliding into the limestone wall caused an eerie sound.

Doctor Luke Gartner, twenty-four hours off a plane, quietly entered the cave. Luke was a friend and a fellow scientist, and now a member of The Holy See's Scientific Advisory Board. Max and Luke previously worked together at Syracuse, where they developed a strong friendship, before Luke accepted the offer by The Holy See to participate in its Scientific Advisory Board, which he now oversaw. He was the only person whom Max trusted in this world - a trust demonstrated time and again by his old friend. In fact, during their time at Syracuse together, the two scientists formed a successful business partnership to commercially exploit opportunities in the genetic coding research they were conducting.

Unfortunately, Max's arrest changed everything, including Luke's own future—and fortunes.

Their company, Genetech, did in fact own certain embryonic scientific discoveries related to human gene coding. These discoveries, though in the early stage of genetics, were valuable assets, and eventually became the basis for most genetic science and research conducted today.

As Max's legal bills mounted into hundreds of thousands of dollars, the need to sell the technology they mutually owned in order to pay Max's legal defense became necessary.

It was Luke who found an obscure biotechnology company based in Northern Italy willing to purchase their business. Though the sum, in comparison to other current economic times was pale, it did provide Max with barely enough funds to mount his legal defense.

Driven by friendship, Luke never took his fifty percent share of the profits obtained from the company's sale, citing the need for Max's need of funds to clear his name. Nor did Luke mention to Max the act of kindness demonstrated. When Max mentioned his intent to repay Luke, Luke continually told him their friendship meant more than any monies, and so Max should "stop insulting him."

The previous morning, Max contacted his trusted friend and shared with him the news of the discovered cave at the site of Calvary, Latin for the Aramaic "Golgotha"—"place of the skull" – where Jesus of Nazareth was executed, and the location where the Christian world believed the most holy event in creation occurred: The Death and Resurrection of Jesus Christ. Luke took the first available flight from Rome to Tel Aviv.

"I see you're figuring out how to expand that passageway," said Gartner as he moved his heavyset frame into the chamber where Max studied the vertical stones forming an obstructive wedge to the second chamber.

"Something like that," Max replied without turning. "This

isn't going to be easy. The rock formations don't appear secure. Probably can come down on us if we sneeze."

"Well, don't sneeze. But you're right, the ceiling looks weak," Luke observed standing next to Max. "I think we should build a support structure to protect us."

"I think I can get in there."

"You sure?"

"Pretty sure. Remember, we don't have much time. Sooner or later the locals are going to start wandering around."

"And then we're out of here," Luke responded, aware Max had not informed the Israeli government of his unexpected dig. "Let's be quick, but careful."

"If I chip three inches off either side of these stones, I can squeeze through."

"Well, at least one of us can," Luke amusingly joked. "The last time I could have fit through a crevice this small was when I was nine."

Max turned to his old friend with an amused smile, "Rome has been good to you. Maybe too good?"

"Maybe," he grinned.

"Do you think these walls will support the ceiling's weight?" Max seriously asked.

"I'm not sure."

"Any ideas?"

"Build support beams –"

"—before you go any further, I know what you're about to say."

"But it's dangerous."

"Don't worry about it. I'm going in alone. We don't have much time before the locals start arriving. Besides, if you get hurt, your lovely wife Eileen will have my head. If something happens to me...well, I have no one to go back to," Max's voice lowered.

"Nonsense, Max. I keep telling you it's time to move on. You have your whole life ahead of you."

"Do me a favor, and tell everyone not to come in here until I tell them it's safe."

"Do you need anything else?" he asked skeptically, knowing it was useless to argue with his old friend.

"No."

Luke nodded, his blonde hair falling across his eyes. "Call if you need any help," he offered while turning to exit the cave.

"I'll be right outside. Be careful."

Max was already focusing on the stone's grain, determining how to chisel away at the thick boulders. Holding a hammer, he skillfully began to pound at the limestone. With every precise blow, he felt as if his heart was going to jump out of his skin. He was moving closer to the unknown, closer to the light, and closer to a potential uncertainty the world was not equipped to face. This was a world of great familiarity: a world of uncertainty.

The hammer struck the chisel, causing a large stone slab to fall to the floor. *If it is possible—*

Another blow. *It must be considered.*

The chisel split the stone again. *The world has great needs.*

Another hardened blow. *And everything to gain if it can be done.*

Another. *Do you really exist?*

Another. *I thought you did - once!*

Again the hammer came down. *But if you do, why have you disappeared?*

Again. *Why did you allow it to be done?*

Stones continued to crumble down to the floor. *Do you remember me?*

Harder. *Do you remember them?*

The hammer hit its mark again. *It must be considered.*

Again. *If it is true?*

He felt his arm burning as he came down on the stone. *Is there really any other choice?*

One careful blow after another, Max began to open a crevice wide enough to slip through. Moving the chisel over his head, he started to chip away at the formations above him. Suddenly, a part of the cave's ceiling began to crumble around him, covering Max in small debris. Locked in, Max was set on entering the second chamber and paid no attention to the falling debris. *It must be considered.*

"Max, are you okay?" screamed Luke from outside the cave's opening, alarmed that Train might have been injured.

The sound of small stones falling combined with Luke's echoing voice reverberated around its entrance, but Max continued hammering away.

"Max!" Luke roared again as he began to move towards the opening.

"I'm fine, but the ceiling is unstable!"

"Get out of there!" Luke screamed.

"Not yet. I think it will stabilize. Stay out."

"What are you doing?" Luke asked, aware of the dangerous position Max was in.

"Trying to secure the outer wall leading into the second chamber," he replied as stones continued to fall on his shoulders.

"I'm coming in!" Gartner screamed.

"It's not safe. Stay out!"

A loud sound of falling rocks in the cave provided Luke with all the incentive he required. "Max, are you hurt?"

"No," he replied, standing inside the cavern's second chamber, "but stay out of here, it's unstable!"

Moments later a thunderous roar filled the cavern as falling rocks hurtled down the cave's entranceway, blockading Max's colleagues from entering.

Focused on exploring the second chamber, Max paid no attention to the fact he was trapped inside.

Pointing the flashlight towards the floor, one excitable step after another followed, as the pull of the unknown lured him deeper into the mountainside.

Moments later Max entered a confined antechamber approximately six meters by seven meters located deep in the earth. The room was cool and odorless, and appeared to have been preserved from time. He scanned the granular silica walls in search of any openings or calligraphy. There were neither. Nor were there any footprints or visible impressions on the sand floor.

Max's muscles tensed. *Where am I?*

Light sprayed over what appeared to be a wide wooden board partially uncovered by the untouched, undisturbed sand floor. Curiously, he approached the plank. The board appeared nearly two inches thick.

A cross?

Crouching down, he began to carefully remove the sand from the surface of the wood. As his hands meticulously pushed aside the earth in order to uncover the wood, he realized the plank reached almost nine feet in length and nearly a foot in width. Both of its ends were shattered. Another wooden board ran horizontally across it. The two planks were joined by four barbaric six inch long rusted iron nails, razor sharp edges still obvious. One end of the horizontal boards was two feet long. The other nearly five feet across. At the long end of the horizontal beam a thick rope was nailed to the back of the board. In the same area of the rope were four sizeable holes. They were seemingly formed by additional nails that had been removed. After carefully inspecting the secured rope, Max realized it was some type of support brace.

Looking down at the rope, he noticed several dark stains and strands of hair. *Blood? There? God—the holes, the nails, the stains – a man's wrist was staked into the damn board! Jeez!*

This can't be. No, no! The Cross they crucified Christ on? Helen, mother of Constantine—she found it. Right? Could this cross be from one of the thousands of crucifixions at the Fall of Jerusalem in 70 AD? Or maybe... you're near the Mount of Olives. There are those who say this is where the Cross actually ended up...No.

His eyes closed in great trepidation. The one thing his mind was hoping to discover was also the one item his heart was not pre-pared to accept. Emotions of every sort rushed at him at once, over-whelming his every sense.

Memories of his wife Lisa flooded his mind. The love he held for her momentarily brought him back to a time when he open-ly loved. A time when he knew peace.

Reflecting in their love, Max's hardened spirit began to thaw and a sense of tranquility touched his embroiled soul. He recalled holding her fair body next to his the day she informed him they were having a child. He also recalled his daughter Anna's birth, and how the sun's godly rays shown bright the day she was born.

Without warning the heavenly light Max visualized began to fade until the stark, twisted nightmarish memories of how he dis-covered the massacred bodies of his family lying mutilated in their respective beds swarmed over him in frigid blackness. His body tightened, ready to attack, as his mouth gnarled shut. Feelings of betrayal once again overcame him.

Who died here, and why?

Crouching over, tears swelled, but he fought them back as the pain he felt was too much to take. Pain so deep and spiritless only a devout *believer* who believed God betrayed him could feel; so angry, so cold, so alone— so very alone—so meaningless.

"Why! Why did you let this happen?" he screamed aloud, the tears now freely falling, as he raised his arms defiantly towards the darkness. "They were my life – and you took them from me!" he wrenched in pain. "You say you're a kind, loving God! But you're not! You didn't have to take them! They had everything... everything to live for! But it didn't matter to you! I didn't matter to you!" his voice echoed. "You say you're a loving God— a kind God! Some loving God you turned out to be, letting my family get hacked to death by a butcher's hand! If you're all so powerful you could have stopped them — but no — no, you didn't! And they believed in you! You let it happen! You—you— butcher!"

Inevitably, Max, exhausted from his painful outcry, gradually composed himself and began to study the cross, looking for any written markings.

Focusing his eyes two feet above the horizontal board where the vertical beam split, his body tensed as he suddenly noticed nailed to the board a small piece of wood, chalky grayish in color, with the faint outlines of some lettering. The piece looked to be no different in shape or thickness than a standard motorcycle license plate. The right portion was quite splintered. He recognized a line of what he was sure were letters similar to ancient Greek.

He slowly rose to get a clearer view. Slowly. His eyes squinted. *What is that letter? These letters seem to be reversed. Is this wood painted? How black at spots the lettering appears. Is that letter beginning the Greek word for king? That letter, does it begin the word for...? No, it can't be. No.*

His heart was pounding. His fingers moved unevenly across the worn lettered tablet.

Is it?

He took a deep breath. Every one of his senses was magnified in a way he never experienced; yet he felt a sense of tranquility overcoming him. *This can't be possible.* Bowing down to the cross tears fell from his face — tears of joy, tears of pain and suffering, tears of reverence, and tears of relief. *I . . . I . . . God! There have been rumors of the Cross-, but this*— "I have abandoned you when I needed you most. I . . . I turned my back from you and claimed you didn't exist in order to ease my pain. I loved them so much, and was unable to understand why you would take them from me. They, we, had so much to live for. All my life . . . I was devoted to you . . . and you could have prevented them from dying. Why . . . why didn't you stop them? Why? They were so innocent. They were my life. God, I miss my wife and my little girl. Why did this happen?" he uncontrollably wept in the darkness of the empty chamber. "Why us? Why us?"

Alone in the cave he continued to weep and ask God why his family was taken from him. Though given no answer, Max was unknowingly taking the first step in *believing* again.

Outside the cave, Luke and the two students desperately tried to remove the fallen stones that entrapped Max, not knowing if he was alive or dead.

Little could they imagine how alive Max was.

Oblivious to the rescue attempt, Max sat cross-legged, his face moist with tears, as his fingers continued to run over the cross – the cross he realized very well could be the actual Cross Jesus of Nazareth was murdered on.

With every stroke of his fingers on the ancient cross, Max felt further removed from himself. The image of the moth appeared again – climbing and dancing towards a higher light. As the moth joyfully ascended, Max felt as if it was carrying his own spirit closer to the all-powerful Creator. This time, as opposed to past visualizations, the moth did not disappear, but alightingly continued to ascend, elevating Max's soul.

It was at this moment of understanding when Max Train, a battered and bruised man tested by one of the most inconceivable hardships the world could throw at him, felt mystic joy. Before him and in his hands could possibly be the bodily remains of the Infinite God.

It was here, in a dark chamber deep in the limestone foothills of Calvary that a believer was reborn.

Chapter II

Two hours passed sitting in the hallowed cave deep in orison and contemplation while his friends continued their rescue efforts. Max wondered what to do. His scientific training told him the wooden cross and tablet, along with the stained adjoining rope and rusted nails needed to be independently analyzed by a group of objective scientists; however, he also realized his friend and colleague for many years, Doctor Luke Gartner, would try to claim the Cross on behalf of the Church in Rome if he became aware of its existence.

Weighing heavily on Max's decision were past stories of scientists who submitted discovered antiquities to The Holy See, only to have them disappear without proper explanation. His complex dilemmas, as Max perceived it, included *who* was actually crucified on the cross, and, *who* should be responsible for verifying its authenticity.

Feeling the colossal burden caused by his unexpected discovery, he pondered what to do. Not lost on him was how the Vatican handled the scientific analysis conducted on The Holy Shroud of Turin, and the Catholic Church's rejection of arguments on the cloth's coated layer that may have preserved the actual linen, thus allowing for possible miscalculations of the carbon-14 testing to occur. From his scientific perspective, Max did not fully object to the dating of the Shroud to *circa* the twelfth or thirteenth century. However, he did have a major problem with how Rome handled the testing methods used to determine the effects of fire and heat on the Shroud weave.

He was aware Rome frowned upon research not conducted by their own appointed scientist – which he was not, and in all likelihood, would never be. He also wondered how Rome would react to his discovery, if indeed what he unearthed were the true Holy Cross of Jesus. How would anyone, himself included, account for the Greek markings located on the *titulus*, the small tablet fastened on the cross beam, with letters that appeared possibly to say 'KING OF'? He knew the Church's *tradition* that pieces of the Holy Cross were spread across the world, including places such as Constantinople, Rome, St. Louis, and Ghent. There was also the tradition of Emperor Heraclius who is said to have rescued the True

Cross from the Persians, and the Church's September 14th feast day commemorating it. Would Rome be willing to accept that he may have discovered the True Cross of Jesus? Would they be willing to say for two thousand years they were mistaken—something seldom done? If the Vatican accepted the unearthed cross, then Rome, and for that matter, the rest of the world would be required to amend their history books – something he knew in all likelihood would not be done in his lifetime.

The fact Rome more likely would initially deny the authenticity and credibility of the discovered cross, even if uncorrupted scientific data showed unequivocally this was the true Holy Cross of Jesus, provided Max with the foundation for the plan developing in his mind. The more he thought about it, the more he realized it was his responsibility to assemble an unbiased team of scientists among which would include theologians from the Christian, Jewish, and Islamic faiths capable of determining how old the Cross was, and if at all possible, who was actually crucified on it.

These were the least of his present concerns. Paramount was the physical characteristic of the cross. There appeared to be human remains of the cross. Did not Jesus Christ's body ascend to Heaven? Or, was the intent of Scripture to tell of Jesus' spiritual body only? What would the world think if physical remnants of Jesus' body were found? Would he be the Christ?

Feeling the drain of the heavy burden, Max decided to wait a day before sharing the news of his historic discovery with his associates. He needed time to think things through despite his deep friendship with Luke.

"I can't believe it took you so long."

"Well, I can't believe you're alive."

Max smiled apprehensively at his former colleague.

"We were sure you were going to be crushed," said John Muir, another of Max Train's students.

"If I was a betting man, I would've bet against me coming out of that cave alive, too."

"Max, maybe you can fool these young students, but trust me everyone," Luke voiced as he amusingly looked into each of the two students eyes, "Doctor Train has more lives than a cat. Isn't that right, Max?"

Max chuckled. "I'm not sure what you mean."

"I mean you have a knack for survival."

As the sun's purple hues set over Jerusalem, Max, Luke, and

the two students dined at a busy, tastefully decorated local outdoor café on Jerusalem's crowded Muristan. Sitting among peoples of all faiths the group found refuge from the grueling desert in which they spent that day. Enjoying the local cuisine and customary wine, they spent the evening discussing their plans to excavate the second chamber the following day, the earthquake that previously occurred, the friendship the two professors forged over the years, and the two students' plans after graduate school.

The wine flowed easily as they spoke.

Still trying to grasp the magnitude of the day's events, Max mentioned nothing to his associates concerning his startling find. However, during dinner and as the conversation turned towards historical relics, Max posed a hypothetical question regarding how each would react if they discovered a religious artifact such as the Holy Cross of Christ.

Luke's interest piqued with Max's question. "All theological relics found in the Holy Land should immediately be delivered to the Roman Church in relative secrecy in order to prevent the local authorities from attempting to retain them." When pressed further by Max on what should be done with the cross, his friend replied, "It belongs to Rome."

Luke's opinion rhetorically reiterated his belief it was Rome's obligation to investigate the accuracy of any Christian related findings. This was no surprise to Max.

Lynn Johnson voiced an opinion that Christ was never crucified on a man-made 'artistic cross'. She cited historical evidence that many barbaric crucifixions that occurred during the time of Jesus of Nazareth occurred by nailing a person to an olive tree.

John Muir added that the endless possibilities of what to do were too much for his mind to imagine. "I'm not sure. If you're asking me, I mean, a discovery like that would bring the worlds of theological beliefs and science together… and distinctly apart. Can you imagine the arguments that would be made, or the lunatics that would try to get their hands on the cross –?"

"—If it turned out to be the True Cross," interjected Max.

"There's but only one Cross," Luke voiced in accordance to his Christian beliefs.

"I'm not saying otherwise," Max replied, aware Luke, like other Christians throughout the world, really had no idea where Jesus' Cross was.

"I see."

"But you know Luke there are many different thoughts about where the Cross is, and if Constantine's mother Helen really found it. Many who accept Helen's claim that she found the True Cross accept her statements as *tradition*, which is different than accepting the physical discovery of the True Cross. Many in Christianity accept Helen's discovered Cross as a matter of faith, not as a matter of scientific prudence.

"Most importantly, the question of what really happened on this cross is paramount to any actions anyone would take. I mean what you're talking about here is if Jesus of Nazareth—the Son of God, according to Christian belief—really was crucified and his physical body form completely ascended into Heaven the way Scripture preaches. Then there hypothetically would not be any physical evidence of Christ's human form. Now you know, as well as I do, that within all of mankind there are debates still brewing nearly two thousand years later about what really happened on that Cross. If a cross could be determined as the True Cross Jesus of Nazareth was murdered on and there was physical evidence of bodily remnants, could this undermine the entire basis of Christianity - Christ's self-sacrifice in order to redeem Mankind and his physical ascension to Heaven? I mean Luke, what we're talking about here is a cross, if this Cross hypothetically was found, that could potentially change the entire perspective of all Christianity—and thus all religions within the world.

"If physical evidence of Jesus is discovered on this Cross— blood, hair, whatever, does that mean that Jesus was not the Christ? When it is said Jesus rose, was it only the body in the tomb that 'rose', or did this include more—as, for example, remnants, if there are any, left on the Cross? If the remnants did not 'rise' with Jesus, but are still on the Cross here on earth today, then are they part of Jesus—especially if he is ascended into Heaven now? And isn't it almost obvious the remnants on the Cross, if it exists, could not have 'risen' with Jesus if they're found on that Cross? Of course there'll be many who will argue the issue one way or the other over whatever scientific evidence is discovered. And this whole hypothesis brings us to another question," Max said slowly as he looked at each person at the table. "If it is true that the Creator molded man in His image and distinguished humanity from the beast by Man's rational powers, what could be said about a discovery of a Cross with remnants of Jesus? What is God's intent if this was found?"

"What do you mean?"

"What would God's Way be if someone were to make such a find? Anyway, this is all so hypothetical. Who knows what's real, what's not?"

"Well, Max, I see you still live in your past," Luke observed. "You have doubts."

"Maybe."

"Faith should remove your doubts."

"Blind obedience—look where that took me."

"Perhaps there is a purpose you don't understand, one that has not yet been revealed."

Flashes of the images of the artifacts he touched raced through Max's mind. "Maybe."

"This reminds me of the story of Job—"

"— Yeah, I'm familiar with the story of God's servant who was continually tested. Didn't He allow the Devil to take away his family? It was as if Job's life really didn't matter, and Job had, if I remember the story correctly, blind obedience. Anyway, in today's real world, filled with bombs of mass destruction controlled by lunatics willing to launch them—in a world where martyrdom fanatics commit jihad, where faith is used—as it always has been to control the masses by ideal threats to a person's soul, or one's unknown promise for spiritual enlightenment—in this real world of complete globalization—the one who finds that cross will have a lot to figure out... a lot of tests, or should I say burdens. What should that person do?"

"What would you do, Max?" Luke asked.

"I'm not sure," he distantly replied as a young Israeli woman brought the table their meals.

"What do you mean?"

"Just that. I would have to think about it before I did anything. If anyone ever found the Cross, there would be so many burdens placed on this person's shoulders. Should it be turned over to the country where it's found . . . which in this case – Israel could be just enough to provide the Islamic, the Jews, and the Catholics with enough reason to kill each other. Or, should it be turned over to a major scientific institute for further study? Or, like you said, should it be turned over to Rome? I just don't know what I would do."

"Well, I think we can agree that turning over a holy artifact of any kind . . . let alone the cross, to political organizations would be a great mistake," Luke responded.

"You're probably right."

"It should be given to the Pope's emissaries," Luke said as he reached for a glass of water.

Max looked at him. "At what point do you do that?"

"I think once they're found. They belong to the Church."

"They do?"

"Of course."

"But isn't it true any artifacts found within the boundary of a country belong to that country?" voiced Lynn.

"Yes. But could you imagine—"

"—If the Holy Cross was found here," interrupted Max as he nodded his head in bewilderment. "Can you imagine how crazy this place would be? You're talking about –"

"—power," whispered John Muir. "So many things about Christ's life could be scientifically answered if *that* cross was found! These answers could —"

"— change the world forever," observed Max. "Think of how it could divide nations, one from the other. How would the people of the world react, if they knew there was a possibility that Jesus' Cross was discovered?"

"Well, it really isn't an issue whether we can link a cross to his physical body. There is no cross," a skeptic Lynn Johnson interjected. "Jesus of Nazareth was crucified on an olive tree the same way the Romans killed everyone else. Pontius Pilate, that charming Roman centurion who killed thousands during his military assignment in Spain, and who was *Procurator* of Judea, was not very wasteful. In fact, he was a cold miser who wouldn't spend the money making crucifixes. That's why there's no cross."

"I wouldn't be so sure of that, Lynn," quickly retorted Luke. "I think there are many eyewitnesses and sufficient scientific evidence stating Jesus Christ was indeed crucified on a man-made cross."

"I'm not disputing Jesus was crucified. I'm saying he was crucified on a tree in accordance with—"

"—but that was not the only custom, Lynn," voiced Max.

"And on the question of ownership, would we not be breaking the law if we didn't inform the Israeli Government that we found it?" Max posed.

"Are you serious?" Muir said. "The Middle East could turn into a murderous hell while everyone tried to get their hands on it.

Besides, what do you think the Israeli Government would do? Support this discovery? I doubt that very much."

"You're probably right about that," Luke agreed. "Which is why, if a cross that could alter the traditional perspective established by Helen was found it should be given immediately to Rome. Government, and its citizens, may have many different opinions on what is actually discovered. You know various interpretations will be voiced. Unfortunately, perspectives on religion can cause harm to others. That's why the Pope, with the support of all other Christians, should issue some type of unifying statement... if this was ever discovered. But this is all rhetoric—we're playing the 'what-if' game."

"You never know for sure what any government will do," Max added, aware of Luke's opinion.

Diners at the surrounding tables glanced over at their table. One couple nearby seemed very interested in their conversation. Max stared back at them and the couple turned their attention back to their meal.

"Can you imagine the debates that would occur?" Max dryly pointed out. "It would be chaos."

The four Americans looked at each other tentatively. Silence fell on the table the remainder of the meal, as each reflected on the hypothetical gravity of what they had discussed.

***

Under a blanketed night aglitter with shooting stars Max quietly left the two-story hotel he and the others were staying at. Once a Templar hospice it was now a quiet, comfortable hotel nestled among greenery and offered tranquil, magnificent views of the Western world's theological citadel.

The cool desert air moving through the strangely quiet night comforted him.

Guided by a luminous moon, he drove the old Ford towards the outskirts of Jerusalem. Leaving the city's limits, Max noticed a vehicle following him. After a second glance, he did not notice the car, and so dismissed it. Approaching the mysterious cave, he wondered about the hypothetical question of Christ's Cross posed during dinner with his friends.

Their previous answers provided him with no answers. *What should I do?*

After parking the truck off the side of the dirt road, he slowly approached the intended foothills. Under a bright orange moon intermittently obscured by fast moving clouds, Max began to remove the small rocks and boulders he earlier placed in front of the cave.

Though by himself, he didn't feel alone.

Once completed, he quickly entered the dark cavern.

Electric currents ran threw his body, painfully sensitizing the balls of his feet. His heart's eagerness to reach the remnants of the hidden cross was elevated by a feeling of overwhelming anxiety.

As the low burning light of the lantern gently bounced off the cave's limestone walls, Max descended step by apprehensive step into the cave's lower chamber where the ancient cross lay hidden.

Kneeling in the second chamber's far corner, his hands carefully brushed away the sandstone covering the buried cross. With each passing stroke of his hand, his heart opened the way a rosebud does when receiving the new day. The apprehension he initially felt was ending. In its place were growing feelings of serenity.

Max managed to tell himself this was his fate. *Why Me?*

Continuing to remove the sand from the cross, images of his past filled his mind and elevated his spirit.

He was no longer alone.

Though scientifically unproven, Max's soul immediately recognized what he may have discovered: The Holy Cross Jesus of Nazareth was crucified on.

For him — Max, this was the instrument used by the Son of God to save Mankind.

I am sorry for all I've done . . . for all I've questioned. I'm not sure what you desire from me, or what I should do now. Please Lord, provide me with direction. I –

Without warning Max heard the echoing sound of a car door slamming shut echo through the cave's chambers. *Who's there?*

Instinctively looking down at the large cross, he focused on the loosely driven iron nails that joined the two beams together.

The sound of a second door closing captured his ears.

His premonition told him something was wrong. *Who's*

there? Taking a deep breath, he accepted that in his possession was possibly one of the most powerful items in the world.

God, forgive me.

Instantly, the two loosely joined wooden boards separated from one another.

Quickly, he covered the longer board with sand. Then picking up the shorter of the two planks, the horizontal cross beam, or, as it was called, the *patibulum*, and the woven rope marked with the dark blood stains and hair strands, his penetrating eyes focused on the stark ascending tunnel which led to the first chamber. Reaching for the small wooden tablet, the *titulus*, which had carried the Greek lettering and had been affixed to the *patibulum*, his heart pumped faster as an overwhelming feeling of being trapped covered him. *The car- I was followed. Damn it!*

Judging from the distance of the noise, he believed there were few seconds remaining before the unknown intruders entered the cave.

Leaving the lantern aside, and holding the crossbeam and tablet, Max ascended up the unlit narrow passageway, his left arm acting as a guide against the stone wall.

Entering the larger chamber, he heard Lynn, Luke and John outside the cave.

Max stepped behind a bending rock formation and out of sight from everyone.

Hidden in silence he watched as his three friends entered the cave. *How did they know I was here?*

"Max?" yelled Luke. "Max, are you here?"

The echoing sound of his name filling the chamber chilled him. *I am not ready. I need to hide these things. But where?*

"Max, it's John Muir," the tall African-American student hollered. "Doctor Train, are you here?"

There was no response.

"Look. Down there," pointed Lynn. "There's a dim light coming from behind the wall to the second chamber," she said as she worked her way deep in the cave, and towards the second chamber. "Max!"

Not lost on any of the three was the fact someone, probably Max, had entered the cave that night. After all, the stones outside the entranceway were removed and they had seen the old Ford Truck parked nearby.

It was decided by the three that John and Lynn would descend onto the second chamber, while Luke would remain behind, unable to slip through the narrow opening.

Max silently watched their movements. *Why am I acting this way? This is ridiculous.*

Within a minute the two students yelled back to Luke, informing him Max was not in the second chamber.

"Where did you go?" Gartner said aloud as his eyes roamed the poorly lit chamber. *What's going on?*

"Dr. Gartner!" yelled the male student.

"Yes?"

"There's a . . . there's a long, old thick piece of wood about ten feet long and some old iron nails down here."

"A what?" hearing perfectly well what Muir said.

John Muir repeated himself.

Luke carefully looked around the cave. *Max old buddy, what in the world are you up to?* "Are you sure?" he asked, reaffirming Muir's description of the vertical beam.

"We're sure," answered Lynn.

"Describe it."

Lynn followed his instructions.

As she did, Luke's own anxiety began to surface. Gartner, a former leader in the genetics field and now a highly respected theological scholar with and the Director of the Church of Rome's Scientific Advisory Board, immediately recognized what Lynn was speaking of.

While Lynn described aloud the board and remaining nails of a Cross, Max had the perfect opportunity to get out of the cave in order to hide his two most sacred finds. Quickly, he rationalized, the vertical beam could not be associated by anyone with the Holy Cross, for its true test was answered only through the Greek markings found on the tablet which had been affixed to the horizontal beam, and thus possibly on the cross beam itself too.

Staying close to the wall, Max left the cave unknown to his colleagues. The awkwardness he felt in sneaking out made him feel foolish. Still, he continued.

While Lynn continued describing her find, Luke was deep in thought. *A hidden cave found here in the outskirts of Jerusalem? A vertical board that would be the size used to make a crucifix that somehow appears in the middle of the night . . . one that Max must have known about. And then he disappears in the middle of the night without telling anyone? What about the other board—the horizontal one—where is that? What's going on?* "Max, buddy, where are you?" he powerfully screamed.

Concern began to drape Luke. "Hey guys, are you okay down there?" he asked the two young students.

"We're fine, Dr. Gartner," replied John. "This is amazing. This wooden board . . . I think it's some type of post. It appears very old."

"Is there anything else down there? Another beam? Another chamber?" Luke yelled excitedly.

"We're looking, but I don't see anything," added Muir.

One board, not two? Odd. What's happened to Max? Peering around the chamber and seeing nothing alarming or disconcerting did not alleviate the growing concern building in Luke. *Strange. Very strange.*

"I'll be right back," Luke screamed to the students, as he turned towards the caves exit. "I want to see if Max is outside."

The sun's violet hues were moving closer to the horizon, its crest nearly breaking the night's darkness as the moon's yellow glow began to evanesce as Luke exited the cave.

He noticed Max's truck still sitting idle off the side of the dirt road. *Odd. Very odd. Why would Max*

"Hey, I think you're looking for me," Max voiced walking towards his friend, relieved Luke didn't see him place the artifacts he wrapped in bed linens taken from his hotel room and placed in the back of his old pickup truck.

"Why didn't you tell anyone you were leaving, and, where have you been?"

"I was restless, so I came up here," he said noticing passing tail lights disappear over one of the small foothills.

Max's stoic reply was not lost on Luke.

"Didn't think it was a big deal," Max added.

"These are dangerous times. You know where you are," Luke emphasized. "We were worried."

"Point taken," he said apologetically.

"Seems like I'm always worrying about you," Luke added with a sense of sarcastic amusement, as he noticed the headlights of a vehicle slowly creeping down the highway.

"I know. Thanks." *I guess I deserved that.*

"What were you doing out here?"

"I don't really know. Couldn't sleep, so I thought I would

take a look around the cave."

"I see. Well, your students are in their looking for you."

"Guess I should tell them to come out."

"That would be the first considerate thing you did all night," Luke playfully responded, not mentioning the beams Lynn and John discovered.

"Okay. You coming?"

"Be there in a minute. I want to get some water from the car."

"Sure," Max replied as he turned towards the small entranceway, wondering where the car he noticed had just vanished to.

***

The sun was edging closer to the new horizon when a violent explosion roared from inside the cave, eerily breaking the morning's peaceful silence blanketing the Holy Land. The crumbling limestone ceiling and walls from within shook the desert ground as if another earthquake had just occurred. Tons of falling rocks covered both chambers, annihilating everything left inside.

Staring alone in the twilight of the oncoming day and at the horrific incident unfolding before his very eyes was a horrified Max Train.

Oh my God!

Train's presence outside the cave surprised the lone observer. From behind a rocky plateau he quickly reached for his deadly Galil assault rifle, knowing he better hit his mark.

The disruptive sound of piercing steel erupting from the rifle ripped through the disturbed, chilled morning air.

The bullet found its deadly mark. *Oh damn, I've been hit!*

Startled and reeling in pain, Max looked down at the gunshot wound that bore into his left shoulder. Hot red blood covering his pale face dripped onto his canvas jacket. *What the hell's going on? Who's out there?*

Instinctively, he took cover by the old Ford as his eyes quickly tried to see through the break of morning's twilight and determine who the shooter was. Dusk still present, it was impossible to clearly see anything in the hilly, desert mountainside. *My shoulder – bastards. Where are they?*

The killer moved towards Max, then aimed the steel barrel

of the rifle.

A second bullet bounced off the front end of the truck's hood as Max reached into his pocket for the ignition keys. *I gotta get out of here. Whoever just killed Luke and the kids . . . Bastards, you're not going to take me! Damn, Luke! No, not him, too!*

The gunman moved closer and aimed at Train's head. *He's unarmed.*

Another bullet came within inches of his head as he fearfully moved to the passenger side of the truck, hoping he was not providing the assassin with a better shot. *Damn, my shoulder. Christ! I'm a sitting target.*

Two more gunshots exploded the truck's windows, throwing shattered glass everywhere.

Max's eyes searched, looking to see how many killers were out there. *Crap, I don't want to be here! Why –*

Without warning a violent wave of bullets erupted from a machine gun, shredding the truck apart.

"Damn!" screamed Max as a bullet burst into his right thigh. "Uggh!" he cried. "What the hell do you want?"

Max's answer came back in a wicked bombardment of bullets.

Heart pounding heavily, the severe pain surged through his leg. The sound of empty metallic clicks of the machine gun was heard in the near distance. *So this is how it ends! Some life it's been! My wife and daughter, and now my best friend and two of my students! Some God you've turned out to be! A loving, gentle God — yeah, right!*

Placing his right hand's fingers around the torn flesh of his leg, Max noticed that the bullet did not deeply enter his quad muscle. He heard the killer release the empty magazine from the machinegun. *My leg! Damnit!*

A ray of the morning's light pierced his eyes as he felt the hot sensation of the two gunshot wounds extend through his frightened body. Holding his right blood-soaked hand in front of his eyes, directly in front of the eastern sun, Max, exhausted, forcefully gritted his teeth. *Why?*

Max heard the distinct sound of the gun cartridge being removed from the firearm. Despite the bullet wounds, Max's adrenaline level elevated to unfamiliar levels. With lightening speed he opened the passenger door of the truck and put the key in the ignition. As he did, another bullet hit the truck's rear glass panel.

The killer was less than 100 feet away, and closing.

Max saw his assassin's gray outline, but it was still too dark to identify him.

Turning over the engine, Max launched the old truck down the dirt road underneath a shell of gunfire that was ripping apart the back of the truck. *Don't hit the damn fuel tank! Gotta get out of here, but where to?*

Another bullet found its way into the dashboard, destroying the speedometer. *Who the hell is that?*

As the decimated truck took on more bullets, Max hurriedly directed it to the paved highway.

"Now what?" he emptily screamed as the truck's speed was beginning to provide enough safe distance from the onslaught of bullets.

Chapter III

Max raced down Ha-Tsankhanim Road leading toward Jaffa Road, away from Jerusalem and his would-be killers as fast as he could. He looked down in horror at the bullet lodged in his bloody right leg, and then at the torn flesh wound oozing blood from his left shoulder. Canvassing the truck's cab for a cloth to slow the bleeding, he knew if he didn't attend to the wounds quickly he too would lose his life.

Unfortunately, there was no cloth in the truck.

Aware he was alone in a foreign country having few immediate resources didn't comfort him. Besides, he thought, whoever was after him more than likely was a religious fanatic, perhaps with political ties. Max knew stopping for help was not an option.

His right hand squeezed down on his bleeding leg. Driving the truck became more difficult, especially with a numb left hand unable to hold the steering wheel.

As he chugged down the highway, Max continued to look into his rear view mirror for any suspect cars. Though it appeared no one was following him, Max sensed foreboding shadows of the Reaper's death hand reaching for him. *Where is that guy?*

Accelerating the truck, he abruptly shifted from one lane to another as drivers left behind looked at his taillights in horror.

Forcing the old 1968 truck to its limit, Max realized whoever killed his colleagues and shot at him was not about to stop now. The word the dead student John Muir whispered over dinner repeated itself over and again. *Power! Power!*

Speeding past several low-rise buildings, Max noticed a sign towards Tel Aviv, Israel's largest city, offering him hope he could get some medical attention and hide from his assassins.

Continuing on Jaffa Road to Sderot Weizmann, Max felt his body weakening. The blood loss was substantial, and there was little probability he would make it all the way to Tel Aviv before passing out unless he stopped the bleeding.

His consciousness began to drift.

An upcoming gas station offered the opportunity to clean his wounds. *Should I stop here? What about the killer?*

There was but one choice.

The Esso station had four separate island pumps, each occupied with morning customers filling their tanks. Max was comforted at the presence of rush hour workers.

Pulling to the back of the building, he noticed an Orthodox man enter a side bathroom. Careful not to call attention to himself, he tried to seem preoccupied. All along, his roving brown eyes stayed on the highway, watching for any vehicles coming from Jerusalem. *This is just great! How the hell am I supposed to know who's trying to kill me, or what they look like? I need a plan.*

A black Range Rover slowly entered the gas station. His body tensed. Fortunately the woman driving the vehicle appeared interested in only getting gas. *I have to keep moving, but gotta stop this damn bleeding!*

Two minutes later Max found himself in a clean bathroom. Locking the door, he immediately took off his shirt and then removed his blood soaked pants.

The bullet was superficially lodged in the surface of his skin. He began to clean the wound. After a few minutes, and satisfied the bleeding stopped, he noticed a small pair of needle-nose pliers on the floor, picked them up, and ran them under hot running water.

Sitting on the toilet seat, Max spread open the flesh wound and painfully placed the open pliers' head around the bullet.

Blood began to drain out of the wounded hole.

Tears filled his eyes as pain rushed through his legs. Taking a deep breath, he pulled the slug out of his mangled quadriceps. *Ahhh!*

Finding a useable towel in the bathroom, Max tightly wrapped it around the wound, providing a temporary bandage until he could find proper medical assistance, which he realized, had to be soon.

He turned his attention to his aching shoulder. The blood appeared to be clotting on its own.

Okay, I'm in the middle of nowhere, and I don't have much money on me. If I use my credit cards, it could be possible that whoever is trying to kill me can find me. I have to reach Tel Aviv and lose myself in the city. Then I can figure out what to do.

Opening the bathroom door an inch, he looked outside. Nothing seemed strange.

With eyes agape, he limped back towards the truck parked seventeen meters away. Nearby was the empty cargo van he had seen parked earlier. He walked towards it.

Looking into the passenger window, Max noticed a map.

Quickly, he opened the door and reached for it. As he did, he saw a battered gym-bag containing some oversized clothing.

Moments later, Max was back on Jaffa Road, carefully studying the map while heading towards Tel Aviv. He thought about taking some side roads, but thought against it since the fastest way to get there, he concluded, appeared to be Jaffa.

The short journey into the metropolis was painstaking, as Max fearfully continued to look for his would-be killers on the highway. *Everyone I come close to eventually dies a brutal death. Why? Why is it you allow the world to be so violent? Does human life mean little . . . nothing to you? You know they didn't have to die, either. Lynn, she was a bright young lady filled with promise. Maybe she was right? And John, he somehow found his way and was making something of himself. Now they're both gone. Luke, he was like my brother. He stood by me when I had nobody. You remember that, don't you? And I called him, my best friend, to his death! I should've never asked him to come down from Rome! But I did . . . all because of the cave . . . and none of them ever knew what I think I found . . . or what they died for. I'm not even sure about it. Nothing makes sense- you don't make any sense.*

Why did you put this burden on me? I'm carrying around part of a Cross that may be the one your supposed Son was murdered on. I know, as you do, if this is actually the Cross Jesus died on it could cause so many problems: theological, political- whatever- nobody is going to know what to think, or do if it becomes known this Cross has been uncovered- but every fanatic is going to say they have an answer. The last thing we need are more fanatics running around over a pious claim. And as you know, we men love to wage wars against each other over our desire to have you love us. I don't get you. You have to show me what to do. This is too much for me to handle alone.

Exhausted, Max entered Tel Aviv, a modern city with architecture seemingly as diverse as its history. This gift of Israel to the Mediterranean was vibrant, brash, cosmopolitan but personal, casual yet never fully at rest.

For two days he had not slept. This, combined with his physical wounds, was taking a massive toll on him.

On the outskirts of the city he noticed a single level motel off Havakook that likely would not draw any attention. Max parked the truck in the back of the building, and then quickly changed into the stolen clothes.

At the registration desk he asked an old woman how much a room was. Listening to her response, Max removed twice the amount required from his wallet and handed the monies to the lady. "My name is Bernard Hecht," he nodded.

The woman said nothing, but handed him a key to a room.

"Thank you," he said, grateful the woman asked no questions.

Her blackened eyes looked at his. "One day—we're good here?"

"Yes."

"In the back," she motioned.

Retrieving the wrapped artifacts from the Ford, he found his very ordinary, stale room.

After washing his face, Max cautiously returned to the bullet strewn truck and drove it a few miles from the motel, where he parked it in an industrial zone, hoping nobody would recognize the vehicle's gunshot markings before he left the scene.

So far so good, he thought to himself as an Arab taxi driver dropped him off two blocks from the motel.

Walking tentatively to the motel, Max tried his best not to call attention to himself even though the pain surging through his leg was mounting from overuse. He noticed fresh bloodstains appearing on his khaki pants. *Oh Christ, I've got to get help.*

Knowing if he walked into a hospital his gunshot wounds would be reported to the local authorities, who by now must have become aware of the explosion in Jerusalem, Max thought about who he could seek help from. The idea of contacting any law enforcement officials died over a decade ago.

After returning to the motel and re-bandaging his wounds, he picked up the telephone and dialed a number to a Rabbi now living in Borough Park, Brooklyn.

"Hello," answered an old voice on the other end.

"Rabbi, it's Max Train."

"Ah, my old friend, how are you?"

"Not very good. I need your help," Max weakly responded.

There was a long pause.

"What's the matter?"

"It's a long story—and I'm not even sure where I should

begin."

"You're in trouble?"

"More like in danger."

"Where are you?"

Max told the Rabbi, who he befriended over twenty years ago, that he was in Tel Aviv, had been shot and desperately needed "private medical attention."

The Rabbi, Morton Kohn, realized not to pry. "Max, we know each other a long time. I'll do whatever I can to help you."

Max sighed in relief. *True friends never die.*

Less than an hour later help arrived. An attractive black hair woman in her early thirties, wearing a pair of jeans and a white button down shirt, calling herself Sara, knocked on Max's door, and announced she was "a friend of Rabbi Kohn"

Entering the room, Sara told Max she was Rabbi Kohn's niece, and had practiced medicine for the last five years. Instructing him to lay flat on the bed, she inspected the gunshot wounds, and then reached for her knapsack.

"You're very lucky. They're not serious, though it appears you've lost some blood. You're going to need to keep off that leg for a few days and give it time to heal," she replied, beginning to bandage Max's leg wound.

"I don't have time for that," Max confided in her.

Running her fingers through her long black hair, her deep blue eyes looked into Max's. Life in Israel was not easy, and Sara knew there were things better left alone. "Perhaps it is not safe for you to stay here," she suggested.

He nodded. "Perhaps."

"My most favored uncle suggested that we . . . I help you."

"Thank you," he said with genuine warmth.

"We need to get you out of here. I assume you don't want to be seen?"

"Unseen would be good."

"And some rest for this leg."

"That bad?"

"If you keep staying on it, it will be," she replied, as Max wondered what to do about the burdening items he had in his possession.

"Okay, but—"

"— you'll stay with me for a few days, till you're ready to travel again. Then we'll get you out of here."

Max said nothing back. He knew the feisty, honorable Rabbi Kohn was very active in Israeli politics, and had escaped Auschwitz during the time of the Holocaust.

"I have some items I need to take with me," Max added.

"Whatever," she replied, not paying attention to the two items by the side of the bed. *Who is this stranger, and why is my uncle willing to help him?*

***

The sound of fast moving wooden heels hitting the narrow cobblestone pavement cutting through the old tenements echoed through the manmade gorge. Keeping his face towards the stone-layered street, the pedestrian paid little noticeable attention to the other strollers as he raced along shielded from view by a large black hat. His quickening pace sounded like a determined steed racing to its final destination.

Underneath his wool hat's brim, sunken brown eyes focused on two menacing wooden doors twenty meters away. Slightly altering his gait, he arrived in front of a three hundred year old gray stone building weathered by time. Glancing in both directions for observant eyes, he leaned his frame forward, pushing open one of the heavy doors, and entered into a spacious hallway, satisfied his movements were not of any interest to the street's passersby.

Upon reaching the third level landing, he removed the hat covering his thin, drawn face and receding gray hairline and entered the apartment, not having bothered to knock, for he was expected.

The expansive parlor room he entered was bare but for a lone large rectangular walnut wooden table placed in the center of the room. Six hardened chairs around the table, whose grain matched the deep mahogany of the darkened floor and ornate walls gave the distinct feeling this room was a meeting place. A series of antique flickering candle visconces moving at the beckoning of the faint wind provided hints of light that the four large window shutters attempted to prohibit from entering the room.

On the table was an Etruscan style water pitcher. There were no glasses.

The messenger, for that was what he was, took a seat facing the closed window shutters. Trying to calm his nerves, he began to count the number of wooden veneers on the shutters.

Moments later he heard movements coming from behind a second door and immediately corrected his slouching posture. He knew the one he sought was imperious, and a slouching posture, he was told, was indicative of a person's weakened character.

All things considered, he preferred not to have his constitution questioned.

As the doorknob slowly turned, the messenger's right hand grasped the armchair tightly.

A middle aged man of unremarkable physical features but for a receding hairline framing a pockmarked face accompanied by a three inch scar high on his right cheekbone entered through the door, his presence always a cause of discomfort, and walked to the table.

As he did, the messenger looked respectfully down towards the table.

"What news have you for me, my friend?" asked the patron in a condescending voice as he glided across the wooden floor and took his seat at the head of the table in the cool, lonely looking room.

"I received word two hours ago that he's escaped," he answered, not looking at the man.

The patron squinted in annoyance. "Why?"

"I am not sure."

"Tell me, is it that hard to kill a man in the desert?"

The messenger felt the contempt growing from his superior. "No."

"The items, were they with him?" his voice began to rise.

"There is no way of knowing. It was not yet sunrise when this happened."

The answer was not what the patron wished to hear. He slammed his manicured right hand, dressed with the elaborate diamond and sapphire encrusted ring of his office, onto the table with astonishing speed and force. "Do you realize what's at stake here? For God's sake, the security and well being of our lives and the lives of all others could be turned upside down if that freak escapes us." Vulture like, leaning over the table, his faded green eyes cruelly pierced the mettle of the messenger's cognitive spirit. "I don't care what has to be done to find him—and kill him! Kill him before he comes up with another brilliant idea, one mind you that he better not even ever think of. And make sure that we get our rightful belongings back! And you listen to me carefully," he snarled, starting to rise, veins clearly thickening on his now reddened face. "You tell those imbeciles I don't care what resources or expenses we use. There is only one objective here, and it better be carried out without fault, or I promise you will all die a wicked death," his rapturous voice threatened.

The emissary nodded, knowing full well the man across from him had the will and the way to make good on his threat the way he had often in the past.

"Do we have any idea where he is?"

"Not yet," the messenger replied, finally lifting his head, eyes focused on the thick, aged scar—a scar never asked about by others, though silently questioned as to its origin by all who knew him.

"You said you recently found out about this, which means he must still be in Israel."

"We have no information—he drove away."

"You're saying he could've left Israel?"

"No, I'm not saying this—"

"But it's a possibility."

The subordinate nodded.

"He could have gone directly to the airport and caught a flight to anywhere in the world. Did we have people at ben Gurion?"

"We think so. But we'll find him. We're going to have the flight manifest checked for his name." The messenger knew this was not enough to satisfy his patron's thirst for detail.

"For your sake, you better be right. The last thing I want to hear is a reporting of any sort in a newspaper or on the radio or through the Internet of his whereabouts. If that happens—if he's smart enough to get to the press, the world will never sleep again."

"Could it be possible he may try to contact us?"

The patron licked his fingers with saliva, then walked over to the wall sconce closest to him, and extinguished the burning flame with his fingers. He found a second lit candle, then placing his fingers over the flame, he replied "No."

The idea of the hunted turning to the press for protection never crossed the messenger's mind. The situation's gravity was clear to him. Any given minute the scientist could simply walk into any credible press agency and make an irreversible announcement.

"I want those items brought here, and I want Max Train

dead!"

"I understand."

"You better," the patron whispered. "You better . . . regardless of the price we must pay – find him, and kill him!"

Fearful of the pending threat, the messenger timidly turned his head. "I understand."

As he did, the words *benedicamus Domino* reached his ears.

***

The late afternoon's fading sun began to cool the busy streets of Tel Aviv below where Max and Sara sat. For over an hour the two medical professionals spoke about the bioethical issues related to Max's field of expertise: genetics. What the two concluded after discussing the scientific, medical, evolutionary, sociological, theological, and political ramifications related to DNA research was that the topic was very complicated and filled with many opinions.

"So how do you know my uncle?" Sara asked Max from her kitchen.

"We go back a long time, when I was living in Brooklyn twenty years ago and studying microbiology at Rockefeller University. I met him in a – well, when he crashed his car into mine."

"What?"

"Well, that's how we met."

"That's a strange way to meet someone," Sara said as she brought dinner out.

"I could think of other ways, such as someone I now know who came to a perfect stranger's hotel room and rescued him from, well your guess is as good as mine," his voice trailed off.

"You really have no idea who did this to you?"

"None."

Though Max had previously told her about the tragic death of his friends, she didn't want to press him to go to the police. Rabbi Kohn had already filled her in on Max's past history with law enforcement.

"So you're telling me you met my uncle in a car accident. I don't know who is stranger, you or him," she laughed. "Whose fault was it?" *I'm sure this is true, Max, but there must be some-*

thing else that neither of you is willing to tell me. As for you being shot, you must have angered someone. Why else would an attempt on your life- after all, you have nothing to do with the affairs of the Holy Land- occur so early in the morning?

"I guess you can say we're both peculiar... but the car accident was definitely his fault," Max chuckled, not telling her about the night of the accident. That was when Rabbi Kohn was coming home from a party, and more than likely would have failed the inevitable breathalyzer test had Max called the police to report the accident, which he did not.

"Were either of you hurt?"

"Fortunately my car was the only one that came out of it banged up," Max said with a smile. "I guess the rest is history. We've been friends ever since."

"That's what he told me," Sara acknowledged as she took a seat opposite Max. "You look much better from earlier today. Sleep has helped you. How are those wounds?"

A warm grin spread across his face as he reached for his glass of ice tea. Not noticing until now how attractive Sara actually was, he could not take his eyes off her. "I have a good doctor who deserves all the credit for my quick recovery."

"True, but seriously, how's your leg?"

"Is that sea bass?" Max asked, taking notice of the grilled fish.

Sara nodded. "Max, your leg?"

"I know I won't be running anytime soon, but other than that, I think I'm going to be fine."

"Well, you do have a very good doctor treating you."

"You're right," he smiled back. "I've heard of house calls, but this is probably one of the first times when a doctor takes the patient home to ensure his well-being."

She looked at him cautiously, but with a hint of respectful understanding. "I'm supposed to help you. Now you better eat your dinner before it gets cold," Sara insisted, reaching for Max's empty plate. "Besides, you need some food," she added with a warm smile.

The remainder of the evening Max told Sara about distinct portions of his life. He mentioned his studies and the loss of his family, but stayed away from the grueling court trial he endured.

When she asked what brought him to Israel, Max told her that over the years he fell in love with archaeology, and though his stellar professional accomplishments evolved around biogenetics, a science he still was active in, "trying to understand man's social behavior has become a love of mine."

As the evening passed in enjoyable conversation, Max's subconscious felt a disturbing shadow grasping at him, summoning him to the pious relics he had unearthed from the cave's sleeping tomb.

Thoughts of his dead friends, for there was no possible way they survived, suddenly began to consume him. *I need to let some-body know where they're buried. I need to call their families. How am I going to break this to them? What reason do I give?*

He tried his best not to let Sara know his trepidation, and listened to her tell of life in war torn Israel. Though he intended to place an unidentified call to the local police once he left Israel concerning the cave's collapse, he wondered if he was not doing the right thing by acting sooner. After all, his friend's bodies were buried in the limestone foothills.

But the scars left from his past reminded him of the brutal interactions he had with the law. The last thing he wanted was to get blamed for more deaths.

The call would have to wait until he left Tel Aviv.

Laying eyes wide-open in Sara's guestroom later that night Max became engulfed with the decisions he would have to make. *Should I contact the U.S. embassy, and let them know what I have discovered? Or, should I contact the Israel Department of Antiquities? Perhaps Luke was right; maybe I should contact the Church in Rome and let them know what I have discovered. Luke seemed to believe strongly that would be the right thing to do. But will Rome's Scientific Advisory Board do the right thing? Will they share with the world this discovery, or will they take their time in trying to determine what to do? If I were in charge . . . I have no idea what I would do. I wonder how the average person would act if they were in my position and found what appears to be the actual Cross Jesus was crucified on. Would they be able to think through their options, or feel as confused as I am?*

Warily rising, he retrieved the wrapped *titulus.* Carefully unfolding the cloth, his eyes gazed at the indigo ink marking on the thin board. The Greek letters were better seen now under the white light of the lamp in his room, by which he was now viewing the tablet. He took a glass of water, placed it over the *titulus,* in an attempt to magnify the lettering. *If the second word's first letter begins the word for king... and the first two letters of the first word do seem to be, or are they... I'm not sure- letters are missing.*

Max felt his chest tighten as enigmatic crests of bewilderment surged their hazy peaks towards his wanting soul. The magnetic force of confusion pulled his human spirit to suspiciousness.

Are you not supposed to be a God of love? This is what I was taught... and it is what the world wants to think. But all around is murder and unnecessary killing. I don't know why I thought it would stop, but it hasn't. Brutal death still follows me. Why is it that those I come close to are met by cruel death? Perhaps if I die, those I care for will not have to suffer? Is that your desire? Tell me, for if it is not, show me what to do. Or perhaps . . . perhaps you do not exist?

Max got out of bed and retrieved the *patibulum*. Laying it down, he unwrapped the sheet. A wicked chill ran down his spine as he took note of one of the iron spikes used to nail a body to the wood. Thoughts of Jesus' painful crucifixion and his blessed Resurrection began to engulf him, yet in his contemplation, the painful murder of Christ caused only further confusion. *Why did you really allow your Son to die? His death was suppose to make this world a better place, but has it? Has it? Look around this world—there is so much pain.*

That night Max lay sleepless in bed wondering about God's existence, and what to do next. Over and over again, the notion he had held the possible remains of Jesus of Nazareth in his own hands repeated itself in his mind like dripping water from a faucet that wouldn't let you sleep at night. *If this is the remains of Jesus, and he is Christ, did I hold God in my hands? Did I hold God in my hands?*

Eventually morning's sun rose, and with it, Max finally fell into a deeply needed sleep, unaware killers had descended upon Israel during the night looking for him.

Awakening in the early afternoon, a note from Sara informed him she had gone to work, but would return around 3:00 p.m., giving him less than two hours alone to figure out his next steps. He felt, whatever his pain, he must leave Jerusalem as soon as he could in case the shooting was not an isolated attack. He recalled the passing car that suddenly disappeared that night.

An hour passed when Max decided to make two telephone calls. The first was to Brooklyn, to Rabbi Kohn's home. The second was to an old colleague, Francesco Pellegrino, who was at the

University of Bologna's Medical School, and who had received his doctorate in genetics.

Arriving back at her home, Sara noticed Max on her telephone, smiled, and gestured not to get up.

Five minutes later Max hung up on his call to Italy.

"How are you feeling?" Sara asked as she entered the living room.

"Much better. My wounds seem to be healing faster than I expected."

"For the most part they were both surface wounds, though you should be mindful of your leg."

"I know," he replied tentatively. "Sara, I don't think it's safe for me to stay here, and the quicker I get out of Israel, the safer we'll both be."

Sara nodded.

"Your uncle said you might be able to help," Max suggested, knowing Rabbi Kohn's ties with the Mossad, the Israeli government's formidable intelligence service.

For the next few hours they discussed what Max had in mind. As they did, Sara carefully re-wrapped his injuries, applying extra gauze in order to protect the wounds.

Early the next morning a car arrived in front of Sara's nondescript concrete high-rise building.

Five minutes later, Max, holding the smaller of the two wrapped artifacts, and accompanied by Sara, who was holding the other, descended into the lobby of her high rise building and quickly entered the vehicle, their destination: ben Gurion Airport, twelve miles outside of Tel Aviv

As the blue sedan traveled towards ben Gurion, where Max would take a flight to Rome's Leonardo da Vinci Airport, he cautiously kept his eyes open for any further threats. The road he was traveling, Ha-Shomron, was jammed with vehicles of all kinds, giving Max this time safety in numbers.

In the back of the car Sara reiterated her advice to appear calm while going through the airport. As she spoke, Max was handed an envelope.

Opening it, he found a British passport, and a Canadian, along with the equivalent of ten thousand American dollars in Italian Lira. Two credit cards bore the name on the British passport, and two others the name John Burns, the name on the Canadian. Inspecting the passport, he asked. "How did you manage that?"

"While you were sleeping yesterday I took the liberty thinking that it may be useful, Mr. O'Brian."

Grinning, "Do I look like a 'Keith O'Brian'?"

"You do now."

The car entered onto the airport's grounds and pulled up to the El Al terminal.

"I'll walk you to the gate. Your ticket will find us."

"You've thought of everything."

"Israel has many enemies. We need to think of everything."

Max felt a surging level of trust towards the woman. "I need to tell you something."

She leaned towards him.

For the next minute he informed her about the explosion outside of Jerusalem, and how his three friends were crushed to their death inside the cave.

Max, what were you doing there and what is it that you're carrying? Quickly, Sara's eyes looked upon the cardboard boxes. Reaching for Max's hand, "I'm sorry."

Her discretion was not lost on Max, who asked her if it might be possible to get word out to the police of the unfortunate incident in order to retrieve the bodies.

"I can arrange this."

The driver got out of the car and removed Max's carefully boxed items from the trunk. As he did, a luggage attendant approached Sara, nodded, and placed Max's belongings on a small pushcart.

"These are some of my friends," she told him while taking his left arm. "Pretend we're lovers," she whispered as they slowly walked into the terminal.

With each step of the new day Max's tension built.

Unseen to Max, a second attendant approached them. Quickly, an envelope was handed to Sara containing Max's ticket to Rome.

"We need to take your items," Sara told him before turning to the attendant. "We'll have to carry them through the gate."

An imposing Israeli soldier dressed in army fatigues and equipped with a deadly micro Uzi SMG, discreetly waved to Sara, directing her towards him.

Max squeezed Sara's hand.

As they came closer, the soldier removed the red rope used

to cordon off passengers and waved them on.

Through the gates, Max realized he had fifteen minutes remaining before his flight departed.

"I think I'll grab something to read," he told her, eyeing the small kiosk nearby the departure gate.

"Okay, but don't drift. I'll go check on the flight."

Threatening eyes observed Max and Sara from a nearby passenger seating area.

The onlooker, a middle-aged man of ordinary appearance, wearing a blue business suit, stood as he watched the Mossad agent walk towards the gate.

His attention turned to Max, who was carrying the two packages while meandering towards the kiosk. *Hello, Max Train.*

Purposefully, the spectator's eyes roamed the terminal landscape in search of any other Mossad. He noticed one powerless agent, whose abilities had already been immobilized.

He approached his target.

Steps from where Max stood, the killer discreetly placed his hand in his pocket. *You're mine, Max Train, and you have been condemned to death.*

Max reached down for a *U. S. A. Today* newspaper, unaware of the assassin's approach.

The killer went directly towards him. *Your time has come.*

Max looked up towards the gate where Sara was talking to an attendant, blind to the approaching threat.

A specially made synthetic Gazio dart gun containing a needle laced with deadly cyanide was removed from the pants pocket of the blue suit.

Keeping his concealed hand to his side, bland gray eyes unassumingly met Max's.

Max met the stranger's look.

"Hi," the would be businessman casually responded, his right hand's fingers tightening around the concealed weapon.

Max nodded. "Hello."

A friendly smile was returned.

Good-bye, scientist. The killer nodded in passing as he squeezed the deadly trigger.

A venomous dart landed in Max's leg.

Train, you fool, you're a dead man. And when you fall I'll take those boxes of yours.

Undeterred, Max stepped towards the cashier. Unknown to

him, the deadly dart fell to the floor, the poisonous threat momentarily gone.

The assassin, trying to appear preoccupied, waited for Max to keel over, his eyes on the two boxes Max had beside him. *These are your last steps before you go to hell, Train!*

"They're getting ready to board." It was Sara.

Why is he standing? I know I hit his right leg!

"Be right there," he answered.

"I think you should go now," she replied while turning her attention towards the cashier. "I'll take care of these later, Emily," she told the young woman brusquely as she reached for the magazines and newspapers Max had taken. "Let's go," Sara finished as she then reached for the two cardboard boxes.

What the hell was that? The bastard is still standing, and about to get onto a plane. Hell!

Unaware of the attempted threat on his life, Max, accompanied by Sara, walked towards the gate.

"Sara, I can't thank you enough for everything."

"I was told to treat you like one of us, so you don't need to thank me. Just be careful."

"Well, thank you anyway," Max replied under the dark gaze of the confused assassin, who unknowingly directed the mortal dart into Max's heavily bandaged leg.

"You're welcome."

"I guess I'll be in touch."

"I hope so," she said squeezing his hand. "I hope so."

They both heard another boarding call for flight 45 to Rome.

He turned to his rescuer. "I won't forget all of your help."

"I know. Now get onto the plane."

He nodded before turning. "Thanks."

As Max handed his boarding pass to the gate attendant, the *patibulum* and *titulus* in a neatly wrapped box by his side, the killer took out his cell phone, and called a local telephone number. After three relay connections, the caller was eventually connected to a seldom-used telephone in Rome.

Chapter IV

The El Al flight cut through ominous clouds as it approached Italy's fabled capitol city of Rome without delay en route to its expected 10 a.m. arrival. In the bulkhead passenger seat close to the exit door, Max cautiously allowed his body to rest, relieved he was able to depart from Israel unnoticed.

As the plane descended towards the airport, he began to stir deep in thought over his decision to travel to Rome, a city he frequented, and his resolve not to contact any law enforcement officials about the murders that took place outside Jerusalem's walls until after he left Israel.

Once again, I am alone.

Looking out the window, he saw distant remnants of the Roman Emperor Vespasian's infamous Coliseum, built in 72 A.D. A colossal statue of Emperor Nero, who blamed the Christians for Rome's destructive conflagration in 64 A.D., once could be seen afar from this oval structure, formerly named the Ampithheatrum Flavianum. Here the sport of martyrdom, defenseless Christians by the tens of thousands being mercilessly devoured by starved lions, was a popular Roman entertainment. Slaughtered gladiators, in many cases slaves, and in some instances, disgraced former Roman soldiers, added to the amusements for the spectators, numbering at times as many as fifty thousand.

The glorified death-arena was not lost on Max.

Searching the Tiber, Rome's historic river, from his plane, Max looked for the famed Milvian Bridge. Legend had it that in preparing to battle Maxentius in 312 AD for rule of the Roman Empire, Constantine had a vision of the Holy Cross. The vision, as it has been told through time, said Constantine witnessed a large white cross mystically afloat in the sky. Upon his revelation he noticed the words "CONQUER BY THIS" surrounding the cross. Believing it was the Christian God's intervention, Constantine ordered the emblem of the Cross to be affixed to the shields of each and every one of his warriors. A great battle ensued that day. Bloodshed fell from the heavens, as brother turned against brother, and one-time friends became foes. As the night faded and the sun awoke to the new day, it was Constantine, Helen's son, standing victoriously with the sign of the Holy Cross, as Rome's emperor, and so the world's new leader. The divine intervention branded in his soul, Constantine swore the Holy Cross was alone the reason for his victory. A year after the battle he issued the Edict of Milan in gratitude. This made the previously outlawed Christian religion free from persecution throughout the Roman Empire.

Eyes moving towards the great plaza, Max realized he was viewing St. Peter's Square, designed by Lorenzo Benin in the 17th century during the reign of Pope Alexander VII. The plane was now flying over the world's smallest country, the 108-acre sovereign state of Vatican City. It had survived the carnage of the Roman Empire, the greed of would be pretenders to its governance, and the decadence of some of its own Popes to stand as a symbol of eternity to over one billion Christians today.

As he momentarily scanned the buildings of the Vatican below, he wondered what building Luke once occupied. Painfully, Max questioned what he should tell Luke's family, and when.

Max clenched his fist. The need to stay invisible, at least for the moment, was troublesome.

The sound of the jet's engines roaring as the plane sharply descended on approach to the airport runway intensified the knot tightly forming in his stomach. *I need to let Luke's wife Eileen know he's been killed. This whole thing is way over my head. Hopefully, Luke's associates at the Vatican will know what to do.*

***

The robe, a bleeding red in color, draped well over the ascetic frame of Anselm Mugant.

For years he ascended in his quest to obtain the responsibility associated with the handmade garments only select few were chosen to wear. In many ways, the drapery he wore was more protective than the thickest armor, more powerful than the mightiest sword, and to many, more visible than the sun.

A French Canadian from the Laurentian Mountain region north of Montreal, his parents, now deceased had operated a small tourist lodging at Saint-Saveur. Mugant's mother had a special devotion to Blessed Brother Andre Bassette, and would bring Anselm with her yearly to the Oratory in Montreal, founded by the

Holy Cross Brother. It was here, exposed to the many miracle stories of the Brother, that Andre's lessons in religion began. He decided on the religious life when he had attended a Mass celebrated at the Oratory by the Cardinal Archbishop of Toronto. As he told the story of his calling later in life, some who heard it believed it was the finery of the Archbishop's vestments that had motivated Mugant, not the content of the Archbishop's sermon that day at the Oratory.

Accepted into the Montreal archdiocese high school seminary program, Mugant's ability at studies brought him to Rome's Pontifical Gregorian University, where his superiors sent him to study Canon Law upon graduation from the Preparatory Seminary. Canon lawyers rose quickly in the Church, Mugant soon was to find out, and the Church's law for that reason became almost his sole object of learning. His other courses in Rome were simply tolerated as necessary distractions as he learned the subtleties and distinctions of legal argument he knew he needed to master in order to impress his teachers in Rome.

Now at 56, Mugant was a Cardinal fifteen years, a feat of great achievement not lost on any of the faithful. Asked to draft a canonical code for rules on biogenetics some eighteen years earlier, Mugant's reward for his work was the Cardinals' red hat and a seat of power near the Pope. He had been appointed to the secretive Roman Curia, the Catholic Church's governing bureaucracy.

"Your Eminence, good morning." It was 9:45 a.m., and Anslem Cardinal Mugant had just entered the shadowy, bare walled vestibule of the ancient chapel Sant' Agnesi fuori la Mura, where he was to celebrate, by special dispensation, the Mass of the Resurrection for a Redemptorist cleric, Mugant's personal confessor, who had suddenly died at the Redemptorist Roman college, the Alfonsiana where he was stationed, three days prior. Saint' Agnesi, it is said, was built by the Emperor Constantine's daughter, Constantia, who suffered from leprosy and often prayed at the Church for a healing which never came.

Mugant's eyes fixed on the priest who had just greeted him. "Is it done?"

"He made it out of Tel Aviv alive, your Eminence. But we are awaiting his arrival at da Vinci airport now."

"What?" Mugant stopped short. "He's not dead? How did he escape, how did he get out of Tel Aviv?"

"We're not sure, Your Eminence. Our associate adamantly

swears that the poisonous dart hit him."

"Yet the man walked on the plane?"

"Yes."

"Could he have died in the air?" Mugant lowly voiced.

"We're not sure. The poison was lethal," the cleric answered.

Two young altar servers entered the hallway to the sacristy where the two clergymen now stood face to face. A deep stare advised them they were intruding on a conversation of privacy. Bowing their heads respectfully, they immediately left the room.

"I see. And the chemical used, it was checked?" Mugant asked as he removed a bothersome piece of linen from his sleeve.

"Yes. I know that for fact."

"Look, my friend," the Cardinal shot back as he shook his finger at the messenger. "I warned you there better be no mistakes. And now he's arriving here in Rome, the one place in the world I didn't want him to come to!"

"Perhaps he's coming to bring the items to the Church?"

Mugant's hand grabbed the clergyman's cassock sleeve and pulled him closer. "Listen, you imbecile of hideous peculiarities, I've protected your hide for years under the guise of my office, but my patience with you is nearly over. You—"

"—but, Eminence—"

"—Don't give me *that* rhetoric," Mugant hardened three stale inches away from the shaken cleric. "I know what you're about to say, but you must be the biggest fool on earth. Max Train believes in nothing. He is a scientist possessing abilities that cannot be permitted. For the Holy Father's sake these abilities of his must never be used. Never!" he vowed, moving just a hair's breadth away from the priest. "Regardless of his intent—which we have no way of knowing—he can create commotions that must be avoided. This institution already has enough to deal with. I don't need another issue to attend to."

"We will get him. I promise," the shaken cleric responded as he stepped back from Mugant's sudden release.

"You better not fail this time. None of you better fail!"

"We won't," he responded.

"If the items are not in my possession today, I promise you'll not see tomorrow's sun," the Cardinal warned.

"Yes, Your Eminence."

Turning his attention away from the cleric, Mugant fastened

his gaze admiringly on the sheen on his silk-clothed vestments. *Why am I surrounded by incompetent, weak buffoons? Must I do everything myself?*

The ancient bell tower's cry signaled the morning congregation to the Mass. From inside his private anteroom, alto voices chanting *O Bello Dio, del Paradiso* were heard.

Turning to the cleric he had just rebuked, Mugant told him "I will vest for Mass. Where is the Brother who is to assist me? I need my alb and cincture. It must be the gold cincture. And I want the Gothic vestments, not the Roman, for this ceremony. Hot though it is, I am being photographed at this Mass and want it to look just right."

The altar server rang the bells at the sacristy entranceway onto the altar, and Mugant sensed a satisfaction that all eyes in the small church would now look towards him as he made his way to the altar. Outside the church speakers had been set up the day before so that the many Redemptorists who sought to pray for their deceased brother would be able to pray with the Cardinal. Mugant was pleased knowing he would have the attention of both those inside and outside Sant' Agnesi.

"The Mass today will be celebrated in English," the lector began as Mugant approached the altar. "Father Linus, our deceased confrere, spoke English as his native language."

An altar server on either side of him now, Mugant bowed to the crucifix hanging from the gray stone wall of the centuries-old Church, and then turned to face the assembled. White was the color of his liturgical garb, with gold trimming setting it off from the stark interior that characterized the setting for this Mass of the Resurrection. Mugant wanted no flowers anywhere near the altar where he was to say the Mass. His possible allergic reaction to the scent of them was more important to him than the feeling of calm that flowers were known to bring to grievers.

"In the Name of the Father and of the Son..." Mugant began, but his thoughts were on his quarry, Max Train. *"Let us call to mind our sins,"* he intoned, as the faithful both inside and outside the Church began to recite the Confession of sin. While he heard their recitation, Mugant looked at the stained glass window to his left, the sun shining brilliantly, and moved his chalice over to its light to catch the effect for his sacred vessel. A look of annoyance crossed his face as he questioned to himself why the altar server had not placed the chalice there originally. *Incompetence every-*

where.

"You were sent to heal the contrite," he began, and the choir took up Mozart's 1766 Paris *Kyrie*, which thrilled the Cardinal. "It is fitting that only the best chant be heard at a Cardinal's Mass," he told the Redemptorist choirmaster earlier who had flown to the Mass from St. Michael's in Toronto. "I must have only the great compositions. Nothing less will do."

"A reading from the Book of Proverbs," began the lector once the choir had finished the grand Kyrie. Mugant seated himself in the velvet-cushioned chair brought especially to the Church for him and listened to the counsel of Holy Writ on how to view death. He had heard it all before, and was more pre-occupied with a death he wished to have occur than over one he was asked to pray.

"I am the Resurrection and the Life, he who believes in me, even if he die shall live..." Mugant began in his most sonorous tone, giving these words from Christ to all within the sound of his voice at this Mass of the Resurrection. He had first heard these words at the Mass celebrated when his father died, and again when his mother died. Inspirational though these words were to so many, to Mugant they were more like rote sayings that kept mourners mollified. As he continued reading the Gospel passage, his eye caught the fraying green velvet on the pulpit's right side.

"The word of the Lord" the lector responded with the congregation as Mugant kissed the bible from which he had just read the Lord's gospel.

The Church was quiet as Mugant cast his eyes on the casket some seventeen meters from him in the Church's center aisle, before refocusing his eyes on the frayed cloth. "Dear people of God," he began. "Father Linus' passing to eternal beatitude is our opportunity to remember that we must be open to the call of the Lord to love each other, and care for the sick and the burdened. We must exercise great good towards all, and respect their contributions, just as we do Father Linus' today."

***

The plane landed two minutes shy of its expected arrival time from the Holy Land. *This is a good omen.*

Carefully removing the precious luggage from the coat

closet near his bulkhead seat, Max limped off the plane towards a preoccupied gate attendant who was attempting to speak to an Algerian traveler having difficulties.

Italy's busiest airport was just that on this early Friday morning: crowded with passengers from throughout the world en route to destinations near and far. For Rome's da Vinci, it did not matter time or season, the world was becoming smaller, and Rome was a hub for its connectivity.

A squat looking Italian *carabiniere* with a lethal Beretta 38/44 sub-machine gun carefully looked at each of El Al's arriving passenger as they exited out of the passenger gate. His stare was penetrating and suggested a lack of tolerance for any antagonist.

Close by was another *carabiniere* holding the leash of a large German shepherd dog.

The short *carabiniere* looked down at a piece of paper he was holding, then back towards the arriving passengers.

Sullen eyes carefully moved from one person to the next, looking, searching for someone.

His eyes shortly met Max's.

The Italian police officer glanced at the paper — a photograph, then shifted restlessly.

Max tried not to notice the officer's interest. *What's going on?*

Eye's darting back to Max, the *carabiniere* adjusted the machine gun under his arm.

Max's muscles tensed at the policeman's obvious unease. *Stay calm.* Max tried to appear patient as he waited, for what seemed to him an eternity, his turn in line.

The *carabiniere* stared menacingly at Max as he moved towards the passenger gate.

Max instinctively tightened his grip on the long corrugated box. *Stay calm, like you belong.* He noticed the gun's barrel rising towards him. *Something's wrong!*

Max's body visibly tightened.

The guard's body tensed as he gazed back at the paper in his hand.

Remember, you belong. You haven't done anything wrong. Max was seven meters away from the muscular *carabiniere*.

Max sensed the threatening tension building as he waited in line to pass the watching policeman. He looked straight ahead.

The cop moved to his left, forcing his eyes to meet Max's.

His heart racing, Max casually nodded at him. Stuck in the tunnel, he had one of two places to go - either back onto the plane or out through the gate.

A sullen nod acknowledged him back.

Three steps later he was side by side with the Italian police officer.

Max felt the intense stare of the suspicious officer, now looking at the box. *Keep walking!*

Another tentative step followed. Taking an additional step and noticing there was no tap on his shoulder he let out a sigh of relief. *Thank God.*

With a small tote over his good shoulder, along with the concealed artifacts, Max purposefully walked towards the Italian Customs line pretending a confident stride.

His senses were on alert, but relief swept over him as he continued alongside the other passengers to the Customs security check.

Remember, if anyone asks why you're carrying a piece of wood with you, stay calm and tell them you're an artist.

Approaching the annoying bright halogen lights above the Italian Customs clearing area, Max wondered if the suspicious idea of claiming the ancient artifacts were artistic remnants that he created would work with the Italian immigration officers.

Twenty minutes later, Keith O'Brian handed his British passport to an Italian immigration officer. As the young man punched in the passport numbers into his computer, Max's nervousness caused him to shift his weight from his good leg to his bad one.

"What's your purpose in Italy?" he asked in English.

"I'm on holiday," Max responded with a slight British accent.

"How long do you intend to stay?"

"Two weeks."

"Do you have a return ticket?"

Max paused. "No."

The Italian looked hesitantly at Max. "No return ticket?"

"No. I'll travel by train back to London."

He studied Max's El Al plane ticket. "Why were you in Israel?"

"On a holiday. I'm an artist. I wanted to visit the Holy Land."

"What do you have in the box?"

Max swallowed hard. "Wood."

The inspector's eyebrows arched curiously. "You carry wood with you?"

"I'm an artist—a sculptor."

The agent's lips tightened. "An artist?" he asked suspiciously. "Are you sure?"

"Yes."

The immigration agent flipped through O'Brian's passport. "A new passport," he said skeptically, eyeballing Max carefully. He stamped the European Passport and returned it to Max without looking at him. "Next in line."

Accepting the British passport, Max nodded to the officer, took the unquestioned, uninspected corrugated box from the Customs table, and walked out a doorway into the busy main terminal.

Now all I have to do is find a hotel to wash up in, then I can make the calls I need to.

Anxious to get out of the airport and into the crowded streets of Rome, Max increased his pace best he could. His leg throbbed with pain, but he believed his safety was secure outside the airport terminal.

"Keep walking straight ahead," hushed a male voice as he snuck up unnoticed alongside Max.

Surprised, Max glanced to his left and noticed a well-dressed bald man in his sixties next to him, his face looking forward.

"Max, say nothing, and look straight ahead," he urged.

"Who are you?" Max asked, following the odd man's instructions.

"A friend. You're being watched."

Max instantly felt like he was back in the cave and rocks were falling down all over him. "Who are you?" he asked, trying to keep a steady gait.

"A friend from Tel Aviv," he answered, keeping stride with Max in a manner that did not give away his mission. "Someone is desperately trying to find you."

Max felt his stomach fall like a lead weight on hearing the words. *I thought this was over. I need to get to Luke's people . . . to the Vatican.* He looked down at the cumbersome box he held in his right hand.

"What should I do?" Max asked while looking down at the

floor.

"Keep walking towards the exit sign. Do you see it? It's about 70 meters straight ahead."

"Okay."

"I'll find you and bring you to a safe house," the old man said before directing his pace away from Max.

"What's going on?"

"We're not sure, but someone wants you dead."

"What?"

"One of our agents was murdered at the airport in Tel Aviv."

"When?"

"A few hours ago while you were there. He was trying to keep an eye on you."

His mind became hazy as Max realized he was now involved in a deadly game. The images of people passing by blurred as the awareness that his life was at stake even here in Rome rushed at him.

"Max, you have a caring friend somewhere, and he—we're sure you have been marked. Explosives were used in the cave at the Mount of Olives."

Clarity began to come back. "Who did this? Who wants me dead?"

"I'm not sure."

Max's eyes scanned the airport landscape. Peoples of all persuasions were moving around indistinguishable as to intent. "Great."

"Keep walking. I'll be right behind you."

Unintentionally, Max slowed his stride as he searched for anyone suspicious. *Who in the world is that? A safe house?*

With the flood of travelers in the airport, it was difficult to notice anyone odd looking. He kept walking. *You gotta get out of the airport.*

A woman wearing a stylish black dress cut below the knees, appearing to be in her mid- forties carefully monitored the move-ments of the Israeli informer. She was certain he had relayed a message to Max Train. *Why in the world are the Mossad involved with him? This is not good. If Train gets out of the airport, we will never find him if they're involved.*

Realizing Max was at a manageable pace 35 meters from the airport's exit, she reached inside her black purse. Two deter-mined associates familiar with Max's appearance stood near the exit aiming to further assure against any possible escape by Train. Eyes scanning the crowd, she looked for other Mossad. *How many agents do they have here?*

Her heart pumped, excitedly. This was what she was trained to do. However, the last thing she wanted was to provoke a clash with the Mossad. *Peace or no peace, I have my orders: stop Max Train at all costs, and take the items he's in possession of.*

She quickened her pace, gaining on the courier.

A concealed Gazio dart gun suddenly emerged from her purse.

The courier noticed a young man seated nearby begin turning the pages of a newspaper. *A signal! What's wrong?*

Stopping and turning quickly, his eyes at once locked onto the approaching woman. *Damn!*

A deadly, fleeting glance was returned.

Suddenly, the burning sting of the poisonous dart found the older man's chest. Eyes focused on the small deadly shaft lodged in his torso, the old courier felt the freezing acid-like poison immediately enter his bloodstream and rush agonizingly through his veins. As the toxin's surging arctic coldness raced to his brain, immobilizing his limbs, he knew it was now his time to die. His chest immediately tightened as his lungs valiantly fought for air. Heartbeat racing painfully, his heart feeling like it was ready to burst, he could not move. The poison overtaking him had paralyzed his central nervous system.

Unable to do anything, his expressionless, fading eyes watched the woman focus her attention on Max. It was a look confirming everything to him; he was believed to be no longer a threat to whoever was attempting to stop Max. It was an accurate assumption.

The Mossad agent stood, his fleeting remaining seconds observing two unknown men approaching him, waiting for him to die. *What is it about Max Train?*

A warm sensation eased down his right leg. *God have mercy.*

His pounding heart literally exploded moments later.

The coroner would eventually report that his death was from an acute heart attack.

Unbothered and undeterred by her killing, the assassin quickened her steps towards Max, inconspicuously reloading the Gazio gun with another deadly dart.

The young Mossad agent had already dropped the newspaper and was briskly walking towards Max, who was less than 20 meters from the exit gate.

Max turned his head and noticed the woman toying with something in her hand. The look on the woman's hurried face told him everything. *Something's wrong!*

"*Senora!*' exclaimed the charging Israeli agent. "*Mi scusi, mi scusi!*" he yelled as he raced ahead, attempting to distract the killer.

Surprised, the woman turned towards the young commando wearing a stylish gray Ferragamo suit.

Max turned to see the young man approach the attractive Italian looking woman. *That guy's face, I've seen it before in Israel. But where?*

The Mossad agent pressed on, to the surprise of the Italian *contessa*, who was lifting the Gazio gun towards him in public. "*Uno momento, Senora. Uno momento!*"

The woman ignored him.

Max cautiously kept moving, when suddenly his eye caught something odd. *The woman! Oh, my God, she has a gun!*

Max spun to his left while lifting the corrugated box in front of him.

The woman's two male associates moved towards her, not sure what was next.

Max moved diagonally towards a second exit door, and away from the gun. *I have to get out of here.*

"No! Stop him!" roared the woman, startling everyone in earshot of her penetrating voice. "Get the box!"

Max turned to look at the woman and saw the lethal firearm rising towards him twenty feet away.

The Mossad agent charged hard, trying to prevent her shot. *Get the box! Who is she?* Train's heart pounded.

The two henchmen raced to form a protective barrier in front of the *contessa*.

The Israeli got closer to the young woman.

An Eastern European gypsy wearing a T-shirt with the logo of a taxi medallion company entered through the airport's revolving doors in search of a customer.

Max, his back facing the doors, collided suddenly with the unsuspecting gypsy and dropped the box.

The woman aimed her weapon at the scientist.

Max's eyes caught the woman's aim.

The Israeli lunged for her, knocking down the larger of the two co-conspirators in the process.

The female assassin's steel like finger pressed down on the Gazio as the Mossad agent crashed into her.

The lethal dart propelled out of the chamber towards Max.

Max moved to his right.

The cyanide-laced dart missed him.

"Ugghhh!" It was the gypsy, eyes ajar in horrified bewilderment.

"Stop him, in the name of God!" urged the fallen woman as she wrestled the Mossad agent.

"Get out of here," screamed the Israeli towards the American.

The second henchman concentrated his attention on Max, who was reeling in pain from the collision he had with the dying gypsy.

"Stop him. Stop Train!" screamed the female executioner again before the Mossad's fist neutralized her.

Max felt the clutching hand of the dying gypsy on his shoulder, the man's face completely contorted from the venomous dart wedged in his throat. *Good God!*

The gypsy's body convulsed, as he struggled to tell Max something.

Max saw the gypsy's eyes bulging to the right.

Train turned back to the killer and noticed the young commando making his way free. "Get out of here, Max," he repeated before turning his attention to the larger male thug, who was now reaching for a gun.

As he did, the other henchman aggressively moved towards an unsuspecting Max, ready to carry out his virtuous orders.

Max heard the metallic sound of keys falling to the floor. He turned back to the innocent Hungarian man readying for death.

The charging Italian assailant reached into his suit coat—a knife!

The Hungarian's eyes widened in painful disbelief at Max, who turned immediately, grasping the dying man's warning.

Two *carabiniere,* startled by the commotion, raced towards the fuss from a distant cambio exchange.

"God bless you," Max said, as he reached towards the dying man's throat, and removed the deadly dart. Noticing his precious cargo nearby, he turned back towards the killer.

Raw determination filled the professionals' face. His hand held the deadly steel blade as he bore down on Max.

Adrenaline flowing, Max charged towards the onrushing assailant.

Four meters away, the killer arched the deadly stiletto.

The knife's merciless blade descended towards Max.

Max's body tightened in mortal anticipation as his eyes caught the glisten of the cold steel.

The killer charged like a deadly bull.

Airborne, Max forcefully wedged the poisonous dart from the dead gypsy's throat into the stalker's stomach, as his wounded left shoulder crashed into the man's body and toppled him over.

Pain surged throughout Max's body, but the endorphin driven sensation of revenge he felt upon seeing the agonizing eyes of the killer becoming overtaken by the deadly poison comforted him for the moment.

Startled, and reeling in unfathomable burning pain, the killer reached for his knife.

Crouching on the floor, Max sprang at the assailant, his hands gripping hard at its mark between the killer's legs.

"Ughhh!" The man's eyes rolled back, revealing intolerable pain as Max crushed his find, causing him to drop the knife.

Years of pent-up rage exploded as Max's hands squeezed harder. "You son-of-a-bitch! How do you bastards know my name?"

In unbearable internal and external suffering, the henchman's eyes bulged. His mouth opened emptily as his chest tightened in shock from the unrelenting pressure on his groin. His body trembled as death suddenly claimed him.

"Max, go!" the Israeli barked as he wrestled with the other thug.

Max looked up and saw the police getting closer.

Glimpsing over at the dead gypsy's T-shirt, he released the iron grip on his fallen assassin. *A taxi driver?*

"Stop right there!" ordered a machine-gun totting carabiniere from a closing distance.

Seeing the dead man's car keys on the floor, he picked them up, and then reached for the artifacts.

"Stop or I'll shoot!"

Using every bit of remaining energy, Max scrambled

towards the exit door, and onto the airport sidewalk. Passersby moved out of his determined way.

His eyes immediately noticed an empty taxi – the gypsy's car? *Please!*

With deafening speed he found the ignition key and jumped into the old red Fiat. The ancient artifacts alongside him, Max sped off just as the *carabiniere* reached the terminal exit door.

Chapter V

"Let us go in peace to love and serve the Lord" Anselm Mugant urged the faithful as he brought to a close the Mass just celebrated for the repose of the soul of his Redemptorist confessor. Taking the gold chalice and ciborium into his hands, he turned to leave the marble altar for the gray sacristy where only earlier he had given instructions to have Max Train killed. The contrast did not faze him. "The Church is forever, her doctrines eternal," Mugant had written on receiving the red hat. Any threat to doctrine in his eyes had to be handled swiftly. The greater the threat, the more decisive the means needed to halt the threat. He persuaded himself rather easily of this. His order to end Train's life followed this rule.

***

Max's heart pounded as he raced the stolen taxi out of the airport and away from the unknown stalled assassins who somehow were expecting his arrival into Rome. With each passing highway marker, he felt he was moving faster towards the tantamount epicenter of an unavoidable constrictive black hole, its magnetic force too powerful to escape, its final determination impossible to see.

He had seen death's cruelty once again, but now, as opposed to in the past, he was the one responsible for calling upon the Reaper.

Around him surreal images of speeding cars and buildings were left behind as he pushed the old Fiat taxi engine to its limits. Bedazzled over more killings, Max struggled with the feeling he was drowning in a cesspool of unavoidable impious disorder, its overwhelming destructive force reeking fervently as it clutched at his dwindling spirit.

Unbearable reflections of the twisted faces of the dying Mossad courier, the dead gypsy, and the Italian assassin he killed, all agonizing in horror as the grip of painful death overtook each of them, converged on him. The destructive image of the exploding cave crushing his three friends outside of Jerusalem seared its way into his memory. Yet none of these awful recollections compared to the cruel, shadowy vision desperately trying to resurface of the bloodstained walls tinted with the bludgeoned remains of his beloved wife and daughter the night he arrived at his home in Syracuse, New York.

It was apparent whoever was responsible for the killings in the Holy Land two days ago had a great purpose: to see him dead and they would stop at no cost or effort to succeed in their plans.

As Max entered Rome, the taxi light turned off, dashing from one lane to another in order to secure his safety, racing past the Coliseum on Via S. Gregorio, he made an unexpected right turn and headed towards the Termini rail station, near the Piazza della Republica. Knowing there was safety in numbers, traveling in the city's heavily visited tourist areas made sense.

Now in the center of Rome, a place of great familiarity, Max carefully recalled the incident that unfolded earlier that day. While he remembered the unexpected warning from the old courier from Israel, the image of the business traveler at the kiosk in ben Gurion flashed in his mind.

Coincidence? Max was beginning to realize there was no such thing – not when his life was continually being threatened. After all, how did the female assailant know his name, and what did she really mean when she said 'stop him in the name of God'?

He glanced over at the box containing parts of the cross. He was beginning to understand a part of the burden Jesus of Nazareth had to endure.

Continuing on through the crowded maze that is Rome's city highway with fluency, the arduous burden of the profound cross grew. *Six deaths – six murders in two days, all over a wooden relic used to crucify Jesus. This is not what Christ died for, yet it becomes more prominent with each passing day. Whoever is trying to find and kill me is fearless. Good God, they killed a Mossad agent in an Israeli airport, and took out another one of them here. And they're able to move so quickly. And how did they know I was on the flight? Were they looking for me or O'Brian?*

While driving on Via Nazionale, Max made a right turn onto Via Crispi and noticed a parking garage. He looked down at his left leg. There were no bloodstains, something that might not stand out in Israel, but this was Rome.

After parking the taxi and grabbing his belongings, Max returned onto Via Crispi and hailed a cab.

It was time to get some answers.

***

The Mass had ended and Cardinal Mugant was now in black cassock and the cardinals' red piping in his Curial office, located on the third floor of the Palace of the Holy Office, Vatican City.

In many instances small and insufficiently ventilated, the Curial offices were where the Vatican hierarchy frequently deliberated on the most sensitive issues in the Church. Slow to modernize, conveniences such as air-conditioning and central heating were deeply appreciated if an office had them.

"Cardinal Mugant, there is news to be announced tomorrow that a renowned French scientist claims he has discovered the means to clone human cells that can develop into a fetus," said Father Flavio Rinaldi, Mugant's Curial assistant for scientific affairs. He had come to his post after studies in England at Oxford. Roman by birth and culture, Rinaldi was responsible for reviewing and summarizing all scientific publications on which the Church expressed moral opinions. His expertise in genetics had brought him to Mugant's office at the Vatican after the new Curial decastery for Human Life had been established. Mugant was its head.

"It's coming out in *Paris Match* that the French have made major strides in the genetics of fetal development, your Eminence. Sister Pasquale Cordesco notified me this morning. The Cardinal Secretary of State has called a meeting for all Curial heads to meet tomorrow at the Curia so as to prepare an official Church response."

"They cannot have gotten that far," Mugant told his aide.

"Your Eminence, could it be that there are so many genetic research projects ongoing around the world that it's impossible to keep up with all of them?"

"Don't be naive. My office has our ways. Nothing escapes us."

"Yes, Eminence."

"Who are these doctors that dare the word of Our Lord?" said Mugant suddenly. "I'm sure we are going to hear this same moronic rhetoric from these scientists. They have the audacity to publicly state—as if they know—that Our Holy Father has held back the march of knowledge so that they can freely rationalize their deplorable sacrilegious actions in the name of science. These are the same murderers willing to abort the living fetus in the name of stem cell research. They're willing to interfere with God's Nature. Rinaldi, is it not these very same ideas that the madman Hitler tried to foist on the world in the name of a supreme Aryan race? Of course it is. We've seen this before. This is not new. For all that is in me I will not permit this to happen."

Flavio Rinaldi stared silently at the Cardinal.

"I want all the information you can obtain on these Frenchmen. You and Sister...Doctor Cordesco have that assignment. I need everything by tonight."

"As you request, Cardinal Mugant."

"These individuals believe they can get away with this?" Mugant arrogantly muttered to himself, rising to leave his office. "Rinaldi, my briefcase there. And those papers."

Leaving his office, Mugant turned right down the newly carpeted third floor of the Palace of the Holy Office. Nearing a corner stairwell, he walked down the three flights onto the main floor. Approaching the exit door onto the grounds he saw one of the Pallottine Brothers assigned to assist the Cardinals officed at the Palace. "Take me to my apartment, Brother Leo. Go the quickest route possible. I need to change my attire before I pay an unexpected visit to the Cardinal Secretary of State. By the way, have you received a message for me from Father Cavaldi?"

"No," the Brother responded. "I have only received glowing messages on the Mass for your confessor, and on how uplifting your sermon was, Eminence."

"I have, by the way, that special cross of Saint Benedict your mother asked for, Brother Leo. I'll get it to you soon."

"Thank you Cardinal Mugant," the Pallottine responded. "It will make her so happy."

***

A monsignor from the Secretary's chambers approached Cardinal Mugant, who was seated in the Cardinal Secretary of State's reading room. Mugant had been musing to himself at the absence of rare books anywhere in the Cardinal Secretary's collection. A 1589 Gutenberg Bible had passed into the Canadian's possession not a month prior, which he thought of as complementing his Dutch 1741

Keurbijbel. His most prized Bible was a binding believed to have been the 1143 work of the Carthusians from Chartreuse. It was never known how this came into his possession.

"He is ready, Eminence." Rising from his chair, and adjusting his cassock sleeves, Mugant nodded to the Monsignor and looked at the clock on the office wall. *This time he is not making me wait*, Mugant said to himself. *This is good, he knows this is serious.*

"Will you have some water, Anselm?" the Cardinal Secretary asked Mugant as the Canadian entered the library antechamber of the Pope's senior diplomat. "Something to refresh you?" A master of moderation, with an envied ability to hold all confidences, the sixty-eight year old black hair Spaniard had served his entire Priesthood in the Vatican Diplomatic Corp. Rarely given to expressing his own views, the frail statured Ferdinand de Salvoyar had swiftly risen through the Vatican bureaucracy after having served as a mediator for the Holy See in tense, but successful, discussions over seven years with the People's Republic of China on property rights in China for several of the Church's missionary orders there. Summoned back to the Vatican de Salvoyar held different sensitive diplomatic portfolios till appointed four years previous to his current post. If silence ever needed an advocate, it had one in this diplomat.

"Water will do," Anselm Mugant responded, taking a glass from de Salvoyar's attendant. At a nod from the Cardinal Secretary, the attendant left the room, closing the Secretary of State's office door.

"I am here to speak with you about an urgent matter that has arisen, doubtless some of which you may already know."

"Take a seat, please. Tell me what you think is necessary. A telephone would not do?" the Pope's most senior aide began.

Mugant seated himself in one of the deep cushioned chairs that had been in the Secretary of State's library as a gift from Mussolini at the signing of the 1929 Lateran Treaty. This concordat assured the Vatican of its permanent status as a free and independent country.

"Telephones have their place, Eminence. But not in this circumstance," Mugant replied. The Canadian placed his water glass on the table next to him.

He went on. "We are in 'the brave new world'. It started years ago, Cardinal de Salvoyar. And now we have this report in

Paris Match."

The Vatican's senior diplomat sat himself behind his desk. "I am listening, Cardinal Mugant."

"Half a century ago, the trans-humanists took control of the science labs. With 'the pill' artificial contraception gave freedom of conception. The Church's response? 'Natural family planning.' Then two decades pass and we start getting whispers of artificial procreation, or should I call it 'creation'? Contraception was not enough. *In vitro* fertilization, Petrie dishes, artificial insemination, test tube babies. The Church's response? Muted, to say the least. Who was condemned in all this time?"

"We had *Humane Vitae*, Anselm. The Church reaffirmed the sacredness of life and married love."

"An encyclical from a Pope who devastated the Church's liturgy many say, and whose own advisors, it was rumored, opposed his stand in the encyclical. He was not forceful enough as a result. Platitudes, some said. Where was the one sentence in it that absolutely forbade violating Church teaching? Not some phrase simply counseling against artificial birth control—but a sentence in that encyclical unconditionally forbidding it?"

The Cardinal Secretary placed his index finger to his lip. "Go on Mugant."

"Now we have scientists taking embryos and wanting to destroy them for the sake of medicine. They call it 'harvesting', 'therapeutic cloning'— extract the code of life from the embryonic cells, inject it into an egg, and you have a liver, a pancreas, an arm. My God, are not these embryos persons too? Where is the Church in this?"

The Pope's senior advisor said nothing as Mugant continued. "Now we supposedly have news that not only has science been able to give you spare body organs, it is rumored that genetic programming capability has been developed to grow a full fledged human from the cloned cell. This is unacceptable Cardinal de Salvoyar. Scientists are not free to be God.

"The Church has played with science through this half century of one transgression after the other of God's procreative law. It has waxed and waned, been indecisive, failing to make the statement that would show its full opposition."

"Cardinal Mugant, the Pope's and Bishops have come out continually criticizing—"

"—But not in dogma! They have not stated infallibly that

'We solemnly assert to our brethren any tampering with the process of procreation violates the very law of God and causes the agent in this case to incur excommunication.' We don't excommunicate any more, Eminence —and we are loath to speak infallibly, or to preach a dogma. We must now speak so, and that is the reason I am meeting with you now. Insist in no uncertain terms to the Holy Father to condemn infallibly, from the Chair of Peter, all tampering with life. Assert as dogma that human life is only the Creator's work, and no else. The *Paris Match* piece gives the right opportunity and timing for such an announcement. Time is of the essence."

"You know that dogmatic pronouncements are rare. The last was in 1950 with Pius XII, and that was on his own, without a council. He made the Assumption a matter of dogma, which all the Church is required to believe."

"Precisely. Pius did it on his own. There was no council called. We have Vatican 1 that gives Peter infallibility. Now his Holiness can invoke it once more on this matter of the violations of life. Surely he has the strength to face this. Anyone who has fought cancer and put it in remission, as the Holy Father did his prostate cancer, is of the right mettle, the right depth. Once and for all, the Pope needs speak *ex cathedra*. Hell will be the punishment for those who make themselves the gods of life. This has to be his instruction to the world."

"Anselm, this is the 21st century. We no longer have the ability to coerce, to bring fear into the world and expect the world to respond to our wishes. We must teach, not threaten. We must persuade, not demand. If we are to reach our flock, including those who have strayed for whatever reasons, we must continue to evolve into a Church of understanding. Secularism does not work. We have seen this over and again, politically and otherwise. Your way has not worked, as our history shows."

"I expect the Cardinal Secretary will inform His Holiness of my view" Mugant chafed. "Our Holy Father gave me the red hat for the expertise I brought to this issue in canon law—"

"—I know, Mugant, however—"

"—there is no 'however', Eminence, is there? Either life is sacred and inviolate—dogmatically so — or it is not. And we can continue to play and experiment if it is not.

"You have my view, and I of course will feel free to continue to express it. I shall take my leave now. We have discussed much. I am sure the Holy Father is interested in all the conversations you have with his Cardinals, Cardinal de Salvoyar."

***

John Burns, a citizen of Vancouver, British Columbia checked into the small hotel on the celebrated Via Condotti, Rome's grand shopping mecca housing Italy's leading couture fashionistas such as Valentino, Bulgari, Versace, Cartier, Ferragamo, and Armani. With a view of the famous Spanish Steps in the fabled er ghetto de l'inglesi - the English ghetto section of Rome, the hotel's location was ideal for vacationers. Handing his Canadian passport to the hotel attendant, Mr. Burns peeked down at the long corrugated box.

Refusing assistance from the bell captain, the hotel guest soon found his way to a spacious studio flat on the third floor of the hotel. The room was inviting: rich antiques carefully appointed accessorized the grand view of Francesco De Sanctis' world famous marble staircase, the crowded Scalinata di Trinita dei Monti.

It was early in the afternoon, and Max felt like hell.

After inspecting his healing wounds, his eyes peered out the gothic shuttered windows and focused on the Piazza di Spagna and the ingenious large boat Barcaccia fountain at the base of the Spanish Steps.

Eyes ascending, Max noticed how the famous architectural landscape presently inhabited by tourists from all over the world had twelve flights of steps of varying width. In a petrification of dancing rhythm, Max's eyes, similar to the fabled steps, moved upwards towards the magnificent Piazza Trinita' dei Monti and the Greek Catholic Church of St. Atanasio, located on Via del Babuino, named literally 'Baboon street' after a hideous statue that is situated near the church.

Under the bright afternoon sky peddlers from the southern continent and eastern Europe hawked their imitation wares while musicians from a near and a far performed their craft to engaged visitors only too happy to participate in the entertaining spirit of the environment.

This was Rome just like Max recalled it to be.

And Rome, as it was known, had the fingerprints of Vatican City all over it.

To his right were five machine-toting *carabinieri* excitedly engaging one another near the imaginative Trevi Fountain, completed in celebration of ancient Rome's abundance by Nicola Salvi around 1750.

Partially closing the window's shutters, he moved to the walnut desk and picked up the telephone.

Weathered eyes looked towards the loud ringing phone in the small study an ocean away. "I'll be right back," said Rabbi Kohn as he put down the food he was feeding to the fish in his stunning salt-water tank.

"Yes?"

"Marty, it's Max."

"Are you okay?"

"I'm not hurt any less than I was two days ago, if that's what you mean."

"Good. I heard about today."

"They were waiting for me."

"Max, do you have any idea who *they* are?"

"I'm clueless –"

"—well, someone it appears is desperate to find you, my friend. They killed my two associates in Rome that went to greet you today."

"What?"

"It's true."

Max shook his head in disbelief. "The young fellow, too?"

"Shot by the local police – purposefully, from what I understand."

"What do you mean, Marty?"

"I'm saying that according to my source at the airport, the *carabiniere* had no need to use a firearm. They could have easily detained him, but chose not to."

"Good God," Max whispered. "I'm sorry. I don't know what to say, other than thank you for all of your help."

Rabbi Kohn let Max linger on the line for a moment.

"It was a risk anticipated. It's always a risk for us. You know what happened at the airport in Tel Aviv?"

"I think so. Whoever is trying to find me –"

"—kill you," the cleric corrected.

"Yes, kill me . . . well, they're willing to do almost anything to get to me," Max said as he looked at the digital clock. It was 2:00 p.m. in Italy.

"Max, I'm sure you would tell me if you could why these

people are after you. For the moment, I'll think that for some reason it's in my best interest not to know. Is that, umm, correct?"

Max hesitated. "For the moment."

"Okay," the Auschwitz survivor surmised. "It would be accurate for me to say that you haven't intentionally hurt anyone, correct?"

"No."

Max's answer caught his friend by surprise. "What do you mean?"

"I killed one of those bastards at the airport."

"Yes Max, I'm aware of that, but that's different. Your life was a stake. What I meant was –"

"—not before anything that happened today, no."

"Well, there is only one thing that comes out of the Holy Land, Max," the Rabbi sullenly voiced. "I think I'll assume whoever is after you belong to some type of fanatical group of religious zealots, and you have something they want. Fair?"

"Fair," he answered, reflecting on how the woman screeched the name of God against him at the airport.

"There's something else I need to tell you."

"What?"

"Do you remember what you mentioned to Sara?"

"I mentioned several things," Max responded.

"About the cave," Rabbi Kohn added.

"I do. My friends were there."

"I know," the rabbinical man said as he rubbed his long beard. "I guess it will not be a surprise to you to know dynamite caused the cave-in."

"I thought so," Max poignantly said.

"There's more."

Max leaned into the phone. "Yes?"

"Well, a search and rescue operation began a few hours ago, but the explosion caused the cave's roof to collapse. According to Sara, there's no way anyone survived, and it will take weeks before the site is excavated – if it can be done at all. The area is still unstable."

Over the last few days Max had accepted that his friends were no longer alive. What was hard to accept was that the three bodies might not be recovered. "I understand."

"I'm sorry," the Rabbi offered.

"Yeah."

Rabbi Kohn waited a moment to allow Max to collect his thoughts. "Max, what are you going to do?"

"I'm not sure."

"Why don't you come back home?"

"I can't."

"Are you sure, or is it that you choose not to?"

"Probably both," he responded.

"Do you know what you're doing?"

"I'm not sure, but I'm tired of running. I need some answers."

"I see, but remember Max, these people, they know what they're doing."

"I know – but it's too big, Rabbi."

Max's words were understood by his loyal friend.

"Max, are you using the identifications you were given?"

"I'm under 'John Burns'."

"Good. Don't use any others. The credit cards are good for up to twenty thousand dollars – ten thousand apiece. I'll monitor them in case you're running low, but be smart."

"Marty, thanks. I'm not sure where I'm going, or what's going to happen next, but I want you to know I appreciate everything."

"You would have done the same, and in many ways my friend, I have a grandson because of you. I told you I would never forget," Marty reminded Max of a promise made when Max assisted the Rabbi's family years ago.

After a few minutes, Max hung up the telephone to the States.

Nervously, he dialed the telephone numbers to Luke and Eileen Gartner's home outside of Vatican City.

After three sterile rings, Eileen picked up the phone. "Hello," she said in English.

"Eileen?"

"Max, is that you?" she asked, warily.

"Yes." *I can't believe I have to do this.* "Eileen, you know Luke came down to see me in Israel?" he began.

"Yes, a few days ago," she hesitantly replied.

He was my friend – you're both my friends.

"Eileen, there's been an accident involving Luke," Max confided.

"Eileen?" Max voiced.

"What . . . what happened?"

"It was bizarre. There was a cave-in, and Luke was inside."

"Oh?"

"He didn't make it out."

Eileen Gartner vacillated. "I don't understand, Max. Luke – he's dead?"

"Yes. I'm sorry, Eileen," Max said stoically. "Listen, I need to see you. There are things going on that don't make any sense, and I'm not sure if you're at risk the way Luke and I were."

Hunched over is her chair, Eileen despondently whispered "what?"

"Eileen, I need you not to mention anything to anyone until after I see you, and if anyone calls looking for me, you haven't heard from me. Okay?"

"What are you saying?"

"I think Luke was . . . murdered."

"What?"

"Eileen, listen to me. You can't say anything to anyone until I talk to you. Do you understand?" he forcefully said.

"I . . . I guess."

"Good. Can you meet me at the Barcaccia Fountain by the Spanish steps at 7:00 p.m. tonight?"

"Yes," she answered in shock.

"I'm sorry Eileen. I'll explain more to you in a few hours. I'm sorry to burden you in asking to keep this to yourself until I see you, but it's important."

"Max?" Eileen said emotionlessly.

"Yes," he replied as he was ready to hang up the phone.

"Are you sure . . . he was --"

"—I don't know for sure. I'll see you in a few hours."

* * *

"We just got him making a call."

"Vatican Radio, one moment please."

"Come down the hall and tell me. No names on this line."

Putting aside his radio programming list for that day the tall, gray hair Director of Vatican Radio got up from behind the digital console and turned to his assistant. "Take care of any incoming calls. I'll be back momentarily."

"Before you leave, sir, where do you want these satellite photos that came in?"

"I've seen them, send them to the Vatican Observatory." He looked at his watch, noticeably conscious of the time passing.

"You have these briefings called in this morning on the Bosnia dispute."

"They go to the Secretary of State's office. You know that. Send them there now."

"The sender requested you read the notes."

"Photocopy them, and I will."

Walking past the newsroom, he met the English technician who had just called him on a secured line.

"Did you tell anyone?"

"No, no," the Englishman whispered. "I called you as soon as they hung up. It was only moments ago. The tap on the line came in very clear. We heard the whole conversation, and I have it on tape."

"Move over here, out of the way."

"How about where the call came from? Did you get that?"

"No, it was too short to pinpoint. We do know the relay switch line is located somewhere near the Trevi Fountain which means Train must be nearby."

"We need to know *where* he is."

"Did they say anything about the cross, where it was, who has it? Anything on the next plan of action?"

"No, but he seemed concerned. They're planning to meet at the Barcaccia Fountain by the Spanish Steps at 7 p.m."

"Get the conversation typed up. I'll get it to his Eminence. He suspected Train would seek Gartner's wife out."

"What made him think that?"

"What else would a man fearful for his life do when he can't reach his best friend? You call the wife."

***

Max felt like an isolated man on a barren island struggling to withstand brutal, overpowering gusts of wind smashing into his face, his chilled feet sinking deeper into the cold sand of the raging seashore as dark omnipotent clouds of destruction approached the unprotected beachfront he was unable to leave.

He stared at the carefully wrapped box on the floor.

Until now he would never have imagined how troublesome the sacred artifacts could be. But reality was sinking in. Death's putrefied hand continued reaching for him in the name of God, relentlessly butchering anyone standing in his allegiance.

His decision on what to do with the remnants of the Holy Cross was wavering. Too many things didn't make any sense, and the news of the Italian police killing the young Mossad agent, coupled with the need to speak to Eileen Gartner, only increased his wariness on turning over the artifacts to the Vatican.

Standing up, he looked out the window, his eyes escalating up the hill towards Santo Atanasio Church. *Why is this happening? When will it all end? You have not given me any direction, yet more killings occur by the day. Why?*

Moving back to the desk he dialed a telephone number to Doctor Francesco Pellegrino in Bologna.

A two-minute conversation ensued.

Afterwards, Max quickly left the hotel, the neatly corrugated box under his arm, and into the sun drenched city streets of Rome.

***

"Good, the funds are sufficient," Mugant said to himself hanging the phone up after confirming a wire transfer.

The time has come. And there is not much left.

Garbed in a hand crafted full-length coat, Mugant exited his apartment building just off Rome's Via della Conciliaziaone. Walking briskly down the narrow streets leading away from the Vatican his figure cast a shortening shadow on the ancient cobblestone pavement as oncoming dusk dismissed the sun for another day. His Borsalino fedora, the one he bought in Lisbon for the Fatima celebration, hid his worried brow from the pedestrians hurrying by.

What are the consequences if this is the Cross, and this Train decides to try something? What will be said if there is evidence of a body on the Cross? This could cause serious issues to arise. Can he clone? Can any cell be cloned? How can we take a chance? The horror and sacrilege to attempt to bring Christ back.

What if Train fails at cloning? He murders Christ? And who will provide the egg?

What if Train went to the media? The news would be every-where, and all would look at him as the one with the power, the power to bring Christ back from his Cross!

Nothing's worked though. He is like a lizard slithering away from every bullet. What has brought man to this day? How is it possible that I would ever see this day, this moment of abuse of the most sacred?

The Canadian's pace quickened as he turned down a narrow alley onto the street of his destination, where stood a four story gray building. It showed little activity within it as he looked at its shut-tered windows. Entering the building, he ascended its dimly lit stairway.

As he reached the third floor, he turned to open the door. An unexpected hand firmly grasped his shoulder.

Mugant quickly turned around.

"You have more issues, your Eminence?" the voice said.

"Where did you come from?"

"From above."

"You could not have come from above - especially you."

"I watched you from the roof, waiting for our meeting. You're on time, Cardinal Mugant."

"Good, man! I am never late," he said as the resolve of the dead bolt opening echoed through the hallway. "Move on. This must be done quickly," he directed entering the darkened loft. "I'm not impressed with you waiting on the roof. You should have been in here waiting for me."

"I never knew I had to impress you. I work as I want. Unlike your New Testament's Roman centurion, I have no one who says 'Go, and I go, come and I come'."

"Even the devil can quote Scripture, can't he, and you do. No, you work for me. What if someone had seen you?"

Mugant's visitor defiantly chuckled.

"If you want your soul free from your sins, you will obey me," the Cardinal hostilely declared.

"What is this sin you speak of, *Eminenza*? For you know its meaning. I recall my first visit with you in the confessional. It was a day our union was bound forever," the visitor whispered in the shadow-cast room.

"I remember that day well. You came to me filled with sin,

your hands covered with the blood of many you murdered in your lifetime. How many innocent did you actually kill?" Cardinal Mugant probed.

"But did I really? I was just a tool. Cardinal, it was Man's intent to call upon me. Their hearts—and there were many—they were filled with darkness. It was this darkness that beckoned to them to call upon me. For I did not condemn those to death. That was the decision of others."

"Your hand is now used in His Name."

"As you wish," the visitor slyly grinned.

The room had been untouched since Mugant's last departure. The desk and its chairs were as they had been. Mugant used this flat only rarely.

"Let us be seated," Mugant began as they approached the table. The color in the sky was almost gone. No one from the outside could see into the unlit room. Inside their two faces were just shadows.

"I need some business taken care of. The individual I have in mind is now in Rome."

Mugant paused, moistening his dry lips before proceeding. The 7 p.m. church bells sounding the *Panis Angelicus* could be heard in the background.

Reaching into his suit coat pocket, Mugant produced two photos and slid them across the table.

Taking them, the shadowy figure studied the image of a man's face.

"His name is Max Train."

The assassin didn't bother to look up.

"He has some old wooden boards in his possession. I want them back."

The killer slowly lifted his head, eyes sparkling. "Oh?"

Chapter VI

"Sir, may I interest you in anything?" the stunning young woman asked.

"I'm browsing at the moment, but I'll let you know if I need assistance," the casual shopper said. Of average height and wearing traditional olive khaki pants and white oxford shirt underneath a blue Burbar raincoat, he politely looked at, and then over the petite woman. His itinerant brown eyes darted onto the dim city street outside.

"But of course," the woman said in schooled English, a common trait for Rome's most elite rag handlers. "If you need anything, do not hesitate."

Pretending to ably inspect the knitted garments of Italy's most favored fashion designer's boutique, Giorgio Armani, the lingering customer replied "thank you," as he gradually drifted towards the large bay window accompanied by three "fashionista" mannequins outfitted in the coming season's trendy attire.

From within the brightly lit store, the unassuming visitor heard the expansive resonance of the brass bells ringing in unison from the gothic bell towers of the Franciscan Church of Trinita dei Monti sitting high above the Spanish Steps.

It was 8:00 p.m.

Wandering eyes peered out the glass window and onto the crowded street ahead in search of his target. Experience advised him to conceal himself; after all, it was best to remain invisible in the face of conspiracy and death.

Thirty paces away was Pietro Bernini's Barcaccia Fountain. Congested with visiting tourists some there were at the Keats-Shelley House, and others sitting in front of the foundation of the Spanish Steps ingratiating themselves with Rome's magical custom of frivolousness. Trying to inspect the faces of each loitering person, displeasure crept up on the lone observer as the annoying darkness of nightfall prevented him from distinguishing the face sought from memory.

He needed to get closer.

Patience was not a virtue he was born with, but his life's journey became his cruel teacher. Endurance was now a tool he mastered.

Stepping out onto the busy cobbled sidewalk, the traveler walked away from the Barcaccia, and towards the renowned Greco Café' meters away from the clothier. Eyeballing an empty outdoor table, he thought otherwise and continued to amble unremarkably down the well traveled Via Condotti, careful of his surroundings.

Thirty meters down the street, he darted across the road. Continuing, he suddenly turned around near one of the many old street lamps illuminating the sidewalk and traveled in the other direction. Approaching the intended meeting location, he cautiously adjusted his waistband, his gait indifferent.

Pausing, eyes focused on the passing crowds dead ahead.

The colorful sounds of festive Rome filled his ears.

A cool breeze passing by did nothing for him.

His body tensed in anticipation.

Standing towards the stairs, eyes' scanning the ascending stairway was his objective!

Alone, or are others there?

He was a predator, regardless if he wanted to believe it or not. Rationalization of his behavior was not lost – and though it was not consciously evident, the murkiness of his actions was distantly beckoning him, reminding him of his violence. Thirst for knowledge or thirst for revenge – it did not matter: very little now did.

An old car, its thick exhaust fumes heavily polluting the street passed him by, the dark smoke it emitted of no concern to him. Nor were the two motor scooters recklessly tailing the sedan.

Seated on the crowded third level terra firma forty feet above the city street were a group of tourists enjoying the soft voice of an American musician playing her acoustic guitar.

Under the guise of a lighthearted traveler was a man wearing a light raincoat who was most familiar with Rome. His face beamed with merriment while his hands clapped in rhythm to the musician's song. Careful of his movements and gestures, the sightseer scrutinized the piazza below as well as the ascending steps leading to the Trinita dei Monti above him in search of any undesired interlopers soaking up the inviting panorama.

His seated position provided the perfect view of the Barcaccia.

He clapped his hands in song, participating in the gypsy-like festivities that occurred daily on the Spanish Steps for centuries.

Down below, a middle-aged woman was lingering around the fountain by herself.

The perched man leaned forward in interest, his gleeful face suddenly gone. He started to tap his fingers on the marble stairwell.

From the café' nearby, the conservatively dressed shopper recognized the unaccompanied woman surrounded by a dozen people.

Increasing his gait to a determined pace, eyes racing in question, he purposefully passed her by and joined the bustling crowd in the open piazza. Stopping twenty paces away, in the front of a retailer's window, he turned once again.

The woman appeared to be detached.

He approached her.

"Eileen, keep walking," Max said, his arm underneath hers, as he took the woman by surprise.

Startled, the woman moved in Max's direction towards the Trevi Fountain. "Max? What's the matter?"

"Eileen, I'm not sure if we're being watched," he replied, directing the woman down the street, "but it may be likely. There's a lot I need to tell you."

The woman, numb over Max's earlier phone call, moved along with him on the crowded street. "What's going on? Where's Luke?"

The brief encounter by the Barcaccia Fountain did not go unnoticed by the traveler sitting on the steps, who quickly stood up and began walking down the stairs, careful not to appear to act hastily.

He squeezed her arm. "I'm sorry. There was an accident of sorts in the cave – Luke was inside," Max continued.

Eileen Gartner tried to stop and turn, but Max steered her pace.

"Eileen, over the last few days many crazy things have happened. You know, I called Luke from Jerusalem and asked him to help me figure out how to proceed with an amateur dig," Max began, as he continued his pace towards the Ponte Cavour.

Keeping a mindful distance behind Max and Eileen Gartner were the careful eyes of the indistinguishable watcher. *They appear hurried. I know this trait. What is he telling her?*

Aware of the severity of which he was called upon to immediately exterminate his wealthy employer's obvious threat, the assassin increased his stealthy pace. Killing in gangland fashion on the open street was not ideal; however, this was Rome, his familiar streets, and his convenient customs. He had killed in public forums all over the world, doing the bidding for heads of state and governments alike in the name of power and righteousness. *This will be easy money, and more, Eminence!*

Few knew of him, but for those who did, he was the merciless facilitator of decisive judgment.

He was the assassin's assassin.

A chameleon of disguise, his approach undetectable, his deathblow always purposeful of the intended message, if a meaning was desired.

A preacher, banker, poet, waiter, doctor, journalist, electrician, dignitary, tourist, philosopher it mattered not. He was a believer in nothing other than himself.

He was *The Scorpion*.

Invisible to all except for one: his previous confessor, who no longer acted like a guide in the mist of his dark storms, but who now had become the pitiless, formidable undercurrent responsible for destroying any thoughts he may have once had of salvation, if salvation was a possibility.

Train's guarded movements as he continued to walk with the woman down the Via dei Condotti clearly indicated his target was sharing information with the woman, more than likely material his long-time patron Mugant would not want shared. A public double homicide on the crowded streets was not his first choice, but if it had to be done to protect his client – and his own reputation – so be it. An insignificant, but rather sizeable sum of monies collected weekly in baskets from around the world that eventually found its way to several numbered accounts located in nations near and far would provide for a nice holiday if necessary. That holiday in all likelihood, would not be. *I know he wants the items returned, but I'm sure I can always find where Train was staying and recover them.*

Besides, killing was the only nutrient his soul craved. Being the hand of ruthless anguish and pain was a drug he once tried desperately to give up. Now, it was all that mattered.

"Max, I don't understand this. You're telling me Luke's body was left behind . . . how could you have done that?" Eileen Gartner asked again, still feeling numb from the tragic news Max just shared with her of her husband Luke's death.

"I'm sorry Eileen . . . but the Israeli Government is now conducting a search and rescue mission and attempting to excavate the cave," Max explained as they continued their walk past the Palazzo Borghese and towards Ponte Cavour. He felt like he betrayed Eileen. After all, he didn't attempt to go back to save Luke or the two students, even if it were nearly impossible. Luke never had abandoned him. "We should know more soon, Eileen, but as I had said, that explosion shook the earth. I can't imagine anything or anyone having survived. You know, I wanted to go back, but there's something else that happened there . . . something difficult to make sense of."

Tears painfully fell from the troubled woman's face as she slowed her pace. "You know, I can't understand what you're telling me. Why would anyone try to stop you and Luke from a dig? For God's sake you're scientists."

Max looked at the approaching bridge empty of pedestrians, its stone expanse crossing the Tiber River and leading to Vatican City. The breeze cresting over the river felt stale in his lungs as his leg pained from too much movement. "I'm not sure, Eileen. And I can't tell you how guilty and sorry I feel about everything. Luke was like a brother to me, you know that. But I have several gun-shot wounds reminding me the cave-in was no accident, not to mention what I went through today." He stopped on the foot of the bridge, and turned towards his friend. "Eileen, was there anything odd going on at work with Luke?"

"Gunshot wounds? That's why you're limping, she said incredulously."

"When the cave exploded, it shook everything around me. I was about to run back to it, but the next thing I knew, I was pinned in, and getting shot out – for what reason, I have no idea."

"My God! You have no idea who did this," she exclaimed.

"None. But I knew I had to get the hell out of there. As I said, there was no way the mountain didn't completely collapse –"

"—I get the idea. Max, Luke loved you a great deal. He always talked about you, wondering what you were investigating in your labs, if you were keeping yourself busy, if you were happy . . . if you were willing to get back on with your life," she said lowering her voice.

"I know he cared, and you know how I feel," Max added.

"I know."

"Thanks. Eileen, was there anything odd going on in

Luke's life? Nothing makes any sense to me."

Her eyes dashed around introspectively at the moving cars on the low, two-lane bridge. "Not that I know of. Luke was very busy as usual, but I don't recall anything odd," she replied entering onto the viaduct.

"Oh, I see. I was just —"

"—you have some concerns?" she asked inquisitively wiping another tear from her face. "What's the matter?"

"It appears that I somehow got involved in things others are very concerned about," Max said, trying to figure out the language to tell her that he thought he might have found the True Cross of Jesus of Nazareth.

"What do you mean, Max?" she asked, aware of Max's past.

"I don't know for sure, but have you ever had the feeling there's something dangerous following you?"

She looked deeply into Max's telling eyes as they moved onto the bridge. She saw a determined man seeking for answers to questions he did not even know. "I'm not sure."

They heard the dark rushing waters of the Tiber as they silently crossed the bridge. Max looked down into the river and noticed how unusually fast the river's currents were moving._

"It's frustrating, Eileen," Max said, turning to his friend. "Wherever I seem to go, disasters follow. And now Luke's gone. I'm sorry."

Eileen Gartner said nothing back.

Walking discretely across the other side of the bridge was the confessor's lethal hand.

The assassin looked around the bridge, confirming no others were nearby. His shadowy pace quickened, moving directly opposite to Max and Eileen from the other side of the road.

Two trucks rumbled down the causeway amongst fleeting, nondescript cars.

A second glance confirmed there were no others on foot nearby. His targets were alone on the bridge, nearing the mouth to Vatican City. *This is perfect. Death will be delivered to the front door of his kingdom!*

The killer removed a 9mm firearm from his coat, the deadly gun kept concealed on his side, away from eyes in the passing cars. Pausing for a moment in the middle of the bridge, he raised his arm.

"Max, why didn't you call me — or Luke's office at the

Vatican to tell them what happened? They might have known—"

A deadly projectile tore into the air and instantly burst through the left side of Eileen's chest, viciously ripping through her white skin until it pierced her heart and the bullet's shrapnel exploded, obliterating her innocent heart.

Her warm blood and fleshy organs sprayed over a horrified Max, covering his hair, face, and body in remains. He gasped in horror, his eyes locked on Eileen's wide-open sockets, frozen dead in shock as she fell to the floor.

Ghost-like images of the faces of those he was close to who met their untimely death suddenly pursued his soul. In a nanosecond Max recalled the brutality of death he was too familiar with.

Trying to wipe the dead woman's hot blood from his face, he frenetically searched the bridge.

The Scorpion, filled with loathing adulation, began to salivate seeing Max's frantic movements. His malevolent heart swelled in excitement as familiar dark clouds of madness and mayhem rushed through his brain. He raised the gun towards Max. *Train, or whoever you are – I'll see you in Hell, too!*

Max turned and noticed the assailant thirty meters away from him taking aim. "Christ!" he screamed as he dove to the floor, landing in his dead friend's pooling blood now staining the concrete pavement.

A bullet barely missed Max as he dove to the ground.

I have to keep moving. Christ, this blood!

"It's your time, Mr. Train," the killer piously called to him. "Time to die. 'To everything there is a season…'"

Several cars passed onto the bridge, their headlights picking up the blood-soaked bodies on the sidewalk. The lead car, noticing the death-scene, sped by as fast as it could.

Max was up on his feet, moving away from the psychotic.

"Train, where are you going? God wants you dead!"

I have to get off this bridge. Should I jump into the river? Keep moving

The assassin raced onto the asphalt roadway, his gun pointed towards Max, who was now fleeing the bridge.

A blue four-door car suddenly screeched short, the driver fearful of hitting the alarming stalker now in the middle of the street, gun in hand.

Another bullet hit a metal lamp pole, barely missing Max, who was running as fast as his damaged leg could take him.

A second car suddenly crashed into the halted blue sedan.

The Scorpion smiled at one of the drivers as he passed by.

The young girl appearing in her twenties and seated in the blue car screamed as the assassin passed her by.

"No worry my love," the assailant said as he approached the frightened woman buckled into her car seat.

"No! Please!" she screamed.

"That will not solve your problem. Stop it! You won't need this car any longer," he smiled right before he shot her in the head.

Now Mr. Train, it is your turn. Don't think you can escape me. I see you're unable to run. Life has its way, doesn't it? Were we born with our destiny, or do we create it? No one really knows, it's all so convoluted, but what's not complicated or difficult Mr. Train is that I am going to kill you.

The sounds of the second car's tires screeching as the driver attempted to flee the hellacious death scene on the ominous bridge awakened the killer from his momentary lapse.

With one eye on his slow moving primary target, the assassin quickly turned his attention onto the passengers in the immobile second automobile. "Hello," eyes glistening with horror as he pointed the gun towards a terrified middle-aged man and his wife. "No one alive knows this, but my first name is Sergio," he began as the gun descended towards the startled family.

"Please!" the woman seated in the passenger seat begged, "we see nothing," she begged.

He walked closer to the driver's side of the car. "I'm sorry, but I can't help you. Nobody alive knows my name. But now you do. And for the record, you may have heard of me. I am *The Scorpion.*"

The couple timidly gawked at the lunatic.

With a hideous smile, the killer gently squeezed the trigger of the semi-automatic, instantly killing the last two remaining individuals who could identify him.

Hearing the violent eruption of the killer's firearm coupled with a heinous laugh from the killer, Max raced down the dimly lit street of Via Grescenzio, whose street lights were not working, towards Vatican City. His arms and legs pumped as fast as he could move his injured frame, the increasing severity of his situation at the forefront of his mind. *I need to distance myself from that madman. How did they know where I was? This is crazy! Who the hell are these bastards? Where is he now?*

The killer turned his attention to his racing target. *Life is so meaningless, unless you control life itself* "'Vanity of vanities, is not all vanity?' Max, Max Train – I'm coming for you!" the executioner amusingly screamed. *This is excitement, isn't it?*

An electric current seemed to shoot through Max's racing body from the shock of hearing his name aloud. *These bastards know my real identity. I gotta get out of here.*

It was nearing 9:00 p.m., and like any other day the great Piazza San Pietro built by Bernini for Pope Alexander VII on The Vatican's grounds was still crowded with tourists and believers alike.

Max entered the wide oval piazza, standing grounds for the hundreds of thousands who would on solemn occasions gather to hear the Pope's *urbi et orbe*, "the blessing on the city and the world." Streaming fountains and magnificent Doric columns were part of its great historic beauty. Its Egyptian obelisk built for the Roman Circus' chariot races at the order of Emperor Nero accentuated its antiquity. Nero's blood thirst surged viewing steeds trained for one objective only—trampling underfoot Rome's dispossessed. The lifeless eyes of marbleized statues of Christian saints looked from across the piazza at the crowds of believers from all nations, statues sculptured to commemorate the heroic lives the Church of Rome felt they led. Around these very same grounds the Apostle Simon Peter, who was to become the Christian world's first Pope, was crucified upside down, tradition held, because this Pope felt unworthy to be crucified the way his Redeemer, Jesus Christ, was. He had come from Jerusalem to Rome to lead a new way of belief, by which Rome gained the name "the eternal city."

He eyed a large group of visitors walking onto a nearby tourist bus. *There's safety in crowds in the dark. I hope they don't see these damn blood stains.*

Max moved into the crowd of believers as a line formed to re-enter the bus.

As he did, he noticed the killer enter the piazza's grounds, the man's eyes searching for him.

Train moved quickly around the bus, and away from the murderer. From the corner of his eye he noticed the killer moving towards the bus!

Max removed his blue raincoat and tied it around his waist, exposing his white shirt. *Alter your demeanor, change your appearance.*

Keeping his head hunched down and slowing his steps, he walked alongside an older couple, towards a dimly lit side street.

The assassin carefully looked into the crowded square for Train. *You're here somewhere. I'll find you.*

Moments later Max was waving for a taxi near Ponte Amedo, heading back across the Tiber, and into Rome's inner city.

As he entered the cab, the confessor's henchman noticed a man purposefully look around before entering the taxi. *There you are. The night is young, and the game is too much fun for it to end now.*

Standing in front of a slow moving car, the assassin removed his firearm, and beckoned the driver to get out of the car. The man did as he was told. Approaching the surprised citizen, the stalker crashed the blunt end of the gun onto the man's skull, knocking him unconscious.

Urging the driver to quickly head towards the Stazione Centrale Roma Termini, Max sat in the back seat of the small taxi, his heart raced as he let out a deep breath of relief. Just witnessing four separate brutal murders on the city's street, it was evident to him that whoever was stalking him feared nothing and no one.

After crossing the bridge and driving along the banks of the Tiber, the taxi entered onto Via del Circo Massimo and onto Via di Gregorio. To his left, Max noticed Mount Palatino leading up from the Farnese Gardens, once the festival plain of the Vestal Virgins in the days when Rome was *the world.* Fable had it that the Palatino was one of the Seven Hills that made up this great city founded by Romulus and Remus, who were nursed by a she-wolf, it is said, after finding the twin brothers left for dead on the banks of the Tiber. The Seven Hills corresponded to the seven known planets, and on the Palatino was where the greatest Emperor of Rome, Augustus Caesar, had lived. Under him had begun the *Pax Romana*, the era of lasting peace throughout the empire. Here also had lived once the great orator Cicero.

To his right stood the Roman Coliseum. Max could almost feel the history.

Suddenly, and out of no where, the thunderous impact of an assaulting vehicle colliding with the taxi shook Max and the cab's driver, as their vehicle spun out of control outside of the Coliseum. As the driver's body crashed into the steering column, instantly breaking his rib cage, Max was tossed around in the back seat of the car, his head slamming into the plexi-glass passenger divider.

Hello, Mr. Train! I bet you didn't think you would have this much fun!

The spinning taxi twisted and turned until it rammed into a concrete barrier placed outside the Coliseum. "Christ!" Max screamed as his body took most of the impact from the collision. This is no accident, he thought to himself.

"Are you okay?" Max asked the driver in his fluent tongue, noticing blood flowing from his nose.

"*Si*," the man wearily answered, unaware that the onslaught was not over.

From the back seat, Max saw a vehicle backing up so to realign itself with the taxi in order to continue the relentless assault.

"*Andiamo, Senor! Andiamo!*" Max screamed at the driver. "Oh, God!"

Removing himself from the passenger's back seat of the vehicle, Max quickly opened the front door of the taxi, and tugged at the old man from the passenger side, trying desperately to remove him from the car. Eye-level, he noticed the menacing assailant's vehicle backing up one more time – a perfect, deadly line of impact only moments away.

"You have to help me if you want to live," Max screamed as he used every remaining ounce of strength he had to pull the limp body of the fatigued Italian taxi driver out of the car. "Please," he urged as the man's body went into shock, "you have to help me!"

The old taxi driver was unable to move on his own.

The sound of screeching wheels from hell made time stand still.

Max looked up and saw the lethal steel box racing towards him.

"Help me," whispered the beaten man. "Please."

The car was now picking up speed.

Please, help me!

With what he believed would be his last breath, Max suddenly lifted the man's comatose body from the car, and fell backwards behind the three feet high, thick concrete barricades surrounding the Coliseum.

Horns from passing cars screamed in confusion as the madman raced ahead. *Good-bye Max Train. Good-bye!*

Max struggled to get on his feet in order to get behind the concrete barriers. They were his only hope if he was going to live.

He grabbed the motionless man by his shoulders and pulled him along the floor, behind the barricades.

The killer bore down, unaware of Max's movements.

Max, covered in blood dragged the man as far as he could.

The headlights glared into Max's face as the killer pushed hard on the accelerator.

Max tugged one more time at the man, hoping the ten-meter separation from the barricade would be enough to protect the driver. As he pulled, Max tripped.

The sound of steel on screeching steel clawed at his ears as the killer's sedan crushed into the taxi, sending the twisted cab into the unmovable concrete blockades.

The impact on his body had little immediate affect on the killer, who was strung out on the excitement of the kill.

Within moments the assassin removed his seat belt, shook away the broken glass of the shattered window, and made his way out of the large sedan. He removed his firearm once again. *You're not a meek lamb, are you, Train? Now, where are you!*

Passing spectators slowed their vehicles in stupefaction over the deadly scene that was unfolding in front of their eyes!

The killer raced towards the twisted taxi, his trigger finger ready to release the entire sixteen round cartridge of shells. Moving carefully around the vehicle, he noticed a bleeding body lying motionless on the cold pavement. He sensed something was wrong! Approaching the figure, he soon realized it wasn't Train. *Bullshit! Where are you, you piece of shit?*

Standing in the shadows of the Coliseum, the killer heard the loud piercing sound of the *carabiniere* racing to the scene. *I'll find you Max Train. I'll find you, and bring you to Hell with me.*

The assassin lowered his head and walked in the darkness of the Coliseum towards the Metro, towards the Termini, Rome's central rail station. Careful of his pace, and aware of the failed public attempt on Train's life, he knew he needed to take on an ordinary appearance, if possible. Running for cover was out of the question.

Fortunately, the stark backdrop of the ancient killing cathedral provided him with just enough cover to walk towards Via G. Lanzia and Rome's Metro's B Line.

Standing on the top steps of the descending stairwell to the same subway line nearly one hundred meters away was Max. In his right hand he held a ticket that would bring him to the Termini, where he intended to take another train that would leave Rome in less than twenty minutes, taking him north. As his eyes carefully inspected the piazza he just left, Max noticed a single figure walking towards him. *It's him! He doesn't give up. He's relentless!*

The sound of an oncoming train echoed up into the stairwell.

Max clearly made out the approaching figure. It was the killer!

He turned, moving down the stairwell and towards the platform of the oncoming train – one heading towards the central station!

Entering through a modern turnstile, Max untied the raincoat around his waist, placed it over his shoulders and began to walk up the scarcely populated platform filled with tourists finishing their sightseeing for the day.

The oncoming subway rushed into the station, its doors quickly opening. Max, along with the other passengers on the front end of the platform immediately entered into the congested train.

Towards the back of the train entered *The Scorpion,* blindly bent on finding Train.

Max moved two subway cars forward, unaware his deadly, unknown adversary boarded the train and was working his way towards him.

Two minutes later the subway arrived at its next stop. As the doors were about to close, Max darted onto the platform – just as the now familiar face of the killer entered the subway car.

Max, standing on the platform, and the confessor's killer, stuck inside the moving subway car, looked hard at one another.

The killer blew Max a kiss, then pointed at him, his fingers gesturing the image of a gun.

Max shook his head defiantly, and then gave the killer the finger. "Not today."

As the subway car moved away an evil smirk covered the assassin's face. His eyes deadened on Max, who did not flinch. Mockingly gesturing the sign of the Cross, he then dashed for the stairwell leading to the city streets of Rome.

***

Placing his coat on the green velvet sofa in his Borgo Pio apartment, Anselm Mugant was ready to pour himself a sniff of Remy.

His den phone ringing interrupted him. The voice on the other end was Flavio Rinaldi's.

"Good evening, Cardinal. Father Rinaldi. The meeting for tomorrow that the Cardinal Secretary called earlier today has been rescheduled for this evening, your Eminence," the cleric began. "And it will be in the Pope's library, on the fifth floor of the residence, not the palace of the Holy Office. At 9:00 p.m. Some of the Cardinals are already on their way."

"I know where the Pope's library is, Rinaldi," an annoyed Mugant responded. "The meeting about the *Paris Match* piece has been rescheduled?"

"Exactly, Cardinal Mugant. The meeting has been pushed up to this evening. I tried to reach you earlier but..."

"Of course, Father Rinaldi. Thank you."

Abruptly hanging up on the phone, Mugant went to retrieve his coat. *Well, so much for cognac. This meeting can't be because of what I said earlier this evening about dogmatically forbidding genetic engineering.* He looked at the hand carved Swiss clock on his dining room wall. *Plenty of time.*

Mugant barely acknowledged the Swiss Guard, in his Medici colors, holding open for him the heavy bronze door to the Apostolic Palace. The basilica clock in St. Peter's had just struck 9:00 p.m. Entering this Renaissance architectural marvel, he proceeded past a guests' reception area in the Palace towards a door that led to a little known underground passage. A second Swiss guard opened this entranceway to Mugant. Descending a steep stairwell, he came to a weathered metal door. With a bronze teeth key he opened it. Closing it behind him, he walked some 40 meters through the dimly lit walled underground passage. Reaching a second matching door Mugant used the same key to open it, and, closing the door behind him walked up the steps now before him.

The polished marble of the Papal apartments met his feet as he took his first step out of the stairwell. By the Oakwood statue of St. John Vianney, Patron of Catholic Priests was standing the Vatican's senior diplomat in discussion with a priest Mugant did not recognize. The Cardinal Prefect for the Doctrine of the Faith, the tall, silver hair Frenchman Etienne Rostreau who had received his agregè in Philosophy from Louvain and doctorate in Sacred Theology from Rome's Pontifical University of Saint Thomas, was looking at a painting that was the gift of Salvatore Dali. Further down the hallway, near the stairs that led to the Pope's Library, were Laurian Lisawara, Prefect for Religious, and the Cardinal from Mauritania. The first African to be Dean of the College of Cardinals, his command of languages was unmatched by any in the Vatican. He spoke eighteen. The Archbishop who headed the Holy Roman *Rota*, Calvar Sastrini, the Church's marriage tribunal, was speaking to him. The *Rota* kept all requests sent to the Vatican dealing with scientific advances in human reproduction.

"Cardinal Mugant, welcome. I see you got the message in time. Your aide informed my office he had reached you about the rescheduling, which was so important for this meeting."

Mugant looked at Cardinal de Salvoyar. "Shall we keep His Holiness waiting, or begin the meeting?"

"Of course, let us go."

The four Vatican prelates walked past the two Swiss guards at the top of the stairway towards the Pope's Library and were greeted by the Pope's personal secretary. In silence the four followed him into the Pope's library where they saw sitting at the head of a long Oakwood table the spiritual head of one billion believers. He appeared to be signing a document that had just been handed him. Seeing the Cardinal Secretary of State, the Pope arose from his red velvet cushioned chair, which one of the Priest chamberlains behind him helped pull away from him. Tall and thin, health robust after defeating his cancer, his penetrating blue eyes looked through rimless eyeglasses at his most trusted advisor. His white robes, the symbol of his high spiritual office, accented his sun beaten face. "Let us get to the task at hand," he said softly to his senior advisor. "We will avoid any formalities. Let us first pray for the guidance of the Spirit."

The prayer finished, the Pope began to speak. "I have called this meeting, as you know, on sudden notice. It appears that a bio-geneticist in France has perfected, at least he claims to have, a mitosis technique for artificial human reproduction. Of course, I speak of cell division, the scientific details of which Cardinal Mugant can apprise any of you here."

The Pope continued, walking towards a wall bookshelf, from which he removed one volume. "I know of the proposed technique in some fashion. This text discusses it in some detail." The Pope opened the book to a page and placed it on the oak wood table.

"This is a matter of moment. If what the report indicates in any way is near fact, the Church has a most profound issue at hand.

Research on means of human reproduction, on the relation between reproductive cellular development and the relief of crippling pain is extensive today. This could not be imagined when I was a student here in Rome 45 years ago.

"Now there is venomous rhetoric, and it is escalating. 'Man has fought God, has fought himself. Now he asserts a power reserved previously to the Creator.' This is what some are saying. This form of speech does nothing to help resolve what is before us.

"Scientists are being murdered from different labs, in different countries, for their work in genetic blueprinting and embryo cell research, and no one claims responsibility for the violence. What of the commandment given to Moses on the mount, Thou shalt not kill? When is it that one just chooses, picks, without jury or judge, who should live or die?

"We preach the Fatherhood of God. The religion whence we come preaches this. Our separated brethren, those who left us and with whom we have now sought reconciliation, our faithful Protestant brothers and sisters—they preach it to the world, where all are brothers and sisters.

"These murderers stand fast in opposition to everything all religions—the Koran, our Scripture— all religions of the world preach.

"The Church is not above man, some power of laws or beliefs dictating to listeners below. We are all on the road together seeking truth—Jew, Muslim, Coptic, Catholic, Hindu, and Buddhist. We are summoned in unity to reach the truth and to learn from it. Buddha and those that follow the Eastern way believe that kindness is the first act of wisdom. And it is this wisdom of kindness for which all humanity strives. It is this wisdom of kindness that our Heavenly Father tries to instill in all of us through His Son in the Gospels."

The Pope moved towards his high library window, and looked out at the sky now dark blue. "More than a dozen of these researched have died. They have families. They have children. No one knows who the murderers are. We have never condoned these brutal murders. We have condemned them even though some claim in their assaults on these scientists that they're like the Crusaders of old hunting down the heathen. All 'in the name of God' say this group, while on the other progress is proclaimed all in 'the name of science'.

"Man must not murder man, whatever the belief, whatever

the issue. These deaths go against everything for which the Church has stood over these two millennia."

Out of the corner of his eye, Mugant saw the Pope's Secretary of State look in his direction.

The Church's Pontiff continued. "We have at this precise moment the opportunity to set forth a ringing statement for the cooperation between science and faith, to put behind us all the animosity and suspicion of the past. We are in the age of progress towards the improvement of the human condition. Surely when there are ways to bring radical and complete reversal of horrifying bodily conditions to any person the Church must find a way to cooperate with science in overcoming those physical hardships. Man was given the mind to decipher the very building blocks of the body—he was given so by the Creator. Surely we cannot ignore this, but instead must move with science to appropriate this knowledge to the ethical healing of suffering man. We must find the way to overcome the obstacles that have been put in the way of both faith and science on this path to relieving bodily pain.

"Science and faith together, discussing, reasoning, interacting for the betterment of man. This was the purpose of the Scientific Advisory Board established over a half century ago by our Predecessor. Our dogma is not to condemn. It is to bring man closer to the goodness that only science and revelation working together, not in conflict, can provide."

Mugant's look was distant now, realizing his call for a dogmatic announcement of excommunication for scientists daring to ignore centuries old guidelines that some believed no longer applied as they once did was being dismissed. He let his gaze move over the framed photos on the library wall. One was of the Pope's senior statesman addressing a UN delegation. *This is who the Vicar of Christ listens to?*

"Thus, my dear Cardinals, I have asked the Cardinal Secretary to establish a Curial commission of Science and Theology, and to announce it tomorrow in *L'Osservatore Romano*. It will be a Commission separate from the office of Human Life that Cardinal Mugant heads. It will work with the Scientific Advisory Board, but will not be part of it. It will be under the auspices of the Prefecture for the Congregation of the Faith. However, the Cardinal Secretary of State will announce the Commission's formation to show the gravity with which we see the current developments. Since it will be a Curial commission, the world will know the importance I place on this subject now. The announcement of the new Commission will follow along the lines of what I have said here, and it will be our response to the report from France. This initiative will be timely, given my planned trip to America next week. The end to our present violence and the end to the animosity and centuries of suspicion must begin now."

Not a word was said in response to what the Cardinals knew was a final decision. Anselm Mugant sat with a cold stare. The Pope's Secretary of State took a sip of water from the glass next to him. The Cardinal from Mauritania placed his hands on his leather bound Breviary.

Moving back to his chair, at the end of the oak wood table, the Pope lifted his arms, saying "Let us invoke the *Veni Sancte Spiritus*."

Chapter VII

Max sat attentive, but quietly in the rear seat of the taxi en route
from Rome to the Etruscan city of Bologna. With each passing
moment the weight of leaving Rome, filled with its many brutal
contradictions, colorful complexities, and masqueraded intents,
relieved the wary scientist. As he traveled north from the only city
in the world whose perimeters enclosed the capitals of two nation-
states, The Republic of Italy, and, Vatican City, a desolate feeling of
fateful loneliness initiated by a sense of abandonment overtook
him.

What exactly was going on? It was just five days ago that
he was enjoying a historical sightseeing visit to the Holy Land with
two of his students. Now, with every passing turn there appeared
killer – different faceless assassins – remorselessly attempting to
annihilate his very existence. But that wasn't enough; there was
something else that wasn't right. Whoever was behind the multi-
tude of recent deaths was powerful, organized, well financed, and
ruthless. They had access to the most powerful tool of all; information. They knew, he deemed, that he had uncovered a buried artifact. Could it be possible there existed individuals or a group who
were charged with protecting the Cross, and securing it never left
its final resting place? Of course it was. How else could someone
have known the four Americans were in the cave early that morning? And the cave's collapse – there was no question it erupted
from a planted explosive discharge. Whatever lives he came in contact with, for the most part, were all dead. Luke and Eileen Gartner;
dead. The Syracuse University students, John Muir and Lynn
Johnson; dead. The gypsy taxi driver and the old Mossad agent in
Rome's airport; dead. The list seemed endless. All that remained,
he supposed, was the woman Sara in Israel.

As shadowy images of the bountiful Tuscan countryside
passed him by, exhausted, Max sat pensively. There was something
subtle, something hinted at which could provide him with a clue to
who was behind the chaos now in his life. Whatever the hidden
clues were would only be potential keys to the first mystery. Max
realized he somehow had entered into a deadly maze of hidden
agendas, clandestine movement, and zealot fanaticism. Spiraling,

as one door opened, it appeared as if two killers were always await-ing him. Alone, surrounded by death, uncertainty of tomorrow, under a belief more pain would be forthcoming, Max believed he entered Hell.

It was nearing 2:00 a.m. when the taxi entered the medieval looking city of Bologna. The driver, a native son of Italy's most famous culinary city, drove towards the address Max previously had given him.

Odd, Max thought to himself, how different Bologna was from Rome. Though he had been here twice before this was the first time Max sensed the city's subliminal, yet powerful, personal-ity. Not only was Bologna's fortress-like buildings decorated with over forty kilometer of porticoes designed during early fifteenth century Papal rule through the late eighteenth century different than anything of Rome, but there was a different sense, a distinct invisi-ble undercurrent of defiant centralism running through this town.

Bologna was everything not Rome.

Centuries ago, under the auspiciousness of Antonio di Vincenzo, the first foundation stone was laid in 1390 A.D. as Bologna initiated the construction of the Church of San Petronio, located in the center of Piazza Maggiore, Bologna's central square. Centuries of continued construction, and the church, till this day, was never completed. Jealousies were a common trait held between archbishops and Cardinals alike during the Middle Ages. All fought for *blessed consent* from their Popes, who were at times completely corrupt. With learned knowledge that Bologna had architectural designs and aspirations of grandeur even St. Peter's did not obtain, the Church of Rome, filled with envy, ceased financ-ing the construction of San Petronio. Till this day the façade of San Petronio was purposefully left unfinished by its citizens. For those familiar with the intimate relations of these two cities, Bologna's statement to sister Rome was clear.

The taxi pulled up to a winding street in the gothic environs of the University of Bologna. The world's oldest university was built in 1088 A.D. So great of an impact did this citadel of higher education have on the city that Bologna at times was referred to as "Bologna the Learned."

Within moments the taxi stopped in front of a four story, centuries old building set in front of a modest sized courtyard gar-den. Seeing this was the expected address, Max gave the driver the other half of the toll due him, thanked him, and made sure there were no other vehicles behind him before he quickly exited the taxi.

As the taxi drove off, Max noticed a light was on in the second floor.

Exhausted, he approached the door, wondering skeptically, what was next?

As he reached for the doorbell, the large wooden door quickly opened. In the doorway stood Francesco Pellegrino, a man in his fifties whose brilliant eyes darted into the night. "Max? Are you all right?" The man said, curious to find Max Train at his doorstep in the middle of the night.

For the next hour Max told his friend and scientific colleague whom he befriended over the years in part due to their mutual scientific research in the field of genetics everything that occurred the past few days. Max was careful not to leave out any details.

Dr. Pellegrino, still upset over the news Luke Gartner had died, was further shaken over the new information that his wife, Eileen, was murdered in public too.

Fighting closing eye-lids, Max reiterated his concerns about the Holy Cross, and its many possible implications in today's world, which he had left in Rome's Excelsior Hotel, under the name of his Bolognese friend at the suggestion of Dr. Pellegrino.

"Max, you know what I need to do," suggested Francesco. "Quickly."

"You'll need to rest. It's late and I'm sure your body is exhausted, not to mention those flesh wounds you sustained in Jerusalem need to be re-attended to."

"You remember the hotel?"

"Of course. A friend of mine works there. It is in safekeeping."

***

It was nearing 7 p.m. as Pellegrino and Train sat in the Bologna scientist's office situated in a gothic tower in the middle of the university's thousand-year-old grounds. Both men still weary from little sleep pushed on.

"The test results are not infallible, Max. You have a lot of 'variables' that can provide a wrong answer." Francesco Pellegrino was Director of Testing at the University of Bologna's prestigious

Radiation Measurements Lab, and now found himself with what he knew could be "the relic of the ages." Graduate Studies at Ruprecht-Karl Universität in Heidelberg and Baltimore's Johns Hopkins, as well as numerous authoritative monographs in his specialty, had brought him to the position of *Direttore* at this world renowned scientific facility of "non-destructive evaluation" at Università di Bologna. Academically trained as a biogeneticist, Pellegrino's talents brought him into many fields of science, and his colleagues were not surprised when he was named to this highly visible appointment at Bologna. Pellegrino's personality and approach to academics showed an evenness that was to gain him respect throughout university labs specializing in the same field of dating artifacts ten million years old or simply two thousand years old.

"What you told me on your hastened arrival last night has given me cause for much thought, Max. I know you have trepidation. So do I."

"With good reason."

"If what you're thinking has possibility, and it just might, then this is not simply a scientific experiment we are carrying out here." Pellegrino paused, as he poured himself a glass of water. He knew even in science the possibility of the unexplainable must be recognized. Some things were in God's hands.

"I think you need some espresso, Max," he said rising from his office chair.

"Thanks."

"I have said nothing to anyone. At the Excelsior I made as if the packages I was picking up were simply a routine matter. The trip back here from Rome—nothing happened. The roads I took were almost empty, so I would have known if someone was watching."

"Are you sure?"

"Yes."

"Francesco, are the cross and *titulus* safe?"

"Yes, Max. As I told you I have safely placed them at Albergo Acconciamessa. A friend of mine works at the charming hotel. I think it is best for the moment to leave the items away from the university. They're secure."

Max shifted uneasily in his chair. He knew Francesco was correct. Keeping the artifacts near him could jeopardize the welfare of the remnants; however, something was growing inside him that sought possession of the holy remnants.

"And here I am doing the tests myself. Of course no one else can have an inkling where you are, or what you think these artifacts might be."

Looking through sleepless eyes, Max was intent upon what his friend, to whom he had desperately now turned, was saying. Pellegrino knew his friend felt mortal fear. The killings also had him worried for his own life. But a forged friendship based upon scientific research and professional respect in the field of genetics, coupled with historical and theological intrigue, was more than enough for Dr. Pellegrino to shelter and assist Max.

"Max, we're going to be all right. Can I get you anything else?"

"No, the espresso will be fine."

"I hope I'm not putting you to sleep, Max," Pellegrino joked, intentionally trying to make his friend laugh.

"Let me go on. A sliver from the wooden beam is being tested right now, Max. That is all anyone knows in the lab. We frequently have cases where a client asks for an immediate test of an artifact. This has been my cover. Everything has the appearance of routine. So I believe that this wood, and the thin piece with the lettering, will get by as normal processing— unnoticed. The specimens are numbered, and other tests on other unrelated items are underway in the lab as usual. I think we are safe with the lettering not being deciphered or understood by the way. Languages are not usually a lab technician's forte," Pellegrino smiled. "But what do you say to yourself when before you, at your fingertips, in your hands, you have what may bring us in this age into actual physical contact with Jesus?" A somber look came across the Bologna scientist's face.

"This is—part of the dilemma," Max solemnly responded, recalling the physical characteristics of the cross.

"We are so fortunate to have an accelerator mass spectrometry radiocarbon instrumentation that can within hours give us a preliminary scientific approximation on the age of a piece of material. Our procedure is far better than the Gove model in reaching an initial approximation that matches the final results. We can come within fifty years in the preliminary count of accurate dating. This is no little thing… nothing we're doing is."

"I know Francesco. Others apparently are thinking the same thing. That may explain the hell of this past week I've lived.

I have someone very worried, that's obvious."

Pellegrino looked intently at Max. "I'd say so."

"But they're invisible."

"It's hard to fight back against an unseen enemy. We're going to need to figure out how to stop this. Max, you have no idea, do you?"

"I see blackened images, it seems, before me, Francesco. I see the twisted faces from the airport in Rome, the face of a vagrant cab driver—dead because of me. I see the shiny black steel of weapons I have never seen before pointed at my face. I am hearing gunshots. My closest friend Luke—we were like brothers—has died, while I am still living. His wife was killed, shot, right before my eyes—for reasons I cannot know, but can only wonder. Had I not asked to meet her, she would still be alive. When she was shot on the bridge where we were walking, her blood covered me. I feel so responsible. But more than this, I see a dark mass growing bigger and more dangerous by the minute, and it's hunting me—and will not stop until I am dead. It's near impossible to defend yourself from a faceless assassin, isn't it? For I myself too have now killed."

"Max, at the end of every masquerade, the costume does come off. And you too, or should I say we," Francesco said with a defiant smile, "shall know who is behind the dark shadows. We must be measured and careful. Do not jump to conclusions. Do not persecute yourself. The killing was in self-defense. Let us take this one step at a time. Things will work themselves out, and even though it might sound improbable, you need to hold on to your faith."

Both men, the only two persons alive, who knew of the possibilities which they now possessed, stared at one another in silence. Men of science, they too were men of faith.

Dr. Francisco Pellegrino sighed. "Still, we have here a possible find that could put the lab in some danger."

"I do not know if anyone knows I am here, Francesco. I do not know if I was seen coming here."

"You're talking to me right now. If they knew where you were we both would be dead, I suppose. Besides, the lab does have highly trained professional guards employed by our clients, individuals once with Interpol and other law enforcement background, Max. You don't see them, but they're here even now as we're doing some tests on a find for the Nigerian government. The security people are trained on a number of different fronts. They trained to expect anything, and operate at the highest level. We will assume no difference in the tests I am doing on the two pieces."

"I hope so," Max said.

"We can make public our findings to the press immediately, too. As soon as we see the results, we can get a conference call with a number of our colleagues so that more than just we two are involved. A televised conference call with the worldwide press asking questions—it could be put together in a day or two— will give us wide publicity and be a deterrent to any group looking for foul play."

"You're right, Francesco. This would help take much of the burden off our shoulders."

"As well as help protect our lives, Max, if necessary."

Pellegrino took a sheaf of papers from his desk. "Let's go over the testing issue. I know certitude is what you want here, and we all do.

"There is much dispute, Max, about the Shroud of Turin and Carbon 14 testing," Pellegrino began.

"There is the famous C14 misdating of the Egyptian mummy No. 1770 from England's Manchester Museum, as we all know," Train responded. "I have spent part of my life understanding this science. I know the carbon-14 tests are only the first step in determining what it is I unearthed."

Pellegrino nodded. "The Catholic Church has control and ownership of the Shroud now. It is no longer in the possession of King Umberto's family. The ownership issue makes it difficult to get access to the cloth, but this is not to blame the Church. Any owner would be just as careful and protective. Some say the Oxford and Arizona carbon 14 testing of the Shroud in 1988 A.D. did not deal with the possible contaminant issues or the charge of carbonization of the cloth from the 1532 A.D. fire, and the like."

"The dispute over the Mayan Itzamna Tun carving as it relates to questions of 'bioplastic coating' also has made radiocarbon-14 dating a bit more problematic," Train noted in agreement.

"Yes, Max, and as for the Shroud there is no way to resolve its age, even were carbon-14 testing infallible, till the Church releases the relic again."

Pellegrino paused, as Max Train rubbed his wounded thigh. "Every once in a while I have a shooting pain that runs through my leg that makes my hair stand up." Train winced. "It's getting better, though."

Pellegrino showed a look of concern, as he continued. "The testing results we should have sometime today. The test is rather straightforward. Simply, what we do is calculate, by extremely sophisticated radiation counters, the amount of nitrogen 14 into which the Carbon isotope, C14, has decayed. I could show you these counters in the lab, but you have seen many labs Max. Blue tinted light looks the same everywhere glancing off chrome." Pellegrino smiled, attempting a moment of levity.

"Carbon has three forms, as you know. An exponential decay formula gives us the math to calculate how old any material is—or, I should say, might be. This is what I was making reference to before, about the Shroud. The results are still not certain, so the carbon 14 may not put the matter to rest about the wooden beam piece I chose for testing. It is very splintered. No one knows where it was prior to your finding it; or how it got where it did, either. Also, the explosives you mentioned to me last night or whatever happened there—what sort of effect may they or may they not have had on the piece?"

"What of the piece with the faded inscription on it?" Max asked.

"The same rules hold for the carbon dating, although we will be able to read the inscription without trouble with the x-ray process we have."

"The inscriptions on the *titulus*, they seem to be real, didn't they?" Max asked.

"I looked at the inscription myself under different lightings. You remember, while you were looking at some Internet news services. There are many letters, for sure, I can tell that myself from looking at it. We'll get to see the exact inscription shortly."

"Given what is going on in the terrorist fights in Jerusalem, who knows if this find or the explosion may not be something bigger than we have right now, Max? Could some terrorist group seeking to undermine relations between the Christian Church and Israel have orchestrated an elaborate hoax? I mean, maybe your articles were placed where they were, with some purpose of having them found in a pre-arranged explosion, an explosion timed for when it was known visitors would be at that site?"

"Anything's possible, Francesco, but that would be going far."

"Maybe, maybe not. Much has been done and happened in

the name of religion. Conflict and hatred often times have resulted—centuries of it. Organized religion could be a tool of world forces, but not my faith in Jesus. That cannot be anyone's tool."

"You always were a man of conviction and truthfulness, Francesco. I appreciate your help."

Pellegrino looked at his digital clock on his office wall. "Well, it looks like the test results should be available. Let's go and see what they say."

Max Train followed Francesco Pellegrino out of his office, and waited as Pellegrino locked the door behind him. Together they then proceeded wordlessly down the end of the university corridor and entered on an elevator to the third floor. Max noted the walls of this elevator had soft leather padding, but said nothing about it.

"This way, Max" Pellegrino told him as they exited the elevator. "The lab is down the hall to the right."

Taking out a special key, Pellegrino placed it in the metal door bolt. It clicked. He then tapped out a number sequence on the combination lock pad above the door bolt. Turning the doorknob, he pulled the door towards him. It opened.

Closing the door behind him, Pellegrino walked towards a computer monitor. "This way, Max." Soft white lighting filled the room, one of the most advanced lab facilities in Europe. Birchwood cabinets on three walls offset the austere cold look of highly polished chromium tables and drawers. Occasionally a soft bell tone could be heard from one of the computers, indicating a testing procedure was either finished or entering a new phase.

"Okay, let's see what we have, Max. I did not write down the number of the items, obviously. The first one is 11990—that's the boy's birth date." Typing in his lab password, and then the number into the computer bank, a whole series of columns and rows appeared on the monitor.

"Let me see, where is the number?" Pellegrino said, squinting at the screen. "Here it is."

Pausing, he then went on. "Well, the wooden beam looks to be in the range, 1950 years old plus on this reading."

Max's eyes froze. "This cross, it is possible then is the True Cross. After all these years God may have now revealed it to us."

"It is possible, Max. I can't believe what I am looking at, but we need to stay scientific. Remember, there is a long way to go."

"But it is possible."

Pellegrino looked at his friend of many years. "Yes, but remember, Max, we're only approximating, and remember this is a fast test indication. It is not the laborious and detailed kind we would usually…"

"Francesco, I know. But the results have to be within range, right?"

"Everything being equal, yes, Max, the results have to be within range of accuracy."

Max watched with amazement as Francesco commanded the high tech gadgets and computers in the labs.

"Let's go on. Let's see for the other piece—the *titulus*." Typing in a different number sequence, the answer Pellegrino was looking for appeared. "Same result Max. They're both from the time of Jesus, give or take a few years. We also need to deduct the age of the wood for the beam. Remember, it came from a dead tree" Francesco slowly said, his voice guarded with bewildered enthusiasm. "I can't believe what I am seeing. Do you know what this possibly means?" Pellegrino excitingly asked.

Max nodded. "And are you aware of the heavy burdens of this Cross?"

"I'm beginning to."

"Your world has changed forever, my friend."

"I feel that."

"Let's hope we're doing the right thing. I don't know what others would do if they discovered these relics. You know, Francesco, I was going to Rome to bring these items to the Church. But so much has happened, so much interference, not to mention the continual threats on my life. I thought it was prudent to first determine what it is we are now in possession of. We need to document everything," Max added as his thoughts went back to the image of the burning cross pushing through the darkness that had formed in his head. "I hope that nothing happens to you over this."

"You did the right thing coming here," Francesco said as he sipped his water. "Once we determine the authenticity of these items, if it is at all possible, then you'll have to decide what to do next."

"That is one of the many burdens of this cross. Who will accept it, or will anyone accept it, when we uncover its true identity?"

"That's a good question."

"And another burden."

"I'm sensing that. Now as to the inscription. I had that isolated by a certain x-ray technique. It's part of a Heidelberg University "*Epigraphisch*" protocol. The image the computer generates should give us what exactly is on that piece. Do you want to go on?"

"We have to, Francesco."

Pellegrino typed in another number series. "It's the reverse of the first series, Max," Pellegrino smiled.

"Here we go, this is what we have."

גנק אזאנ ש צ

I τλιαεβ ντίτ οἔ Bἡ̵I

r duI x R unerazaN SI

"This is from the piece with the wooden beam, Francesco?"

"Yes it is, Max. It is."

Pellegrino pointed to the screen, his index finger even with the top line. What do you see in the letters?"

"You see the 'SI' there?" Max said, ignoring where Pellegrino was pointing.

"Yes."

"See the word after it, it's backwards."

"Yes, oddly we have a piece here where the writing is not from right to left, but left to right. I can see it in the bottom line"

"Well, Hebrew is written right to left. That's what's going on here. The letters are right to left in accordance with Jewish script. The word after '' is obviously a form of the word Nazareth in Latin. Do you see it? Does that sound right to you, Francesco?"

"Quite plausible, Max, now that you point it out. And above it?"

"That's Greek, Francesco, letters right to left again. It says what I did not want it to say. Though letters are missing, we have an inscription in English translation indicating Jesus of Nazareth, King of the Jews. The word 'Jews' is not that clear, but you can conclude it from the prior three words."

"Well, let's go above—what is the Hebrew script?"

"Alone, the first two letters would mean nothing. They look to be the beginning of the word Yeshua. But the second word seems to be in line with Nazaros, Nazarus—or something akin. We have an important three rows of letters, and the dating indicating this might be something far graver than anyone could have imagined five days ago," Max declared.

"This confirms that the *titulus* prepared somewhere around 2,000 year ago was written about Jesus of Nazareth. For all I know this very well could be the true creed handed out by Pilate. Nothing like this has ever been publicly seen. I doubt anyone would even dare claim a hoax like this 2,000 years ago. Remember—"

"— few back then took Jesus of Nazareth seriously. That was only after centuries and under the direction of Emperor Constantine—"

"—that Christianity began its universal expansion and penetration. The teachings of Jesus have always been about universal love."

"And there's no science to that."

"Max, you know these tests, though formidable in the dating process, are not conclusive. I don't know if we will ever know who was on this cross."

Max looked at his friend seriously. "There is the issue of the blood and hair. They might reveal more than humanity can imagine or accept."

"Are you prepared to move ahead?"

"Are you prepared, Francesco, to move ahead?"

"I'm understanding the burdens you speak of. Do I have a choice?"

"What does your soul tell you?"

"There is but one choice. We move ahead."

"What happens if this is human blood? Is it the blood of a dead man, or of God? And what will this all mean to the world? If blood remained on the Cross, did all of Jesus ascend bodily? After all, if all your memories are retained when you enter the after life, in the same way your entire bodily history would have to be retained. So if part of Jesus' bodily remnants is on the Cross, can we say that he ascended into Heaven entirely, nothing of him left behind? If part of him is here bodily, how did he ascend completely into Heaven?"

"We're also talking about a crime scene. Jesus was murdered. He was not tried by a legitimate tribunal. No, he was murdered. At most crime scenes there is forensic evidence left behind. Hair, blood, saliva, skin, whatever. Do we have that here, and if so

I'm not sure how these potential bodily remains are connected to the Ascension."

There was no answer as yet burdens continued to surface.

"Max, I am going to delete this information," Dr. Pellegrino said. "It is not necessary to have it on file. I simply don't want to take any chances."

"I agree."

In almost clinical fashion, Francesco Pellegrino typed in four rows of three numbers each, excising permanently from the Bologna University computer databank all the results that had just been read and shown on his computer screen in the Radiation Measurements Lab. Satisfied the data was permanently gone, he turned to Max. "Let's go, my friend. These are unusual times, aren't they?"

"They're confusing, but most exciting. Francesco, we might be staring at God."

"This is too much for the simple mind. I never realized how simple and ordinary my mind actually is," Francesco replied. "I don't know what to say or to think, but you might be right. God have mercy on us for what we are about to do."

Max made the sign of the Cross, "God have mercy."

Quietly the two scientists walked towards the heavy lab door, which Pellegrino opened slowly. The lab corridor was empty, as Train walked to the elevator with Pellegrino, who had satisfied himself that the lab door was securely locked.

Train noted the same leather padding on the elevator that he had previously, but his mind now was elsewhere. Stepping off the elevator, Pellegrino and Train returned to the office of the *Direttore*. "Max, I am just going to see my secretary. I'll be right back. Why not just make yourself at home," Pellegrino smiled.

Train walked into Pellegrino's office, and sat down at his friend's computer. Accessing a Yahoo news service his eyes caught a headline:

Polyclinique Normale Lab Bombed in Paris, Casualties Feared

Train stood motionless. *This is the genetics lab where Mousoir works. Damn!*

At the doorway was Francesco Pellegrino looking at his frazzled colleague. "Max?"

"The Associated Press is reporting over the internet a bombing at the Polyclinique Normale genetics lab in Paris. I can't believe this. Do you know who Rene Mousoir is? He is a friend of mine. Do you think this could be all tied in?"

"What happened?"

"Another genetic lab was bombed."

"You're not serious, are you?"

Max looked at Francesco; his stare indicated the severity of the situation.

And now another burden.

"Max, I'm not sure if it is an isolated incident. What does it have to do with a Jerusalem excavation? It may merely be—"

"No, Francesco. There is no such thing as coincidence. Biogenetic scientists have mysteriously begun to die. There have been seven suspicious deaths over this last year. I heard rumors that Polyclinique was on the verge of a major breakthrough in human reproduction."

"Coincidence is just an excuse for one's desire not to face truth. Let me see the online article."

Polyclinique Normale Lab Bombed in Paris
Casualties Feared

(Associated Press)

At 8: 00 p.m. this evening a devastating explosion erupted inside the scientific laboratory of Polyclinic Normale Laboratories (PNL), located on the outskirts of Paris. PNL is a leading biogenetics research company specializing in human fertility and stem cell research.

According to local Parisian authorities at the scene, there are no reports confirming or denying any injuries or deaths, though several principal scientist of PNL have not been accounted for. According to local firefighters rushing to the scene, the PNL building imploded from within, knocking down two of the three-story building's floors. At the time of this report, firefighters are still wrestling with the intense fire, believed to be burning due to chemicals PNL may have had on the premises.

PNL has scene its share of controversy this past year. Over the last six months, Doctor Rene Mousoir has become an outspoken proponent of both stem cell research and human cloning. Though unconfirmed at this time, it was rumored that PNL was intending to hold a press conference within the next few days regarding their technologies.

In addition, PNL **(PNLI : NASDAQ & PNL: PARIS)**, a closely held publicly traded firm listed on both the American NASDAQ and the French bourses made the press when its Board of Directors rejected a sizable tender offer for acquisition by little known Como Ventures of Milan, Italy five weeks ago. According to public records, the PNL Board instituted a 'poison pill', enabling the company to retain its sovereignty in lieu of Como Ventures tender offer of twice the market value at the time. Shares of PNL have traded heavily these last few weeks in response to an anticipated counter from Como Ventures, as well as potentially other suitors.

A spokesperson for PNL was not available for comment; however, Dr. William Seto, spokesperson for Como Ventures, when reached at his home, was startled by the news. "This is a tragic event. I know I share the same sentiments with everyone here at Como Ventures that we hope no persons were seriously injured or killed."

When pressed about the intent of Como Ventures to acquire PNL, Dr. Seto stated "there are more pressing matters at hand."

"My God."
"What is it, Max?"
"Seto. Como Ventures. A name from my past."
"What?"
"They were the company that acquired my research a decade ago. Something isn't right. I no longer believe in coincidence."

Both men looked at each other, fear in their eyes.

Chapter VIII

"I thank you O Lord that I am not like the rest of men."

The Gospel passage from the 6 a.m. Mass he had just finished in his Borgo Pio apartment chapel was pleasing to Anselm Mugant, although his recitation of it did not possess the meaning he gave it. A Gospel admonition against hypocrisy, the passage was read by Mugant as a prayer of gratitude to a Power he believed kept him strong and single of intent. It was the passage with which the Canadian began his "thanksgiving after mass" only hours after having heard his Pope call for reconciliation and brotherhood among the scientists of the world late the previous night.

Kneeling at his velvet cushioned predieu, as he did daily for this thanksgiving, he continued. "Your will is that your commandments be obeyed. You have called your few, Father in Heaven, to secure your Church and teaching. A people set apart, O God, we few who heed your word invoke your teaching as our shield in a world unwilling to follow your law."

Mugant paused, seeming as if expecting a response.

"Defend us O Lord from the wiles and snares of the devil," he began again. "Righteous in your eyes, like Peter of old we will use the sword to protect the Church of our Master, your Son Jesus Christ. Your law is our light. Whatever is needed for Your law to be carried out we who follow Your commandments will accomplish. Like the archangel Michael we will slay the dragons who fester at your throne.

"There are those who amidst us that do harm to your way, O Lord. Father, they do not understand the way I do that Way You have shared with me what Your true will is. Even now they choose not to make a formidable stand. For they choose rhetoric, and rhetoric does not conquer the might of Your sword.

"But I, Father, I understand. I shall wield Your might in order to restore everlasting obedience throughout Your kingdom. No wall will be too thick, no miscreed unreachable.

"Divine Father, there is another matter I must attend to, as you know. It is because of the 'rhetoric speakers' that this issue has now come to be, and our very Church's foundation, already weakened, can potentially shatter in two. This devil may have discovered a cross that he may claim is the True Cross of Your Son. The scientists of this mad world may attempt to dismiss their faith—and so will seek scientific evidence of the validity of its origins. And it is possible that this science, so easily manipulated, can cause enough disturbance in man's already weakened faith as to undermine belief in Christ's very existence as the Redeemer. For remnants on the Cross —if they exist—could cause even greater speculation of Your Way, and His sacrifice. Especially if the media, our scourge, get a hold of this news and choose to sensationalize this lie."

Slightly beginning to perspire, Mugant took a handkerchief from his mohair suit trouser pocket and dabbed his brow. The handkerchiefs were always white Irish linen, laundered by a religious order of Catholic Sisters whose members Mugant never saw. But the clamminess he would sometimes feel when in prayer or meditation would somehow always be relieved by the clean and starched handkerchiefs that the Sisters' servitude provided him.

Mugant noticed at that moment the flickering of a bone white light at the end of his desk's phone turret. No phones ever rang in the Cardinal's apartment. Silence was Mugant's preference. Only a light suddenly flashing on three six-button phone banks, the identical bank of six in three of his apartment's rooms, told him of an incoming call. Rising from his predieu, he walked into his office immediately across the hall from his private chapel. Mugant knew by the number being called that it was the balding Fausto Cavaldi, the Franciscan cleric who served as the press attaché for his Curial office.

"Who is this?" Mugant began.

"Your Eminence, Cavaldi here. Do you remember *the Paris Match* news floating around the other day?"

"Get to the point, Fausto. What is it?"

"Polyclinique Normale, it is being reported, was bombed—blown to bits yesterday evening. The *Paris Match* story supposedly had to do with that lab and some news on a major advance in cell division."

"Is there anything else in the news on it?"

"I'll get you the full story as it was reported so far. But that is the—"

A second phone light flashed. Without pause, Mugant hit its phone button, cutting off at the same time Cavaldi's call on the other line.

"Your Eminence, Flavio Rinaldi speaking. I'm sorry to call you so early in the morning. You've heard about the explosion in Polyclinique, I would assume."

"I've heard nothing till this moment. Polyclinique, is that not something with the *Paris Match* story that you and Dr. Cordesco were working on for me, and one of the reasons Cardinal Fernando de Salvoyar had us meet with His Holiness last night?"

"Precisely, Eminence. The lab, reports as late as ten minutes ago tell us, was very badly hit. According to the nuncio in Paris, who had two eye witnesses at the scene afterwards, pretty much nothing is left. Obviously His Holiness is concerned with the possible loss of life.

"Sounds like terrorists to me, something the Israelis and Palestinians get involved in."

"Eminence, there is no reason for nationalists to be bombing a genetics lab."

"Is there anything else, Rinaldi?"

"Yes, thank you Cardinal Mugant. The Cardinal Secretary of State has asked that you make remarks this morning on your Vatican Radio "Life" program setting forth the Holy Father's comments last night. The Secretary has indicated this is actually the Holy Father's request."

"Well, we don't do political commentary, Rinaldi. We eschew that, remember?"

"His note for you on this matter is here, typewritten, and I can fax it to you."

"No, no. What does it say? Just give me the nub of it."

Rinaldi paused. "In solidarity with the Holy Father, Anselm, we feel it apt that you, as Curial Head of the Congregation for Human Life, re-iterate the Church's absolute abhorrence of all violence and her centuries old teaching on the sanctity and respect for all human life. This will be in accord, of course, with the Holy Father's meeting of last night, as I know this is what you want to bring forth also to your listeners at this time—"

"—fine, Rinaldi, I have it."

What a fool! A simpleton Curial cleric who has no idea of the gravity or dimensions of what is going on reads this note from de Salvoyar. Solidarity with human life? Tampering with God's handiwork is a sacrilege to the Almighty—that is what solidarity with human life tells us, not this other confection about respect for all life. Had we not used that 'respect for life' line at Hitler's time, maybe someone would have thought differently about what to do with his life.

The Swiss cuckoo clock on Mugant's apartment wall chimed 7 a.m. Mugant, his black mohair suit fitting exactly as he liked it, with the silk white Roman collar fitting just as well, walked to his closet door to retrieve his coat.

Another phone light flashed. Quickly, Mugant moved to answer the line.

"Yes?"

"We didn't get him."

"I am aware of everything already."

"The guy's slippery."

"Jerusalem, Tel Aviv—maybe I can understand. But Rome? Right here? The exact time and location was given, how could it be missed? It was the perfect way."

Mugant placed his black coat on top of his desk and sat himself in his high back leather chair. "You better know where he is now."

"He might be in Bologna, at the university there. Can't tell yet. It seems that Train kept contacts at one or two universities in Italy. Someone may have slipped under our radar. We have been targeting Train's geneticist goons, but at two universities there are individuals now teaching who once were in genetics, but switched to other fields."

"Right, anyone who was ever involved in genetics research must be tracked down. I've got to be moving on. What's this scientist's name?"

"We have only narrowed the list right now. At Bologna, if that's where he's at, there is Flavio Zechetto, Gaetano Ianni, and Francesco Pellegrino—all have geneticist backgrounds but are now doing other work there. If Bologna is not the place, Milano has an Achille Firneno. If we can connect Train to any one of these scientists, we probably know where he is."

"Get me the curriculum vitae of every scientist at any gene lab in Europe. There are 14 of these labs left. You know which ones they are. I do not want any further misses, excuses, and incompetence. We are on a holy mission. Now get on it." *No wonder we are still fighting these battles. No one gets the job done.*

***

"I understand Sister Pasquale. I need to right now get my bearings for my 8 am program." Dr. Pasquale Cordesco, the Ursuline Sister that worked with Flavio Rinaldi in the Curia's Human Life office, had just repeated to Mugant news he already knew. Though her religious garb, which she wore when occasion required, partly concealed her long black hair, it did not her deep blue eyes. "This morning is chilly, Sister Pasquale. I would like to have some coffee, if you would be so gracious."

"I'll get it, Sister," the Vatican Radio receptionist said, seeing Mugant was out of earshot. "You didn't go through all that schooling to fetch black coffee."

"Did we have any personality scheduled today for my show?" Mugant, reaching the doorway of the Vatican Radio control room, said to its respected director of programming, Terzo Amato.

"No, Cardinal. You were going to make some comments on *Humane Vitae* as it applied to the science of today. Some notes, a remembrance you have written for a Cardinal Cicognani, are on the—"

"—Ah, yes. Correct. I remember. Well, I'll have to make some comments on other matters this morning before that. There will be a slight change to format."

"Will you be here for the whole 30 minutes, Cardinal?"

"Of course. Do I ever miss a beat or cue?"

"This is Vatican Radio" the announcer's voice could be heard. "On the internet, on satellite radio, and in Rome. Ladies and gentlemen, "Life" with his Eminence, Anselm Cardinal Mugant, Prefect of the Congregation of Human Life."

"We are going to chat today on the work of the Cardinals who supported our venerable Holy Father, Pope Paul VI, in his courageous statement on human life, the 1968 encyclical *Humane Vitae*, presented to the world on July 25th of that year. One Cardinal in particular we wanted to especially honor and discuss today for his work in this encyclical. He is the great Vatican Secretary of State who served Holy Father Paul VI so well, Amletto Cicognani.

"However, first it is necessary to address an event

from yesterday news of which is now known worldwide. Human life scientists, who are braving the frontiers of nature's long held secrets, are being killed almost indiscriminately now. In Paris yesterday, a famous and respected genetics lab was bombed. The latest news is that seven are feared dead, twelve wounded critically."

Mugant looked at the clock wall.

"Last night I was with the Holy Father and other Cardinals. We assembled in the Pontiff's library, from where as dusk commences can be seen the *chameleon* like nature of the sky as it changes its many colors. *Flashing across* the sky, the lights seem to dart *from the Eternal City to Bologna* if you will. But our charge was to hear His Holiness' ringing condemnation of violence against scientists in life experiments, in cellular management systems, in embryo experimentations. Any *university* even is hostage possibly to violence if it carries out experiments that seek to understand the code of life. A university here, a *university in Bologna*, a university in Toronto, where I once lived—our youth are now in danger from these infidels who use science as a means to defy God. *We must take from these scientists, however they seek to conceal it, whatever it is they carry to destroy our creed.* They are like a *scorpion's* venom. It is up to all believers in God's Way to stand in unison against those who harbor violence of any sort. For we peaceful believers of the Way are the true bearers, soldiers, I might say, of Christ. And as peaceful warriors we must show the world the light."

***

A sullen figure only blocks away sat in his Rome flat. *The Scorpion must dart to the University of Bologna. Somebody there's got a concealed package it sounds like that he wants.* The speaker's voice from Vatican Radio could still be heard on his set as he closed the door behind him to descend into the streets below. *Bologna it is.*

***

"Sister, I've taken a walk to stretch my legs. I thought you might like to know things are still quiet here," a gentle voice said on the phone. "Nothing seems out of the ordinary."

"Have you had any luck at all?"

"No," the blue-eyed speaker softly responded, looking around to make sure no one was within earshot.

"Is there any further news on him?" her sister asked.

"Not yet, I'll give you a call tonight."

***

Train and Pellegrino had been up for the last three hours, scouring over various news wire services in search of further information regarding Polyclinique and Como Ventures. Successful in locating informative current and past articles regarding the biogenetic company, they were equally unsuccessful in finding any information on Como Ventures other than several small articles mentioning their failed attempt to acquire the Paris-based entity. Though still surprised to see the Italian based company mentioned in the news, Max was more surprised there was little else mentioned of the company anywhere on the internet. The name William Seto, Como's spokesperson, was familiar to him since Max recalled seeing the man's signature on documents when he had sold his and Luke's company to them. However, Dr. Margarita Sanchez, the company's chief executive officer, was not known to Max. Any attempt to locate Dr. Sanchez on the Net was meaningless. Peculiarly, these were the only two names mentioned in the eight news articles discussed on the Internet; a company no less, that recently attempted to offer several hundred million dollars for a now surely defunct bio-genetic start-up company, which according to the news reports, had lost the majority of its senior scientist in last nights explosion.

As Max was further investigating Polyclinique, knowing the company was rumored to be planning a major announcement, Francesco was on the telephone behind his office desk attempting to find an address and telephone number for Como Ventures.

There was no need to look up Polyclinique's information: little was left of the company. In fact, the company's stock did not open that morning on Paris' bourse, and more than likely would not open in the American markets later that day. On the surface they were an open book.

The Milanese operator told Pellegrino Como Ventures did not list an address, but the first four digits of the published telephone number appear to be located in the small town of Cernobbio, on Italy's Lake Como. Pellegrino jotted down the number, then reset his telephone. "Max, I have a number for Como Ventures."

Max paused from conducting his Internet search. "Oh? Where are they?" his interest peaked, as he sipped his cold espresso.

"There was no address listed, just a phone number. The operator believes the first four digits are a prefix for Cernobbio, a small town—"

"—I know it. My wife and I spent five days of our honeymoon at Villa d'Estaing. It's one of the most beautiful places in the world. So, "he continued, turning in Pellegrino's office chair, "Como Ventures is somewhere in the Italian Alps— or, at least a phone number is. I find it odd that they're still around—under that name, and I wonder why they don't list an address."

"What are you thinking?"

"That I don't believe in coincidence."

"And?"

"We're going to have to test the remnants of the Cross to determine what is on there. Then maybe we should contact the Vatican — but not until we complete our tests, and arrange for a press conference. A matter of fact, we should make sure we invite the heads of every major theological religion — Christians, Catholics, Protestants, Jews, Muslims, and Buddhist — even atheist. Everyone. And before I forget, when we study what appears to be the blood and hair remains on the Cross, we need to video tape everything. I also think we should test the items again to verify their ages today. We need to be careful with how we procure and attain all data."

"Contaminated data, or any questionable methods, regardless of how careful we are, could render our studies useless. I have a digital video recorder. We can set it up on a tripod. Perhaps we can arrange for a press conference in two or three days."

"That makes sense, but remember, like you said, 'we still have a long way to go'."

"We do - but," Francesco said lowly, awe of what his eyes

had witness the previous day taking hold of him.

"It's the Cross, isn't it? Kind of strange how it attaches to your soul."

Francesco, seated behind his desk, ran his fingers through his graying hair, then nodded agreeing towards Max. "It's very strange. I feel weird not having it by me. Are you sure it'll be safe?"

"At the Albergo Acconciamessa? You're the one who put it there."

"Right."

"Are you going to be all right?"

"Yes. I am aware of my desire to hold it. It's so odd, Max. I think I have heard the Cross calling me . . . asking me to come and get it. I won't though. I'm not supposed to feel this way, you know? I'm a man of science."

"You sure you want to go through with this?"

"Testing the remnants?"

"Testing of what appears to be blood and hair," Max inter jected.

"What if it is unlike anything we have ever seen?"

"I don't know, Francesco. The same can be asked if what we discover is human, right."

"Like we're entering into a magnetic hole. We have no way of knowing what's going to come out on the other side."

"Or in a certain way, being able to stop. Right?" Max specifically asked.

"I guess so. We need to find out if this is God's remains."

Max realized another burden had appeared. "Francesco, it is easy to be lured to wanting to hold the Cross . . . potentially hold God in your own hands. But you have to remember, we are only human. Only human," Max finished, realizing that he needed to move the cross Pellegrino placed at the hotel in Bologna.

Train's point was understood by Pellegrino.

"Francesco, what's the number to Como Ventures?"

Dialing the number spoken to him, Max received a sterile recording on the telephone line instructing him to leave a message. Odd, he thought to himself.

Hanging up the telephone, Max stood up, "Francesco, an answering machine picked up. I left no message, but I find it all very strange," Max said with a sense of skepticism. "I suddenly have a great need to visit my old suitors."

117

"Como Ventures?"
"Yes."
"How are you going to find them?"
"I have an idea," Max said affirmatively.

***

A bell echoed throughout the crowded open plaza as a lone stranger with short blonde hair and blue eyes briskly walked towards an outdoor cafe in Bologna's Piazza Migorrio. His long raincoat concealed two Berretta 9mm semi-automatic pistols. Tucked neatly inside the coat's inside pocket was an envelope containing the names, addresses, telephone numbers and pictures of each scientist he was to seek out.

He looked at his watch, now showing the correct time was 2:55 p.m. *Idiots. They can't even get time right.*

***

Having borrowed Francesco's Fiat, Max arrived back in the land of Caesars and Emperors precisely at 2:55 p.m., twenty minutes earlier than expected. From a previous phone call made earlier that morning from Bologna he obtained funeral 'showing' arrangements for Eileen Gartner who had not been waked yet. This information was shared with him via a chance phone call he made to Luke's office at the Vatican, under the pretense of a false friend looking to speak to Luke. The secretary, not knowing it was Max calling, who made sure not to hint otherwise, informed him of the tragic news that Ms. Gartner had been killed two nights ago, in all likelihood by some 'foreigners now living in Rome'. The woman went on to say Luke himself was missing, and her office was frantically looking for him.

Driving over the same blood infested bridge where he witnessed Eileen's, as well as the other innocent murders occur, Max entered the environs of Vatican City. The neighborhood was where the home that Luke and Eileen once lived.

From memory, he recalled the address of the dead couple's residency. As he passively moved the car out of the notorious traffic, Max felt his heart racing. Somewhere in the shadows there was a deadly cobra hungry for him, and he just entered into the snake's den.

Nevertheless, Max knew he was not a free man, and the assassins would continue until they found and killed him. His only hope was to find answers to questions he did not even know, other than the fact somebody knew what he found and was willing to do anything possible. No human life was too sacred to prevent him from keeping the Cross. Why else would they want him dead?

Noticing a parked car exiting its spot, Max pulled to the side and awaited the vehicle to depart. Less than a minute later, Pellegrino's Fiat was parked on the city street. As he stepped out of the car, the now too familiar shooting pain pulsed up his injured leg like an electrical current.

The mid-afternoon sun beat down on him as exhaust fumes from an old truck slowly rumbled by, the soot it expelled seemingly directed into his squinting eyes. Tentative moving steps barely outpacing the congestion on the city asphalt followed one after another, his heart's rhythm racing four beats for every forced step.

Max knew where he was: one block away from where the Gartner's lived.

Forcing him onward, the plan he developed in his head earlier that morning began to evaporate the way the poisonous truck fumes disappeared into the haze that was covering Rome.

Amongst the crowded street located in Vatican City's external grounds filled with pilgrims seeking to pay tribute to The Holy Father, Max moved snail-like, similar to the other tourist in the area. Moments later he noticed Via Anisole, a small non-connecting cul-de-sac. He turned right and noticed 3 Via Anisole: the building that housed the Gartner's flat.

Feelings of self-betrayal crept up on him. The reality, as he viewed it, was the only two people in the world who really gave a damn about him were now dead because of the calls he made to them. Attempting to tell himself their deaths were not his fault was something he didn't bother to rationalize to himself as he stared at the street. He had tried to do so each day. It never worked.

The cross he discovered which he expected would bear him great peace and comfort had brought nothing but agony. With each passing day greater burdens were placed on his shoulders. At some point anybody would weaken from heavy weights. Train's body was nearing the breaking point. Looking around the streets of a city where too many people died, he once again recalled the images of death.

Everything around him appeared to be a facade. The ancient buildings, though handsomely crafted, once housed hypocrites who perhaps never really left. The people next to him, *humanity*, able to love and share with each other in community, also was able to purposefully kill. The government of Italy, similar to many political structures around the world, intended to develop fair regimes so all citizens could be provided for. Yet that too was a far reach as politicians' blind eyes of compromise and self-elation too often prevented their intentions from being accomplished. Even at this moment there were sinful pilgrims who would enter the mother-Church basilica of St. Peter's, filled with numerous monuments of sinful Popes scattered among true men of the Lord's Way, Emperors and Caesars who helped expand "righteous Christianity", who in their crusade acted in every conceivable way Christ taught not to. The country— for that is what Vatican City is— was the only nation in the world, Israel included, which dictated all policy under the pretext of "God's Way." Complex, confusing, contradictory in action and belief, the modern Papacy and his constituency were honorable with intent, yet they too had to cope with the realities that the teachers of their flock were human.

It was difficult for Max to know what was real and what was a lie. What was true, what was a façade? What was "God's Way", and the manipulated intent of man? For a spiritually beaten down man possessing a scientific mind nothing was clear.

Unexpectedly, the six bells of Saint Peter's sounded through the cool air. Max looked up, and noticed from afar the grand dome built to commemorate the father of Christianity, Simon Peter, constructed and reconstructed by Italian's of legendary fame who themselves sought grandeur and riches in the name of the Church.

The towering basilica was 212 meters long, 140 meters wide, and its height from pavement to the cross on the dome 137 meters. It was a colossus, yet diminutive in comparison to its global reach.

Max felt the muscles in his body tense, as a new sense of strength and courage began to form within him. *If you're a loving God, why is the world like this? Look at my life now. I thought it could not have gotten worse than it was when you my wife and daughter were taken from me, but it has. It sure has. If I die, which I am sure I will fairly soon, it doesn't matter. I don't believe in this*

— this place you created. Nothing you do can harm me any longer. Nothing!

Taking a deep breath, Max forced himself to cross the street along with the other city visitors, and now stood less than sixty feet away from the door entrance that would lead to the second floor apartment.

He was a man left with very little. As he saw it, his life was really no life at all. The Cross he had found, as profound as it may be, was nothing more than an invitation to chaos, havoc, and destruction. Max realized that with the alleged holy artifacts discovery commenced his free-fall into Dante's inferno. A hell he descended deeper into with each passing day.

I'll find those who have sought me. I will hunt them down the way they have hunted and killed all those that mattered to me — and then I will destroy them. And if I need to scour the earth looking for you, you invisible bastard, I will use every remaining piece of energy to do so. Hide like you do coward, but somewhere you have made a mistake. And I will find that one error, as tiny and insignificant as it might be and use it to hunt you down. I promise you'll know the suffering and the pain that I have come to know. You'll know the horror of suffocating as you gasp for air. You'll know the nothingness of bullet lodging into your skin, right before warmth turns to agonizing pain. You'll know what Hell is like the way I do.

Max looked around the street once more, noticing passers-by continuing on their way. He walked directly towards the Gartner's home. Without looking back, he put his hand on the large brass doorknob attached to a large double wooden door and turned it.

The door opened. Max quickly entered a dimly lit stairway. Walking up to the second floor landing, he listened carefully for anyone inside the Gartner's home. There appeared to be no one. Pausing, he listened to hear sounds from the apartment above. It also appeared empty.

His heart had slowed down and the images that were in his mind only moments ago were gone. The only thing on Max's mind was revenge - revenge against those who turned his life into the nothingness it was.

Removing two thin wires from his pocket, he quickly put them in the keyhole. The trick he learned from his childhood had worked, as he heard the tumbling of the door's cylinders line up together.

Pressing down on the door handle, he heard it unlock. He entered the apartment and quietly closed the door behind him.

Max carefully looked around Luke and Eileen's apartment in search of any clues indicating a lead that would provide him the direction needed to locate the invisible lunatic.

It became apparent the apartment was not touched in two days. Ready for the unexpected, Max, carrying a large knife he found in the kitchen, carefully entered each of the remaining rooms of the three-bedroom flat. Everything appeared untouched.

He walked back into the living room and noticed a flashing light attached to a telephone answering machine. On the digital display appeared the red blinking number '2', indicating there were two new messages.

"That's strange. Someone must have been here arranging for Eileen's funeral arrangements," he said as he looked around the room once again. "To hell with it," he continued, as he pressed down on the answering machine's 'play' button.

A woman's voice, identifying herself as Amy left a message for Eileen to give her a call when she had the chance. No return number was left.

The second caller was a male's voice. The message was for Luke, informing him that everything was set for next week. No return number was left.

Unexpectedly, Max felt an unseen shadow reaching for him. He turned, wielding the large steel knife in his hand!

There was no one there.

"You got to get a grip of yourself," he said aloud as he slowly turned his attention back to the answering machine. Pressing the 'record' button, he listened to the happy voices of Luke and Eileen telling their would-be callers to leave a message. "They'll never have a chance to return your calls," Max added. "I'm sorry it has turned out the way it has."

Walking back into one of the bedrooms Luke used as a home office, Train looked at a large glass dining room table now used as a desk covered with photographs. There were many pictures of Luke and Eileen together, as well as three photos taken of him and The Holy Father. Four pictures on a near-by shelf captured the avid skier Luke and some friends skiing in the Alps. The remaining items on the desk were stacks of cluttered papers and files appearing to be associated with Luke's work with the Pontiff's

Scientific Advisory Board.

Max began to carefully go through each draw in search of old files Luke may have saved regarding the Como Ventures deal. Within twenty minutes he came across an old folder titled "Como Ventures Sales Documents".

He opened the folder. Inside was only one sheet of paper. It indicated an address in Cernobbio. There was no phone number, or any legible names on the file. Folding it, he placed it in his pocket, and returned the file from the credenza behind the desk from where he found it.

Two minutes later Max was back on the busy street's of Rome. Five minutes later, he was seated behind the wheel of Francesco's car, and pulling out of the parking lot.

***

Sixty-two year old Doctor Flavio Zechetto walked quickly up the wide flight of stairs leading to his spacious two-story home built in 1658 A.D. located in the center of Bologna's Piazza Maggiore. Whistling a carefree tune, Bologna's celebrated medical bachelor removed his keys from his stylish plaid cashmere sports coat and placed them in the door lock. As he did, he noticed the day's mail on the floor, and reached to pick it up. "Ah, I thought I told the postman to slip my mail under the door," Flavio said in a gentle demeanor as he reached for the items. "Look at that, he must have dropped some of this. Well, it must be a difficult position," he continued as he began to thumb through the postals.

Entering his elegant apartment, Flavio immediately walked over to the large windows overlooking the grand Palazzo dell'Archiginnasio, Italy's most important public library with over 700,000 books, rare manuscripts and codices, and the first seat of the University of Bologna in the 16th century. Lifting the large, heavy window up from its shut position, a fresh breeze entered the spacious loft. "Ah, I must prepare myself for this evening. First, I change, then I do twenty minutes of this new 'pilates' to get the blood moving. But first, I put some music on. Perhaps some *Mango*."

Taking off his expensive coat and tossing it on a goose-down couch, the colorful Bolognese walked over to his stereo system console and flipped through his CD's. Finding what he desired, he bent down and placed the CD in the machine.

As he hit the 'play' button, he noticed the reflection of a man behind him.

The next thing the bleeding Dr. Zechetto realized was that his mouth was skillfully gagged tight from one of his Zegna ties, and his arms and legs were immovably fastened to one of his antique dining room chairs, so much so that he felt a lack of blood in his extremities. The smooth voice of the Italian performer Mango played loudly in the background, but it did nothing to sooth his aching head, still lightly bleeding from the pistol blunt that descended on his skull.

In front of him, Flavio was able to see the radiant orange sun setting over Bologna. Orange crests with flares of volcanic red set in the backdrop of the Piazza's gray-blue skies, the setting would have been "ideal for lovemaking", but that he was so viciously bound. Instead of admiring the two Towers of Bologna; the Torre Della Garisenda and the Torre degli Asinelli the way he typically did if at home during this time of day from his windows, Flavio looked forebodingly at the Pavaglione, a mass of buildings whose famous porticoes provided a place to meet for many Bolognesi over the centuries. The Pavaglione was made up of two buildings designed by Terribilia: the Palazzo dell' Archiginnasio, built between 1562 and 1563, and housed the great library. The second building, the Palazzo dell'Ospedale della Morte, construct-ed and reconstructed during the 16th century set off subconscious fears for the mischievous doctor. Half conscious, he could not take his eyes off dell' Ospedale — the Palace of the Death Hospital.

What happened to him and by whom, he had no idea. Flavio was aware that any attempt to free his limbs would be use-less, as the thick rope was too tight.

Turning his head around to see who had done this to him, Flavio noticed nobody in the room. He looked into the fading sun and new he was without physical choice.

Flavio's physical freedom was gone, but that did not prevent him from taking his mind elsewhere. If his body was to be a sacri-ficial lamb of some sort, so be it, he thought to himself. Taking a deep breath through his nostrils, he closed his eyes and allowed his mind to journey to the Greek island of Santorini.

Moments of tranquility passed in his head, when suddenly the burning sting of an open fist smashing into the right side of his face abruptly shattered any peaceful thoughts. The power of the blow threw Flavio onto the floor, still bound to the old oak chair.

Suddenly lifted upright in the chair, Flavio looked into the tinted gray-blue eyes of a voidless face, one without any expression whatsoever.

"Where is Max Train?" *The Scorpion* asked, his mouth inches now away from Flavio.

Who? Flavio stared in shock.

"Where is Max Train?" asked the killer once again, his hand removing the knotted tie in placed in the doctor's mouth.

"I do not know who you're talking about," he weakly answered.

Placing his face inches away from Flavio's, "I will only ask you one last time, then I'll use this," *The Scorpion* said, removing a long sharp razor. "Do not make a mistake. I will not hesitate to slit your throat. Where's Max Train and the items he carries?"

"I tell you the truth. I am a doctor. I know not of this Max Train. Please, don't."

"You tell me the truth?"

"Yes."

"You're not lying?"

"No. Have mercy," begged Flavio.

"Mercy? There is no such thing."

"For Christ's sake—"

"—he doesn't hear your voice. He doesn't hear any voices," the killer spewed.

Flavio stared in disbelief at the blonde psychopath.

"Well it is too bad you have seen my face," the killer said right before the steel blade was forced deep into the innocent doctor's throat, killing him instantly.

Within moments *The Scorpion* was back on the streets of Bologna, his killing having gone unnoticed by anyone. As he walked across the great square, he removed the list in his pocket. Meticulous, he checked off Dr. Zechetto's name from the list before concentrating on the next person named.

Seeing a vacant taxi lingering around the great library, he hailed it down. Moments later he was dropped off a few blocks from his next destination. Departing from the cab, he heard the bell towers of Torre Della Garisenda and Torre degli Asinelli and realized it was 6 p.m.

Under the dusk filled sky he carefully walked to the cobbled residential street of Via Tommasso, his eyes passively scrutinizing the passing faces on the street. Noticing the numbered direction of the addresses listed on the homes, he turned right and continued his ordinary walk. Within minutes he slowly passed the targeted address, noticing a light on in the second floor.

He continued walking up the street, inspecting the scene for any potential inconveniences. There appeared as if there were none.

Purposefully turning on the right heel of his foot, the killer reversed his movements and walked back towards the address on his short list.

Normal appearances are the easiest way to disarm someone. That fool wants this done, and so I shall comply. There still is another on my list living in this foul place I may need to attend to before I possibly travel to Milan tonight.

Opening the gate to a small courtyard, he went directly to the door and rang the bell to the second floor apartment. As he waited he took out a white envelope.

"Who is it?" asked a voice on the intercom.

"I have a package for a Doctor Francesco Pellegrino from Dr. Flavio Zechetto, *Senor*. It needs to be signed for."

"Doctor Zechetto? Come to the second floor," Francesco Pellegrino suggested as he buzzed the killer into his home.

"Grazie." Entering onto the second floor landing, *The Scorpion* removed one of his firearms, assembled with a silencer, from his waist side. As he did, Francesco opened the door.

"What do you have —?"

There was no chance to complete his sentence, as the steel barrel of the gun was instantly placed less than a foot from his forehead.

"Are you alone, Doctor?"

"Si."

"You say a word, you die. *Capisce?*"

"Capisco."

"Move slowly into your place," said the killer as he moved the gun inches closer to Pellegrino's head.

Closing the door quietly behind him, the madman looked around the room. It appeared that nobody was there. "Doctor, this can be made simple or difficult. You know why I am here?"

Pellegrino's heart raced, but words eluded him.

It was all The *Scorpion* needed. "Where is Max Train?"

"I . . . I don't know," the doctor replied.

The gun's cold barrel was now touching his forehead. "Do not lie to me. You may save your life by telling me the truth. I have no qualm with you. It is Train who I want. Where is he?"

"I . . . I . . . I'm not sure. He borrowed my car early this morning. I'm not sure where he went or when he will be back," he answered, innately knowing that the blonde man was not playing with him.

"Move inside — towards the dining room."

Pellegrino did what was asked of him.

"Tell me Doctor, why did Max Train come to you?"

Breathless, Pellegrino hesitated.

Without warning, the killer pointed the gun at Pellegrino's left leg, and squeezed the trigger.

As the bullet exploded into the Doctor's leg, the powerful lunatic quickly was on top of him, his long cold hand over Francesco's mouth in order to muffle any outcry. "Do not lie to me. Do not. You understand?" he coldly said to the terrified scientist, who was frantically nodding his head in full apprehension as tears swelled in his eyes.

"I'm going to ask you again: why did Train show up at your door?"

"He . . . he needed a place to hide," Pellegrino whimpered.

The Scorpion smiled a sickly smile. "Now we're making progress, no? Yes. Good. But Doctor, it is my understanding that he may have had some items friends of mine are very anxious to get back, and Train has no intent to return them. You can save your own life by giving them back to me."

As beads of sweat mixed with the warm blood pouring out of his leg, Francesco closed his eyes. "Please don't hurt me. I'll tell you what I know, which isn't very much. He — Train showed up at my home a few days ago, in the middle of the night saying that some people in Rome were after him. He said he found some items dating back to the time of Jesus. He wanted them dated. That's what I do. I date things using carbon tests for the University here."

"What things?"

"I'm not sure. I haven't seen them yet. He —"

The gun was instantly stuck in Francesco's mouth, his eyes ajar in a terror he could never have imagined. "If you lie to me once more, you're dead. I will also find any living relative of yours and painfully torture them before killing them. Do I make myself clear?"

With the gun stuck in his face, Francesco Pellegrino fearfully nodded.

"What things?" he asked again slowly moves the gun barrel out of Pellegrino's mouth.

"Train said he thought he may have found the True Cross of Christ."

The Scorpion smiled. "Oh, really?" *So that's why Mugant called me. He wants the Cross back. I should have known it was something of significance for him to awaken me from sleep. That bastard's fees are going up.*

"Yes, but like I said, I haven't seen it. I think he left it at a hotel."

"And why haven't you gone to get it?"

"I . . . I doubt it is real. The Church is supposed to have it."

"Where is this hotel?" the killer asked, moving the gun closer to the frightened trembling man.

"I'm not sure. Please, please put the gun away. I'm telling you the truth," he begged.

"In good time. What is the name of the hotel?"

"It's . . . I think it's called the Albergo Acconciamessa, but I'm not sure."

"And Train, when is he expected back?"

"I told you, I'm not sure. I think he was going to Rome."

"Rome?"

"Yes. A friend of ours died," Pellegrino began, now realizing he was looking at the face of Eileen Gartner's killer. "The bridge . . . it was you!"

"Yes. That bridge and many others, Doctor."

"Oh, God!"

"There is no such person. You're a person of science. You should know that."

"Please, don't —"

"Doctor, I have a secret to tell you."

Pellegrino's mouth opened, agape. "What?" he asked stunned.

"My name is Sergio."

"Huh?"

"Now that you know my name, I have to kill you. Ask your God for help," the lunatic said in an icy even voice.

Francesco Pellegrino knew he was to die. "God, have mercy."

"He knows of no such thing, Doctor," *The Scorpion* smirked before sending a bullet into Francesco's forehead.

Looking around the blood and gut-splattered dining room, the killer looked at his watch. "It's time to visit this hotel, then I'll call Mugant, and discuss my new price to return his precious items."

Walking over to an antique writing desk in the corner of Francesco's apartment, cold fingers picked up several Internet articles dated yesterday and today. Circled on two of these articles were the names Dr. William Seto and Dr. Margarita Sanchez. "Interesting. Como Venture. Where have I heard this name before?"

***

It was a half hour since *The Scorpion* entered Francesco Pellegrino's dwelling when a man of average height and demeanor walked up to the Doctor's home, opened the door, and ascended to the second floor landing. Noticing the door to the flat partially opened, he cautiously entered the apartment. With startled eyes Max Train realized the Reaper's sickle had sliced yet again.

There were to be no answers or discoveries to be found in Bologna. The madmen who wanted him dead had found him once again. *My God, look at what has been done. I need to leave before I get attached to this killing, too. Maybe Como can provide the answer. If there is a God, listen to me, and listen to me now. Stop this, stop this right now!*

Chapter IX

Two cars were filling their gas tanks at the 24 hour petrol station located a half hour north of Bologna.

Another friend who tried to help Max was dead. Bologna, the fourth city he traveled to in less than one week now too had innocent blood on its streets. Wherever he traveled his hunters awaited his arrival. Luckily, they were moments behind him each time. Sooner or later, Max realized, his luck would end, and if he didn't uncover who and why he was being hunted — then no doubt he too was a dead man.

In his mind he heard the loud ticks of an imaginary time clock closing in near to a resounding vibration that time — his time here had ended.

Returning to Rome appeared to be an option equally as undesirable as staying in Bologna. Como Ventures, located on the shores of Cernobbio on Lake Como was worth investigating, but there were little reassurances remaining other than the $9,000 American and the credit card issued under the name of John Burns he had in his possession. It wasn't enough.

Now seated in Francesco's Fiat with the "package" Pellegrino left at Albergo Acconciamessa which Max picked-up earlier this morning before his departure to Rome, he stretched his tired limbs, fighting off his body's fatigue.

The station attendant waved him on to the island pump. It was his turn to fill-up his tank.

The artifact no doubt had turned out to have more ramifications than he could have imagined — continual disasters included. The fact remained that since it's unearthing, nothing good had come about. Was this some type of cruel joke orchestrated by a demonic madman on earth or elsewhere? Circumstances strongly suggested so . . . at least to Max. For if there was a God, then why the continual tests? Why the murders — why him?

Perhaps, Max reflected, the ordeal was a test that would bring him to a higher station. This thought, coupled with any accepting thoughts of a Higher Being were quickly dismissed as Max noticed a man approximately his age holding the delicate hand of a young girl as they walked into the kiosk of the gas station.

He squeezed his hand before focusing his attention on the wedding band on his hand. More than ever he felt alone and betrayed. *I wish you were here. It all is so confusing, and so dangerous. I'm not sure what I should do, or who I should contact. Everyone I turn to dies. Not that I have many persons to turn to, you know? The Cross, what of it? All that occurs are the things Jesus of Nazareth, who died on that barbaric thing, preached not to do. Yet evil surrounds it. Whoever is hunting me is also hunting Him . . . if there really is a Him. You know, if he existed, I wish he was here — but who knows what's real and what's not. God, I miss you and our daughter so much. So much!*

As the attendant filled the car, Max looked carefully at the wrapped boxes placed in the passenger seat. "Who are you?"

The service attendant interrupted his trance when he came over to collect the monies due.

As Max paid him, the idea that had been forming in his head was now becoming clear. From what he knew, there were no arrest warrants related to the incidents in Rome issued against him — though he would have to be sure first before he did anything. He was an American citizen, and The United States Mission in Milan should offer him a safe haven.

He would turn over the artifacts to the U.S. Consulate and let them deal with the problem.

The lab tests that were conducted in Francesco's lab were enough for him: the wood was nearly two millennia old. The test to determine who was on the cross would have to be done by someone else, or left undone. All that mattered was staying alive at this point. And as much as it was appealing for him to bury the items in some open field, he knew that was only a temporary solution. Max was smart enough to realize most temporary solutions only created larger problems in the future. *The American Mission it is, and then back to New York. Maybe it's time to do something else. Maybe time to get a life.*

Directing the car to the public restroom in the rear of the building, Max gingerly got out of the car, stretched his beaten body under the stale night lights of the modern gas station, and walked towards the pay phone. Moments later an Italian operator informed Rabbi Kohn he had a "collect call" from Italy. The Rabbi immediately accepted the charges.

"Max, where are you?" Marty Kohn assumed as he walked to his study in his newly constructed home in Brooklyn.

"Outside of Bologna. Maybe 30 kilometers. Things have gone from bad to rotten here."

Rabbi Kohn sat in his deep leather black chair behind a pile of books on his desk. "Max, I have been very worried about you. Are you safe?"

"Not really," Train said sarcastically. Someone is trying to kill me—"

"—I know that. Do you know who it might be?"

"No. But I did see the face of one bastard on the bridge, and the face of that woman at the airport."

"The woman, she's dead. We don't know how. But this man, you saw him, what did he look like?"

Max realized whoever was stalking him was covering his tracks. He went on to then describe the masqueraded face of *The Scorpion,* though neither person realized whom he really described, nor that what Max saw was not the monster's true face.

"Why is it some mysterious group may want you dead? You're not a violent person, Max."

"I may have taken something of theirs that I shouldn't have. I'm not sure."

"What do you mean? You're not a thief."

"No, I'm not."

"Then what is it, friend?" the Rabbi asked in a warm, genuine voice.

"Before I tell you Rabbi, have any of my friends' bodies been found?" Max asked as he swatted away several flies by the outdoor telephone booth.

"Yes. The girl was found so far."

"Lynn. Lynn Johnson?"

"According to my friends, they have a way to go. By the way, they found gunpowder in the cave. There's no question someone was trying to hurt you in Jerusalem . . . and it appears they have found you to the land of Caesars."

"When was her body found?"

"Yesterday. I believe her family was notified by the Israeli government. The others — you said there were two more —"

"— yes, Luke Gartner and John Muir."

"Well, they haven't been found yet. It's a matter of time. I guess that was a big cave."

"It was, I suppose."

"I'm sorry," the Rabbi offered.

"Thank you. Marty, did Sara tell you I was carrying a box when I left Israel?"

"Yes. A long, thin rectangular box. Tell me, what is it that was in this box that now has killers looking all over the world for you."

"Marty, we're friends, right?"

Marty let out a friendly chuckle. "What makes you ask that? Of course we are."

Max swatted away another annoying mosquito. "How would you feel if I was to tell you I think I discovered the Cross Jesus of Nazareth was crucified on?"

Rabbi Kohn hunched deeper in his chair. "Max, are you sure of what you're saying?" he slowly asked.

"I think there is a strong possibility it might be. That's what I found on the Mount of Olives."

"What makes you think this?"

"I read the languages of old, remember? I also had the wood tested in Bologna."

Everything so far, at least preliminarily seems genuine. There's even remnants left on the cross that very well might be —
"

"—Max, do you understand what you're suggesting?"

Train took a deep breath as he noticed a car pulling out onto the open road. "I'm aware of what only I see, but yes, I think I do."

"Max, in my faith, Jesus was a man, but a very special man. In yours, well he is the Son of God. Are you sure there were body parts on this cross?"

"Possibly. They have to be tested," Max answered.

"I understand, I think, why you're being hunted. Max, two thousand years of humanity's divisiveness in *faith* may, in a certain way, be attached to that cross. There may be more answers on the items you carry than what the world can accept — or undo."

"What do you mean?"

"Think of the geopolitical consequences of what you have found. The possibilities are endless, one way or another. History books would need to be altered. Institutions that have been built around theological beliefs—at least man's perspective of God's Way—Judaism, Christianity, — even Islam, would be forced to changing—of possibly undoing themselves and the way they operate. Humanity could have eternal peace or face Armageddon. The extremes are very real."

"I've thought of this. I've also thought of throwing the cross into the sea."

"But that does no good for two reasons, Max. You know this. First, Jesus was special to everyone. You simply can't discard him. And secondly, for you, whoever is hunting you — well, let's say that they're pretty damn good at it. They got by my friends, you understand?"

"I'm aware of that."

"What are you intending to do?"

"Go to Milan and turn it over to the United States Mission. The American Constitution, for what it's worth, calls for a separation of power and religion. I think that Constitution may be able to handle the burdens of what I have found. I know I can't."

"You ask a great deal from government."

"I didn't want any of this. I'm just a man."

"Perhaps a chosen one, Max," the Rabbi countered.

"Don't be ridiculous. I want out."

The Jewish Rabbi said nothing.

"Marty, so much evil is drawn to this cross. It's not what Jesus taught or represented."

"I understand your fears, Max. But Jesus, in his lessons, was a resilient person, was he not? You're alive, and I trust, the cross has not been damaged, has it?"

Max thought briefly about it. "I guess so."

"Good. I do think going to the American Embassy is a good idea. At least you should have some safety there."

"That's what I was thinking, but I was wondering if you can do me a favor?"

"Yes?"

"I'm not sure, but can you check to see if there is an arrest warrant out for me in Italy?"

"I already have, Max. There is nothing anywhere. Be careful, and get to Milan. The Embassy will offer you refuge. It's a good idea. You can figure out the meanings behind everything later. The most important thing is to know you're okay."

"Thanks. I have a few hour trips ahead of me."

"I know, Max. Remember, I lived in Rome for two years after the war."

"I know," Max responded, aware Rabbi Kohn had escaped not only the brutality of Auschwitz but also renegade clerics who were rumored to have commanded Hitler's army in Croatia during

World War II. He also knew his wise friend now living in Brooklyn now found it in his heart to forgive those who killed in the name of God.

"Max, do you have enough money?"

"I'm fine. Thank you, Marty."

"Good, now listen, I think it's best that you go to the consulate in the mid-morning. And before you do, please call me. Collect is fine."

"Okay," Max replied.

"Max, be careful and hold onto your faith. God is a loving God. 'My refuge, my stronghold, my God in Whom I trust'."

***

Outside, lonely bells indicated it was 10 p.m. in the Eternal City.

"Someone is not guiding the Holy Father correctly. He is getting the wrong advice. We have had two emergency meetings with him in the past 36 hours, both called by his unremarkable Secretary of State. Instead of saying how horrific mitosis advancement in human cell manipulation would be to God's creation, he is bemoaning today the violence against those who need it—the brave new world doctors and bloodthirsty financiers of genetic counterfeiting!"

Six large candles were burning in the same room where the Canadian *watchman of the laws of life* had commissioned only three days earlier a murderer for hire who had once been his penitent. Shadows of six figures moved back and forth on the dull gray walls as the candle lights flickered first one way, then another. No one would ever be able to identify who these shadows were of. The Canadian prelate was a practiced hand at concealment.

"This is the first time you have used the word 'chameleon' on your Vatican Radio program. We had to be sure that it still was the password to meet here," said one of the seated visitors who flew to Rome on moment's notice. His eyes, like all visiting eyes in the room, recognized the familiar scar on the face of the one who had summoned them there.

Mugant had little use for the Argentinean oil magnate's droning. Scion of the founders of the century old German construction giant, Mühlor Fabrik, long rumored to have helped finance Hitler's rise to power, the middle age blue-eyed Hernando Mühlor,

135

blond hair thinning, was key to inaccessible money sources for institutions and projects in which he believed. Mühlor's usefulness to the Curial Cardinal was his ability to conceal money collection efforts for goals they both supported. Raising funds for hospitals and orphanages was a cover he had mastered well, and which had caught Mugant's eye when he had served on a Vatican commission examining the financial apparatuses of the Holy See. An oversight that was never really lost, but disappeared, was his hook. "The Crusader vision of our equestrian order is at the service of our faith" were words from Mühlor's investiture into a centuries old order of Church knighthood that he carried with him everywhere… so too was the fact these records still remained on this physical earth.

"It is good that you did pick up on the word, obvious as it was to others. You function well as the chairman *ex officio* of Mühlor Empressa" Mugant responded. "No one asks questions, Mühlor is very profitable, and you can look charitable to the citizens of Buenos Aires sending out requests to donors for hospital care and schools while you go on assisting in obtaining the funds our Fifth Crusade needs without them even knowing. Funding it through a Brunei petrol facility has a nice feel to it. Perhaps you'll eventually know salvation from your many sins."

A soft wind could be heard winding through the shadows filled meeting room. It was a backdrop in which Mugant felt he could work.

"We continue to be creative in our financial reporting, Eminence," the Argentinean replied, causing a muffled laughter to start in the room.

"The issue is serious," Mugant barked. "We are at an inflection point. There cannot be distractions from what we are doing here. You must make sure that funding is available at whatever moment." Mugant's thin fingers tapped the cast iron candleholder nearest him. All were aware of the bank accounts containing huge sums of money secretly held in Switzerland, Grand Cayman, and Cyprus.

"Vatican Bank has provided all here today with ample cover. Comments about a country's financial reporting standards are not relevant to our funding since only three have access to the Bank records, I being one of them, and the records that could provide each of you with unbelievable disturbance are tucked secretly away in my sole possession. Of course, if I was to mysteriously die, they'll become public record. So if any of you think of harming me while I do God's work, I'll make sure that each of you go directly to Hell. As they say, one for all and all for one," he said with a piercing snicker. "You're all here today because as a Commission Member looking into the Banks' staggering losses from the stock market crash thirteen years ago, I personally assured each of you cover for some questionable transactions—or should I say illegal transactions— that your governments would love to know about which you and your families executed through Vatican Bank."

All five looked at Mugant passively. Clearly they were his puppets, but puppets of great power and influence.

"Guillermo Schemmizzi, washing billions of lira through silver contracts pledged to Catholic Action," Mugant went on, his lizard like eyes showing pleasure at the eighty-one year old Italian media mogul's obvious discomfort. "You certainly had large ambitions, Guillermo. Your faith in the traditional Church, and how you expressed your conviction to me when you were notified you had been caught, moved me to provide you with financial cover. Is your conviction still strong?"

"This Pope I cannot support, *Eminenza*. The Church is so changed, and we must do whatever we can to stop its destruction."

"Exactly, and well-said, Guillermo.

"Adrianna Corvoso de Sa. Armaments trafficking for years and yet you, as almost a *femme fatale*, as it were are here today for Holy Mother Church."

"My family will do anything for the Church, you know that most reverend Cardinal. We have supplied arms for the fighters of Communism in Brazil, in Colombia, in Venezuela. We saved the continent for Christ," the stylishly clad woman in her early forties replied as she exhaled cigarette smoke from her lungs.

"For sure, and the Bank was a clearing agent since World War II for those funds you received defending the continent for our Savior. Your government never knew how profitable fighting Communism was."

"McGeorge Previn. We can review your work for the intelligence community in America, but some of that is, shall we say, confidential? Family money has given you the liberty and means to work for your Church."

"We believe in the sacredness of human life, my family, and we have watched as the battle lines have been drawn. We continue with you, Cardinal Mugant," the thin, athletic gray suited figure responded.

"Not that you had much leeway, Previn, given the scandal that would be made public if your family was known to have used Vatican Bank for its support of Franco in Spain.

"And Rupert Hawkins, an Englishman running global investment finance conglomerate bearing his surname, and might I add one that rumors continue to persist has an interest in biogenetic investments. And now also charged with overseeing our financial sword, which I named Como Ventures. By the way, if you all recall I chose that name because I love spending time in the Lake region. As a matter of fact, this whole thing should be headquartered there. Delicious how Como has so many different interests, from brewery to global investment banking," the Canadian prelate said, seeming hardly able to contain himself.

"This is a far cry from rumors of your family financings of the Habsburgs through a secret account in World War II, though, Rupert. You remember that. You're old enough. So is Guillermo. They were going to finance forced opposed to the psychopath, the Fuehrer, in an attempt to rebuild the Holy Roman Empire, to which they were fantastic pretenders. A noble objective, but do it legally."

Hawkins' ice gray eyes looked at Mugant. "Hawkins Investment Services has no interest in renegade scientists or scientist entrepreneurs running amuck in genetics. It gives a bad name to legitimate corporations—"

"—Of course, Rupert. It having nothing to do with keeping past money trails hidden?" Mugant quietly replied, his smirk barely concealable. "But we are now all beyond this."

None of the five in the room believed they were beyond anything Cardinal Mugant held or stored. At his fingertips was enough information to destroy each of the empires they or their families had built. In their potential fall, there surely would be worldwide outcries for long-term jail sentences, significant financial restitution, and the complete destruction of their individual empires. None were willing to see if Mugant was bluffing.

Mugant folded his hands. "It is believed that the True Cross of Christ may have been found."

All five in the room at once looked at Mugant.

"What?" asked McGeorge Previn.

"Now I know," Mugant quickly interjected, "that many hold

to the Cross of Helena as the True Cross, the relics of which our devout believe the Franciscan have at the Church of the Holy Sepulchre in Jerusalem. But there is no proof this is the Cross. It is pious tradition. Holy Mother Church has never confirmed that the Cross of Christ has been discovered. The fact that some have held it is still at the Mount of Olives may give believability to the rumor now circulating." Mugant paused to let his announcement take the effect he wanted on his listeners.

"The person who found what may be the Cross is one Dr. Max Train of Syracuse, New York who was at an excavation site at the Mount of Olives in Jerusalem when an explosion occurred."

"Train is an iconoclast. He is, I fear, a cloner." Mugant paused, eyes fierce. "He believes in the inevitable progress of nuclear transfer cloning. He worships it! He is obsessed with fused cells research, and there are some who say that we are at the days from which the first actual cloning of a human cell will occur."

Mugant rose from his chair. "It must not happen!" Slamming his clenched fist on the heavy walnut table, Mugant glared at the members of his Fifth Crusade. "Never, in the name of God!" he yelled.

"We have heard rumors of this, these human cloning break-throughs Your Eminence. This is why we attempted to acquire Polyclinique," began Rupert Hawkins. "It is fortuitous that there was an accident—"

"—That was no accident!" *Why do I have to do everything myself even here? I am surrounded by children.*

"I am going to end this. There are 14 genetic labs in the world working to be the first to bring forth the horror of the ages a human clone. If human creation occurs, it will be the work of Satan. This world will think it does not need our Holy Father, for *man* may think he is God himself. And as you know that is the work of Satan. We can either liquidate those diseased vessels of filth, as happened in Paris, or buy them out—shelving their technology forever from the world so that it could never be used. If we liquidate them, it cannot be done as was done at Polyclinique Normale. It has to be neat, not sloppy. The press is becoming more interested in these heathens and their deaths. Time is passing and we must act soon. Funds abound for buying these labs out—Como Ventures can force it." Mugant looked at Rupert Hawkins. "I'll accept nothing less, and you know that I can bring heavy pressure to bear against anyone—including those here—who dawdle. I will ruin anyone who does not comply.

"And this scientist Train has to go. This is where Previn comes in." Mugant, beginning to sweat, wiped his forehead. "Even as we meet, he is hunted. But he, like the devil, is a snake."

Each industrialist looked attentively at Cardinal Mugant. To themselves each wondered what His Eminence meant by *True Cross of Christ*.

"Previn, you can use your powerful office in the United States government to pull this murderer in. First, McGeorge, you can run a story through the US wires that Train is wanted for questioning in the case of the young woman whose body was found in Lake Geneva, New York recently. Of course, you're going to have to actually get the arrest warrant issued out for him, but that should-n't be a big deal since your office can fabricate that. Use your reach, good man. Local police can be easily manipulated—especially by your office. Be smart and fastidious. No mistakes. I am sure none of you are aware that Train was arrested, but eventually cleared, for the murder of his young wife and handicapped, autistic daughter over a decade ago. What we have here is a criminal who has never repented, but who has reached for the hand extended to him from Hell. For God's sake, he killed his own wife and handi-capped daughter. And this I know firsthand because I followed his trial extensively during my time in Toronto. We can now go after him with this new trumpeted murder charge. Previn you can also have some rape allegations thrown in... show that this bastard is a sexual predator as well. That should excite the newspapers. Perhaps your office can issue out a modest bounty. The Lord knows how excitable American prosecutor offices are. Sometimes I wonder if the whole American economy is based upon jailing its citizens. What's the percentage of American adults being held right now? It's close to 3%. One more arrest should go unnoticed. Get the US police on the lookout for him, and broadcast stories on the case, even if not true, on Train as a deviant."

McGeorge Previn looked tentatively at Cardinal Mugant. Previn's tentacles in America's international and homeland security intelligence ran deeper than any living American citizens.

His family's bloodline coursed deep through an assortment of American law enforcement agencies. He now ran a secretive intelligence organization created by the sitting President of the United States of America that charged Previn with overseeing all agencies protecting American interests.

"That could be difficult."

"Don't dare give me that," hardened Mugant. "This you'll do. Do I make myself clear?"

The American nodded, not willing to take that fight. It would be done.

"Schemmizzi, do you know what has happened right here in your own broadcasting area, Italy? Of course not. I can't believe you. Here you are with ten satellites orbiting this earth, Internet infrastructure backbone built throughout all of Europe— including two major Internet provider services, twenty-one newspapers worldwide, and I don't know how many television or radio stations. Let me tell you. This Train killed a woman on the Ponte Cavour, after fleeing da Vinci airport, where he killed a handful of other Italian citizens. And what is reported of these murders? I have seen nothing. You'll put out a sensationalized report, Guillermo that Max Train killed two, three—don't be precise just yet—at da Vinci and is now on the run. You can contact our man Allesandro Galina, *Commandante in Capo* of the Roman *carabiniere*. He will give you the names of the people that died at the airport whom Train murdered. Of course, I'll let our Allesandro know that Train is the murderer. Sensationalize him the same way I suggested to McGeorge. He rapes women and then kills them. I want you to run Train's picture on Italian TV, float the story out to CNN, and have SES Astra beam it on their BBC channel. You're on their Board. The Italian press will pick it up, and we will have a man who wishes he had never been born. Job's life will look like a day in Paradise compared to the hell in store for Max Train. He will never clone the body of Christ."

Each man seated at the rectangular walnut table felt in his own way a sudden chill run through his body. For the first time they actually understood Mugant's fears. A man, a sinner with no morals, and obviously no convictions was possibly in possession of the True Cross of Jesus of Nazareth. A man with knowledge and associates in the field of genetics. A man who had already played God by taking the life of his wife and daughter. A man who no doubt could attempt to play God again, but this time a man who had gone too far. For everything that they believed in the one denominator that tied each of these men together was their devout commitment to prevent cloning of all sorts.

Adrianna Corvoso de Sa adjusted a gold bracelet her deceased father had given her some thirty years earlier, and which she always wore on her right wrist. "This man Train," she began. "You're sure he would clone remains of Christ's body if they were left behind on His Cross? And you really think he's in possession of our Redeemer's Cross?"

"As sure as I am of the Word of the Lord."

"We were taught Christ's Body ascended," she said, reaching for another cigarette.

"Christ did ascend. But Train's a scientist... and a Lucifer. He can invent things. And as you know, our Church has become weakened by those not strong or able enough to carry the Lord's work. We have had many scandals to deal with—and to my dismay I have had to use some of the monies you have all assembled to silence troublemakers and opportunists. But nothing can do more damage to our establishment if Train begins building credible myths—scientific lies. We must use every resource to stop him."

"What do the police do when they find him?" Schemmizzi asked Mugant.

"Make sure he can never utter another recognizable word. But more importantly you're to bring me the cross. Remember, this is about reclaiming the cross. Train can never live to tell his story. *Capisce*?

"*Si*," they answered at once.

"The Pope will be in America next week, the first country he visits on his much publicized tour of North America. He is to be in America one week. He has a formal address scheduled for his delivery at the United Nations. He will not be firm with them, I fear. In precisely twenty-four hours we will assemble again, in the *camera di Giada* at Como, to further plan and review the mission to which we are all committed. There are not many remaining who see the gravity of the monstrosity before us. Making man in his own image, that is what cloning is. It will not go forward."

***

"I have tried reaching you for the last hour."

"I was meeting with someone close. Something strange is going on, but it was not made clear."

The wise friend and sponsor of many Eastern European

refugees stretched his neck backwards, eyes looking at the spinning ceiling fan. "I am left with concern."

"And the one you seek, what of his whereabouts?"

"He is traveling to Milan, and he is definitely frightened. You're to get there immediately."

"Where is he going?"

"I'm not sure, but he will arrive sometime tonight."

"A hotel?"

"Not that I know of. He probably doesn't trust anything now."

"Then how do I find him?"

"He will find us. Stay in the city center. Be accessible."

"I understand."

***

The police who first entered the ramshackled hotel could not comprehend the blood bath in front of their eyes. Amongst the butchered were four adult males, three women and a child. An infant boy cried hysterically in a small cradle grasping at a teddy bear, his frenzied outburst for his mother enough to crush their hearts. Of the dead, the four men, two children, and the child had been shot in the head. A knife in the heart had ended the other woman's life.

The eight souls were, at the time, the only individuals at the small hotel. Only the husband and wife, along with their two children, one dead and one crying aloud, were not employees of the inn.

The dead staff members were unable to answer the questions of a stranger who had entered the hotel, though the police were not aware of this. Nor were they aware this stranger sought a package he was there to claim.

The *carabiniere* knew the reasons behind the brutal events which unfolded at the Albergo Acconciamessa more than likely would be lost forever unless a witness appeared from the heavens, which, in all likelihood would not happen. After all, this was Bologna.

"I'll have another glass of wine my beltline," ordered a handsome man whose azure eyes sparkled reflectively against the

143

flashing red, blue, and white lights passing him by as he sat on the wind swept patio of a local outdoor cafe in Bologna. He lifted the deep Chianti wine filled glass to the sky. *"Scusa bellalina, grappa,"* he said, changing his drink.

The waitress smiled and nodded before returning inside.

Slightly turning in his seat, he looked down at the liquid remains in his wine glass, spun it in his hand, then focused on the scene unfolding down the street from where he sat. Wine was always soothing to him, and his past escapade thirty minutes ago was too close for his own comfort. Still, he needed to watch the story he created unfold, one he knew would make the local newspapers tomorrow, whose clippings would be in his treasured portfolio.

Moments later, the ordinary looking brunette waitress came back to his table with the *grappa*. He nodded, but did not say anything, as his thoughts were elsewhere.

Lifting the *grappa*, he sniffed it, and then swallowed. The pleasing fiery sensation of the alcohol burning down his throat was only surpassed by the memories of the adrenaline roaring through him as he squeezed the trigger of his gun earlier. The peaceful cloud of the blazing drink settling his uneasy mind was similar to the nirvana he felt moments ago when flowing hot blood caused by his steel bullets exploded into unexpected innocence. To him, this was salvation.

The open rage he had felt was rare, even for him. Initially, he had no intent to kill the way he did, but someone had gotten in the way of his plans. *Train, I know you're out there somewhere, and now, as opposed to before, it is now about you and me — and that bastard in Rome, who I'll have a very enjoyable talk with soon enough. You think you can outsmart me? Are you kidding? Not even He can do that! But you, Max Train, you have what I want! You hold the key for great riches, but more than that, you hold the key to life itself, the key to the kingdom — and I'll take it from you.*

When I devour you Train, and I will, my eyes will turn to Rome. I'll conquer the empire that sits quietly like the grazing lamb; a charade that has fooled many but not me! I know the truth! There in Rome I'll take the throne of the entire Kingdom, even as those who parade in white or red continue to pose as they do. For if what you have is true - - and Mugant is not foolish — just a fool, then the Church will come to me. And I like those who masquerade there, are familiar with the lies. They'll beg me for my blessing! They'll pay tribute and homage to me! They'll accept who sits on the throne of this earthly Kingdom!

The world will be mine — and no price they offer will be enough. For they do not know who sleeps amongst them. Nor do they know the secrets of the world leaders the way I do. And Mugant, he thinks he is my master! The fool!

Let the fool think I am his puppet. Let him think I am from Hell! But I will take the throne of the Kingdom!

"*Bellalina, grappa,*" he said, lifting his empty glass, his empty eyes catching her innocent gaze. "*Grappa.*"

Chapter X

"On the contrary, Cardinal Furth, you will vote with my group. The Pontiff needs to see that there is not agreement with his way."

"I will disgrace neither the college of Belvedere, nor Louvain, Cardinal Mugant. Do you actually think anyone wants the Church to say it understands the emotions and views of those who bombed the Polyclinique Company? That's what you're asking me to support. There is not a prelate alive who would possibly allow such a view to come from Rome, or anywhere."

Mugant's face twitched, as an iron silence suddenly deadened the walkway towards the statue of Saint Peter, where the two were on an early morning walk in the Giardini Vaticani. The lush green verdure, carefully bricked pathway, and soft green well-tended bushes all added to the beauty of the violets and tulips encircling the memorial to the Church's first Pope. The soft-spoken Cardinal Furth, consecrated Cardinal priest only one year earlier, had been in silent thought in the Giardini till Mugant had approached him. He was now domiciled in Rome in appreciation for his service as Secretary in the 15th World Synod of Bishops. It was rewarded by the Curial post he now occupied, *Prefect for Pastoral Administration.*

"You have not been here long Furth," Mugant replied, rubbing his freshly shaven face. His left hand tightened its grip on the brass tip of the hand carved Birchwood cane he sometimes used when walking.

"Length of time has nothing to do with correctness of vision, Mugant. Surely you cannot believe what you have said to me reflects views of the Church. Your approach is so divisive, so contrary to all that we have been trying to accomplish. I was unaware how hard your outlook is. In that respect I have not been here long, you're right."

Mugant looked up to the sun, and squinted under its bright light. "Don't be a fool, Furth. You'll vote with my group because of what is not in the files at Holy Cross in Dublin."

A blank stare came across the Irishman's face.

"You never informed the diocesan tribunal that approved your entrance to the seminary that you had been married," Mugant went on, stooping to pick up a dandelion that had not yet cast off the morning's dew. "In fact, Lord Cardinal, you have never allowed this to be known. You married a young Irish colleen," Mugant continued smugly, "who died two months after your civil ceremony. That is how you were able to conceal it from the Church, since there was no sacramental wedding. Only a civil ceremony in Phibsboro."

A knot twisted in Cardinal Furth's stomach.

"Horror of horrors, shortly after that, you seem to have had a 'road to Damascus conversion', just like the Apostle Paul did, and felt, you say, what we call 'a calling'."

"You need not go on, Cardinal Mugant."

"Oh, but let me. I want to see if I have the record straight. After you decided you were being 'called' to Orders, you applied for admittance to the Seminary. Notice, I said, 'you decided you were being called'." Mugant laughed with a sound that mimicked a hiss. "Conflicted about the death of your bride, you never revealed your nights in bed with her. And it worked out well, since you could not have risen to your Cardinalate today, Furth, had you been married once. For what Committee in the Vatican, what nuncio in Dublin would recommend anyone who had at one time been married to this high appointment, "the red hat?"

Furth, a moderate within the Church, knew Mugant cornered him. A married man was still unable to wear the holy white collar regardless of how good that man was—a very real issue that was part of today's Achilles heel in the Church; diversity based upon a single male having "a calling" had limits, and in many ways created diverse problems.

"I have it all correct, don't I Cardinal Furth? There are more details, but we can stop here, no?"

There was no answer.

"Silence is consent, my Lord Cardinal. I expect your full support. For some reason, you're a favorite of our Holy Father. Push him in the direction that the tradition demands. Leave it to me, a canon lawyer, to find that little discrepancy in your record, eh Furth?"

Suddenly turning around in the direction opposite to the stunned Irish prelate, Mugant's face sported a broad sneer as his eyes squinted at the dome of St. Peter's.

***

"Cardinal Jayant, see how lovely the view of the Piazza from this height is, and the cupola design by della Porta shows so much of faith and belief in our Church's holy mysteries."

"The view from this roof level is clearly elegant. And such a bright day, Cardinal Mugant. I have never been up to this level before." Looking at the cross on the Dome of Saint Peter's, the Indian Cardinal's wide face beamed. "I must thank you for such an opportunity to see the Basilica this way. The Vatican Gardens below, and look, those are the Apennines. And the Albanian Hills. Fortunately, Anselm, we did not have to climb 537 steps to reach here. Once that would have been the only way to come here.

"So what are your thoughts on this meeting that has been called this morning by the Pope? I saw you speaking with Furth, and then suddenly turn in my direction."

"An urgent matter has arisen. I want you to hear me." Mugant stared without emotion at Jayant.

"You mentioned, and are right, the Pope has called a meeting—a mid-afternoon meeting today of all Curial department heads. In Ligouri Hall. Obviously, given it is on such short notice, the meeting is important. The Curial office of Human Life, which I head, is especially pivotal in this meeting, since the subject is the destruction of genetics labs around the world, including the most recent disaster in Paris."

Bells announcing the eighth hour of the day could be heard. "I know of the incident."

"You know some of it, Cardinal Jayant." The Indian looked at Mugant, taken aback by the abruptness of his response.

Mugant continued, eyes fixed hard on Jayant. "You represent the country that has the fastest growing population in the world, India. Anything you say at this meeting the Pope will carefully hear."

"India, a lab bombing, the connection?"

"Exactly what I said. You know only part of it," Mugant answered, annoyed at the puzzled expression Jayant gave him.

"Only the night before this bombing the Pope held a meeting called by his State Secretary at the Pontiff's instructions, which I attended. Some had thought a major announcement about the Church's stand on "the new science" was forthcoming, perhaps a statement with the tone of dogma. Instead, he told those there that we must move to a higher plain, as he calls it, of reconciliation with the creators of life."

"'Creators of life'? That phrase is not in the transcript of the meeting we were given. His Holiness would not use such inflammatory language. What troubles you, Anselm?"

Mugant stiffened at the challenge from the former Cardinal Archbishop of Mumbai.

"You're going to tell the Pope at this upcoming meeting this morning that reconciliation with the scientists of the brave new world will bring laughter from them, and scorn and derision towards the Church. You must tell the Holy Father the Church must oppose them all. Holy Mother has a solemn obligation to prevent any tampering with God's master plan. The Church must be ever vigilant and use whatever means to insure God's will in all of creation."

"'Whatever means'?" Jayant folded his hands. "I'm what? I am to challenge his Holiness? It's so bellicose. I cannot challenge Peter."

"The only reason I am speaking to you Jayant is because though you're now here in charge of the Office of the Evangelization of Peoples, you're intimate and influential in the question of human population trends. Your doctorate in sociology from Oxford brings you far beyond the days of your study at the Pontifical Seminary of Kandy in Sri Lanka."

"I serve the Holy Father."

"Jayant, you're a Salesian. Like so many from your area of the world, marriage records at times were not rigorously documented or controlled."

Gabriel Jayant suddenly froze.

"You were born out of wedlock, Monsignor Jayant."

Gabriel Jayant knew that in the Church of Rome a man could not obtain the title of Cardinal if he were born out of wedlock. "Cardinal Mugant—"

"— I know the records that the Salesians do not have. And at the time of your entrance into the order illegitimacy was a canonical impediment to the Salesian Priesthood. Your relatives hid the indiscretion well, Gabriel. But not so well. You're not a licit Salesian, nor licit Priest—no canonical approval—much less a Cardinal."

Mugant's hand went to the pectoral cross hanging from the

gold chain around his neck.

"Your baptismal records are safe with me, Lord Cardinal, of course. Unless we cannot come to an accord on—"

"—It was decades ago. The impediment no longer exists. The Church has changed."

"Ah, but you need a special dispensation from the Holy Father to remain a Cardinal now. And I am sure you enjoy the privilege of your office. Of course, if you're not satisfied you can always descend to the life of an everyday Priest. And what will His Holiness think of your work if he sees that this fact about you, which you knew, was hidden Lo these many years of service to Holy Mother?" Mugant shifted his weight off his walking stick, standing perfectly erect.

"Do you understand Gabriel?"

"What am I to do?"

"Just follow my lead at this meeting today. Affirm my statements in front of His Holiness in your own personal way." The look of satisfaction on Mugant's face could hardly be concealed. "You have influence with many of the Cardinals from the Third World, and the Pope will realize a bloc of sentiment may be opposed to him if you call for condemnation and correction of the abuses of the scientists of 'iniquity'."

The dark skinned Cardinal felt the gold chain around his neck being tugged by Mugant.

"You do realize, Gabriel, how fast we have moved to this day of Armageddon. A decade ago no one would have thought possible that a human could be cloned. An outright defiance of the God of all creation is about to come upon the world if this happens. It is not an issue that can be treated with the unction of reconciliation and understanding. The Church must finally stand *for* something, not *with* something."

"What you're asking of me is to protect 'God's intent of creation'. I am an opponent of this genetic science, and so is our Holy Father. For this matter, I believe all who don our red hat are strongly opposed to all genetic creation, stem cell, and cloning. Perhaps it is time the world hears out strong voices of dissent."

"It is what our Father wants, Gabriel."

Gabriel Jayant looked into the distance, away from Mugant.

"Your secret is unknown to any save me, Cardinal Jayant. This plague against God is to end."

Mugant prepared to leave. "At the meeting, your manner

will be unbending. The bombing of the Polyclinique is not the Church's concern. You're to re-affirm that when I say it to the Pope in this meeting. Others will hear you. The prevention of sacrilege to the laws of creation is what we have been called to, not to commenting on some act of terrorism. There must be no compromise with the world. That is how we serve the Holy Father, Lord Cardinal."

The bells of the basilica tolled once again, reminding Mugant that he had not heard from his penitent in too long a while. More than a day had passed. *Where is that cross? Where is Train?*

***

The alarm clock in his modern Milanese hotel room overlooking the Arco della Pace and the famed luscious greens of Parco Sempione had been going off for twenty minutes before Max, exhausted from the drive from Bologna the previous night turned to his side and shut it off. The time read 8:50 a.m. The extra twenty minutes sleep he received did very little to restore his aching body.

After checking on his leg and shoulder wounds, which were miraculously healing well despite his body's fatigue, he showered and changed into the same clothes he was wearing last night.

Opening the box he placed on the bed, he carefully unwrapped the *titulus*. "Good morning," he said aloud, as he looked solemnly at Jesus' condemnation plate. "Let's hope today is a better day," he said with a tone of optimism, the sun outside lighting the room.

Walking over to an espresso machine located on the vanity near the bathroom, he prepared himself coffee, hoping the caffeine would help him wake up.

Settling on a burgundy cloth desk chair next to the bed, Max carefully picked up the *titulus* by its edges and looked at the inscription before gently placing it back down. "No one should ever have been brutalized the way you were. Life is not supposed to be about violence, but it appears my life is shadowed by it. I know you've had your share of it, too. It's awful to have someone condemn you, isn't it?"

Max didn't expect an answer.

"I just want to go home. Funny, I never thought I would

ever have a strong desire to go back there the way I now do. The best times of my life were spent there with my family. Hopefully I'll be on a plane going back into New York later today," he said as he began to wrap the small tablet back in the box. "I just want all of this to end."

Completing his task, he stretched his weary limbs, and walked over to the phone that was placed on the desk. He looked outside the window and directly at The Arch of Peace, which welcomed all to the gardens of *Sempione. I have a good feeling about today. All I have to do is get to the Consulate, drop off these artifacts . . . I hope they're handled correctly . . . and get on a plane. I'm sure that the American government will make some type of formal announcement that they're now in possession of these items — and then hopefully whoever is trying to kill me will focus their attentions somewhere else.*

Looking out the window, Max suddenly noticed the gothic spires of the Duomo. *I wonder if it really is safe to go back to my home just yet. Well, there's no time like the present. I better get going, the Consulate opens at 10:00 a.m., and I need to call Marty.*

He looked over at the boxed artifacts. "I hope I have not failed you, but I think this is best."

The Rabbi was surprisingly alert, considering it was only after three in the morning back in New York when he picked up the phone. "Max, where are you?" the Brooklynite quickly asked.

"In a hotel in Milan."

"Hmm. Okay."

Max sensed the immediate tension in his friend's voice. "What's the matter?"

Marty stood up from behind his desk and started to pace in his expansive library filled with thousands of books on every conceivable subject. "Max, there's a problem," he stoically whispered, "here, in the States."

Max felt as if his insides fell out, as his heart jumped. "What? What problems?"

"I don't understand this, but you're wanted for the murder of a Cindy Vale in Upstate New York. It was put out on the wires around midnight tonight. We caught it on Interpol a little while ago."

"What! Who?" *What the hell is this!*

"Stay calm, Max. You're wanted for a murder. I —"

"— what the hell is going on?" he demanded.

"I don't know, but it is obvious that the monster that seeks you has malignant tentacles. It's too ironic, considering the ordeal you've been going through."

"When did this happen?"

"Supposedly, two months ago. You know Lake Geneva?"

"Yes," he slowly replied, now remembering the news story about the unsolved murder of a woman near his hometown of Syracuse. "I recall the new story."

"Someone is trying to pin it on you."

"This is just great," Max said as he sat in the chair, his eyes focused on the "package". "Just great."

"You need to stay calm —"

"— I didn't do it, Marty."

"I know."

"What the hell should I do?"

"The first thing you shouldn't do is go to the US Consulate. They'll arrest you once you tell them who you are. They'll have to run your name through The Department of Justice. Red flags will go up."

Any optimism Max had earlier this morning completely disappeared. "What do I do?"

"We have to get you out of Italy, that's for sure," said Max's protective friend. He still carried with him gratitude towards the fugitive who many years ago identified a gene strand that eventually led to the proper diagnosis of a rare, deadly disease of his only grandson, who was now living a normal life.

"Somehow I'm a fugitive. What's next?"

"We need to find out who's behind this. Once we do, perhaps we can clear your name."

"Right, if I'm alive."

"Think positive. Help is on the way," Marty said, as he sat behind his desk. "Sara should be arriving in Milan within the hour."

Marty's comment upset Max. "No, Marty. Everyone I come close to dies."

"Max, Sara can help you."

"What if these bastards are trying to find me? They'll get her too."

"Do you think you were followed?"

"No, but I've thought that before."

"I know for safety reasons you should meet in a public

place."

"Then what?"

"Out through Switzerland."

Getting out of Italy was most appealing. "How?"

"We have friends there. The Swiss want to make nice with Israel. Those bank accounts of theirs still have a great deal of illegally obtained moneys from the war."

Max thought about it for a moment. "Okay, but I have one thing I want to investigate before we leave. It is on the way to the border."

Max discussed his idea with Rabbi Kohn.

"That sounds like a decent idea, but you must be careful, and listen to what Sara has to say. She's one of the best," he said, making note to secure certain assets near the Swiss-Italian border.

"I realize that. What do you think of the Duomo?"

"In an hour, towards the front," Marty replied.

"Okay. In an hour."

Fifty minutes later, Max exited a taxi traveling down the heavily used Via Dante that left him in front of Italy's largest and most intricate example of Gothic architecture, the renowned Duomo. As his eyes ascended to the twisted spires, he noticed Perego's famous Madonnina standing atop the highest spire, and overlooking all of Milan. The statue of Mary was one of over 3,000 statues placed in the environs of the Duomo.

Waves of apprehension covered him as he looked at the cathedral, his right hand holding the wrapped "package". He was a wanted man, and each day, filled with terrible surprises, had taken a deep toll on him. Eyes darting nervously for the face of the killer and Sara, Max quickly entered the Cathedral.

The Church was magnificent. Statues and rare stain glass windows abounded the five naves, each chamber separated by colossal pillars. For all of its magnificence, Max hardly felt the awe of its inspiring architecture. The alluring grandeur of the Duomo brought one's faith to aspire towards God. The despair of a man usually brought man back to his faith, but in Max's case, faith was becoming a very distant memory.

Walking down the long marble aisle, his steps echoing against the walls of the hallowed church, he took a seat in the fifth pew in front of the gilded altar aglitter with candlelight. His eyes stared at a large gold cross.

Funny, but that's not what it looks like.

As he replayed the events that occurred this past week in his head, he noticed an elderly couple take a seat fifteen feet away from him in the same pew. He turned around in search of Sara. He didn't see her.

His eyes focused on the glorified cross.

"Keep looking straight ahead," said a woman's voice minutes later. It was Sara.

Max nodded. "I'm glad to hear your voice."

"I'm glad to see you, but Italy is not safe for you."

"Is any place safe?"

"I hope so."

"What do we do next?"

"I have a taxi waiting outside. We leave here, together. Okay?"

"Yes."

"Good, lets go," she firmly said.

Little was said while they sat in a taxi heading towards the neoclassic designed Teatro alla Scala. Telling the cab driver to pull over near the front of the world famous opera house built more than two hundred years ago over the ruins of the old church Santa Maria della Scala, the two soon entered a black Audi parked on the city street.

With Sara driving, they drove north towards the Alps, discussing the past days since they left one another in Tel Aviv and Max's plan.

For a man in great despair Max felt an odd sense of comfort in the presence of Sara. Driving north towards Italy's illustrious Lake Region, he periodically gazed at her long black silk hair and tried to understand how a woman so beautiful had become his protector. Underneath her stylish black suit coat Max noticed the bulge of her firearm.

Continuing their drive towards Lake Como, information was shared and scenarios were played out in an attempt to discover who was trying to kill Max. Sara, already informed by Rabbi Kohn, was well aware of what Max possessed in the box. Neither John Muir nor Luke Gartner's body had been found as of yet, the excavation of the cave moving slower than expected. The bodies of the two Mossad agents at ben Gurion were poisoned, as too were all who died at da Vinci except for those who were gunned down. Max also told Sara of the Polyclinique Lab bombing in Paris. She was familiar with the tragedy: seven months ago three genetic scientists in Tel Aviv were murdered, their facilities destroyed by a fire.

On the car's console was a sheet of paper containing the address of Como Ventures.

The car made its winding way around the southern part of the expansive lake, bordered by grand history-tested villas built centuries ago housing many of Europe's financially elite families. Passing Villa d'Este, the noble hotel that once was the summer estate of Queen Anne of England and now was one of the world's elite romantic hotels, Max's body tensed.

Gazing at the basin beneath the Grigna Mountain, Max's eyes stretched across the eastern side of the Y-shaped lake, and noticed the breathtaking poetic peninsula of Bellagio, the town where Franz Liszt, composed his homage to Dante. He remembered the legend that the people of Bellagio, protected from a deadly plague that ravaged Europe in 1630 A.D., avoided being infected due to the geographic conformation of the peninsula. There they grew corn, which they used to make bread for neighboring citizens of Varenna. The bread, once baked, would be left on a large boulder on the shores of the lake. The Varenna buyers, desperate for food, would place money in a jar filled with vinegar so as to decontaminate the currency. Over the years many boating accidents occurred due to that boulder, and it was eventually dynamited.

Max also knew Como was the place where Mussolini was killed by the partisans in 1946 A.D. for inhumane war crimes against all peoples.

"What's wrong?" asked Sara, seeing Max begin to fidget in his seat.

"My wife and I honeymooned there," he wistfully replied as he took note of the small octagon sided chapel overlooking the sailboat dotted lake that was at the foot of the snow-capped mountains on the hotel's grounds of Villa d'Este.

Sara slightly slowed the car around a twisting curve. "I'm sorry Max. I know this is hard for you."

"Yeah."

Sara said nothing back.

"Como Ventures, it's odd they're here on the lake in Cernobbio," Max offered, pointing out that the handsome structures were superbly kept estates guarded for privacy.

"Nothing should surprise you anymore."

"You're right."

"Are you sure you want to do this?"

"Something tells me it's a mistake not to."

Moments later they pulled up to a sprawling three-story neoclassical stone manor home imposingly standing on the peaceful banks of the fabled lake. A well-manicured garden overflowing with hundreds of colorful rose bushes, oleanders, hydrangeas and cypress trees coupled with several marble Roman statues of antiquity offered the eye a majestic sight. On the sunbathed steep slopes across from the villa were large chestnut trees, beeches, walnuts, and confers. Oddly, there were no cars parked in the lengthy driveway.

"Could this be a mailing address of sorts?" Sara asked directing the car into the black-tarred circular driveway.

"I have no idea."

The intense fragrance from the sea of roses filled each of their nostrils as they exited the car.

They walked up to the large walnut door and noticed it slightly ajar.

Sara looked around, before ringing the bell.

"Will this Doctor remember you?"

"I'm not sure. It was a long time ago, but he may."

Sara rang the bell again.

There was no answer.

"I suppose you might want to take a look around," she said, her delicate looking right hand unbuttoning her suit coat as she eased the door open.

"I think the door being left open is an invitation to come in, don't you?"

Sara looked blankly at Max. "Be careful," she said as she reached for her semiautomatic.

Entering the foyer to the manor home, large tapestries centuries old were depicting various historical events of the Church ornamented sixteen-foot high terra-cotta walls. Several paintings from the *Masters* were carefully placed, providing a sense of old-world wealth their eyes had not seen. Hanging from the center of the ceiling an enormous crystal chandelier sparkled, indicating the manor was meticulously kept. Polished black onyx floors confirmed this.

"Odd," Sara whispered.

"For a biotechnology firm, I'd say so."

Carefully, they entered into a large formal living area, complete with a mahogany grand piano and plush furniture. Several paintings hung on the walls. Interestingly, there were five armored suites standing underneath a tapestry of Godfrey of Bullion, the Crusader, seated on a white stallion.

"I wonder if anyone is here," Max said.

"It doesn't appear so, unless whoever lives here is either upstairs or outside."

They walked under a large archway that led into a spacious dining room. A redwood table preset for twelve would have pleased any diner. Standing there, they looked out onto the lake from a large bay window. A small Riva was docked on the lake, whose depth reached 410 meters in certain areas.

"Do you get the feeling something's not right?" Max asked.

"Absolutely."

"There must be a room where records are kept."

"Let's find it and get out of here. But I'll lead," said Sara, her gun ready.

Inspecting the entire first floor for what would appear to be an office, the only thing found were formal entertaining rooms, decorated in the most expensive and rich style the eye could fathom. To themselves, each wondered how little known Como Ventures could obtain the wealth evident by their opulent surroundings.

Sara made her way to a wide marble staircase. "Stay behind me."

"You've got the gun."

"Anything happens, get to the floor, okay?" she said looking up the menacing flight. "I don't like this."

"We could leave."

"We've come this far."

Step by careful step the two ascended to the second floor. Six closed doors lined the dim hallway.

"Max, you need to stay behind me, remember."

"I know, but be careful," Max replied, knowing Sara was trained for such ordeals.

Her heart beating fast, she opened the first door on her left. It was an empty library that appeared to be filled with bibles.

Sara looked at the door opposite where she and Max stood. "That's next."

Max reached for her shoulder. "Be careful."

"I am," she replied as she entered the hallway, Max right

behind her, both listening for any sudden movements.

Opening the door, a series of computer terminals were stacked on two credenzas, the desk in the room filled with unorganized, shuffled papers.

"I think we found the electronic brain," Max said.

"Do you know what you're looking for?"

"Yes," he said moving aside from her. "Purchases."

She understood.

With lightning speed Max rushed behind the computer terminal and began to navigate his way in search of Como Ventures' banking records. With each passing stroke on the keyboard, he was met with a firewall, effectively stonewalling him from entering the company's data systems.

As Max diligently continued trying to hack the information system, Sara scoured the desk. Seeing a gold-foil letterhead from Zurich Investment Services Group, she noticed the name Alpha Acquisitions LLC written boldly in red ink. In addition down at the bottom of the paper scribbled in black was the notation. "225 B". She placed the paper in her pocket.

"I can't seem to break their code," Max anxiously said. "Whoever built this system knew what—"

"—Max" Sara suddenly stopped, hearing a light whimper coming from a closet in the room.

Max raced to the closet door.

"No!" exclaimed Sara, pointing the gun towards the closet as Max opened the door.

To his shock, lying in a puddle of blood on the floor, his face badly bruised, and clothes red-soaked was a terrified Doctor Seto, shaking his head frantically.

Sara immediately turned towards the hallway door. Nothing.

As Max reached over to help his beaten colleague, Sara turned to Max. "Get him out of here, back to the car. You have your lead, I think."

Sara entered the hallway as Max helped the bound man up to his feet.

"He's here," whimpered Seto, gasping hysterically.

"Who's here?"

"He… he…he…"

"Who?"

"I…I…"

"Who's here?"

"The... d... the devil...he's—"

Max's eyes bulged. He knew who Seto spoke of. "Where is he?"

"The devil . . . he's in this house. Oh, God - my hands!" Dr. Seto wailed in absolute pain.

"Where is he?" Max said.

"My hands!" Seto cried.

Max instinctively looked at the man's hands. Only his thumbs and pinkies remained. *Good God! Sara!*

Leaving the brutalized man, Max rushed out into the hallway. He noticed Sara standing in the doorway of the middle door on the left side of the hall. "Sara," he muttered, when suddenly he saw from the corner of his eye the door opposite her move a fraction of an inch.

Using every ounce of energy in him, Max rushed the door, slamming it with his full force.

A loud thud on the other side indicated there was someone else there.

"Let's get the hell out of here!" Max roared, not knowing his unexpected charge knocked the person concealed behind the door to the floor.

That bastard is going to die the most brutal death man has ever known. Peter's death was nothing! The key bearer is here — and he's mine! No one ever gets away. Staggering to his feet, the fallen assassin covered his now bleeding nose. Rage and loathing filled him. "Mine shall not be the last blood to fall Max Train!" he screamed, as he swung the door open, pulling out his gun.

Rushing down the stairway, Sara and Max having grabbed the inconceivably brutalized Seto, heard the howl of the killer as he rushed to the second floor landing.

Max froze in his tracks.

"Train, you're dead!" screamed the outraged voice defiantly.

Sara, spinning on the staircase, let off a round of gunfire towards the lunatic.

As bullets hurtled towards him, the searcher of the key let out his own round of bullets.

One found Dr. Seto's skull, the steel exploding the back of his head, its warm, bloody remnants instantly covering Max, Sara, and the entire staircase.

"Aargh!" screamed Max as parts of Seto's brain went into his eye.

"Keep moving!" Sara yelled as she let off another round of bullets, her feet, along with Max's now, on the first floor marble landing. "Get to the car!" she ordered, dropping the dead man's body to the floor. "Go!"

Max followed her instructions.

Bullets were exchanged with no abatement, as both focused shooters relied on unspoken skills, when suddenly the bullets descending from above stopped.

Sara paused for a moment, listening attentively as she wiped the wet human tissue covering her face.

She heard the sound of the Audi's ignition. *Damn!*

Sara darted outside, her gun raised to the windows above.

As she did, Sergio, *The Scorpion*, hesitatingly descended the flight of stairs, his wounded calf now an obstacle. *You bitch; you shall know the endless fires of Hell!*

Seeing Sara, Max reversed the car towards the front door, his arm opening the passenger side. "Hurry!" he screamed as Sara raced towards him.

A bullet missed Sara's head by inches, as she turned back towards the foyer of the estate. She glanced at the car, and then let out a violent round of bullets towards the large door before, darting towards the awaiting vehicle.

Lethal bullets erupted passed her, mocking the tranquility of the sleepless lake. She continued firing her weapon as she dove into the car, already moving towards the grounds' exit.

Placing his hand on his throbbing calf muscle, the killer looked at the blood now on his trigger finger. *This ain't done, bitch.*

Inserting a new clip into his Beretta 9mm, *The Scorpion* stood defiantly outside the sprawling garden and unleashed a hailstorm of bullets.

Cold steel fell on the Audi, piercing the car's metal and shattering its glass tail light and windows until it reached the narrow winding road along the lake shore, and headed north—towards the Swiss border.

Chapter XI

"Do you have what I asked for, Cavaldi?"

Mugant's Franciscan aide removed a suede binder from the briefcase he had carried to his superior's Curial office. "Here they are *Eminenza*. You do know the arrest warrants here and in the United States have been sworn out for the American?"

"Who do you think ordered them? Of course I do. Now let's see what we have here, Cavaldi. Nine, ten—yes, thirteen genetics labs now. Fine," the Canadian said, rubbing the paper with his thumb and index finger for the feel of its cotton texture.

"Let me have the other folder," Mugant brusquely ordered the Franciscan.

Mugant sorted through a number of pages. "Finances are strong. Nine different currencies, eleven different locations, three countries. Yes. This is correct. Good."

Mugant looked at the Franciscan. "It is the desire for money, not money itself, Father Cavaldi, that is evil. And we have money." Then looking out his office window at the pebbled pavement below he said, "You can leave the papers here as you exit."

As his office door was closed, suddenly a phone light flickered. Mugant picked up the receiver, waiting to hear the voice on the other side. "Had a problem, Your Eminence. I followed your man to Como this morning. He went to a villa I think you're familiar with. There are several dead bodies still there, but his isn't one of them."

The sound of Mugant wetting his lips could be heard by the speaker on the other end. "More bad stuff, Eminence. He had a female with him. The place was a mess— papers everywhere. I think they may have tried to break into your computer system. I got there just in time. I followed them for a while but a damn truck broke down in a tunnel underpass while I was chasing them."

"Where was he going?"

"Switzerland."

"Where are you?"

"The lake area."

"Stay there."

"Your fees are going up."

"Whatever."

"This is going to be much more expensive, *Eminenza*."

"Who's the lady?" Mugant replied, paying little attention to the *increased* price. "Don't know, except she knows how to use a firearm."

Mugant's ornate diamond and sapphire Cardinal's ring was cutting into the plastic phone receiver, his fist had tightened so much. "Get off the phone. We will use the same means to communicate as we always do. When you get the next message from me, be absolutely punctual."

***

The white cassocked leader of Catholicism entered the tense Curial conference room. Standing at the long highly polished mahogany table were eleven Cardinals attired in simple black. At the chair immediately to the right of the red velvet-back chair the Pope would occupy was the Cardinal Secretary of State. Nationalities broadly representative of the Church's diverse population of believers were represented here. This was the Church of Rome's earthly leadership.

Standing attentive at his chair the Pope, his thumb and index finger on the gold chain holding his Papal cross, looked out the high wave-paned window nearest him. There he saw the sunlight dancing off a stream of water bubbling in a fountain he knew well. Frequently he would stop at it to leave food for birds that alighted on the small wooden aviary the gardeners fashioned at his request when first arriving in the Vatican. His face now seemed wrenched with pain and deep concern, and perhaps he was looking for some sign of peace in the flight of those little birds.

Looking at a black cassocked cleric at the door to the conference hall, the Cardinal Secretary of State nodded. The door was closed.

The Pope motioned for those in the room to be seated.

"Too much killing, too much death. When will we see respect for life, our most precious gift? We have condemned these acts of violence against biogenetic scientists repeatedly, at every chance. Now the media seek to hold us responsible because we, they say, create the climate that makes such killings 'understandable'. That is in an editorial in today's *London Times*. Our teaching that life cannot be tampered with gives ammunition, it reads, to those who would attack researchers studying the genomic elements involved in the reproduction and fortification of human life. It reads that by misconstrued virtue, some of our sheep are wolves in disguise. That these intolerable acts are ignored by this Church with a blind eye. Well, I am here to say that the true Light will brighten the darkness. The author's opinion in the London paper is not accurate. Not accurate at all. It is a tragedy, it is against all that we stand for, it is against all that He desires from us. Labs of science in New York, San Francisco, Tokyo, Tel Aviv, Copenhagen, Paris, and even in our own Milan have been bombed by fanatics who claim to be part of the flock of Jesus. They are not, nor do we support them."

A slight smug crossed the face of one Curial Prefect.

"We who have through two world wars in the last century, through the barbarism of capital punishment, through the grave issue of abortion and euthanasia condemned all violence against life—we are now held responsible for 'a climate of fear'. The life of one, the life of many. No life shall be forsaken."

The severity of the Pope's tone was clear to all.

"The brutality at Paris yesterday is nothing our teaching on life could have brought about," the Pope continued.

All eyes were affixed on the faithful leader of over one billion people.

"I have called this meeting to get thoughts on how we can effectively preach our word on life so as to eliminate any misunderstanding of our central teaching: we unconditionally abhor all the killings done in the name of God, or in the name of the Church. We do not condone any violence. This is not some Fifth Crusade, nor are we barbarians. And this position must be fully and completely understood by those who continue to act in hatred. If it is possible to have our voices heard by those adrift in righteousness, we must spread His word everywhere. It is a simple message; do not kill."

There were nods of agreement around the room, and each Cardinal understood the gravity of tone their peaceful Holy Father spoke in.

"I have called all of you here so as to get a plenary statement out to the world, a statement that will leave no doubt where we stand. Because of so many killings that have occurred, the joint statement from all here will leave no doubt in the media's mind that there is no division among us in any condemnation of violence against life."

"Do you mean to suggest that the statement have the flavor that 'The Holy Father, and all bishops of the world, etcetera, etcetera?" asked the thin, dark complexioned Humberto Relor, the Colombian born Prefect for the Congregation of Bishops.

"More than that," the Cardinal Secretary of State responded. "His Holiness wants the world to see that his highest body of advisors, all of us here, are in unison with him—not simply the bishops of the world but the Church's governmental leaders."

"The media have always spoken against us. What good will any new statement from us make to them? They'll only distort it," commented the Curia's newest Prefect, Cameroon's Daniel Umbota.

Very good, Anselm Mugant thought to himself. *Umbota's conservative credentials, strengthened at the University of Navarro, come into play nicely.*

"We will, however, be in print as to what we believe. All can read our statement, which I'll instruct be read from the pulpit in every Church throughout the world. The advantage of a written statement today is that all can read what our position is, whatever the media attempts at distortion," the Holy Father answered.

"Anselm, have you any thoughts as to how we should proceed?" the Pope continued.

"I am only one among a number of Cardinals, Your Holiness. Perhaps another one of the Prefects here should be heard, since it is well known my solidarity with your view as Prefect for Human Life." Mugant looked down the table at Gabriel Jayant. The Pope's senior diplomat, the Secretary of State, watching Mugant's eyes, looked at Jayant too.

"Perhaps the Lord Cardinals can put in writing their thoughts—"

"—I do not think that is 'collegial' Cardinal Secretary. We should hear what each has to say and learn from one another. The written word does not have the life of actual speech," Mugant replied. He again looked at Gabriel Jayant.

"Your Holiness, I believe the Church must place an emphasis on the perpetrators of genetic manipulation as the higher evil here," began the Cardinal from Mumbai and now a Curial Prefect. "They are, after all, in violation of the laws of God."

Australia's Jeremy Noth, schooled on three continents and

holder of a doctorate in Philosophy and one in History, decided to speak. "God gave man the brain, Gabriel, to proceed to these new scientific achievements beneficial to man. Not all geneticists—if in fact there are any at all— are evil. The Holy Father has asked for the coordination of vision between faith and science. Why did God give man the mental capacity to plummet the depths of His genetic language, unless man were to benefit by such knowledge when studying the ways of life? The benefit is to assist man in curing devastating ills. We must be mindful that most genetic researchers do not believe in human cloning. Their science is intended to help man's body. The labs that have been bombed—what, thirteen over the last year—possibly hold the key for tomorrow's medical cures. Remember, man was thrown out of Eden, but our merciful God did not take away humanity's ability to understand and better its plight."

"That is pure error, it appears to me, Cardinal Noth," Mugant answered. "Your reasoning would have allowed the likes of the lunatic Mengele and his evil ilk in Germany. How many embryonic fetuses must die in the name of curing the common cold?"

The Cardinals looked at Mugant, as if at once. His point was well understood. Each Cardinal believed that embryonic testing ended human life.

"The Holy Father, Anselm, has not taken that route. You said you're in solidarity with him a few moments ago," the Cardinal Secretary of State responded, remembering Mugant's demand of him to instruct the Pope to issue a dogma with language condemning, as Mugant referred to them, the "gene doctors".

"I am in accord with His Holiness, of course, Cardinal Secretary. I am merely, I believe, adding on to His Holiness' overall statement. The Holy Father has called us here, however, for our wisdom. Cardinals are selected, among other reasons, to give advice. Have we done enough preaching, your Holiness, in the past to share our message on life? I believe we have. Mugant suddenly told the Pope. "Look at the issue of abortion? Millions each year. What has been the Church of Peter's response? Did we condemn the doctors, call them murderers—which they are? No, we prefer to speak about caring for the woman, understanding her needs, rather than make clear and plain that it is the doctor who is the tool of Satan. We do little to mention the dead child. Our Holy Father's voice has moral suasion, but sometimes that is not enough.

Your Holiness, I think that if you called for the faithful to stop the doctors, which does not mean be violent, that none would have—"

"—My office is one of healing and instruction, not issuing a call to arms, Anselm," replied a surprised Pope.

"What has your instruction thus far accomplished, Holiness? Millions die each year, and the abortionist has his way with his payments for the murders he performs daily. Your instruction has not stopped one butcher from using the saline to snuff out the life—"

"Cardinal Mugant, labeling one a murderer does not prevent the murder," the Pope's Secretary of State answered.

"Holiness, have you called for penalties against these butchers? No. The Church has chosen to ignore identifying the sinner, and this is where the teaching fails. You should have called for the faithful to prevent these abortions, not simply pray to have them end."

The tension in the room mounted, and subconscious sides were drawn.

"The faithful would put themselves at legal risks with their government if they attacked life or property, and this we could not—"

"Precisely, Holiness." Mugant said, once again interrupting the Pope. You're afraid of governments imprisoning members of your flock while millions die each year. It is my strong recommendation that the Chair of Peter needs to issue new instructions on life, which call for the faithful among other things to stop those who destroy human life. Human life in its earliest stages is still a creature of the Almighty. It still has personhood. What, Holiness, is the difference between calling for penalties against someone who has murdered a fully grown human and one who has snuffed out the life of a human just conceived? Both are persons."

"There is no difference. We are all children of God."

"Except the living embryo is defenseless. And it is our responsibility, the responsibility of those who carry the sword in the name of Peter to protect those who are defenseless, the children of the world."

"But Christ said to Peter 'Put your sword away'."

"But God said to Moses 'Thou shalt not kill'."

"But isn't that what you're suggesting, Anselm? Death upon death?"

There was absolute silence in that conference hall.

Mugant's gray eyes turned to Cardinal Furth.

"I believe Cardinal Jayant is right in his suggestion," the Irish Cardinal Furth began, responding to Mugant's cold gaze. "The Church must condemn with all force the artificial creation of life, for who knows what wrath it shall bring upon us if we go forward as we are."

The Pope stood. "I cannot understand this shift in opinion so suddenly. Ours is a Church of forgiveness and mercy, of progress and cooperation. A Church of love. We cannot go back to the days of condemning science out of fear that we may in ignorance harbor as man's understanding and knowledge evolve. When we were the Church that condemned by cold steel, we had all sorts of abuses within our ruling body. The Medicis, the Borgias. This is not the religion Jesus brought to earth, and by which He promises we are given eternal joy as our reward if we but follow His message of brotherhood."

A number of the Curial Prefects showed obvious relief, now that the Pope was ending discussion with these remarks.

The Pope continued. "Anselm, I know of your commitment to our call for tolerance and cooperation so that together science and the Church may benefit—and at the same time— respect man. Science does not benefit man unless it shows respect for man at all stages of human life. Religion does not aid science unless it shows science how respect for man is part and parcel of science's mission to improve man's physical plight. You'll continue to promote that view, I am confident. We must change hearts, as we all agree. We cannot change laws by revolution and more violence. We must do it by the conviction of our teaching authority. Cardinal Noth speaks eloquently, and may I suggest, Cardinal Secretary, we incorporate his statements here today as part of our unanimous communiqué that we will issue this afternoon in our condemnation of the violence against life throughout the world."

The Pope's senior collaborator nodded.

"We will then speak to the media today with one voice and make it clear that science and the Church are co-promoters in the well-being of man. We each shall share this view over Mass, and over Vatican Radio. This is important for the Church as I prepare to leave for America in a few days."

Cardinal Mugant sat quietly in his chair.

"I think, further, that some statement with the leaders of other religions regarding this momentous advance of science in our day—the science of biogenetics—is helpful. I have had indications from a number of them that a general statement advocating the improvement of life through the judicious means of scientific advancement is in order. Science and the religions of man must advance together. In understanding and respect." The Pope smiled. "Look at the warbling that has just flown by. So precious to our Heavenly Father. The life of all our people is also of such value, and even more so, to Him."

The wooden doors of Ligouri Hall opened. The leader of the Church of Rome walked out into the gleaming marble hallway, thanking the cleric who had opened the doors. The Secretary of State walked behind him, as the Canadian Curial Prefect said no more.

"It is good the Pontiff has emphasized peace, Anselm, is it not?" said the Pope's Prefect for the Doctrine of the Faith.

Mugant ignored the question as he watched Gabriel Jayant and Jeremy Noth in animated discussion as the sun's last rays cast themselves over Rome.

***

Two black Mercedes limousines wound their way through the dimly lit streets of Como. Passing the Gothic cathedral in the shadow-lined small city center, their presence was ignored by most there whom the limousines passed. Such caravans were a common occurrence in this home of the fabulously rich. No one there would be surprised if they were told the limousines were completely bullet proof and capable of speeds twice that of other luxury vehicles. Heading north under the full moon on the lake's eastern shore the two vehicles made their way around the tight fitting roadway towards the town of Bellagio. Influence and wealth had its price, and the iron gates and high brick walls of Como's Ventura Villa, Cardinal Mugant's hideaway, located on the peninsula shores of Belaggio on the grand lake of Como, to where these autos were heading were added proof of that. Not even drivers commissioned by Como Ventures to drive its fleet were allowed access through those electronic gates without first a thorough search by armed guards. Security was the handmaiden of power and had to be well tended.

Arriving at the front of a two-story granite fortress, dwarfing all other residences on the lake, five figures were quickly ushered up its pillared steps and through its regal front entrance. Walking up a wide flight of stairs, two security detail accompanying them, they reached a room closed off to the second story hall by two heavy bronze doors. It was the *camera di Giade* of Mugant's private dwelling.

The room, to one inside it, seemed completely hewn out of a rare Singapore bright green jade. The floor, the four walls, the ceiling and the large table with its six chairs were completely carved from the rock, its intricately carved design would have been the envious focus of Eastern Dynasty. Four high synthetic windows let the sunlight in by day, or the twinkling from distant stars by night. Electric lights had no place in this room. Anselm Mugant, for all his appreciation of the conveniences electrical power provided, never lost his fondness for light by candle. Candles had always been with him by his bedside as a child. As late as this stage in his life frequently they were still his only source of light.

Once inside, the bronze doors were closed behind the five. As if from a hidden entrance, Anselm Mugant entered the room, and took the seat at the end of the magnificent jade table.

"We have made no progress in cleaning up what has to be cleaned up," the Curial Cardinal began. "We are no nearer to victory today than we were 24 hours ago. The fugitive has not been caught. His Holiness, *your Pope*, still chooses the featherless weight of rhetoric to oppose the blasphemous scientists who condone murder. He does not understand that public intrigue would already allow the weak minded to pursue genomics. And the Church still remains exposed to the possibility of extortion."

Each of the five shadows edged forward, "extortion" and "usury" being synonymous words they were each quite familiar with. So too, were they familiar with the Pope's position to sheathe their sword. His word and ideology, pedantic to all seated in the opulent room.

As if to catch his breath, Mugant paused. "And there was some unnecessary unpleasantness last night at Cernobbio. There may have been some exposure."

"You're saying what?" McGeorge Previn voiced before all others could.

"I am saying our meeting just a day ago was for naught.

The fugitive Train is a criminal, and I told both Previn and Schemmizzi to have American and global news reports plastering his face everywhere."

McGeorge Previn, a Mugant operative with firmly established credentials of fear and respect in the US intelligence apparatus, looked at the Canadian. Known for his efficient execution of complicated "wet ops", and privately praised by a succession of American leaders for such attention to detail, the aficionado of finely tailored blue pinstripe suits was not given to criticism easily. Sole heir to his family's incredible agricultural companies wealth, the tall, bespectacled Previn did not feel as constrained as others more sensitive to oversight. Wealth gave him "more freedom of expression", which took the form of questionable legality in interpreting the laws of his government. A believer in his Church's traditions, Mugant's hold on him was not religious, but financial. Previn was in the *Fifth Crusade* to protect his family's secrets, and his assets.

"Now I know Previn can't get coverage from *Die Frankfurter allgemeine Zeitung*," Mugant continued, "but Schemmizzi—you have contacts there."

Guillermo Schemmizzi knew his extortionist well. From a family of ardent anti-Communists, the rotund, but well manicured Schemmizzi had grown his media empire by taking big bets with heavily borrowed funds. Clever to build his business operations through core "brick and mortar" media companies, he had avoided the initial Internet craze until the devalued industry was ripe for control. And then acquire one steal after another he did. The vast majority of fiber optic cable that supported Europe's Internet infrastructure, along with his vast assortment of orbiting satellites transmitting wireless messages across the continent was only a part of his media and global information empire. By far, Guillermo was the wealthiest of the crusaders, in part due to the stock valuation held on several of his publicly traded companies. His financial acumen was nearly impeccable. His fanatical devotion to Italy's *Catholic Action* caused him to fund it at the avoidance of paying taxes he felt his government should not have extracted from him. When Anselm Mugant needed a foot soldier, however, he would use whatever means necessary. Guillermo Schemmizzi's trust of Vatican Bank is what did him in.

"Run this charlatan's face in all European papers, every edition," Mugant went on. "This scientist may have a passport, he may have an assumed name he can use. He might be so clever as to have others assist him in his travels to escape our hunt. He must be stopped, and right now all I have are snivelings that he is still on the loose."

"What of this *exposure*, Anselm?" Guillermo Schemmizzi asked, already aware of what the Cardinal had mentioned.

"I'll tell you how foolish this is getting," Mugant leaned forward, paying no attention to Schemmizzi, his composure giving way to beads of sweat and trembling hands. "Someone may have got into our records today, possibly stealing financial records of our transactions in Zurich."

"Bank records? Bank records? We each have billions all interconnected with our individual empires hidden there. You're not saying that we have exposure—"

"—Silence Adrianna!" Mugant shouted at the female Brazilian arms financier. "We are all exposed to far greater calamities you fool than your picayune financial bantering!"

Adrianna Corvoso de Sa, an opponent of the same Marxism Mugant loathed, had become a Mugant ally out of her dread for a life the Brazilian prison system could bring if her family's decades old arms trafficking and other illicit operations she was now charged to oversee as the family's *patrona* was ever made known. Mugant, the seductive Brazilian believed, was right in his cause—but not at the cost of a person's soul. Her family's portfolio of nearly $5 billion helped finance Mugant's war.

"*Eminenza*, these are large financial pools—"

"—As large as you lost when you needed Vatican Bank as a conduit for your illegal transactions—for yours and your families before you?"

The English financier Rupert Hawkins leaned back on the hard jade chair. "*Eminenza*, there is no need to point out any of our histories," said the only Protestant in the group. Hawkins was of the Church of England.

Mugant lowered his voice, and seethed at the five in the room with him: "Holy Mother the Church is under siege because a scientist has not been caught. What he can do is a mockery to your cause and your beliefs. And to the world itself. Forget the laundered and embezzled moneys that brought you into this lair, forget the blood money of your past. Money means nothing when we are faced with this devil's existence."

To each of them, leaders of the *Fifth Crusade*, the silent, deadly arm of righteousness, of which Peter's Church knew nothing, great concern over Mugant's news grew.

Mugant, dabbing his brow with a white Irish linen handkerchief, looked at the five, confident he had regained the upper hand. Not a sound was made as he sipped a glass of mineral water, which had beaded just as his brow had only moments before. The trembling in his hand had moderated, but his anger was rebuilding. The polished jade was not having its usual calming effect on him.

"So, let us review our necessities. Previn, your task is to make sure there is no accomplice in Train's work. Certify that no group or individual is aiding him." Mugant's fists tightened. "So far I see no results from your end, but perhaps a day may not be enough. Something gnaws at my bones, tells me this American is not in this alone. The British can give you leads, as if I have to tell you. But maybe I must since I have not seen any convincing results from your intelligence forces."

Mugant paused to let the reprimand have its full effect.

Previn, the American intelligence conduit leaned forward. "I thought you were addressing these issues? Have you failed—?"

"—Fail? Don't be absurd. It is that this Train may have received intelligence from within," Mugant slithered, eyes piercing at each individual in the room. "I am not completely sure this is so, but it will be evident by the one who fails in the tasks I shall order. Then our Judas will have to answer to all. Previn, my dear friend, you know I do not fail," the Cardinal bluntly said.

Frowns of confusion and puzzlement were everywhere.

"The news wires in the States have Train's name and the Lake Geneva woman on them. I expect his face to be on the cover of many newspapers tomorrow, Cardinal Mugant," Previn went on. "I have even arranged for two prime cable news shows to run the story over the next two nights in America, covering especially, as you instructed, the rape angle."

"I have another concern." From his black suit coat's inside vest pocket he pulled out a thin lizard skin billfold. In gold the initials AM could be clearly seen against the black. "Two photos here show the face of someone who may be a rogue, may be an aid to the American. In fact I think he had something to do with last night's unpleasantness to which I before alluded. Three people are dead at the facilities in Cernobbio," Mugant smirked, watching McGeorge Previn's expression. "You'll take these photos and run it through to see who this man is. He may be a murderer who has to be taken down for the cause of justice. I'll know more of him in a day or two. Until then, there is no need to kill a possibly innocent man—if that is what he is. I'll let you know my intent soon. For now get information on him."

McGeorge Previn looked at the Canadian. "Is he an intelligence asset?"

"Maybe. Run the photo and see what you find. Make sure everyone gets a copy of these," he said, tossing the pictures on the table. "Previn, I know those computers back in Washington can magnify a man's retina, and in lieu of all the disasters going on in the world that your country is involved with, I am sure a retina scan may be helpful. Get people close to you on this one," Mugant instructed, hedging his bets. "He might have a history."

"And of course you will not let me in on where you got these photos?"

"That information would be of no use to you, Previn."

The narrow faced Rupert Hawkins moved forward on the rectangular jade chair on which he was seated. "You have the names, Eminence, of those who were killed?" Hawkins asked his tired eyes bloodshot, indicative of the lack of sleep the last twenty-four hours had caused him.

"Yes, and you'll issue the appropriate condolences," Mugant brusquely replied.

Hawkins nodded.

"Things must not get out of control. Part of success in destroying an enemy is having complete secrecy. Already I suspect someone in this operation may have leaked. Secrecy served the cause well in Paris. The American government was completely off guard when the Kentucky explosions succeeded. The deaths, discretely timed, of different Japanese geneticists has had a marvelous effect of slowing down their rot. Panama, attempting to conceal harboring these madmen for money, has gotten the message, thanks to our Argentinean confrere Hernando here, but it has yet to thank the messenger," Mugant continued with a self-absorbing smile.

Hernando Mühlor, still sporting an athletic build under his salt and pepper hair, ruefully recalled Mugant's persistence in demanding his family use their funds to pay off Panamanian government officials to block all genetics lab construction in Panama. Plans for construction of an industrial park facility for two such labs outside Panama City were shelved when the bribery amount was enough.

"This is what I am talking about," Mugant's voice bellowed. "We have had many successes in staving off the enemy; Satan on earth. Well-financed operatives, operations expertly executed, sources in every country on the lookout for the peddlers of filth that threaten us all. Now we have our supreme test after all these years. Would our Lord want His Body desecrated by a fanatic? This is whom we are now, in the greatest struggle yet in the Church, called to stop.

"Cardinal, what type of *exposure* do we have?" the Argentinean of Aryan bloodline solemnly asked.

"There are many, I am afraid, my friends."

"Please, can you elaborate?"

"Earlier today I believe this fellow Train broke into Como Ventures offices across the lake, killing those courageous souls who worked each day in the name of God's intent. So brutal and purposeful was Max Train's attempted message to all of you, that he chopped off the three middle fingers on each hand of Dr. Seto. What is this message? He left behind the symbol of the devil— and now he is here on this earth walking amongst us. Hernando, that is but only one of our concerns. The place where Seto's fingers were found was in one of our computer rooms. Financial papers and records were scattered everywhere. I need not tell you what some of those records may have contained."

"Zurich?" Mühlor exclaimed.

"Unfortunately, my fellow soldiers of Christ, there is more as I had mentioned yesterday. This man knows the ways of human cloning. In his possession may be the Cross of our beloved Savior. He is in a position to either destroy each of your financial empires... or worse, cause many of our flock to scatter."

"What do you mean?" asked Adrianna, perplexed.

"I need not tell you there are real questions existing today whether Christ's crucifix was ever found, regardless of what history's words to the world may indicate. I have further reason to believe Max Train has found and is in possession of the True Cross.

"There have been many thoughts and perspectives if all of Christ's Body ascended upon His great Sacrifice. The truth is I thought we would never know, and perhaps we will not. It is in our Faith that compels us to believe Christ completely ascended. Unfortunately," his voice slowly lowering, "we now live in a world where science detracts greatly from man's faith. There are times when our intellect subtracts from our intelligence. The world now moves too fast. Mankind's image grows in his reflective mirror. Now, if Train reveals the Cross and it does contain bodily remnants, what will be the reaction of our faithful? Saints Peter and Paul built our Church proclaiming Christ, in his totality, ascended into Heaven. Nothing of Him was left behind. Until now there has never been a true scientific challenge on Christ's disappearance. He was not in the cave when Mary returned. He ascended to Heaven. The remnants on the Cross also had to ascend. As Paul said, 'Unless Christ be risen from the dead, our faith is in vain'. The vast majority of our faithful, in their own interpretation of their faith, believe in the physical Ascension. And this is possibly an issue."

Mugant's beliefs were not lost on any of them. Each understood the difference in Ascension theories. Arguments and perspectives had abounded throughout time within all the churches of Christ. Never before, other than in its days before Constantine's vision on the battlefield, was the Church so vulnerable.

"What makes you think there may be remnants left behind?" Adrianna asked what the others were thinking.

"I do not believe His remnants were. But Train—he is the devil. I would not be surprised if the Satan tries to create—invent something through science that will attempt to undermine Christ's Way. He wants nothing more than for our flock to lose their faith in our almighty Savior."

Confounded gazes abounded, as all eyes focused on Mugant.

"Your fortunes and souls ride on the outcome, my confrères. Max Train must be found and stopped. You can do nothing to me, as I know I need not even hint. Your criminal financial records, your manifest lawbreaking, would be known instantly worldwide were any ill fortune to come upon me. I will not have the body of Jesus Christ cloned while I am alive. Nor shall I have our Church divided on a question of faith. It has fallen to me, and to each of you, to stand fast against the abomination modern man seeks to foist upon the community of God's elect. All means are righteous in His eyes to bring to an end the work of Satan's forces. You will strike out with greatest commitment to annihilate the threat where man would make God."

Anselm Mugant closed his eyes, his palms flat on the jade he cherished so much. "The meeting is ended. You now know what has to be done. Previn, I trust you know what must be done to

Train. I'll let you know of the other one Train may be traveling with. You can confer amongst yourselves on your approach and mutual use of resources. But now go, for I have to attend to."

Bronze doors opened, the same that had before, and the five who so quickly came to Como Ventura Villa now would so quickly leave it.

***

Milan's granite stoned Castello Sforzesco, built in 1450 A.D. by Francesco Sforza, was always a pleasing sight to Anselm Mugant. It was the fortress he never had, but whose history and architecture he knew as well as his own Como Ventura Villa. Now it housed magnificent artwork such as Michelangelo's unfinished marble sculpture, his last work, the Rondaninni Pieta, the Arrazi Trivulzio tapestry, and works by Giovanni Bellini, and Dutch masters. Mugant's own interest in the museum was the Castello's *Biblioteca Trivulziana*, for it contained a favorite chant of the Canadian Cardinal, Saint Ambrose's *Hic est dies verus Dei*. Each time he listened to its being sung, he would recall with approval the definition of music as "the science of moving well" given by Ambrose's student, the brilliant St. Augustine.

At the middle of the fortress's front entrance was a three tiered tower that overlooked a capacious courtyard. Pacing below it, outside the fortress walls, Anselm Mugant waited for his expected acquaintance before another Milanese dawn made its way to Lake Como. A candle lit in an opening two floors above the ground in the fortress rarely patronized circular south tower suddenly caught Mugant's eye. It was the signal his caller had pre-arranged, who remained in the tower behind the candle, not wanting to be easily seen by the Cardinal. Knowing the Castello's passageways and ambits, the caller felt secure in meeting with the Canadian this way.

"So Your Eminence, what news have you for me?" he said as Mugant stood beneath the window.

Mugant countered with a question. "They went through the records?"

"Maybe," the voice said.

"Why do you answer with 'maybe'?"

"I do not have the key to your answer, Eminence, the key that loosens to you the answer you seek. 'Whatsoever you loose on earth, shall be loosed in Heaven, and whatsoever you bind on earth, shall be bound in Heaven'." A sardonic laugh seemed to swoop past Mugant's ears.

"Didn't you watch them?"

"There was not much to watch, Eminence, as I moved swiftly to stop them."

"Seems to me you only stopped the wrong people, three of them in fact."

A crow flew past the south tower.

"You're to go to Zurich. Get into Zurich Investment Services. So far all you have to show for the past days are mishaps upon mistakes."

The shadow in the tower was already gone. His destination, Zurich, as the crow flies, was only a sunlight away.

Chapter XII

The rising sun's golden rays delicately nudged the darkness below the colossal snowcap mountains until they reached the majestic, tranquil blue lake situated in the center plains of the canton of Zurich.

From a large leather back chair, Max watched as the radiant rays of hope brought in the new day, fancifully bouncing off the deep waters of Switzerland's renowned lakefront. Their glimmering reflective hues met his brown weary eyes. He perched forward out the large window of the exclusive high-rise apartment on the banks of the Limmat River, located on the edge of Zurich's fashionable and trendy Bahnhofstrasse. Meticulous 'greened' promenades overflowing in abundance with roses and expensive houses built like castles neatly situated themselves on the crisp shoreline, making Zurich's environs stunning to view.

Synonymous with international banking, gold is the armature of which Zurich built and sustained its material beauty. First inhabited by the Romans, the Swiss people gained their independence from the Holy Roman Emperor Maximilian I in 1499. During the Swiss Reformation that took place during the sixteenth century, and under the guidance of *Zwingli the Reformer*, the theory of 'pray and work' had taken root in this Alpine enclave; an attribute not lost today. Unfortunately, there were times when the 'neutral' perspectives of the Swiss interfered with proper judgment and facilitated crimes against humanity, their storied vaults protected by the imposing mountains still filled with untold wealth stolen from victims of the Second World War, and more.

The spacious, pleasant apartment Sara brought them to last evening was one of several in this city used by associates of Sara.

Max gazed down the beautiful lime-tree lined Bahnhofstrasse, the epicenter of the banking industry for all of Switzerland, and home to many exclusive boutiques. Though the street was not paved in gold, pedestrian's everyday literally walked several feet above a majority of the world's precious metals each day. Underneath the Bahnhofstrasse were vast underground steel vaults reaching hundreds of meters in length filled with gold bullion and silver.

Max stood and quietly entered the kitchen, pouring himself a cup of American coffee he prepared after rising from the couch an hour earlier, awoken by dark thoughts of the ordeal he and his family were forced to face over a decade ago. He looked at a large grandfather clock, its gold gilded arms barely visible since dawn was only now awakening.

It was 6:30 a.m.

Placing the coffee on the kitchen table, Max returned to the leather chair and watched the fingering rays continue to ascend over the tremendous mountain range.

This was a town Max was familiar with, having traveled here on six separate occasions in the past to attend conferences and meetings at the Institute of Molecular Biology, the prestigious wing of the University of Zurich, renown throughout the world for advances in medicine.

Feeling the heaviness of his eyelids beginning to close, Max shifted comfortably in the chair, not trying to fight his body's fatigue.

Each day since the fatal night in Jerusalem had been exhausting. After escaping the madman awaiting their arrival yesterday in Cernobbio, Sara and Max switched cars — before entering Switzerland through Chiasso.

After resting for fifteen minutes on the outskirts of Lugano, they continued their drive into the fading day, navigating the narrow roads twisting high above the forbidding ice-capped Ticino and Glarner Alpine ranges. Their only delay, much needed at the time, was due to an avalanche that previously had fallen and covered the winding road near the town of Altdorf.

It had been near 10: 00 p.m. when they finally arrived into Zurich. Hungered from the long day, Sara suggested they dine at the Bierhalle Wolf, the city's best known tavern.

Several pitchers of beer easily flowed that night as the two devoured sauerbraten, potato pancakes and red cabbage as the 'evergreen music' of a local oompah band, dressed in regional garb, roused the friendly atmosphere of bankers who left their work behind. Max, following Sara's lead, found the ability to shed his worries and concerns for several hours and joined in the merriment circulating under the large beer hall adorned with brilliant flags of Switzerland's cantons.

For several hours they laughed and drank together free from

the imminent horrors that continued to follow the scientist. Max took it to heart when Sara said 'we're safe here . . . at least temporarily."

Upon arriving to the apartment, "package" in hand, earlier this morning, Max took refuge on the white goose-down sofa in the living room, where he fell sound asleep, satiated with his share of beer and food.

Stretching his arms as he let out a tiring yawn, Max's eyes searched north, on the western side of the Limmat River that cut across the lake, recognizing the tall steeple clock tower of St. Peter's Church, the clocks face of twenty-eight feet being the largest in all of Europe.

"Max?" said Sara in a gentle voice.

"Hi," he replied, turning towards her as she walked out of the bedroom. "You're up early."

She smiled. "How long have you been up?"

"Not too long."

"How are you feeling?"

"Okay, I guess."

"Well, I want to take a look at those wounds of yours. It's been a while."

"Okay."

Over the next half hour Sara washed and cared for the two bullet wounds. To her surprise, they were healing quite well, considering the physical and mental stress Max's body was going through.

After preparing a quick breakfast, Sara told Max she needed to purchase new clothing for them. Quickly showering, she left the apartment at 9:30 a.m., only to return an hour later with two packages filled with clothing for the two of them.

Attired in her new wardrobe, Sara sat on the couch as Max showered and changed in the bedroom.

"How do I look?" he asked, wearing a pair of denim jeans and a white button down shirt.

"Straight out of one of your American catalogues."

"That good?"

"Not bad," she playfully volleyed, a subtle smile directed towards him.

Having been surrounded by continual violence, he appreciated her warm smile.

"Max, I have a question."

"Sure," he replied, walking towards the couch.

"Can I see the items?"

"Of course." Moments later Max opened the corrugated box and delicately placed the artifacts on the dining room table. With precision he removed the wrapped items, careful to only hold the edges of both items.

"Do you think they're authentic?" Sara asked, somewhat amazed at what was before her eyes.

"They very well could be. Someone is going to great lengths to stop me."

"That's the part I don't understand. Stop you from what?"

He shrugged. "That's what I don't know, but the more I think about it, I think the clue I have searched for has been right in front of me."

"What do you mean?" Sara said as she looked at the ancient items, her shoulder touching Max's.

"You just said it. Are they *'authentic'*?"

"And?"

"And, there appears to be some type of remains left on the long board. Look," he said, pointing out the dark stains on the wood as well as several pieces of hair still embedded into the rope.

"So?"

"There are those who may have great concern if the markings left on it are human. Jesus was believed to have completely ascended forty days after His Resurrection. You probably know that his body was never found, nor claimed to have been found. I already know the items are from the time period he lived on earth, but if these items are human, then there may be a question regarding His Ascension."

"Which Christians believe is the most important part of their faith."

"Well, one of them. Yes."

"And if this is from a body?" she asked, peering down over the dark markings.

"I don't know what that really means."

"Doesn't part of one's *faith* include believing and accepting unknowns or uncertainties?"

"I think so, yes."

"So what would the big deal be if these remains turned out to be those of Jesus, would it detract from Christian's views?"

"I don't know. I hope not."

"But that is *faith,* isn't it? Believing in uncertainties," Sara added.

"I suppose so. Believing in God and God's Way when you may have little reason to do so." Max heard his own words echo in his mind. He knew the significance of what he just said aloud. "In faith, the will must accept what the mind cannot see. That's what faith is—ascending to things unseen. That ability to accept must come from a Power which lifts the will and the mind above simply earthly things."

"It can be easy to lose faith in God, especially when things go wrong in your life. I see people do that everyday. We all do. But Faith would not exist if there was no need to understand our belief in God and each other. I always thought Faith was connected to all mankind and our belief in one another. When you wake up everyday filled with promising expectations, hopeful in your desires, is that not also connected to your faith in God and each other? I think so. I guess in your world of science—which is also my world, our belief in Faith gets tested more often than others since we are trained to questions unknowns—trained to seek answers to mysteries our minds can't solve. Faith in itself is one of those tests. Even now, my homeland has too many people that have lost their faith in God, and in one another. Look at all the fighting that has occurred in the Holy Land," she said, her eyes affixed on the *titulus.* "His teachings of gentleness were that of a wise person."

"Christ?"

She paused. "Jesus was a man in my eyes, Max, but a special man."

"A gentle teacher filled with wisdom."

"And filled with faith in mankind," Sara added.

He nodded. "Can you imagine what he had to endure in his life?"

"I can't," she said, turning her focus onto Max.

"Dying this way, it was brutal."

"Why didn't you just give these items to the Catholic Church?"

"At first I wanted to find out what they were. Get some tests done. Then I was intending to do just that . . . but my plans changed when I entered a hailstorm of gunfire at the airport in Rome. I didn't know what to do, though I still had intent to contact the Vatican . . . until the assassination attempt on my life on the bridge."

"That's why you left Rome?"

"To Bologna."

"And more murders followed—"

"— pushing me further away from everything."

"What do you intend to do?"

"Regarding?"

"These items."

"They're not mine to keep. I thought it was my responsibility to scientifically test the items though. Now," his voice softened, "I'm not sure what to do."

"What do you mean?"

"I know they're not mine to keep. Believe me, I don't want them. These items belong to the world."

"What about turning them over to the Pope?"

"That's what I was intending to do."

"Israel may not stand in the way, but perhaps there is a better way," Sara began.

"What way?"

"I'm not sure, but I have some contacts who may help. It may take a few days, but it's a possibility."

The promise of ridding himself from the burden he shouldered was appealing. "That would be great, but what about my life?"

"We need to find out who wants you dead, right? For the moment we should be safe here in Zurich. Perhaps we should start by investigating Como Ventures and Alpha Acquisitions — they're our only leads at the moment."

"The Library has old records on all companies, including data that may not have appeared on the Internet yet. It has the largest microfiche bank in Europe, Sara."

"And you're confident, Max, that information on Como Ventures and Alpha Acquisitions will be here?" Sara asked him, the latter name being the handwritten name they found on Zurich Investment Services letterhead the night before at Lake Como.

"I've never seen the name Alpha Acquisitions before. Call it a gut feeling, but if there are any public records or statements out there they'll be here. Alpha we know is not on the web. Como we haven't looked for yet. If Polymolecular doesn't have information, I can't see how other libraries would. If we're going to find anything on these organizations the smartest thing is to start here.

People forget before the web there was microfiche," Max said jokingly.

"You're the Professor, Max, so you would know," she said to him. "Let's first see what's on the web," Sara suggested, seeing a free computer terminal from where they stood on the library's third floor."

Getting an Internet online password from the reference desk, Sara typed it in. "Type your name in the search box here, Max," Sara said to him once they got online. "Let's see what it says about your scientific articles that you have written. It will be interesting to see how many of your scholarly papers appear."

Max Train typed in his name, and waited for the website pages to appear. Seeing what astounded him, he looked twice to make sure of what he had just read:

American Scientist Wanted For Questioning In Italian Airport Slaying

The next headline was equally ominous.

Authorities Looking For American Geneticist Max Train In Connection With Explosion In Jerusalem

"Sara, are you reading this?" Max asked incredulously, as he was now "Wanted" around the world. "Am I having a bad dream?" he whispered, conscious of his voice.

"This is ridiculous. It's all nonsense," Sara said, aware there was no arrest warrant for Max in Israel.

Continuing, a *New York Times* article headline read:

Syracuse University Professor Wanted By FBI On Kidnapping Charges

The Mossad agent looked at the first headline, clicking on it.

American Scientist Wanted For Questioning In Italian Airport Slaying

(AP News)
Italian police today announced no progress in the hunt for an American scientist from New York whom they believe was

involved with five da Vinci airport murders two days ago. Federico Bugnini, da Vinci Airport Police Director, commented to reporters that the killings seemed unprovoked. "The suspect Train has left no trail as to his whereabouts. It appears wherever he goes, he leaves a long blood trail. We do not believe he is in Rome. He may have gotten out of the city, and his whereabouts at this time are unknown," the law enforcement officer said.

Sara clicked on the next headline.

Authorities Looking For American Geneticist Max Train In Connection With Explosion In Jerusalem
(Reuters News Services)
Interpol Police chief Reynard Reizmann today denied reports that terrorists were involved in the explosion near Jerusalem's Mount Olive last week that it is believed left three people dead. "Information we have gathered leads us to believe this may be the work of the da Vinci airport killer out to settle a score in the Holy Land," Reizmann told reporters, giving no further details nor reasons for this view.

Train's body tensed, his heart racing. Sara read the next story.

Syracuse University Professor Wanted by FBI On Kidnapping Charges
(USA Today)
Syracuse University Professor Max Train is wanted in the gruesome murder of a woman whose dead body was found on a deserted bank of Lake Geneva, New York early last week. Lake Geneva police chief Arnold Stelling told reporters that fingerprints near the scene were of the Syracuse scientist, who over a decade ago had been charged for the murder of his wife and child, but was later cleared by a jury. Syracuse police were never fully satisfied with that verdict. Lake Geneva's Stelling pointed out that it is not impossible that the Lake Geneva case may reopen the Train case that occurred more than ten years ago. "If new evidence comes forth in our investigation regarding what happened ten years ago, it is my understanding that my colleagues in the Syracuse Police

Department may attempt to reopen the case, testing the Constitutional interpretation of Double Jeopardy," the police chief said. "We would be interested in trying to reopen the case, questioning the valid interpretation of prosecution in this country," Lindon Mitchell, Syracuse's aggressive DA agreed.

"I can't believe this, Sara," Max blurted. It was the nightmare all over again.

"I don't know how this has happened" she responded. "The Israeli story—it's planted."

"I want to call John Wheelock, the Vice-Chancellor at Syracuse. He's a friend. I have to straighten this out. Come with me."

Going down the hall and a flight of stairs to a public phone bank, Max dialed Syracuse University's number, and was able to get Wheelock, an early bird to the office, on the phone almost immediately.

"Dr. Train, where are you?"

"I can't stay on the phone long, John."

"That's fine, where are you?"

"I have read on the Internet I am wanted for the killing of a Lake Geneva woman."

"Can you tell me where you're calling from, Dr. Train? You were supposed to be in Jerusalem, according to your department chairman. Is that where you are?"

Train said nothing, suspicious about Wheelock's repeated questioning as to his whereabouts. *Why isn't he calling me Max?*

"Don't bother coming back Dr. Train," he suddenly heard. "Your position here has been vacated."

Train, without waiting, hung the phone up, "How long was the call I just made, Sara?"

"Not more than 20 seconds. I was timing the call and was going to tell you to hang up before it could be traced. What happened?"

"I guess you could say my former friend at Syracuse asked me three times where I was calling from. It sounded suspicious. And then he told me I'd just been fired," Max said disheartened. "Do you know anyone who's hiring?" he asked, trying to ease his own mounting tensions.

"I could check around," Sara replied reaching for Max's

hand. "You seem like a nice fellow," she added, squeezing Max's hand. "Maybe that guy is acting on someone's instructions, Max."

"But the story about me being wanted for murder is world-wide... everyone is going to see it. It's all lies."

"Max, someone very dangerous has entered the picture, someone not clear to us yet. Let me call my uncle, see what he may know. Let's use a different phone to call, though."

Not reaching Rabbi Kohn after nine rings, Sara looked at Max quizzically. "That's odd. No answer on his cell phone. Maybe he didn't hear it or is in the car. I'll call him back in a few minutes. Let's go and start getting this information we want. Let's find out what this Alpha Acquisitions name is all about, as well as Como Ventures. Maybe there's a link."

Walking back upstairs to the first floor of Polymolecular Library, Max and Sara went to the library's microfiche room. The 20 Swiss franc fee required to use the room Max thought well worth it. Typing in "Alpha Acquisitions" in the microfiche data bank computer, Max came across three newspaper references, the first from the *Washington Post*.

Inserting the required roll of film into the microfiche viewer, Max came across a reference to a Rupert Hawkins in the *Post* piece written five years ago. It identified him as "a new force on the London Exchange", "another Edinburgh University success story, and one of the University's most prominent alumni." The article quoted Hawkins as saying, "We are bound by confidentiality agreements to never discuss the business affairs of any organization our investment company may act as an advisor to. Thus, I am not acknowledging nor denying we have any relationship with Alpha Acquisitions. Officially The Hawkins Group has no comment."

"Sara, do you recognize this name here?"

Getting up from the chair, he let Sara read the microfiche copy he just had finished so she could read the piece.

"You mean 'Rupert Hawkins?'"

"Yes."

"I don't think so. We can check the Net."

"Good idea."

"Edinburgh, I know, is where the sheep Mildred was cloned. There was damage to the Medical Science building there, about six months after the news of the cloning came out. I don't know if anyone linked the damage to the cloning, or maybe there was no link One of the scientists in the labs died. Many think all the data on Mildred the sheep and how she was cloned got destroyed—but it didn't. The other scientist working on the project, a friend of mine, Bernard Darcy, wrote everything out from memory that the both of them did."

"No one has made a connection between the explosion and the cloning?" Sara asked.

"Not that I am aware of," Max answered intrigued by Sara's query.

Train moved through the next microfiche film to see if there was any more information on Alpha that would shed light on what had happened at Lake Como, or to him.

"Here's a story about Alpha having some commodities trading business in agriculture," Train told his Mossad protector. "The name Previn Agriculture appears linked to it. Previn I think makes mayonnaise in the States, if I am not mistaken. That and cooking oil."

"Max, that name sounds familiar."

"It's on mayonnaise jars everywhere."

"No, that's not it. I've seen the name elsewhere."

"I only know it because they make disgusting mayonnaise."

Continuing to the third microfiche roll, Train's face showed a deep frown. "What's wrong Max?" Sara asked."

"Well," he whispered, "here we have the name of Guillermo Schemmizzi involved with Alpha Acquisitions. Pretty heavy stuff. He is one of the richest men around. Schemmizzi is a real philanthropist. A matter of fact, I think he gave Edinburgh 50 million pounds to rebuild its scientific research facilities that were lost in the explosion. Says here that apparently this guy made a fortune swooping up Internet companies for pennies on the dollar after the market crashed. Calls him a devout Roman Catholic, too."

"At least there are some people out there who care about science. 50 million—that's a lot of money."

"He's supposed to be a good guy. Bernard Darcy—my friend in Edinburgh, said the new building should be up in four months when I spoke to him two weeks ago."

Sara looked at him. "Let's get more microfiche, old newspaper clippings, on Hawkins."

Max waited about ten minutes to get the new microfiche roll that the databank called for on Rupert Hawkins. It contained an article from the *London Times*. Finishing the article, Max turned to Sara. "That's odd, very little interesting is mentioned about his finance company. I guess that's because it's privately owned. The articles mention how Hawkins feels his faith is an everyday part of him and how strong his convictions are in it. Do you think it's a coincidence? Schemmizzi and Hawkins, both wearing their religion overtly, and possibly associated with this Alpha Acquisitions?"

"I don't believe in coincidence, Max," Sara replied. He nodded, recalling those were words he uttered before. "We need more information."

"Why did you think of a possible tie-in between the Brit and Schemmizzi, Sara?"

"If there's a conspiracy to get someone, sometimes the people in that effort share similar outlooks. Kind of like a spider web. Each player is a thread. Together, they create a tangled web. I was going on that as my hunch."

"Then who and where is the spider?"

"I'm not sure."

"Thought you'd say that."

"Is that all there is with the microfiche data on Alpha?" Sara asked.

"Yes."

"While we're in the microfiche library, we can check that Edinburgh lab damage story."

Returning the three celluloid rolls he had borrowed, Max returned to the desk they had been using and placed the microfiche roll for the Edinburgh story he had requested into the projector:

University Lab Explosion. Scientist Killed.

(Reuters News Services)

At Edinburgh University's prestigious Medical and Science building, housing the world renowned Genomics Center, an explosion occurred last night, destroying the majority of the Medical and Science building, which was where the laboratory facilities were where the cloning of the sheep Mildred was conducted six months ago. Dr. Michael Nemeth, one of the two scientists credited with the revolutionary accomplishment, was found dead, and is one of nine known fatalities. It is presumed Dr. Nemeth and the other scientists were working late into the evening when the explosion, believed to have been caused from a gas leak, occurred. Damage was substantial to the facility and it is believed the building is beyond repair. Scotland Yard has asked for any information citizens may have on the explosion to contact their Edinburgh office, where an investigative unit has already been assembled. "We cannot say if the explosion was or was not a criminal act," Deputy Inspector Hancock told the press. "We are conducting an investigation just like we would in any case where an explosion has occurred. However, Doctor Nemeth appears to have been murdered."

"I think we should visit Edinburgh if we don't resolve this issue while in Zurich, Sara. I knew Michael, and Bernard Darcy is a friend of mine. We can also see if Bernard has any view on the Paris bombing. Maybe there is or there isn't a connection to Edinburgh."

"I think that's a good idea, Max," Sara nodded, getting out of the chair. "Let's see what else we can find on the web about Como Ventures and Zurich Investment Services."

Handing back the last roll of microfiche to a librarian, Max and Sara walked to the library elevator bank to get to the library's third floor. There the two silently walked down the corridor to the Internet room they had left. The computer they had been using before was free. Their new efforts came up with very little other than what Max previously discovered the other day while researching the Internet.

Striking the keyboards and navigating the mouse through Zurich's extensive WebPages for information on Zurich Investment Services, the two were unaware digital "cookies" raced across the network alerting an ISP control apparatus in Italy of their repeated hits on ZIS web sites. These binary trackers would be activated after a certain number of "hits", usually 15 if it was in a brief time period, and at the Italian ISP control center in Geneva the electronic address for "Polymolecular Library, Zurich" recording the page hits of "Zurich Investment Services" suddenly appeared on a digital readout. After five minutes with the digital readout still in place, the control operator, as instructed, sent the readout to the computer screen of Guillermo Schemmizzi, owner of the mammoth network where the information was being transmitted. Zurich Investment Services had become an issue of *exposure* to the fabulously wealthy Italian. Any references to Zurich Investment Services transmitted through his massive communications network he ordered to be reported directly to him, using whatever electronic means necessary. This was done effectively.

Schemmizzi, on the phone when he saw the electronic readout, immediately contacted his ISP engineering chief in Geneva. "What does this mean, who is this?" Schemmizzi asked.

"You have a computer user in Polymolecular Library who has an awful lot of interest in a company called Zurich Investment Services, sir" came the answer back to Schemmizzi. "Someone is taking their time going through Zurich Investment Services' web pages."

"Zurich" Schemmizzi thought to himself. Polymolecular was the giant Swiss genetics research library center, he knew. Hanging up on the Swiss engineer, Schemmizzi made a call to a private number in Lake Como.

"Your Eminence, there seems to have been unusual activity in a library in Zurich. It appears ZIS information is being sought from the library's Internet."

"You know what he looks like," was the cold response. "The longer you talk to me, the less time you have to get someone there," Mugant said, hanging up the phone before immediately dialing another number.

"Somewhere in the Polymolecular Library, Zurich is the man we want," Schemmizzi told the listener on the phone. "He may still be on the third floor there, at one of their Internet computer terminals. Where in Zurich are you right now?"

"Ten minutes away from your friend's library."

Schemmizzi's heart raced. "You know what he looks like; you were given photographs of him. Get rid of him, whatever you have to do—but remember you must obtain the package I mentioned."

"6:20 p.m. is the time now," Schemmizzi said aloud, looking at his watch. "This should be over soon."

No one took particular note of the two casually dressed men, both in their late 30's, one stocky with a crew cut, the other black hair and wiry, who had entered Polymolecular as the Zurich time struck 6:35 p.m. Having studied the layout of the library facilities once they had been contacted by Guillermo Schemmizzi, they knew exactly where the Polymolecular computer terminals were stationed. Reaching the library's third floor, the two walked quickly to the large room where they expected to see Max Train. Dinner hour had thinned the room population significantly, so scanning the desks for his presence was much easier.

Train was not there.

Schemmizzi's stocky operative quickly went to the terminals not being occupied looking for any sign on the screens their prey may be coming back, or that he had used a particular terminal. Only Polymolecular's screensaver showed on the monitors.

Motioning to his black hair accomplice to leave with him, the stocky Schemmizzi henchman walked out of the Internet area towards the floor's male restroom. A lone, dark suited figure, sitting at a desk behind a sheaf of papers watched them. As Schemmizzi's stocky operative walked into the lavatory, his partner stayed outside watching for Train in the hallway.

There was no sign of their target.

"Get to the library entrance, and stay there," commanded the obvious leader of the two. "I'll check these floors."

Casually walking the library's long floors, so as to avoid any inquiring glances, Schemmizzi's hire checked all the rooms a library patron would visit.

Train was nowhere in Polymolecular.

"Let's go," the lead operative told his accomplice. "We were called too late. The guy is gone. I'll make the telephone call."

Schemmizzi's two henchmen exited the library, and quickly walked to the black Volkswagen they had parked on Neiderdorfstrasse, a block from Polymolecular. Speeding their auto to the Qual Brücke, from where they were instructed to call Schemmizzi, Schemmizzi's henchmen did not notice a blue van following. The evening's darkness laid heavily on their route to the Zurichsee.

A few kilometers into the ride, taking advantage of a sudden absence of cars ahead of him, the driver of the blue van sped towards the Volkswagen, and smashed head on from the left lane on to the driver's side of the attacked vehicle. Schemmizzi's driver, not expecting the blue van to hit him, struggled to take control of the spinning car. The blue van hit it a second time, knocking the car off the road down a deep ravine. The Volkswagen rolled violently, until it came to a stand still 150 feet below the highway and suddenly exploded. The blue van continued on its way, not paying any attention to the demolished car's dead occupants. *The pins work all the time* the driver of the van chortled. *Max Train is mine and no one must ever forget it!*

***

Some 30 miles from the Italian frontier in Monte Lema, right outside the Swiss city of Lugano, sprawled the magnificent estate of Guillermo Schemmizzi. Its main house, topped by a dome the color of alabaster, was of a reddish granite hue, carved precisely to best reflect the sunlight that came over the Valais Alps. Wondrously manicured gardens, displaying tulips, daffodils, roses, and azaleas gave a pleasing scent to the visitor walking its marble pebbled pathways The same granite hue colored the estate's smaller guest houses, which were separated from each other by glistening blue ponds, home of the gray and white flecked ducks whose placid ways always seemed to calm Italy's wealthiest son.

On the second floor of the main house, almost a day after their meeting at Como Ventura Villa, were assembled at a black onyx table the same five industrialists who had first met Anselm Mugant, at his bidding from Vatican Radio, 48 hours before. This time they were meeting without the leader of the Fifth Crusade. Dusk had just fallen when the room's ceiling lights came on, giving the room a quiet glow.

"The exposure issue, and our possible resultant financial risks, must be discussed," Guillermo Schemmizzi began. "I have called us all together at this locale so that we may have time alone from the Cardinal. His cause is right, but we have to have a contingency plan just in case he has floundered, as we all think he may have with the incident at Lake Como." Schemmizzi's watch read 7:15, as a telephone call interrupted his opening remarks. "I ordered no interruptions," the Italian magnate softly said into the phone's mouthpiece. "This is urgent, Senor Schemmizzi. The call is from Geneva. The caller insists he speak to you. Lucerne and Vladivistok are words he said you would recognize."

"Put him through," the Italian said, motioning with his index finger to his guests.

"Rencilier?"

"Yes, Senor Schemmizzi. We have indications again of multiple, quick Zurich Investment Services web page hits. The origin of the hits indicated by the router, however, is an apartment complex in Zurich itself. It is not the library this time. In 12 minutes there were 36 page hits from this one location."

Schemmizzi looked at his watch. *I wonder if they got him.* "Stay on it, Rencilier," Schemmizzi responded, and hung the phone up.

"I was just talking about exposure, confreres. I have been having all Internet traffic at Zurich Investment Services websites and related websites monitored since early this morning. We have been able to determine an unusual amount of interest from one party—first from a floor at Polymolecular library in Zurich, and now from an apartment residence in Zurich. If I had to guess, it is the same party or persons."

"Well, there is no evidence of getting into records," Rupert Hawkins interjected.

"Not records, yet, Rupert. But there is a peculiar amount of interest suddenly in ZIS, with special emphasis, apparently, being targeted towards the history of its officers and board members."

7:35 p.m. Still no information Schemmizzi thought to himself. *I'll give them a half hour. If I don't hear anything I'll have to send out reinforcements.*

"I have a marker on Train," McGeorge Previn said, removing his glasses. "Wherever he's been we will know. Shortly, within a day or two, we should be able to tail him everywhere. I have already ordered checks into his past to see if there are any Zurich red flags. If there's anybody in his past who has had anything to do with Zurich, we'll know and be able to act accordingly."

"He needs to be stopped soon," the Brazilian, Adrianna Corvoso de Sa spoke. "He is just one man, how is it he gets away from the surveillance? He seems almost a professional escapist," she said, a hint of exasperation in her demeanor.

"If he has someone or some group aiding him, it is not on the radar yet," Previn responded. "Mugant did suggest he may be getting help, and we'll see if that is true very soon."

"What will be our contingency plan if we have been compromised at Zurich Investments?" Guillermo. "Previn is getting intelligence resources behind the Train matter. What about us?"

"Hernando, I'll advise Cardinal Mugant that the exposure issue must be addressed quickly. He needs to have Vatican Bank ready for an immediate shift of funds from ZIS to the Bank so that this becomes a non-issue. In fact, he may be working on having that done now, to have every trace of any of our moneys completely erased from there. Zurich Investment owes the Vatican since World War II, and the debt is still outstanding.

"Mugant will do whatever it takes to assure our solvency, the security of our capital, and his. We are all in this deeply, and we have agreed that science has gone too far. If we, who are able, do not prevent the affront to God which Mugant fears, how will we answer for this upon our deaths? The riches of this world have not been given us for no reason," Guillermo Schemmizzi continued. "We have been given them for a purpose, and it may very well be that the purpose is right before us. To protect the Body of God from a second desecration."

There was no dissent.

"Let us repair to the dining room," the Italian host told his four guests. *Still no news* he remarked to himself as he looked at the bronze framed wall clock. *Did they get him?*

Chapter XIII

Progress made during the day, for now there existed a possible starting point, allowed Max to enjoy the casual, mindful walk down Zurich's Bahnhofstrasse towards *the Urania Observatory*. After a long day of research that followed few hours of sleep, the cool breeze coming off the peaceful lakefront was refreshing. For the first time, Max actually felt a tangible sense of optimism.

The two brass bells high above the Grossmunster Church resonated over the quiet city, indicating it was now 8:00 p.m. In an hour he was to meet Sara back at the apartment, who hopefully may have made further leeway in obtaining information on both Como Ventures and Alpha Acquisitions via the meeting she was now having with her banking 'source' here in Zurich.

Strolling along the clean sidewalk, Max noticed a small cigar shop. On occasion he was known to enjoy lighting up, and now, feeling less stress than previously, he entered the boutique. Unlike America, Switzerland sold Cubans. Purchasing an expensive import and a lighter, he walked outside and lit up, placing the thin butane lighter in the back of his blue denim jeans.

His lungs inhaled the sweet aroma flavors of oak and cherry as his eyes ascended to the Orion Constellation reaching out over the night. The Milky Way was to its left, its serene indefinite overcast brushing the pleasant night. With no particular direction in mind, he headed towards the river.

With the cigar in hand, intermittent clouds beginning to gather, Max continued idly alone amongst bountiful rose bushes located on the well-kept promenade along the river's edge adjacent to the Bahnofbrücke Bridge, which was across from the Zurich Haupbahnhof, the city's rail station. His heartbeat slowed. He could feel the heavy tension in his neck and shoulders begin to ease. Looking around the riverbank, he noticed no one. This pleased him.

Sitting on a wooden bench, he looked towards the heavens, and reflected on the day. Sara was correct in her observation of faith, he thought to himself, as he gazed at the North Star high above his head. So many terrible events had occurred in his life, and to those who he loved or cared about. Was this a test without cause placed in front of him by God, or was there a greater, unknown purpose he was not yet aware of? Neither her nor his own words spoken earlier this morning had gone adrift, as loving thoughts of God overwhelmed him.

A shooting star raced overhead. Max smiled. "Hi, my little girl. I miss and love you, too."

There was no pain or despair in his words. Simply love. Love and acceptance.

Standing, Max looked towards the heavens, their cloud formations thickening. "I know you're looking out after me, somehow," he said aloud in an easy tone, "Thank you."

Seeing the enormous clock of St. Peters, Max decided to return to the apartment in the event Sara arrived early with helpful news.

His gait along the sidewalk was quick, but not hurried.

Entering the building, Max gestured to the doorman he previously met last night, reminding him he was staying with Sara.

The doorman nodded, recalling last night's introduction.

Pressing the button for the 28th floor, Max leaned against the elevator wall as it ascended up Zurich's tallest residential tower.

Taking out his key while exiting the elevator, he turned towards the apartment.

Anxious to see Sara, his pace quickened towards the door. He noticed it was slightly ajar. The television was on inside. *She must have gotten here first.*

Cautiously entering the apartment, Max noticed CNN was on. "Sara?" he asked, when suddenly he heard the sound of shower water running in the bathroom. "Hmm."

He walked over to the computer terminal and noticed the home page of Zurich Investment Services. *Hopefully, she got lucky.*

Sitting on the white couch in front of the television, Max turned his attention to the news. Brian Gaughan, the CNN anchor was talking idly about the American financial markets. Max decided to flip through the channels, wondering if there was any news being broadcast about him. Ten minutes, and thirty-eight stations later, there was nothing. *Well, that's a relief. Boy, that's some shower.*

Relaxed, Max entered the kitchen and opened the refrigerator door, looking to quench his growing thirst. Two scaffold ropes were swaying by the apartment's dining area window, but Max took little note of it.

With a bottle of water in hand, he returned back to the desk and typed in the web address for the local Syracuse newspaper. When the page appeared, Max was looking at his own face on the computer screen. The words written about him made any serial killer look like a saint. *This is garbage. I know it's not true, and that's all that matters. Sara also knows I didn't do anything. Sara?*

Getting up, Max reached for the television remote control, and shut off the television. He walked towards the bathroom door. "Sara?"

He heard nothing back.

"Sara? Are you in there?" he asked, concern's shadows rising.

Max listened carefully. The shower's running water was steady, as if not being reflected off a body the way it usually does when someone is bathing.

"Sara, are you there?"

There was no response.

"Strange."

Turning towards the partially closed bedroom door, he nudged it open. The light was on.

She wasn't there.

Tension's heavy hand tapped him on his shoulder, as he spun around.

"Max," said the familiar face as the assassin's fist dropped Max unconscious to the floor.

For the twenty minutes prior to Max's arrival to the apartment, the Confessor's killer had meticulously searched everywhere for his sought trophy. In an ironic twist, he had decided that if he found the artifacts Mugant sent him in search of prior to Max's return to the apartment, he would have allowed the scientist to live. This was not due to any sense of sympathy being extended towards Max Train, but was purposefully planned to infuriate Cardinal Mugant.

Unfortunately, the items were not there.

Tilting Max's motionless head upright, *The Scorpion* unleashed another powerful blow directly onto the bridge of Max's nose drawing a gush of blood. The crazed lunatic sneered at his victim's still body, as the narcotic-like power he wielded in his lethal hands enjoyably overwhelmed him. "You ass, I would have preferred it the other way. But it really doesn't matter. I'll take what is rightfully mine."

Lifting Max's bludgeoned body, *The Scorpion* carried him out of the apartment and towards the stairwell leading to the barren roof deck high above all of Zurich.

Standing three hundred feet above the city street below, the lunatic dropped Max to the roof floor. He looked out into the darkness towards the strong winds emanating from the ominous mountains. The long-sought taste of victory was only moments away. *You may have thought you were able to silence me, but you were wrong! The key to your kingdom you desperately tried to protect will soon be mine! Your flock will come to know and worship me, as I take the throne of this kingdom! Those who believed in you will no longer. Even now, there is continual doubt of you! When I am done, it is you who will be viewed as the fraud!*

Satisfied Max was unconscious, the rapturous figure moved towards the buildings ledge, his eyes immediately focusing on St. Peter's Church. The howling gusts of the powerful winds now escalating off the mountains filled his ears. Reckless metal banging off the window scaffolding hitting the building seemed to applaud his action. *They honor the one who denied you. What nonsense! They actually believe Peter was your loyal follower! That he had himself crucified upside down thinking he wasn't worthy to die the way you did. Your flock was led by a coward! It is time they follow one who knows strength!*

"The day is upon the horizon!" he wailed lifting his massive boa constrictor like arms to the stars. "They'll dwell within devouring fire bearing everlasting flames that will singe their souls! Even now, those who claim to be the loyalist of your flock and lead your sheep have already reached for my hand. Soon, all mankind will reach for my extended arms as flames from Hell ignite the Earth. Skin for skin, all that a man hath will he give to redeem his life here! Humanity will beg for my forgiveness!"

His dark eyes obsessively turned to Max, before gazing back to the stars. "Even now, you shall be denied!"

Like the racing wind blowing off the temperamental mountainside, he rushed towards Train, whose thrashed face swelled blue underneath the streams of blood. "You will prove my point!" He screamed at the unconscious man as the clattering caused by the scaffolding grew.

Removing razor thin fishing cord from his pocket, he lifted Max up and carried him towards a rusty steel ladder used to service the elevator motors of the building. Pushing Max against the steel, he wrapped the strong cord tight around his captive's limp hands that were placed behind him. The blood flowing through his arms slowed, turning Max's fastened hands blue.

Lifting Train's head straight, he proceeded to wrap the sharp cord around his open mouth. It prevented Max's mouth from closing, or making any coherent sound.

Ten times the spool was cruelly whipped around the motionless man's head. With each tug on the cord, the synthetic wire cut deeper into Max's delicate skin, causing blood to stream down his jaw.

Satisfied, he turned his attention to Max's listless body, firmly wrapping his legs and torso to the iron ladder before gazing towards the shadowy mountains.

Above, descending dark clouds trapped between the Swiss Alps gave off a feeling as if they were about to crush anything below. Appearing to swell, they were imprisoned by the monolithic mountain ranges girding the grassy plain's brim below. Obscure dense clusters swiftly forming overhead impeded the moon and stars' cascading light from entering onto the canton's floor. The powerful wind's escalating temperament swept off the distant mountain peaks and raced defiantly across the stirring lake. Darkness descended on the night.

The Scorpion strutted towards the ledge unimpeded by the magnifying winds. He looked down to the calm streets which were undisturbed by the severe storm forming above and unaware of the mayhem waiting to commence. To his right, the resounding applause of the scaffolding magnified sharply. The malevolence growing pleased him, as if he had called upon the omen filled chaos to appear.

He walked over to Max, who was still motionless.

A thick index finger belligerently poked at Max's chest. "Open your eyes, Train."

Max did not move.

Grabbing Max's jaw and shaking his head, the unearthly lunatic suddenly slapped Max's badly bruised left cheek. "Open your eyes, now!"

Still, Max remained silent.

The violent sound of flesh on flesh was heard above the battering winds.

Another open fist descended onto Max's face.

Still, Max was silent.

Squeezing Train's bleeding nose, air was prevented from entering Max's lungs. "Open your eyes!" he screamed again as thunder echoed in the sky. "Open them!"

Max remained motionless as the pressure on his nose was eventually withdrawn.

All at once large raindrops pelted heavily down on Zurich. The surging storm's outburst so severe it prevented pedestrians from seeing two meters ahead. Above all of Zurich, Max's body remained listless, as sheering winds thrust the cold rain onto and past him.

Swirling winds continued sweeping across the rooftop as the storm's intensity bore down. *The Scorpion* raised his hands ecclesiastically, as the brutal forces descended onto the unsuspecting city below.

Suddenly, an enormous lightening bolt directed from the mountains flashed across the sky, as ground-shattering thunder that shook the building followed moments behind.

Pelted by hard rain, Max's awareness was nudged, slowly awakening him from the foggy unconscious state he was knocked into. The taste of blood, which continued dripping down his swollen nose, enveloped his open-wired mouth. He forced himself to swallow the pooled blood. His head pounding from the enormous cold-cocked blow he had taken, Max's left eye flickered, desperate for sight. His body was drenched with cold rain, but he was unable to shiver. His right eye blinked, struggling too for sight. The torrential downpour combined with the sinister cloud covering his mind prevented him from seeing clearly. He had entered Hell.

Struggling half-shut eyes made out a dark shadow moving close by.

Seeing several buildings, Max realized he was on a roof deck. He tried to lean forward. It was impossible.

The attempt he made to move his arms was futile.

A deadly bolt of lightening exploded overhead, as the shadowed figure in front of Max goaded on the storm's flexing rage. "Show me your strength! Show me it now!" screamed the ominous figure brandishing his hands in the air. "The world will be mine!"

Max became fixated with the defiant scene unfolding before his drained eyes. *Who is he?*

Soon, he realized the raving figure was the one who had been stalking him all along. *Where does he come from?*

Another lightening bolt exploded above the tower, causing *The Scorpion* to face his bound victim.

"I see you've decided to join my party," he screamed through the torrential rain falling as he swaggered towards Max. "Good to have you!" his voice carried above the pounding storm.

Max, unable to reply due to the razor sharp fishing wire wrapped around his mouth, looked at the dark figure in disbelief.

"I have been looking for you, Max Train, but you keep running off on me."

Max stared in horror as the dark figure's face emerged in front of him.

"Do you like the storm, Max?"

Max stared defiantly at the menace's familiar face. *My God, who are you? And what have you done to Sara?*

"Oh, I forgot. You can't talk." A wicked heinous laughed followed.

"You must be wondering why you're here?"

A lightening bolt illuminated the sky above as the storm raged on.

"Well, Max, you have something I want."

Max tasted the blood pooling in his mouth. *What does he want?*

"This can all be very simple, you know. All you have to do is tell me where it is," *The Scorpion* grinned, his finger driving at Max's chest as he pronounced each word.

Max squinted his eyes.

The defiant gesture was not lost on *The Scorpion*, who punishingly slapped Max's wet face with his large open hand. "Do you know who I am, fool?" he bellowed.

Max noticed an unmistakable dark void in the madman's eyes.

"All I want are the items that were hidden from me. Two thousand years they have been concealed! I promise you freedom once I have them."

Max slowly looked up. There was no fear left inside him to cling to. His muscles tensed. *You're the one responsible for the killings.*

"Now we can do this my way, or no way at all," Max was told as a deadly box cutter appeared in front of his eyes, before being placed under his chin.

Feeling the sharp cold steel, he did not breathe.

"Max, many over time have said I am not fair. They say I only think of myself. But I'll show you they're wrong."

Max looked stunned as the brutal wire wrapped around his head was cut loose.

"See. I keep my word," he shrieked.

"Who . . . are . . . you?" Max vaguely asked, the corners of his mouth ripped open as the rain persisted.

"Me? What do you mean, Max Train?"

"Who . . . why are you doin' this?"

"I am you, Max Train."

Max looked at the lunatic. *What!*

"You think that I am not you?" the Confessor's killer asked, a freakish laugh resonating from his stomach. "How many have you killed, Max? How many?" he demanded.

Max couldn't say a word.

"Yes, Max, you know what it's like to take away life. But do you realize how many have died because of you?"

Max's eyes stayed in horror.

The sound of the steel scaffolding desperately trying to free itself was heard over the howling, rain-swept wind.

The Scorpion glared.

"What of your actions, Max? You had choices."

"What are you talking about?" Max responded. "You're a monster."

The figure snickered. "Max, I'll give you part of this kingdom. Just tell me where the items that you took are."

"What do you mean? Where's Sara?"

"In due time you'll see her. You have no idea who I am, do you?"

Max shook his head. *Yeah, you're a monster who kills innocent people.* "I've seen your face before . . . in Rome, and —"

"— yes, yes, in Como. That's not what I mean, my dear Max."

"Who are you?" Max screamed.

"Look around you, Max," the animated figure gestured, spinning around to make his point. "The mountains, the wind, the water, the sky, and the fire! That is who I am! Everything is right here for you. All you have to do is give me what I want, and you can have any earthly possessions."

"The earth?"

"Yes, everything!"

A ferocious wave of lightning bolts lit up the heavens. Thunder rocked the building where the two visible figures stood.

Max's heart slowed as he glanced towards the sky. "Do you know what has happened to me? Do you?"

Battering rams of thunder pounded the air, shaking the building once again as the rain increased.

"Of course I do. I know everything."

"Then why don't you answer my question? Who are you?"

A perfect smile met Max's eyes. "I am the one willing to give you anything you desire. All you need to do is tell me where the wooden items are. Then you'll be free."

"Free to do what, die?" Max spat back to him.

"The life you've lived Max has been dead for some time. You have nothing, and you believe in nothing! I can change all that for you. I offer you life!"

"A bound life?"

"Freedom!"

"Yeah, right. The way you freed those people in Rome."

The Scorpion smiled.

"The way you have—"

"—Silence!" he screamed. "The Cross, where is it?"

Oh God, he wants the Cross Jesus died on. "Why do you want it?" Max was more than prepared to die. Accepting his mortality, he accepted his destiny. This gave him strength.

The question caught *The Scorpion* off guard. "I am its rightful owner."

You're a liar. "Is there a rightful owner?"

"Yes. Now where is it?"

"I don't have it!" Max yelled as the rain continued to pour down on them.

"Where is it, Max? You're in no position to lie to me," the killer whispered, glaring into Max's eyes.

"You've killed innocent people."

"I know your history, my old friend."

Max didn't move.

"I know what happened to your family!" the psychopath laughed aloud. "It must have been awful for them! 'Vengeance is mine, and mine alone, thus sayeth the Lord'."

Rages of anger swelled within Max, yet he remained defiantly silent.

"Where's my Ba-ba?" the madman chided. "You remember

your little girl, don't you? How old would she be today if she was alive?"

Max clenched his teeth, fighting the torment.

"Max, wouldn't you like to know the truth? I can give it to you."

Max looked to the heavens before closing his astounded eyes. He swallowed more of his own pooled blood.

"You can know who killed your family, Max. I can tell you! 'With vengeance I will repay my foes, and requite those who hate me'."

Bastard!

"Don't you care?"

Max swallowed hard, and did not answer.

"I guess I was right, Max. You're like me—and I am you!"

"You're nothing. Kill me, but you'll never know anything!"

"Max, you can go free. Free from worries, free from pain, free from any needs. Look," *The Scorpion* said, pointing to the mountains as another lightening bold flashed across the portentous horizon. "You can walk free from worry in the new kingdom!"

"I'm supposed to believe you? Look at me," Max shot back.

"Where are the items?"

Max soaked in the cold air, his eyes closing. *I know who you're not!* "They're gone," he defiantly replied, feeling slightly bending his fingers.

"Where are they?"

"Gone."

"Do you cherish your life, Max Train?" *The Scorpion* asked as he fastened his hand around Max's throat.

My soul doesn't belong to you. "More than you," he muttered.

"I am offering you freedom!" he roared back. "I am offering you your life."

"You can kill me. You'll never find them!"

The Scorpion became so incensed that he let loose his grip on Max. "You'll know Hell!"

"I know Hell because of you!"

"You'll burn, Train. Burn!"

"I already have burned because of you, bastard! Kill me! Do whatever you want to my body, but you'll never get them," Max said, finding strength in his resolve. "You'll never take my soul!"

"You'll tell me, Max. Believe me! While your body burns on top of this building, you will tell me."

"Go to Hell!"

The Scorpion looked at Max wickedly. "I am Hell!" he cried, before turning towards the stairwell. "I'll be back quickly. Then I'll show you my Hell!" as he entered the stairwell.

Max was dumbfounded. Raising his head to the pouring rain, he wondered where the lunatic was going, when he realized that Sara should be home by now!

Trying to free himself from the cord that bound his hands, the cutting wire dug deeper into his skin. The cord was impossible to break.

Suddenly, an idea came to him.

Moving his numbed fingers towards his back pocket, Max reached inside for the butane lighter. It was too far down. *Damn!*

His heart raced. Raising his toes slightly, his hand descended deeper into his pants.

He felt the lighter, and forced it into his hand as he went back down on his toes.

A lightening bolt exploded over the Gussmunster Church as he clutched it in his hand.

Please work. Pressing down on the lighter, he felt the gas flame jettison out. He moved the fire towards his wrist. The heat surged through the falling rain, descending onto his wet skin and the synthetic cord. Max closed his eyes in pain as the hot flame hit his skin. He could feel the fire charring his flesh as he tried pulling his hands apart, until the heat burned through the cord, freeing his hands.

Moments later, he freed himself completely.

He staggered towards the exit door, his body exhausted. As he did, he heard the voice of the killer ascend towards the roof deck.

Looking at the scaffolding rope nearby, he raced towards the building's ledge, then hurled himself over the wall, and onto the clattering scaffolding.

The Scorpion entered the roof deck, a steel canister of gasoline in hand, and immediately noticed Train was gone. *Damn!* He looked around. *Where did the bastard go?*

Carefully, his eyes scanned the roof deck. Train wasn't there.

"Max, are you there?" a voice rose from the stairwell. It

was Sara.

"Max Train, are you there?" It was a male voice joining Sara's.

Another voice followed.

The Scorpion's body tightened, realizing there were three individuals moving towards him. Remembering the shootout in Como, he looked towards the ledge. Train wasn't as important as the items he sought, and they had to be somewhere in Zurich.

He raced towards the ledge, where the scaffolding was, and jumped over the side and on it.

The storm was at its highest peak.

Max heard the killer's body land on the dangling platform.

Standing on the aluminum ledge, *The Scorpion* looked down at the streets far below, unaware Max was holding on for life underneath the scaffolding. There was nothing separating Train from the city pavement three hundred feet below.

"Max!" Sara's voice screamed.

The Scorpion eyed the rope, noticing it fell several feet short of the ground below. He wrapped his body around the thick cord, and began to descend, his eyes directed towards the ground.

Max stared in disbelief as the killer dangled in the air less than five feet from him.

"Max Train, where are you?" screamed a male voice.

Lightning flashed across the sky as the madman began his quick descent to the street, unaware of Max's presence.

"Max!" Sara's voice yelled nearby.

"Over here!" he screamed, the muscles in his body burning from overuse.

Looking up, *The Scorpion* saw his prey dangling underneath the scaffolding. *He's too far away. It's too late.* Dropping onto the pavement, he disappeared into the night.

Sara immediately rushed towards the scaffolding as she heard Max repeat his outcry for help. "Oh, my God!" she said, realizing Max was underneath the dangling platform. "He's over here," she yelled to her two colleagues, as she climbed onto the aluminum ledge.

Moments later, with the help of one of the men, Sara pulled Max's badly bruised body up onto the top of the platform, unknown at the time the killer had made a clean getaway.

Later that night, sitting in a different apartment on the outskirts of Zurich, Sara explained staying in Zurich was no longer a possibility since their presence had been compromised. The two men, Mossad agents, kept quiet, other than for one of them, a man in his mid-twenties telling him, "The only record I was able to locate regarding Alpha Acquisitions was a bank wire transfer to Queen's Bank located on the Isle of Mann, in the United Kingdom. As you're probably aware," the agent went on to tell him, "both Switzerland and the Isle of Mann have stringent privacy laws. It may take a while for me to find out anything else, if I do at all."

After describing the killer to the second man, who appeared in his late forties, Max asked Sara what they intended to do since staying in Switzerland no longer was an option.

The next stop was to England, using the Israeli Consulate as a ruse.

The younger of the men informed Max that a private plane would be made available in several hours, at 6:00 a.m., and take them into London's Gatwick Airport.

Sara handed Max's passport identifying him as 'John Burns' to the older man. "You need to change his identification. Who knows who we're dealing with, and what they know?"

Taking it, the man told her he would be back in two hours, along with "the items you left with me earlier today," before leaving.

Chapter XIV

Blackness filled the Borgo apartment of Anselm Mugant, where suddenly a phone light began flickering in the middle of the night. Heavy satin red curtains blocked the apartment bedroom he had just entered from almost all the starlight that the heavens gave so generously to the people of Rome. The apartment's deep thick carpeting silenced any movement of feet that might interrupt the quiet choral and hymnal sounds to which he frequently listened.

"I didn't get the bastard." Hearing nothing for a few moments the caller repeated "I didn't get him. Do you hear me?"

"Yes," Mugant dryly responded. The Canadian pushed aside the red curtain covering the window nearest his bed that he had just been about to enter. The street outside was absolutely still.

"Train is not alone, then," he continued. "Someone is helping him. Do not hang up. I am making a call on another line."

Mugant began to perspire. His forehead felt a cold sweat.

Mugant pressed a button on his phone, and waited.

"Yes," the voice on the other end answered.

"What is happening with our Crusade, Guillermo?"

"We've apparently tracked down, through Internet cookie markers, a computer user from two different locations pulling up information on Zurich Investment Services and just hours ago information on Edinburgh University, Eminence."

"Nothing else? This is all you have?"

The Italian paused. "Nothing else," he replied, choosing not to inform his caller of what he now concluded was a failed attempt by his men to get Train at Polymolecular.

The phone call ended as abruptly as it began, as the Canadian pressed another phone button.

"Where are we in the Crusade, Previn?"

"We have identified all of Train's past associations now, and any new contacts should be fully known within hours." Previn was a man of remarkable resources. Access to "raw" data bases that not only included secure American government files, but also banking transactions, telephone records, Internet e-mail, health records, and the like. He was the epitome of "Big Brother". If information was recorded on a person, Previn's tentacles had access to it. He also had at his disposal an elite group of former commandos who, under questionable hidden employ that would make the Iran Contra incident inconsequential, would follow Previn's every directive. "Your Eminence, I have resources being assembled as we speak to hunt the threat down. In the name of Mother Church, I will find him."

"Train has been tracked apparently looking into the ZIS Internet web sites by Schemmizzi's organization," Mugant told Previn. "I've had all our ZIS files purged so your flanks are no longer exposed, and each of your financial records has been placed in my possession. That limits exposure of the Crusade as far as the Zurich matter goes."

"So the purpose of this call would be what, Your Eminence?"

"Train has also been looking into the University of Edinburgh web pages. You well know about the explosion a few months ago at the Edinburgh Medical and Science Building, and Guillermo's generous donation of 50 million pounds after it. Too much searching may get Train to make a connection to Alpha Acquisitions, which must not happen. We can't have a tie-in to Alpha Acquisitions."

"Alpha is not on any internet site."

"I know that, but there were newspapers once," Mugant sarcastically responded, "or did you forget? He may go to a microfiche facility, for example, and some newspaper may have Schemmizzi's name tied into Alpha and he'll see it and your name. Hawkins Investment Group was mentioned in some newspaper a few years ago in connection with it. I want you to send several of your most trusted resources immediately to that library in Zurich and look into the microfiche stored there. Have them look for Alpha, and follow it. Train will dig further, and if he digs deep enough he'll connect all the dots to all your families and their pasts and then to Vatican Bank. And you know what that means. Train is getting help, Previn. He has to be stopped! If he is getting help from some one, I am sure they're telling him to get to Edinburgh now. Why else all the interest in it? Track him, find him, Previn! You have enormous resources for this."

"Are you sure he may not stay in Switzerland, or try exiting the country by one of its many border crossings?"

"I'm not able to give you definites, don't be a buffoon! Schemmizzi and you—you'd better have a talk when we're done— have resources available to have the border crossings immediately notified. I also—"

"—don't forget the airport."

"Those, too," Mugant agreed. "Now listen, every resource we have must be used. If Train gets to a newspaper or radio station not in our *Brother's* control—one who, let's say is adversarial to his media empire, and Train could tell an unbelievable tale."

"Who'd believe him?"

"That's not the point. He'd be an interesting story. He—"

"—needs to die. I understand, Eminence."

"Make sure you call Schemmizzi. We should have men on the ground in Zurich, Geneva, Como, as well as Edinburgh."

"I'm making the calls now," Previn said, hanging the phone up.

Mugant saw the light from the first caller still flickering. Pressing the button, he told the caller "Get to the University of Edinburgh. He's going there."

Pressing another phone button, Mugant waited for his call to be answered.

"Yes?"

"It's me," Mugant said, recognizing the voice on the other end. "Do you know if Train has any contacts at the University of Edinburgh?"

"Of course he does, Eminence."

"Living contacts?"

"I can immediately think of, off hand, Preston Ross, Michael Moore, Brian Darcy—"

"—Has he been in contact with these recently?"

"Train doesn't keep in contact with anyone on a regular basis. But people do not dislike him."

Disconnecting the call, Mugant took a pen and pad from a night table drawer and wrote the names down he had just been told. The street below his apartment window was still empty as he looked out it once more before finally attempting sleep.

"Something doesn't appear to make sense, Marc. I know it's staring me right in front of my eyes, but I don't see it," Rabbi Kohn said to his trusted associate of twenty-one years. Marc Perlowitz was an accountant to the ordinary observer. Honest, intelligent, and opinionated, he was also one of many who were trained in the ways of the Mossad and operated out of New York City. Perlowitz's main job, his financial acumen included, was to protect the unusual Rabbi. "There must be something universal—mathematical here, Marty. But I can't see it, either."

"It just doesn't make sense. Max Train is not a killer. A little temperamental, yes. But these news stories," his voice escalated, "that's not my friend."

Perlowitz picked up the newspapers on the table and glanced through them. Stories from Italy, Switzerland, Germany, France, England, and America were stacked an inch high. "This news of Train has traveled quickly."

"There are a lot of alleged killings," the Rabbi sadly noted. "You're sure about him?"

"I'm sure," Rabbi Kohn said as he gazed pensively out his window at the dark sky. "Now Marc, have you any idea as of yet how the news picked up the story that Max was wanted for questioning in Israel?"

"No, not yet," the six foot two inch tall muscular man with enormous hands replied.

***

The Papal Library occupant sat alone at his desk. He kept an hour to himself alone in this terracotta gilded room everyday where he could read and concentrate without distraction. Here he also prepared his encyclicals and major addresses before others came in to assist him later on in this very important process. "Cardinal de Salvoyar," the Pope said into the phone he just picked up. "Who prepared the gene science explanations I received? They're so concise and easy to summarize."

"A Sister Pasquale Cordesco, one of Cardinal Mugant's aides" your Holiness.

"She has saved me much reading before my trip to America."

"I'll be sure to report your satisfaction to Cardinal Mugant, Holiness."

"You may, Cardinal de Salvoyar. I'll personally pen our Sister a note of thanks," he said with a sense of familiarity of the Sister's work. "All the work being done to bring the message of peace to the conflict before us needs our gratitude."

***

The early flight from Zurich's Kloten Airport on the privately chartered plane bypassed the expected stopover into London's Gatwick and went directly to Edinburgh Airport, landing at 11:20 a.m. Through the night preceding the flight, Sara and her two fellow Mossad agents tended to Max Train's wounds. Ice packs and anti-swelling injections reduced the throbbing pain in his face, and the tranzene injection he was given sent him into a deep sleep before he was awoken by his protectors at 6 a.m. the next morning. Feeling almost new from the treatment, he had a new name given to him, Michael Landers, on a newly issued American passport. The luggage most important to Max was stored in the cargo hold below on his flight.

Landing at a private, little used runway at Edinburgh airport, the four deplaned. A limousine took them to a handsome, well-kept brick home owned by a supporter of the Mossad's causes minutes away by auto from Edinburgh University in Edinburgh Old Town. Satisfied that Max and Sara would be safe, Sara's fellow agents left the house, leaving her and Max to discuss the ordeal Max had suffered the previous night.

"The Cross carries with it a heavy burden," Max remarked to Sara, seeming to grow more despondent, unable to figure out who was chasing him, and why the suffering had to be so great. The brutal ordeal he endured with the savage hours ago was still at the forefront of his mind.

"It is not something that surpasses our ability to handle, Max, and handle it we will," Sara said to him. "The *Edinburgh Evening News* right here has a news article which repeats the pieces we saw yesterday, saying you're wanted for the murder of five people. Your picture is also here," she went on, handing him the newspaper that was on the dining room table when they walked in. "The story is a fraud. We're going to find out who's spreading these lies. Do not lose hope."

Max looked at the unflattering portrayal written of him. "This has become comical if it weren't that the bullets were real."

Max's accomplice went to the phone that was on the end table to the sofa they were both sitting on. Dialing a number, Sara began speaking to an unidentified party. "We are in Edinburgh now."

"Is everything all right?"

"A few hitches along the way, but we're fine. There is really nothing new except that I think we're beginning to piecemeal who may be behind this whole thing. I think we may have more to talk about later."

"Any possibilities?" the voice whispered as the sound of bells echoed over the telephone line.

"We'll know more soon."

"I'm still keeping tabs on everything. I'll make contact if anything comes up. The trip to New York is only a few days away, you know."

"Yes."

Sara hung the phone up, and smiled at Max. "Just a friend."

"You have friends everywhere," Max smiled in response.

Sara was on the phone again, calling to Rabbi Kohn, "Max, I am now talking to your friend."

"We are in Edinburgh, just arrived from Zurich."

"How's Max doing?" Max's Brooklyn friend asked with concern, still awake and deep in thought.

"He's doing fine after the bruising that we had to treat. Though far from Jerusalem, he's still being hunted."

"Are there any others watching out for your and Max's safety?"

"A number of the agents are keeping watch. We're in the house in Old Town Edinburgh."

"Ah, exactly," responded the Rabbi. "You should be safe, since the house is specially equipped to protect its guests," Sara's uncle said.

"This is bizarre. I thought I've seen conspiracies before, but not like this. He's not what they say," she lowered her voice.

"The stories about the Israeli search warrant, you know, Sara is a total fabrication. There was no such warrant."

"We both felt that when we saw the statement that Israel had issue a warrant for Max."

"The news has spread fast, Sara," Rabbi Kohn said to her.

"Like it's dropped in."

"Hold on a moment," the Rabbi said as he lifted the news articles to his eyes. "Odd, the language is different in the articles, but the context and format are nearly identical in the full-story coverage," he said after a few minutes.

"Maybe they were taken off the news wires. It's common."

"Perhaps."

"We're going to the University of Edinburgh; it seems there are some people there worth seeing. Max has a friend there who survived the explosion at the University Medical and Science Building six months ago. Max is thinking of seeing if any more tests can be run on the relics from the Holy Land. Maybe a blood test is possible. There may be an answer on the Cross."

"Is it necessary?"

"I'm not sure."

"What does Max think?"

"He's not sure, either. But he does think it has to be identified."

"Protect yourselves, and be careful, Sara."

"Always, Uncle Marty. Want to talk to Max?"

"Put him on, of course."

"Hello Marty. Sara was mentioning something about the Israeli warrant?"

"The story that Israel wanted you is totally false, Max. Someone else does, and we're doing what we can to find out and end this matter for you. We all want you to be able to get back to normal."

"Maybe once you have the Cross in your life, nothing is ever back to normal, Marty."

"Come on, Max. We will get this done with. We're on your side."

"Thanks Marty, it means more than I can express."

"Be well, Max. We'll talk soon."

***

The heavy set Bernard Darcy appeared surprised when the Edinburgh University receptionist told him a caller on hold asked to speak to him, requesting the receptionist to "Tell Bernard to stop smoking those filterless cigarettes. The last time I had one with him I nearly coughed my lungs out." Darcy let out a laugh, and asked the Scottish woman at the desk to speak to his mystery caller.

"Bernard?"

"Max?" Bernard Darcy responded, recognizing the speaker's voice. "Where are you? You've been busy, I see."

"Right here in your town, Bernard. I thought, we thought, we'd stop in: take a chance you might be here as my lady friend and I visit Edinburgh. What magnificent hills, and the lush green. The castles are a sight to behold, Bernard."

"The Athens of the North, Max" is what it's called," Darcy responded. "The festivals here, especially the New Year's Hogmanay —it's a great place."

"What's this about 'a lady friend'?' Good for you Max," the Edinburgh doctor responded, fully aware of Max's plight. Call it a bond between genetic scientists—too many who had been killed the last year, but Darcy intended to help Max.

"No, nothing like that Bernard. She is special enough, though. How's your schedule today?"

"I happen to have a free day today, no classes at all. I normally would not be here, but today I decided to break the routine. Why don't we meet in the Library? This is where my office is now because of the explosion here six months ago at the King's campus. To this day no real information as to how or why has come forth, just rumors. Where in Edinburgh are you?"

"We are actually at George Square, Bernard. At the College Liaison Services Office."

"Right on Campus. Why not have your friend ask for directions? The Library is at George Square. Be sure to get a map. I'll be waiting for you. Let's say in 15 minutes?"

"Looking forward to it, Bernard," Max Train said, hanging up the line.

Minutes later Sara and Max were by the Edinburgh University library. "Is that him?" Sara asked Max as a burly, brown hair man, smoking a pipe, came towards them.

"It certainly is, Sara," Max said, as they both began to walk in Darcy's direction.

"How are you good man," the Edinburgh Professor said as Max extended his hand in greeting.

"Bernard, this is my friend, Sara."

Greetings were exchanged.

"Let's go to my office. I have some coffee and tea ready, if you like. We have a lot of ground to cover."

Darcy's office was meticulously kept. Not a paper was out of order, and the library shelves bore their books alphabetically by the author's last name. Max, Sara standing next to him, looked at the large collection of the Edinburgh faculty member's numerous texts, and said "I see you have the two Genomic textbooks you authored on the shelf. I thought you would have more of them here," Max said, smiling.

"All the copies sold out, Max, and these are the only two copies left," Darcy said, bringing laughter from the three in the room.

"Let's sit down," Darcy said, pulling his pipe lighter out of his vest pocket.

"What's happened Max?" he began, once the three had seated themselves. "I've seen some of the news clippings. You're wanted for murder everywhere... it is such a fantastic tale. If you read the news, everything seems to be happening to scientists and their facilities worldwide."

Max and Sara looked at each other in silence.

"Well, I'm not at Syracuse any more Bernard. Too much has happened since you and I last spoke. I guess it is one year, right?"

Darcy placed the lighter on his desk, opting not to smoke. "What happened in Jerusalem? What are they talking about?"

Train, still hurting from his ordeal of the previous day, openly recounted the events of the past nine days in a summary fashion, as Darcy sat quietly and listened. Occasional expressions of disbeliefs and concern crossed the Edinburgh's scientist face.

"So with the cross as it is, Bernard," Train said, coming to the end of his harrowing narrative, "I wanted to check the blood samples on it, and see what we come up with."

"Well, the serological lab is gone, Max. Everything was destroyed in that explosion. And while they're rebuilding as fast as possible, we have had to use other labs in the area. I purchased some equipment to continue testing, and have leased some equipment. We can do some blood DNA work. I have kept everything at a private facility off campus because of the explosion. No one knows about the work. I've kept things quiet. That may be why I have not been able to get any real funding for further research. I do not want to let out too much of exactly how much progress we made with Mildred, or what I am actually doing now. I have had to cut back on publications for the same reason."

"I know they thought that all the data on Mildred was lost when the labs blew up, and your partner in that project died. Francesco, I can't believe he's dead, was telling me at Bologna how none of the material for the process was lost by you."

"A noble man Pellegrino was indeed," Darcy answered, clearly shaken by what Max Train had told him. "Yes, Max, I did reconstruct the tables and wrote out the procedures, all of which is in safe keeping. I haven't really let any of the data out."

Train stood up, and leaned on the chair next to him. "Can we do serological tests for the cross at your facility? See what we come up with?"

"Let's do that, at least get preliminary results," Darcy answered Max. "I can get there later on, after lunch. Let's say 2:30 p.m.? 64/2 Burgess. It's an out of the way address, on a fairly quiet side street. The only real business on it besides the building where the lab is is a warehouse. Where will you be? You can't walk around, obviously."

We'll be at the lab at 2: 30 p.m., Bernard. And thanks."

"Max," Sara said, suddenly stopping. "Let's send my two agents to the lab first. Have them see what's going on, and then give us the green light to go there."

"Do you suspect anything, Sara?"

"We have to be careful every step of the way," she responded.

"Okay, we'll wait to hear from them before we go to the house and get the artifacts."

***

"Here's the lab. It certainly is out of the way, as the map pointed out," said the Mossad agent sent with his counterpart to inspect the Darcy lab before Max and Sara were to visit it. Exiting the white Audi, which brought the two to the Burgess Street site, the senior Mossad agent cautiously looked around the quiet street and at the windows in the building nearby. Satisfied all was clear, he knocked on the door.

A pair of eyes watched from a window angle that hid the observer to anyone on the street below.

Receiving no answer, the Mossad agent went over to a ground floor window. A partly torn curtain showed a room totally in shambles. Motioning emphatically to the other agent, he pulled from a vest billfold a window cutter and sliced out the pane of glass. The window lock was right above his hand as he reached in and turned it to open. Pushing the window up, the two agents entered the room, the sound of glass breaking under their shoes.

"We can't stay here long. We don't know what's around or if there's a timer set to go off." the agent said. "Check the open closets. I'll check these two rooms out and then we'll get out."

The agent carefully noted exposed wires pulled from a smashed cylindrical container in one wall of the room. Three monitor screens affixed to the walls were also smashed, with twisted chrome drawers thrown up against another wall. Printouts of graphs and molecular bonding sequences were strewn everywhere.

"Nothing in the closets. Whoever was here had it in for the owner. All the towels and cleansers were thrown on the floor in the closets. It looks like someone was looking for something."

Moving to the back of the room, the lead Mossad agent noticed red drops on the floor where the door was. Opening the door, he saw more red drops, which suddenly ended. "We're getting out of here," he said. "I am telling them not to come."

"The lab on Burgess Street has been pilfered, Sara" the Mossad agent told her. "You can't come here."

"I was wondering why we hadn't heard from you," Sara said looking at her watch.

"Papers are everywhere, instruments have been hammered to bits. Windows smashed, and all over the floor are lab utensils and broken glass from beakers. It looks like someone has gone through the place very thoroughly, looking for something, and in all likelihood, not finding it, wrecked the place. We also noticed tiny blood droplets by the door out the back, but there is no sign of Dr. Darcy. It appears he may have been here. I noticed his briefcase on the floor. We left the building quickly in case there was a trip-wire set. You and Max must leave Edinburgh quickly. You know the contingency route we discussed. Take it, and we'll do what has to be done here."

"Something wrong, Sara?" Max asked, seeing the look on her face.

"Darcy's lab has been searched, there's blood on the floor, and he's missing. We're leaving here immediately."

A wave of anger rolled over Max. "Darcy's missing?"

Sara nodded towards Max, while continuing to talk on the phone. "All right, Paul," Sara said to her fellow agent. "We'll follow the alternate plan."

"Darcy is missing Max. Seems like they're here—somewhere," her eyes glanced quickly around the library. "We've got to get out of town."

"What about John?"

"Our friends will handle it. You can't stay here."

Max knew Sara was right. "Where to," he asked, not liking the fact he was on the run again.

"A blue Volkswagen is at George Square, Max, right across from where we were this morning," Sara said, having finished speaking to her Mossad associate. "The keys are under the driver's seat. It was left there for us in case we needed to get out of here quickly." His Mossad protector was already walking ahead of him as the two hurriedly retraced their steps from the Library to the waiting get-away vehicle.

A black Jaguar at the end of Burgess Street caught the tall Mossad agent's eye as he hung up with Sara. "The Jag has two antennas, see it? That one antenna is a special intelligence unit make. It's American. It's an antenna for an American communications satellite. Each receiving antenna design is tailored for a specific satellite signal frequency."

A furtive figure from an empty room in a Burgess Street warehouse set his riflescope on the agent.

"Let's follow it, we've suspected an intelligence element— somebody with great resources who has access to those orbiting satellites," his lean, brown hair partner said, preparing to enter their white Audi.

A shot rang out, scraping the bare ground next to where the Mossad stood. Quickly turning to where the shot sound originated, the Mossad agent took his gun out.

The black Jaguar suddenly began to move as the warehouse gunman let out another shot, catching the moving Jaguar's back headlight. Shots from the Jaguar now speeding up the desolate street immediately rang out, wounding the one Mossad agent racing to the street's corner in the leg. From the warehouse window another shot raced by the second Mossad agent now on the other side of the street, missing him by inches. A figure in the Jaguar, hurtling towards the second agent, let out a round of shots. The wounded Mossad agent on the street corner fired a series of bullets, piercing the car's windshield, and hitting its driver. The Jaguar suddenly began to swerve. Another hail of bullets ripped through the other half of the Jaguar's windshield, when suddenly the Mossad agent's partner took a hit from one of the Jaguar's shooters and dropped to the ground. In horror his struck Mossad partner watched as the Jaguar careened out of control on top of him, steel ripping concrete, instantly killing him. From the warehouse the gunman watched the Jaguar turn on its side, screeching into the first floor of the warehouse below. Firing a third shot, he sneered at the Mossad agent on the street corner suddenly grabbing his chest and then lying limp.

"Fools, all of you. You're no match for what I am," he roared in a laugh that no one on the empty street would hear.

Chapter XV

The wild, breathless landscape of Scotland's bonnie green hills passing before their eyes adjoining the rough North Sea coast mirrored their newest situation. A turbulent past week that increased in grave uncertainty had escalated, though neither was fully aware that additional faceless killers had been sent out after them.

Having left Edinburgh on a moments notice, Sara drove the blue Volkswagen on the unfamiliar roads of Scotland's scenic eastern shore. With London to the south and the industrial town of Glasgow to the west, she hoped the northern direction towards the *Highlands* may finally throw their stalkers off guard, buying them some desperately needed time to regroup. Something had to work, she thought to herself.

At the coast town of Perth, Sara turned inland, traveling west and into the rock edged hills towards Loch Ness, and the bustling capital of the Highlands, Inverness. In the rear passenger seat the pursued artifacts were boxed carefully, as always.

The latest incident, and Max correctly believed there was no question somebody got to Darcy, magnified the deadly swift reach of their detractors. It had only been hours since they arrived in Edinburgh, having left Zurich by private jet two hours before any commercial flights departed any of Switzerland's cities to London. A commercial flight from London to Scotland's capitol was the only route possible. There were no direct flights. Yet the psychopathic stalkers, if that's what they were, didn't miss a beat, evidenced by their known destruction of Darcy's supposedly hidden research facility. This was not lost on Max or Sara.

Access to immediate information, substantial finances, and Max's unrecorded past were evident. The killer on Zurich's roof deck who relentlessly pursued Max and Sara indicated these strengths. So too, did Darcy's disappearance.

Max knew instinctively he more than likely would never see his professional colleague again. Any personal attempt to find the one behind the missing scientist was up to Sara's colleagues. Unfortunately, neither Max nor Sara knew of the brutality that occurred on the unassuming Edinburgh street just hours ago. Nor were they aware how strangling the web being spun was.

He looked at Sara, who carefully navigated the car through the rocky mountain range's twisting turns, the sun's fireball-like hue descending into their eyes. Why was it that she continued to help him, Max wondered, as he curiously looked onto the rolling landscape of *Alba*, the first name given to Scotland five hundred years before Jesus was murdered on the Cross, a piece of which was more than likely in the back seat of the car. The "Alba" name given to the magical, turbulent land was eventually changed to Scotia after the purposeful marriage of a Scoti clansman whose ancestors arrived in Alba from Northern Ireland, and a Pict, whose family descended onto the island from Europe.

This marriage was not of mere love, but of necessity. Though the two Celtic tribes by the end of the eighth century had a stringent common belief in Christianity, which transcended the people of the island's faith, the marriage had other intent. It was said, Max recalled, that the marriage between the Picts and the Scotis was arranged due to the threat of the raiding Norsemen, who arrived on the island and took control of the western seaboard for five hundred years.

Over a centuries of warring occurred when the Conmore Dynasty of Scottish rulers established sporadic peace under King Malcolm III in the 11th Century. Under his rule, the Norman feudal system was adopted, granting land to great Norman families in return for protection. The reach of Feudalism in Scotland, responsible for creating great powerful clans, did not reach the Highlander clans, who remained a law unto themselves for six hundred additional years.

The clashes of Christianity brought about civil wars during the 17th Century. Christians with the common belief in Jesus' Resurrection and Ascension fought one another in the name of God - -and for land. This wasn't the first time, nor would it be the last, the teaching of God's intent was manipulated by mankind to harm one another

Turning his head towards the artifacts, Max recalled the letters on the *titulus*. The signature plaque condemning Jesus was as clear to him now as it was the day he first discovered it. With a saddening frown taking form, he recalled the plight of his Christ. Quickly glancing at Sara, he recalled Jesus' teachings about kindness. Sara demonstrated this to him. Suddenly, images of the lunatic high above the Alps who tried desperately to claim the Cross for himself flashed through his mind. *Who — why would that bastard want the Cross? What did he mean — I am the wind, I am the fire . . . It can't be.*

Max looked back towards Sara. "Can I ask you something?"

"Sure," she replied as the car moved northward.

"Why have you been so kind to me?"

Sara gave him a quick glance. "What do you mean?"

"You don't have to be here."

He was right. As a matter of fact, Sara had a responsibility to arrest him, not protect him. After all, Israel had many international treaties they were obliged to uphold. Sara sensed Max was aware she was breaking international laws since she was an officer of the Israeli Government and was harboring an internationally wanted fugitive. "Where else would I be?" she grinned, not turning towards him.

He smiled. "That smirk on your face is my answer, huh?"

"Is that good enough?"

"I guess for the moment it will have to be," Max said, the deep azure blue eyes of Sara sparkling in the commencing twilight.

"Good."

They continued another fifteen minutes when Sara slowed the car down, aware there were no cars following them. "Look at that," she pointed out below the dipping sun, towards the dark and deep waters of the Loch Ness. "Do you want to stretch your legs for a minute?"

Moments later Sara pulled the blue car over to the side of the road, and along with Max, got out. "Look how beautiful this place is," she said, walking towards Max as the sun's lower crust was hidden behind the western mountains.

"Could make you forget your problems for a day or two," he said wishfully.

"You know, Max, that's not a bad idea, if it were possible," Sara said approaching him. "Maybe soon," she said taking his hand.

Surprised, he wrapped his fingers around hers. "Thanks for everything," he softly said, turning towards Sara as her black silk hair blew in the gentle wind. "You've been a real friend."

"You saved my life in Como."

He squeezed her hand. "You've done that a few times, too."

"How are those bruises feeling, Max?"

"Not bad."

"They're healing nicely. You're a quick healer."

"I guess so . . . but as I keep telling you I have a good doctor," he grinned, squeezing her soft hand again.

"You're not what people say you are," she replied as she squeezed his hand back before letting it go.

Their eyes met. Neither spoke.

The sound of a passing car interrupted the feelings growing between them.

"We better get moving," Max soon suggested. "Are you hungry?"

"Always," Sara laughed, unaware that her colleagues had entered into a mortal gun battle earlier this afternoon. "We're not too far away from Inverness."

Twenty minutes later, Sara stumbled across a magnificent 17th century mansion hotel found frequently in Scotland. "How about it?" she asked, nodding towards the exquisite granite hotel shining above the *Beauly Firth* grass hills west of the distant city of Inverness.

Max looked at the two illuminated steeples of the hotel. "Bunchrew House Hotel. Seems—"

"— perfect. I could use a restful night. Do you think we're safe?" Sara asked.

"I can't imagine we've been followed."

"No, we weren't. But we have to be careful, remember — hotels receive newspapers."

After checking in and paying cash under the name Kara Emily, Sara went back to the car and escorted Max and the "package" back to their hotel room.

"It's beautiful," Max said, looking around the spacious grand suite accompanied by every imaginable accessory. A gold plated pitcher of water sat on the fireplace's marble mantelpiece, as the green Egyptian cloth curtains swayed quietly in the night wind. An antique chandeliers provided soft lighting in the spacious parlor, where were placed two mahogany framed burgundy sofas. Two cedar wood French doors with etched glass windowpanes led into the luxurious bedroom, where canopy of white silk covered the teakwood king size bed.

"I think a fire would be nice, don't you, Max?" Sara asked as she walked towards the large marble fireplace. Turning to Max, she said "I think we're safe. Nobody knows the name I checked under, and the car we are using is under the name Matt Wheeler, the gentleman whose home we stopped off at in Edinburgh."

"Room service?"

"I thought you'd never ask."

"Good, I'm starving," Max said reaching for the room service menus left on an imposing mahogany writing desk, forgetting about his troubles amidst the pleasing setting.

Sara purposefully decided not to make contact with anyone, out of her concern for the continual attacks that followed Max.

Tonight they would disappear from the world.

Later, after enjoying the evening's special of fresh brook trout, Max and Sara sat across from one another sipping ginger wine. They were wearing white bathrobes, each having showered earlier. Before a small fire, they talked in great length about their interests, purposefully choosing not to worry about their next move — a trip to the research library at Aberdeen University the next morning.

✝✝✝

The phone light at his desk could be indicating only one caller; only two individuals knew of its existence. Its connection to the phone in Rome had three untraceable electronic relay connections, each located on a different continent. As it flickered in front of him Anselm Mugant momentarily thought of the caller on the other end having already confessed to failure in the mission assigned to him— to get Max Train. Mugant's face showed disgust as he picked up the phone.

"New developments, my Lord Cardinal," the voice said arrogantly. "Your quarry has others hunting him down. You're not the only one."

"You of course did not get him, is what you're calling to tell me," Mugant testily replied, choosing not to tell his caller that the others he mentioned seeking Train were doing so at his direction. "You can't get him in fact. Isn't that what's happening? You're impotent, powerless. I call you in to protect humanity from the grossest sacrilege. I call you to end the existence of one man who has neither protection nor safeguards and your only message to me is you haven't killed him yet, that others are competing with you-"

"— what is it that you are seeking my old friend?"

Mugant twitched back in his chair. "It's irrelevant to you.

227

All you need to do is kill the demon and return the items," he replied hastily.

"Why is it others seek this package you so desperately desire?"

"My desire is none of your business."

"But it is, *Eminenza*. Tell me who else seeks this mysterious item you choose not to discuss."

"I will tell you nothing. Remember who I am. Remember, your soul—"

"—you cannot speak to me thus. I gave your quarry the chance for the Kingdom, to take it as he would, if only he would surrender to me the most precious possession of Man," *The Scorpion* coldly said.

Suddenly interrupting his voice were the echoing bells of the Basilica indicating it was 11:30 p.m.

"To the worm did I promise anything he asked but only if I took possession of his Redeemer's flesh. This is now my calling, Cardinal. Do you know who I am?"

Mugant leaned forward, his eyes wincing as he gazed into the darkness. "What do you mean?"

"I reached for your hand and *you* accepted mine."

A powerful wave of tension rolled through Mugant's leaning body. "I am the key to your salvation, Sergio."

"Salvation? I am my own salvation."

"You're to find Train. Your soul will burn in Hell if you fail," the Canadian Cardinal responded to his erstwhile penitent now hired killer."

"Bless me Father, for I have sinned. It has been an eternity since my last confession," the Scorpion loudly ridiculed his listener.

Mugant clenched his fist in anger. "How dare you!"

"I dare as I choose, holy Cardinal."

"But you have failed."

"I never fail!"

"Then get him. And return what I seek. Make me a believer and not one who doubts" the Canadian said.

"I shall bring what you seek, but your price has gone up."

Mugant stood from his chair and walked towards the large window overlooking the Vatican Gardens and the statue of the first Pope. "Bring them to me."

Tearing out of the phone booth in the pub at Leith where his call had been made, *The Scorpion* walked without pause of step into the winds from the North Sea. Their chill quickened his desire to find the hated prey and to possess what he was sure was the treasure of the everlasting hope of so many billions throughout history. Grimly, ignoring everything but the stars above him, he envisioned his quarry shot by a round of his weapon's spent shells, alone, with no companion. Just he and Max Train. Before the moon's glitter on the North Sea water he paused and swore to the four winds that he would make the Cross his own, whatever cost Fate charged of him. Whoever interfered with his mission, for which he now believed he had come into this life, he swore to those masters of the ends of the earth a cruelty upon his adversaries not unlike that suffered by the Nazorean, whose Cross had now become his obsession.

***

Mugant stared into the pages of his Carthusian bible, whose letters showed the richest colors its medieval monks were able to apply to its precious parchment. For the last three hours he had stared at the same page portraying the battle of Archangel Michael and Lucifer, his adversary.

"The Pope has instructed you to appear on Vatican Radio, Cardinal Mugant, within the hour," Father Flavio Rinaldi told the Curial Prefect at 6:30 a.m. as he walked into his green-carpeted Curial office.

"You're supposed to knock before entering, Rinaldi—"

"—not when the Holy Father gives instructions, Cardinal Mugant. The message is given without delay. Vatican Radio has made available 30 minutes for you to address the latest incident of violence against geneticists, an issue over which the Pope is visibly shaken."

"What might be this incident, Father Rinaldi?" Mugant responded, rising from his desk chair. "Do those papers in your hand carry the details?"

"Precisely, *Eminenza*. A lab in Edinburgh, linked to an Edinburgh University geneticist, had considerable damage—"

"— I can read Father Rinaldi, thank you," Mugant responded as he took Rinaldi's sheaf of papers. "I'll be right over to

Vatican Radio. Let Senor Amato know I'll be there in 15 minutes."

Once Father Rinaldi departed, Mugant lifted the special high tech satellite telephone receiver in his office and entered a familiar phone number on its pad, one that would never be traced. "I'll be on the air in thirty minutes," he quickly said before disconnecting the call.

At the 'top of the hour' as is said," Mugant smirked. "Now go, Rinaldi, so I can prepare my response for the Holy Father."

Following the assistant out his office, Mugant turned down the wide Curial office hallway and walked the several minutes it took to reach the Vatican Radio facilities.

"I am ready, Terzo, when you give me the go," Mugant said to the Vatican Radio control room director. The seven fingers Terzo Amato held up in response told Mugant he would be on air in seven minutes.

"We have at this time," the announcer began, "a special message from His Eminence, Cardinal Mugant, for the listeners of Vatican Radio."

***

"The Holy Father expresses his deep regret to the world the latest incident in Edinburgh Scotland where, despite the pleas for calm and control, another genetics lab has been attacked, the perpetrators still unknown. As the spokesman for the Holy Father on this broadcast, I ask all peoples of the world to stand in solidarity with the call for reconciliation the Pontiff has preached. As we look *skyward* to the heavens it is our prayer that the Author of Life answers our petitions *quickly*. We feel *more than a day is too long* for the healing and hope for it to take place in the soul of each believer in His Way. It is up to each of us to *record* our own actions; you may consider them the *transactions* of your life. We ask the people of the world to raise their head *skyward* to Heaven and pray for rightful peace. We ask all world leaders to join with the Pope, to use their influence and governments to bring to an end this scourge to the world."

***

As Mugant went on to discuss tolerance and peace, while giving the perspectives of life the leader of the Church of Rome sought, Terzo Amato softly clapped his hands as Mugant continued his oratory, the Canadian prelate pleased that he had again delivered a message that both the world and the Fifth Crusade heard.

***

"We've had no luck with the Cardinal's mission," McGeorge Previn said to his Brazilian guest seated across from him in his large Georgetown townhouse living room, the thick gold tone curtains draped to the floor blocking out the night darkness. Their ears just heard the live broadcast from Rome being transmitted from the Holy See at 8 a.m., carrying Cardinal Mugant's message. It was 2:00 a.m. in Washington.

Adrianna Corvoso de Sa lit a cigarette, ignoring the fact there were no ashtrays visible in Previn's colonial décor living room. "It's been a week ago that we started this hunt," she said to her black pinstripe suited Georgetown host as she straightened the simple sapphire pin in the lapel of her light blue jacket. "Rome, McGeorge, was not built in a day. Still this is becoming problematic. All of our families' wealth and legacy suddenly may have risk. This badger continues to dig, is this not true? Three meetings in four days, for what?"

"I know, Adrianna. The financial exposure our empires may now have is great. Even greater, may I remind you, is the possible detriment that the faithful may be exposed to if what the Cardinal speaks of is true."

"I believe in this Way, but I must also protect what the Sa family has built," she said dragging hard on the cigarette.

"We all have great risks, Adrianna. It's up to each of us to protect one another, and most of all, in doing so, protect his Eminence and his mission. The possibility of this Max Train blackmailing the Church may exist. How much are we willing to pay?"

"There is no room to allow this badger to voice his mouth."

Previn stood and walked over to the freestanding bar and

poured himself a glass of Remy. Turning to Adrianna, who worriedly lit a second smoke, "Do you want a double?"

"Yes."

"I trust you heard about the genetic lab that got hit in Scotland? Two of my guys were in Edinburgh. They're part of the four that were found dead there," the soft-spoken Previn said as he handed her the double Remy.

"I didn't know you lost all those men."

"I didn't. Two of them were mine. I have no idea where the hell the other two came from," Previn said downing the drink.

"What do you mean 'you don't know'?"

"Just that. They came out of nowhere."

"Who killed them?"

"Damn if I know," Previn said as he made his way back to the Remy bottle. "We have to find this bastard."

"McGeorge, do you think Train is capable? I thought I read that he might have known the scientist that died."

"I don't know what to think. In Zurich we got a tip that a privately chartered plane had left Kloten, which was tracked to a runway at Edinburgh's airport."

"So the scientist our Cardinal wants may have skipped to another city?" Adrianna asked. "If he had a chartered plane—"

"—we don't know if he did have one, Adrianna. I just said there was a plane suddenly chartered at Kloten."

"McGeorge, who the hell would charter a plane in the middle of the night and go to Scotland? Normal people do not subject themselves to that cold, desolate land unless they have specific purpose or intent. If the plane was chartered, it had to carry Train. And he has to have help!"

"Precisely, Adrianna. This is why our effort needs to have more back-up. If we're dealing with a sophisticated force aiding Max Train, our operation needs to increase its resources. We don't know what the capability of his support might be," Previn said wearily.

Leaning forward in his red cloth covered chair across from where de Sa sat, Previn lowered his voice. "Sinn Fein has used some of your arms conduits; get someone there who owes your organization to join in the hunt, Adrianna. Give Sinn Fein a promise of added arms assistance. Their units know the hills and isles of Scotland. Have one of your people give promise of a bounty to hunt down Train. Sinn Fein has many operatives that like the word 'bounty'."

"Of course, Previn. I am thinking the same way, and will make the contact to carry this out."

Previn leaned back in his chair, folding his thin, long hands. "Mugant believes this to be the moment of the ages. To him, the most important event in Christendom, if not the world, is upon us. We don't know if this Cross has the remnants of Christ on it, as he thinks it may. But can we chance it? Think about the possibilities that cloning may bring about."

Adrianna pulled hard on her lit cigarette, bitterly recalling the *private* conversation several months ago with her physician. The child the *patrona* desperately wanted to bear would not be. Her womb was barren. Was her Church too severe on some of her teachings, she pensively thought to herself.

"McGeorge, I'll get to work on what we just discussed. We must protect our resources. I can have some of my Paris contacts check on any possible Train associates that others may have missed. Later today we go to the Avalon manor at the Cardinal's Vatican Radio invitation."

"Yes, I am leaving in about four hours," her bespectacled associate responded. "Perhaps you'll have more information from your field resources," de Sa assertively responded. "We need to quickly determine if our past activities are exposed how we can protect them."

"I agree about the money issue, Adrianna. Hernando Mühlor, too, has questions. But we cannot also lose sight of the matter about Train and the Cross."

*****

It was 2:30 a.m. in Brooklyn when Max Trains' protective friend turned to the Israeli intelligence officer. "Marc, two Mossad were killed in Edinburgh, near the University," he said somberly. "That was our agent in London just then on the phone. A bullet torn Jaguar was found where their bodies are," he also said, "and apparently two Americans were found dead in that auto."

"Things appear peculiar, Rabbi. Our careful attempts to collect information through friendly channels have not been successful. I wonder if there's any information at all. It might be possible that there's none—that our friends are flying blind. But I don't know, something tells me there's something bigger going on and for some reason we're being stonewalled."

"It's almost as if the devil is against Max," the Rabbi responded.

"The devil doesn't shoot rifle bullets from warehouse windows and miss his target," Perlowitz responded. "Someone was shooting down onto the street according to Scotland Yard ballistics tests. A gunpowder residue test from where they think the shots were fired, an old warehouse on that street, indicates the shooting was recent. I'll guess it was from yesterday. It's not the devil who was shooting, Rabbi."

"I wouldn't be too sure," he responded.

Chapter XVI

Rising from another short, deep slumber on another couch, Max previously awoke from the sound of a shower falling from within the hotel room's bathroom. Looking around the spacious parlor brightened by natural light, the calming smell of burnt firewood filled his nostrils. Max noticed the empty wine glasses, and smiled.

Grabbing the bathrobe he had placed on the floor before turning in last night, he walked towards the door, hoping the traditional complementary newspaper would be waiting outside the door. He had home delivery back in Syracuse. Max was a creature of habit.

Opening the door, he was in luck. Both the local *Inverness Courier* and the *London Times* were waiting for him. Stooping to pick up the newspapers, the *Times* on top of the *Courier*, he noticed on the London paper's bottom right hand side of the first page a disturbing headline:

Manhunt for Max Train Intensifies

Quickly looking at the *Courier*, his eyes nearly bulged out in horror. As if the *London Times* article wasn't enough, the *Courier* read:

Scientist Murdered, Four Additional Dead

(*Reuters News Services*)

A mysterious series of killings that has taken place over the last year appearing to target genetic researchers and scientist has struck again, this time in Edinburgh. Dr. Bernard Darcy is the latest victim to have been found dead here in Edinburgh. Dr. Darcy's body was found on the roof deck of a warehouse building across from where police say he kept a private research facility. Darcy's body was shot at close range, according to local law enforcement officials.

As most will recall, six months previously, the Edinburgh Medical and Science Building at the University's campus was destroyed from a devastating explosion initially believed to have been caused from a technical related gas leak, killing nine people. With the addition of Dr. Darcy's tragic death, who was— infamously to some— known for the cloning of Mildred the sheep, the University of Edinburgh has now lost another esteemed researcher in the field of biomolecular advancement and genetics.

In addition to Dr. Darcy, four unidentified individuals were murdered by gunshot, though one body appears to have been run down by a black Jaguar registered to a fictitious company. Inspector James Matthews of Scotland Yard has indicated that there may be additional accomplices at large. "In order for four men to have been shot, there more likely is another killer at bay, as evidenced by the bullet removed from Dr. Darcy's skull. It matched a bullet that was discovered in the heart of one of the victims, who had three additional bullet wounds."

Further speculation is that this hit was conducted by individuals opposing genetic testing and research, bringing a total of fourteen genetics labs or test centers that may have been or are targeted.

Max's body pulsated as he looked down the empty hallway, before turning towards the running shower. *Sara! No!*

Racing towards the bathroom, he opened the door, prepared for anything. Misty steam blocked his vision. "Sara?"

"Max? What are you doing?" A few moments later, Sara, dripping wet and wearing her bathrobe, was reading the two news articles. Saddened by the news of the death of her two colleagues, her resolve grew within to find those responsible for the gangland type killings.

Any thoughts they were safe evaporated in the air upon reading the news of the murders in Scotland. Darcy's death emphasized their belief the science of stem cell research and scientists' lives who were at the forefront of the genetic field were gravely endangered. However, the murders of the two Mossad agents reiterated the possibility the resources and resolve of those seeking them out was great.

Deciding they were not safe staying still, Sara went down to the hotel's gift shop while Max showered. Upon her return, Max changed into traditional Scottish clothing Sara purchased before they quietly left the hotel, "package" in tow. Each was nervously conscious that the malevolent storm following them across Europe had descended onto the land of the Highlanders.

Directing the Volkswagen northeast, they found themselves in the granite medieval town of Aberdeen.

Sara removed a map purchased from the hotel and instructed Max towards the University of Aberdeen's campus. Each knew that running would eventually be futile. The only way left was for them to gain information that may provide them with a clue as to who was behind the violent rage trailing them. Not lost on either person was the face of the madman who previously followed them from Italy.

Finding their way to the sprawling collegian campus, Max parked the vehicle in a parking garage nearby. Exiting the vehicle, he removed the artifacts and placed them in the trunk of the car.

As they walked towards the Queen Mother library, Max sadly reminded himself another friend who had tried to help him was dead. The irony, as Max thought about it, was the massive power the Cross possessed. If the remains left on the wood were those of Jesus, was it possible that he held the body of God? And if so, where were the miracles in his life? And what of the continual violence that chased the Cross? Why should one who held the Cross suffer this violence? The lunatic searching for them seemed not to care so much about Max's existence, but wanted the items 'hidden for nearly 2000 years'.

Pretending to be visiting professors, both Sara and Max made their way into the library and located the Internet computer terminals in the building's basement.

With Max managing the keyboards, the name 'Schemmizzi' and 'Hawkins' was typed into the Google search engine. Immediately three 'hits' appeared on the screen. Max clicked on the first story.

Schemmizzi Donates £50 Million to Edinburgh
(Knight Ridder)
Guillermo Schemmizzi, the Italian media tycoon and Edinburgh University alumnus, today donated £50 million to the University of Edinburgh in order to rebuild the University's Medical and Center complex destroyed in a devastating gas explosion last month. Mr. Schemmizzi, in a statement released by his Press Secretary, said "It is critical for individuals and organizations with the means to facilitate proper science to assist in the worthy causes which assist

mankind. The University was a very important part of my life, and I feel obligated to assist in their critical time of need. The new facilities will have the newest state-of-the-art capacity and concentrate on traditional sciences. If additional moneys are required, I will secure these resources through friendships that I have made over the years."

In addition to Mr. Schemmizzi's endowment, it is speculated that Rupert Hawkins, Mr. Schemmizzi close friend and fellow Edinburgh alumnus may contribute moneys.

Max viewed the next article.

Schemmizzi Pledges Medical Building Will Be Completed Ahead of Time

(*Edinburgh News*)

The University of Edinburgh's hopes to open their new Medical and Science Building was given a great boost yesterday when Mr. Rupert Hawkins, the London financier, pledged a 20 million pound credit line to be immediately made available to the University.

Whispered concerns heard around the University stated that the necessary moneys to procure the necessary medical equipment was turning out slower than expected due to insurance claims tied to a little spoken of investigation regarding the cause of the building's implosion.

Mr. Hawkins made his announcement with his old friend Guillermo Schemmizzi by his side. Schemmizzi previously donated the required £50 million to construct the new building. In a public statement made today by Mr. Hawkins it is evident the needed resources to build a top-notch medical facility are now available. "It is important each individual takes responsibility in life. This University was an instrumental learning ground for me while I was a young adult. I am only too happy to be able to assist at this time. Science and continual exploration necessary to aid those with sicknesses are critical, and we hope the new facility will become a launching pad for ethical, traditional medical research."

The third article read:

Financiers Attend Vatican Meeting On Life

(AP Rome)

A diverse group of the world's leading industrialist met today with members of the Holy See's Scientific Advisory Board to discuss their input on the Vatican's position on gene cell research, embryonic testing, and genetic cloning. Included in the meeting were Guillermo Schemmizzi, Rupert Hawkins, John Williams, Patricia Byson, Lillian Renter, Craig Stinson, Adrianna Corvoso de Sa, Lewis Tomas, Brian Crossing, David Boone, Jordon Pincus, Michael Flanders, Kris Hunter, and Hernando Mühlor.

Each of these individuals is an ardent supporter of His Holiness' position on Life, and has vowed full support to the Pope and his Curia's directives.

Mr. Guillermo Schemmizzi, the wealthiest of the group, said "It is important for each responsible person to think about the ramifications for our actions. His Holiness' position is clear, and I fully support it: life is to be respected. This means all life. We have all worked very hard, and several associates of mine are off to now reflect upon the messages given today," Schemmizzi concluded his remarks before leaving with Mr. Hawkins for a few days in northern Scotland's Isle of Skye, where Mr. Hernando Mühlor owns a sprawling estate complete with a picturesque golf course.

Max looked at Sara. "That's a pretty heavy list of moneys."

"And resources," she pointed out. "Let's see if we can find out any further information on any of these people."

For the next two hours they searched the Internet collecting data on the industrialist mentioned in the third article. Nothing unusual appeared, other than each extremely wealthy individual was civic minded and deeply rooted in their faith towards Christ.

"You know Max, that 225B on the Zurich Investment Services letterhead — I think it's an address —"

"— I thought it was just some numbers."

"Maybe, but remember, it also could be an address. There's an Internet site called Infoseek, it lets you look up addresses from all over the world. I wonder if we should have a look."

"It was 225 something?"

"Let's try 225 Broad Street in London."

"It appears to be a private book seller."

"225 Borghese, Rome looks to be some sort of pastry store."

"Let's try 225 Broadway, New York."

Max suddenly stopped as the name Mühlor Industries appeared. "I'm getting a hunch these guys are connected, aren't you," he asked Sara.

She leaned back in her seat and ran her hands through her long black hair. "Remember, I don't believe in coincidences."

"Do you think they're connected to Zurich Financial Services of Alpha Acquisitions?"

"Worth a look," Sara suggested as Max quickly typed in the name Alpha Acquisitions onto the computer screen.

As expected, nothing appeared.

He then typed in the name Zurich Investment Services. "Where do we start?"

"How about in their corporate filings? We didn't check them in Polymolecular. There's a menu for it on the top left hand side."

Max hit the menu bar. "Public filings?"

"It's a good start."

For the next fifteen minutes Max and Sara began to scan the many files online regarding the financial conglomerates many public filings. Nothing appeared to stand out, nor was any of the names listed in the previous news articles listed anywhere.

"You hungry, Sara?" Max asked.

"Getting there."

"I saw a vending machine. I think it has some chips and candy."

"If they have any cookies —"

They stared in each other in horror.

"Zurich — electronic *cookies!* I bet that's how they found us," Max exclaimed as his eyes darted around the basement of the library.

"We've got to get out of here!" Sara immediately stood. "There, an emergency stairwell."

Without saying a word, Max stood and followed her towards the exit.

Outside, their eyes searching for the familiar deadly face, they ran towards their parked car, unaware that several killers were racing towards Aberdeen, including *The Scorpion.*

Once they pulled out of the parking garage, Sara asked Max where he thought they should go now, believing their presence on the ZIS Internet site gave away their location.

"There seems to be one place at the moment. Get your map out."

"What am I looking for?" Sara asked as Max made his way out of the small city.

"The fellow Mühlor, his place was on The Island of Skye?"

"Yes."

Chapter XVII

Max and Sara fled the University of Aberdeen grounds by way of King Street in their blue Volkswagen. The sun was beginning to recede in the sky after their approximate four hour stay at the library's Internet center, and both knew they had to reach the Isle of Skye soon.

"So we may have a number of apparently very wealthy people, somehow connected to what has happened so far," Sara said to Max as they made a turn on one of the back roads out of Aberdeen.

"Well, if you connect the dots, the Internet cookie markers and the access phone number of the user can tell anyone with the resources and commitment where anyone using an Internet terminal is," Max commented. "This Guillermo Schemmizzi certainly would have the resources to track someone down that way since he owns most of the Internet Servers in Europe. His organization could narrow someone's whereabouts almost instantly once cookie markers were programmed to signal a website user."

"There also just might be some religious connection that might be added evidence some organization is interested in you and the artifacts, Max," Sara said. "Think of what we seem to have found now," she went on, making another turn on the roads out of Aberdeen. "It's likely we've been tracked looking for information on Web sites, and those tracking us have indications we were at the University of Aberdeen. Schemmizzi is very religious. So is Hawkins, according to the news pieces. If I'm right, their financial means could get anyone they wanted. And if they have concern about the artifacts assuming they know about them, it would be either because of their religion or maybe they see the artifacts as a bargaining chip somewhere down the road with other organizations or even governments."

"Well, it's not clear they actually know about the artifacts," Max responded, looking at the green hills starting to multiply. "So far all we know is that in Lake Como we found the names Alpha Acquisitions and Zurich Investment Services. Because we were attacked, we decided to see if there was any connection among the three."

"But you're forgetting about the killer on the roof deck in

Zurich," Sara observed. "He said he wanted the items 'hidden for 2,000 years'. Somebody has to know what you've found."

"Maybe, you're right."

Sara nodded in agreement.

"Zurich Investment Services may have a tie-in to Lake Como. Why else would the ZIS letterhead be there? Maybe Schemmizzi knew about Lake Como and subsequently issued orders that any unusual visits to the ZIS sites be reported to him. That way, if he had any connection to Lake Como that night, he could send individuals to the locations the cookies pointed to where the individuals accessing the ZIS website were."

"There appears no other possible way, but maybe there's no connection to the relics. We still have to find out if there's a connection to the killer, and ZIS or Schemmizzi. It sure looks it."

"Take this road here, Sara. It leads to the bridge to the Isle of Skye," Max said as he placed a flashlight onto the roadmap found in the glove compartment.

"First let me call my uncle. He might be wondering about me, us," Sara said, pulling the Volkswagen over to the side of the road. Both could see in the distance the waters if the North Sea.

"We're leaving Aberdeen and on the way to the Isle of Skye," Sara told her Brooklyn listener. "I know you must have been wondering why we hadn't called earlier, but I wasn't sure how we were being followed. I was worried about the phone lines. That's why I'm making this call through the secure relay system."

Rabbi Kohn listened to the echoing, scrambled transmission of Sara's voice. "I was concerned you may have been wounded in Edinburgh, Sara," the Rabbi quietly answered.

"Wounded in Edinburgh? Why?"

"Two more Mossad are dead, Sara, and with them two Americans, it appears."

"We're aware of this. It's all over the papers."

"Yes, I know. Listen, Sara, whoever did this must be a trained assassin. Scotland Yard has verified shootings out of a third story window on that street—three bullets from it."

"Do you think it's the same guy stalking Max?"

"It's possible. He's everywhere."

"We need to get a profile on him."

"I know we do, but that means bringing Max in. We have no time for that. I think we're close."

"What does he look like?" Rabbi Kohn asked.

Sara described the lunatic from memory. As she did Max added the killer had chameleon like eyes.

Asking for the phone from Sara, Max began. "Marty, this lunatic is fearless. I've seen him five times with my own eyes. I've seen him kill Eileen Gartner and others on the Ponte Cavour in Rome. I'm sure he killed my friend Dr. Pellegrino and the other scientist they found butchered in Bologna. He shot Dr. Seto in the back of the skull. And—"

"—no one in the press has picked this up."

"That's not true, Marty. They think it's me."

The Rabbi chuckled. "This is not good. He knows your face, Max. I'm sure he's going to keep coming after you."

"I'm aware of that. I need to find who he's working for."

"It appears—"

"—Wait! I remember something."

"What is it?"

"On the bridge, no wait, it was in the subway when I gave the bastard the finger he made the Sign of the Cross."

"He did what?"

"You heard me."

"Max what does he look like?"

"He's about 6 foot tall and near 200 pounds. His eyes are blue but sometimes they're not. They've been brown and they've been gray. He's Caucasian but blends in. He's unbelievably strong, Marty. And I think he's possessed. The nut offered me anything in the world for the Cross."

Rabbi Kohn removed his yarmulke and ran his fingers over his balding head. "I don't like the sound of this."

"I'll say. He's following me everywhere."

"Max, this is very concerning. Why would someone relentlessly try to get those artifacts—killing anyone who gets in their way?"

"I don't know, but that guy's not from this world. Marty, it appears there may be information in Skye. Hernando Mühlor, the Argentinean industrialist, has a home there. I think he's connected to Hawkins and Schemmizzi."

"Mühlor? His family were Nazis. His father died before we were able to bring him to justice."

"Well, he's close to those two Edinburgh alumni. Call it an instinct, but we're heading toward Mühlor's home."

"Max, be careful," the Rabbi said. "You know the face of

the killer. If I can somehow get a sketch of him, I might be able to identify him, and that could lead us to those he works for, Max. We're shorthanded in London right now. So the sooner you leave that area, the better."

Max handed the phone back to Sara.

"We are going to Isle of the Skye," Sara told her uncle, taking the phone from Max.

"Be careful, Sara," her overseas relative told her. "Be very careful."

***

The blue Volkswagen reached the Skye Bridge from Kyle of Lochalsh where Sara and Max had driven shortly before the moon's first rays cast their silvery charm upon the North Sea Lochs. The two occupants had a more fervent commitment to find those who may be at the source of all their turmoil the past 10 days. Concentrating on the route ahead of them, the two turned off the Skye Bridge on to a side road. "Let's head towards the old Kyleakin ferry depot and lock the artifacts away in one of the lockers. No one would ever look for them there," Max said to Sara as the seriousness of their search was becoming all too clear to them now.

Grimly parking the car, which they had driven on a one-lane road that serviced traffic in both directions, Sara and Max went to the trunk and removed the packages. In the darkness no one saw them as Max went to a tall locker, inserted a coin, and placed in it the two packages.

"There's two helicopters," Max said as he pointed overhead.

"They're Robinson R44's," Sara said quickly. "It's one of the best made. I could pick them out anywhere. They're easily identifiable by the long narrow cabin extended above the twin turbo engines. Let's see where the two are going. These might be our friends, Max," Sara said with caution. "I need to call Daniel Harmon, the agent in London, and see if there's any intelligence on any choppers over Skye. He will be able to tell us where Hernando Mühlor's residence is."

"We're right off the new Skye Bridge," Max heard Sara say on the phone a few minutes after she called agent Harmon. Grabbing a pencil from the car's glove compartment, Sara started to write out directions given by the agent. "Got it," she responded. "We're about 37 kilometers away, let's just see if we can avoid the one lane roads, Max."

Turning down road after side road, careful to slow down on the bumpy dirt roads made thick by a recent drizzle, Sara drove the Volkswagen ever closer to where she and Max both believed they had to reach if any part of this growing nightmare was to be solved. "There's a small fork at the Derin sign. Bear to the left 7 kilometers. I think that's where Mühlor's estate is," Sara said to Max. "He said it's called 'Avalon Manor'."

They both looked at each other incredulously. Not lost on either was the story of the Holy Grail.

Down the narrow road, protected by the rolling rock torn Cullin mountain range, Sara drove, and stopped once she saw in the far distance a three story granite edifice that stood starkly under a distant moon. Only lighting from a few of the building's rooms gave off any signs of habitation as its quiet surroundings bore neither a word nor sound from anyone.

Eight red ground lights indicated two helicopter landing pads about one hundred meters on the eastern side of the manor.

Hiding the car off the side of the road and under a large pine tree, Sara, with Max, followed a dark path in the estate's forest. The sound of the sea smashing into the granite bluffs was pierced by the howl of dogs nearby.

As they blindly navigated in the eerie darkness suffocating them, the large pine trees forbade the moon's light to shine for them.

With no light in hand they stumbled down the dirt path, each of their hearts racing. They moved into the foreboding unknown, faith their only answer, their only light.

The monstrous hungered sound from Hell echoed across the rock ledged peninsula that was part of Avalon Manor.

Sara grabbed Max's hand. "This place is bizarre."

Moving close to her, he held her hand tightly, "We're going to be fine."

Continuing in the menacing dark forest, the harrowing sound of the dogs getting closer, they soon came upon an open field. Across from the rolling green stood Avalon Manor.

Looking behind the magnificent what appeared to be a two hundred year old castle, they both noticed a dog shed housing savage beasts trying to knock down the iron fence that kept them.

"Can you imagine if those dogs got out?" Sara noted.

"I'd rather not."

"We need to stay low," Sara said as her eyes scanned the manor's grounds. "Are you ready?"

"Towards the side of the house, right?"

With Sara leading the two dashed across the dark high field and towards the manor home, careful of any observing eyes. Reaching the waste disposal area on the side of the manor, they noticed a series of lime brick fashioned steps.

Suddenly Sara saw an armed guard walking the ground less than twenty meters away. Guiding Max, they crouched behind the plastic garbage cans, and waited silently.

The guard approached.

Hell! Sara removed her gun. A whistle pierced the still air, causing the guard to turn towards the wooden dog shed. Max looked at Sara, "Do you think they know we're here?"

"No," she replied now leading Max down to the level sandy ground where a cellar entrance door appeared.

Sara tried to open the heavy steel door. It wouldn't move. She looked at Max.

"There's got to be another way," he commented.

The grueling sound of the dogs howling louder as they tried to break free from the prison that bound them became more noticeable. These were not the pets of a sane man.

Sara and Max hugged the cold side of the building, and found stairs leading to the first floor.

Taking each step slowly, Sara halfway up the flight could see two armed guards who appeared to be talking with one another. Up the stairwell and to her left Sara noticed a window partially opened to an unlit room.

The two men began walking towards the middle entrance of the building, away from where Sara and Max hid.

Seeing the two men had walked further away, they climbed four steps and reached the parlor floor level. To their surprise the windowpane had been broken. Shattered glass was on the ground nearby. With gun ready Sara slowly pushed up the windowsill, ready for anything, while Max watched for anyone close by. The window opened silently and Sara, getting on the windowsill, pulled herself into the dark room. Max followed.

"We're in," Sara whispered to Max, the offensive smell of lye filling their nostrils. Droplets of sweat began to form around

Sara's temple. The darkness of the room made it impossible to see if anyone else was there. Her gun aimed by her side, she peered into the blackness.

Max, his hands reaching out in front of him, found the door-knob. "Found it."

The door opened to what appeared to be a long unlit corridor extending on to the main floor. They listened carefully.

Wondering about the broken window, Sara guided Max forward. Suddenly they heard a door to a room close by quietly being shut. Max saw Sara put her finger to her lips signaling he had to be absolutely quiet. Gun ready, she took his arm momentarily as a silent message to him to follow behind her.

Prepared to attack, Max moved protectively towards Sara's side.

Hand on the wall as they continued down the corridor Sara, not knowing whether there was another individual with them now, came to another door. Quietly trying the doorknob, she opened the door to what appeared to be a storeroom of sorts. A black light overhead made it possible to see. Max closed the door behind them, when suddenly a distorted voice resonated through the room

"We know, Cardinal, and we are in agreement."

Sara looked around the room for the source of the voice.

"We can lose tens of billions if this thing gets out of control."

Suddenly Sara pointed to two air grates above them. "That's where the sounds are from," she said.

"Can't hear everything exactly," Max said.

Seven individuals in a stately room, walls the unique color of Wedgwood blue, on the floor immediately above Max and Sara, were seated around a gleaming mahogany table. Three floors, each with three meter high ceilings, each of its 31 rooms a different color, exquisitely woven Iranian carpets to complement the color of each room, chandeliers of Rosenthal crystal that painted their room and floor lighting into many shimmering hues bespoke the elegance of the Mühlor estate. Handcrafted wooden banisters for each stairwell, lavatories of black marble and gold plated faucetry, and a wine cellar with the rarest vintages completed the manor's décor.

"We are all subject to unbelievable recriminations if whoever is helping your fugitive, Cardinal, gets information on you and us. All the past dealings, all the back room deals and money laundering—not to mention the money from arms trafficking—it all could be exposed! Then what? Our families' reputations, *Eminenza*, will be ripped apart if what we have done to help *you* ever gets out."

"The finances are covered, Hawkins," the black suited participant began as his fingers glided over his facial scar. "Do you think I do not know how to protect my own assets and reputation? Don't be a fool! I've protected each and every one of you and your precious families for a long time now. In diverting records to not only the Vatican Bank from Zurich Investment Services, but in also creating subsidiary shell companies in undisclosed locations around the world, I can assure you each of your histories is safe—with me. Don't test me; I'm in no mood. Remember I have these records at my sole disposal. No one shall find out about any indiscretions—unless I reveal them...or something happens to me."

"We're not concerned about you, Cardinal. We're worried about his digging into Alpha and Como Ventures," Previn said.

"I said we're all safe. That part of our discussion is now over. There will be no more discussion on financial exposure. There's no need."

On the floor below the two silent listeners stared at each other.

"We are here to review the mission of *Life* on which we embarked," the Canadian Curia Prefect began.

"*Eminenza*, it is imperative we discuss the teachings on this matter of gene manipulation," the raven hair woman sitting to the right of Rupert Hawkins said. "We are hearing the Pope on a different tone than you."

The Cardinal looked at the female Brazilian supporter intently. "Now, you support human cloning?" Mugant glared.

"Of course not, but surely the Church does not seek to prevent the healing of a life, say, of one with pancreatic cancer, if geneticists can do this, Your Eminence. Or perhaps, even provide fertility to a woman who is barren, Cardinal. For sure, if the means are available to man, should we not explore them to better our condition?"

"The ends do not justify the means. We are given sufferings to bear, and we do so in His Name. Still, there is a place for science, but not man's misguided use of scientific creation in the name of healing. This is unacceptable! Do we want scientists to create embryos in their labs, harvest the living cells as if they were fruits and berries, and then suck the life dry—because that's what they'll do when they kill the embryos! All so a pancreatic duct someday may be healed? Do we want to take away a human life, which science has begun in the lab, to maybe find out a new gene variation that gives you 'blue eyes and blonde hair' to order, Adrianna? There are other ways to cure disease, not just by genetic manipulation. Science is becoming lazy. They are looking for the quick way while dismissing His Way! No, the facilities of those who work in the field of manipulation, those evil genetic labs, must continue to be destroyed!"

"And the woman who cannot bear a child?"

"If it's God's Way for those who cannot bear the fruit of life on their own, they are given the deepest reward for God has chosen them to care for those children who cannot care for themselves. And as you know, Adrianna, there are too many orphaned children in God's world. What is the true difference of loving a needed child left alone to face the hardships Satan has placed in this world and a child born from a watchful mother's womb? I'll tell you—nothing. All children must be protected. For those who bear no fruit there is an orchard of uncared for children for them to love."

"Cardinal, you obviously misstate my position. Each woman unable to bear a child sees the means to now possibly correct that barrenness. Are we to simply tell the woman she cannot hope ever to have her condition corrected? It has nothing to do with loving the innocent who are defenseless."

Max Train and Sara stared at each other incredulously. "I can't believe what I am hearing, Max," Sara said.

"How many labs were destroyed?" Max whispered.

"Your Eminence, we follow and believe that human life is sacred," the Aryan owner of the Avalon Manor joined in. "Adrianna raises a point with which we are all grappling. What of the benefits of cancer cures by way of geneticists and their work on cancer markers? If they can eliminate the strand that causes the mistake to occur where cells just multiply out of control—"

"— not by experimentation on the human person," came the answer.

"This is the first meeting you've attended," Guillermo Schemmizzi replied, looking at the portly middle-aged speaker.

"I am here because of the Pope's departure to New York tomorrow, and came at the request of His Eminence to brief all of you on what our outlook is to be," replied the stranger.

"The ends do not justify the means, members of the Fifth

Crusade," the Canadian clergyman began, interrupting the speaker. "This is why we're here. We have an urgent mission, to which you have all *sworn fealty*, to stop the Mengele-like experimentation on the human person. Hitler cannot rise again, my people. Are we not all agreed?" His eyes darted toward Mühlor.

"The question, Your Eminence, is, Is this Mengele or is this legitimate science which, controlled within the bounds of ethics, can morally aid man?"

"The Church must decide that, Hernando. Our moral theologians and our own Scientific Advisory Board have been addressing the matter, and the Church forbids any experimentation."

"Not quite so, Eminence. Only so long as human life is not destroyed in the process the scientists seeking to understand the genetic mysteries may proceed. Would not the Pope in his bout with prostrate cancer, have possibly benefited from genetic studies which you seem to oppose?"

"You must not speak of His Holiness in such a manner," Mugant glared in reply. "There are those who will always dare His Way. They already have cloned human organs! The company— thank Heavens it's gone from this earth—that was in Boston—they intended to do more. So too did the American and the Italian geneticists. But they were stopped in time. We would not have been in this grave situation if it were not for Max Train. He is the reckless scientist who developed the genetic coding map that allowed for all this scientific manipulation to be possible. He too, pursues scientific creation—life's destruction!"

"And he is godless," added the outsider.

"Right now, dear people, this medical advancement is mostly theory," the black suited Cardinal replied, sitting up hard against his high back mahogany chair. "What is not theory is the fanatic, Max Train, is loose with the Cross of Christ. And he seeks to clone the Body of God!"

All eyes looked at the visitor. "This is true."

Silence fell on the room. One floor below, Max and Sara looked at each other. "My God, they think I'm going to use the Cross and re-create Christ," Max Train said to Sara.

"We must search this man out, who is up to this moment still free to do with what I know he will threaten the Church, not to mention each of you. Does anyone here want that?" the Cardinal shouted, looking at the four seated before him. "Two of you here have already failed in your attempts to get him, isn't that right Guillermo? McGeorge? What sort of stooges did you use when you went after Train? First Zurich, then Edinburgh," Mugant sneered.

A sinister smile swept across the face of another unknown visitor listening intently from a different air duct.

"We did not come here to have a class on ethics, but to state to each other the actions to be taken to get this Max Train. He was only hours away from here yesterday and for all we know he may still be in Edinburgh."

"So this has to be the ringleader of the hunt on me," Max said to Sara, unaware of the identity of this Cardinal. "You were right. There is a group—a rich group—lined up against me. They think I want to use the Cross to get Jesus' remains on the Cross cloned. They're insane. I never even thought of that. Does this man think I'm nuts, too?"

Sara looked at Max. "Let me see if I can get up to the next floor without being seen and look around. Maybe I can identify him."

Max looked at Sara, with fear in his eyes. "Stay in this room. If anything happens, flee out the window and reverse your steps back to the car."

"We need to know who that is up there. I'm only going to the next floor momentarily to get a look at him. Then we can get out of here. Just stay here and wait for me."

Sara left the room, re-entering the unlit corridor. A sudden feeling that someone else might be in the same corridor area came over her. She looked intently down the corridor and saw nothing. Satisfied, she moved towards the corridor's end and found a door. It opened to a carpeted stairwell that Sara cautiously ascended.

Max, meanwhile, listened to the leader of this group continue his pedantic talk about the evils of human cloning—something Max knew every genetic scientist in the world strongly opposed. They, just like himself, believed eventually science's ability to remove harmful genetic strains that caused unnecessary illness would soon be realized. The hopeful dream of a cancer free, Muscular Dystrophy free, AIDS free, world was a possibility.

Reaching the top step, Sara opened the door a crack, and saw a room with two shut mahogany doors. Underneath the doors she could see a crack of light. "Maybe this is where the sounds are coming from," she said to herself.

Opening the steel door halfway, Sara looked up and down the large floor. Seeing no one, she crossed the hallway adjoining the steps and moved towards the room where the voices were emanating,

Suddenly she felt a hard object pushing against her back. "Don't turn around. Just walk real slow, or you are dead, Miss," the voice said to her.

Sara stopped.

"I said move or I'll kill you right here."

Sara began moving forward, as she heard like the trigger of a pistol.

"Just walk slowly, Miss."

Sara and her assailant walked about fifteen steps.

"Open up," the assailant's voice said as they got to the two doors. "Do anything Miss, and I will kill you," he said placing the pistol at the back of her head.

"Look what the cat dragged in," the visiting guest said to the stunned onlookers in the room. "I don't think she has an invitation like I do," he laughed.

Down the end of the hallway, at the foot of the stairs Sara had only minutes prior left, stood another uninvited visitor. *So these are Mugant's buddies, and I'm sure I know who that bitch is. Train must be close by, and so must my treasures.*

The Confessor's killer listened to the sound of the voices above. "Who are you?" demanded Mühlor.

Sara looked harshly at the thinning blond hair Argentinean. "I was lost and tried to find someone. That fat idiot over there put a gun to my head," she said angrily.

"Lost out here? That's hard to believe my dear."

"That's the truth."

Mugant looked at his cherubic guest. "Make sure you keep that by her head," he said referring to the gun. Slowly rising from his chair, he menacingly moved towards the woman. "I don't believe in coincidences," he whispered as his hand began to search the woman's side. His hand suddenly felt what he was looking for. "See my love," he hissed as he removed the small 9mm Sara tried to conceal. "You were not lost. You're the woman that abets the bastard." Raising the gun and shoving the steel into her spine, Mugant glided underneath the extended arm of his invited guest who was holding the other gun barrel to the back of Sara's skull.

The members of the Fifth Crusade watched in awe as

Mugant became their protector in front of their very eyes.

"I will ask you one last time. Who are you?"

Sara stood defiantly and said nothing.

Without pause Mugant grabbed the back of her long black hair and with all his strength yanked the woman down to the floor. In his hand the long strands of black silk hair. "Where is he?" he yelled as the woman, hitting the floor screamed in pain. The brutal display was not lost on anyone.

Max clenched his teeth as he heard Sara's outcry. His body tightened. "Oh God," he said as he stood.

Close by Mugant's killer snickered in appreciation of his puppet's use of violence.

Mugant stared at the woman, the deadly gun pointed right at her. "Hernando, you need to secure this place. Previn, where are those damn guards of yours?"

Neither replied.

"Do I have to do everything myself? Someone get the guards."

"You're a murderer," Sara screamed underneath his feet. "You're all murderers, you're all a bunch of lunatics," she continued, hoping that her moment she was trying to buy would not be lost on Max.

"What do you know? If you don't tell me I have no problem killing you," His Eminence said.

"I know if I were you I would get the hell out of here. You think you're so righteous, but did you ever bother listening to yourself? You're like a *Brooklyn street thug*. I would go. You need help," Sara defiantly yelled.

Max was up and moving towards the exit window, fully understanding what Sara was hinting.

The gun-wielding visitor pulled her up by her hair, the deadly firearm waving in her face. "Listen Miss, we're not playing around here. You'll be able to walk free if you let us know where Max is."

Max suddenly stopped, trying to hear the threatening voice.

Sara looked at the man coolly. "I know what you want, but you'll never get it. It's gone. Trust me, I don't care if you kill me but you will never find him and you will never find those artifacts."

The intensity in the room magnified as it became clear to everyone their exposure was great. Somehow Max Train, an unexpected adversary, was now hunting them. The woman's presence at the Avalon Manor proved it.

Mugant looked at each of his colleagues, then strode to the woman. "You may be more useful alive than dead, you bitch," he hissed, then suddenly fired a bullet into the woman's right leg.

As Sara dropped to the floor, the reverberating sound of the bullet broke the dense silence in the house and its environs. The howling of the dogs going wild covered the landscape as the guards patrolling the grounds raced towards the house.

"You bastard," Sara whispered.

"Previn, get those copters ready. Who knows who else may be around?"

McGeorge Previn stood up and raced down the stairs not known that he just raced by the tormentor from Hell.

Max had heard the Preacher's directive that Sara was valuable more alive than dead. The only way, if there was a way, to save her life was for him to get out of Skye. *But how?*

"I think you should tape her hands and legs together, and tape her mouth as well. We'll have plenty of opportunity to run electric charges through her body. I'm sure she'll have no problem telling us what we need to know then," Adrianna said aloud as her deep brown eyes focused on Sara.

Quickly looking down at his immobilized hostage bleeding on the floor, Mugant turned towards his female guest. "Leave it to a Corvoso de Sa to think of such a thing. Family traits are never lost."

Two armed guards rushed the room up from the stairs, their assault rifles ready. Mugant raised his hand towards them. "Neither of you are obviously proficient at what you're hired to do. Let's see if you can get this one right: wrap her up with electrical tape and then bring her to the helicopter. There's also a possibility that she wasn't alone. Fan this place out and find any one else. I don't need to tell you what will be done if you fail."

Outside, under fast moving clouds intermittently blocking the moon's light, Max ran for his life.

Chapter XVIII

Max's heart pounded as he tried to recover from his all-out sprint across the open fields, and away from the granite stone manor home of Hernando Mühlor.

As he gasped for breath the bright stars overhead unfortunately illuminated the majestic, challenging summit ridges of the Cullin of Skye. Looking out over the breathtaking craggy Hebride Mountains, he felt the winds howling from the Atlantic Ocean sweep across his determined face. Muscles pulsating, he searched for a place to hide from the lunatics inside the manor home. Moving towards the high bluff, he thought to himself how bizarre it was that the concept of global capitalism at the highest possible level found its way to the Gaelic-bound shores of the Hebridean Islands.

The departing sound of the two helicopters' blades cutting through the chilling night minutes ago with Sara on board was replaced by the horrifying vicious sounds of chained dogs desperately trying to free themselves from their handlers. From the rocky heights far above the pounding ocean from where he stood, Max noticed a small sweeping road steeply dropping to a fiord-like coastal reach. Turning to the brightly lit manor nearly a kilometer away, he observed four high-tech hand-held floodlights carried by menacing guards previously instructed to kill him on sight. They began to spread out over the open grass fields in front of him.

He moved towards the rocky cliff. The harsh sound of the ocean's turbulent waves relentlessly basted the fortress-like granite bluff formed millions of years ago from a massive volcanic explosion off Iceland.

As he peered down the dark winding road towards the fiord below, Max's only thoughts were on his survival. If he had any chance of saving Sara's life, he needed to reclaim the desperately wanted artifacts and somehow get off the island.

The approach of the mad barking dogs came closer. So too did the floodlights. Max looked down once again towards the fiord, before looking back up to realize the four armed guards still holding onto their deadly canines essentially formed a deadly perimeter around him.

Unexpectedly, a low flying plane that, unknown to Max, departed from the ancestral homeland of the Clan MacLeod, Dronish, interrupted his momentary trance. Max crouched to the cold ground, hoping the powerful search light overhead would not detect him.

Moving on all fours, he made his way towards the winding road leading to the unknown rocks below, the noise of the revolving blades fading, but not the vicious growl of the approaching attack dogs that appeared to be unleashed from their masters.

As strong winds hit his face, Max ran down the road.

In front of him was a small wooden fishing boat. It was tied to a dock protected from the threatening waters by a rock sea wall. The vessel was no longer than 7 meters long. The chipped blue paint and beaten weathered boards indicated it had survived many brutal storms.

Max darted for it.

Removing two ropes that held the vessel to the dock, he jumped onboard.

Above him, the barking dogs came closer. "I think he's over here," screamed a voice.

Crap! The rolling waves shook the boat as Max looked for the engine keys. *Where are they?*

The always hungry dogs, massive expertly trained man-trailing bloodhounds, had picked up his scent and barked wildly, their indefatigable turbid determination now on the top of the road leading down to the small boat.

He noticed the engine key was in the ignition. He turned it. Nothing happened.

Beads of sweat began to fall down his brow as Max noticed a demon-like reddish hair bloodhound bolting down the dirt road.

He turned the key again. "Work!" Max screamed.

The engine's motor suddenly stirred.

"He's down there!" a voice roared from above.

"Let's go," Max said as a bullet echoed above him. "Come on!" he screamed as the vessel moved off the dock."

Hitting the throttle all the way forward, Max navigated his way around the marginal sea wall, and towards the open sea. As he did, he noticed the powerful bloodhound, determined for the catch, racing alongside the boat, waiting for him near the sea wall Max would inevitably have to pass. *Damn!*

A series of bullets blanketed the waters around him, two of

which hit the trudging vessel desperately trying to escape.

Another bloodthirsty hound raced down the dirt road.

The distance between the sea wall and the waterway the vessel would travel through was less than a meter and a half.

The disturbed bloodhound baring his vicious sharp teeth was waiting on the rocks for Max to pass. It unleashed a howl from Hell.

Lining up the boat so it would pass through the small channel, Max moved starboard, eyeing the savage beast. It was a body length away.

The boat slowly moved towards the sea.

A bullet caromed off the boat deck, just missing Max.

The one hundred thirty pound beast crouched, ready to attack. Saliva foamed from its snarling mouth.

Max raised his hands towards his chest.

Another bullet flew past his head.

The dog barked viciously, coming closer. His loathing eyes locked on Max.

Max's muscles tensed as the boat began to rock heavily. In the corner of his eye, he saw the second hound charging towards the boat.

Less space now divided them.

A meter now separated them.

Arm's distance.

The bloodthirsty hound leaped towards Max.

Max sprang forward, his clenched hands lifted in front of his chest.

Razor sharp teeth lunged towards him!

Using every remaining part of energy he had, Max lunged towards the door in midair, colliding with the airborne beast that was desperately gnawing at him.

The brutal force Max held inside him descended onto the hound, hitting it like a cement truck. It fell into the water.

The boat moved forward, less than a meter from breaking free.

The second hound raced around onto the sea wall.

Another bullet hit the boat, right by the throttle, tearing it off its hinges, and rendering it useless.

Max prepared himself for the second hound. He let out an ear-piercing growl.

Suddenly, the charging dog froze in its tracks, as the vessel made its way out of the enclosed sea wall and into black malevolent ocean waters, the engine's throttle permanently turned towards "full".

As the boat stirred forward, Max moved under the bullet-torn canvas tarp and laid on his stomach as more bullets tore up the wooden craft.

Soon he was out of range of the bullets and stirring the nimble boat through the crested waters of the North Sea west towards the two Caledonian islands of Uist.

Looking out towards the fading murky shadows of the coastline, Max wondered how much fuel remained.

The "wanted fugitive" looked towards the brightly lit sky, feeling an odd sense of empowerment that he survived another attack, yet gravely sullen because of Sara's capture. For the first time he knew the faces of several of his stalkers. Knowledge provided strength. Caring built resolve. Max had both.

His anxiety was far from over. He was now a walking threat filled with information on the activities of those who visited the remote estate of Hernando Mühlor. Max was no fool. Without question a flotilla of gun-wielding boats would soon search the waters for him. Though he didn't know for sure, Max did not notice any additional docks alongside the granite bluffs by Mühlor's fortress. If anything, the boats would come from the shoreline of Skye. Something he intended to stay away from.

Sara, his protector, was gone, but Max believed she wasn't dead. Why else would they have taken her off the island? But where did they take her?

The Cross he desperately had wanted to rid himself of was now something he needed to reclaim. Sara's life likely depended on it. The problem was how did he get back into the town of Kyleleakin — if he even got that far?

Out at sea for nearly thirty minutes, a single engine plane from out of nowhere raced overhead and towards the shoreline.

Max spun around to see it. To his dismay he noticed floodlights from three racing boats in the distance coming closer.

The plane turned, lowering its nose towards the sea, coming directly towards him.

Max moved towards the right side of the craft.

The plane slowed, traveling at less than seven meters off the water, passed him again before turning once again.

Max noticed it had water landing gear. His eyes immediately focused on the charging boats now only several hundred meters away.

The plane headed directly back towards him, its nose directly behind the boat. Max hit the floor waiting for gunfire to shred apart the wooden craft.

Suddenly, he heard a loud splash as the plane's landing gear tore into the strong currents of the dangerous sea.

Max stood up and realized the pilot was waving towards him.

"I'm a friend of the Rabbi!" screamed the male pilot.

Good God! How did you know where I am?

"Shut your throttle!" screamed the pilot.

"I can't," replied Max over the loud engine and swirling propeller.

"You have to jump!"

Max turned towards the menacing boats closing on them. He nodded, then looked at the waters below him. Gazing at the electronic gear on the boat, he realized he was moving at fifteen knots.

"You know what you're doing?"

"Jump! There's no time!"

Max looked up to the North Star, then leaped into the dark cold waters.

The pilot directed the seaplane towards him, when suddenly a rocket grenade launched from one of the approaching boats exploded near the aircraft.

"Hurry!" screamed the pilot as Max swam towards him.

A moment later Max moved his body onto the fiberglass water skis. The pilot lifted him into the plane as he revved the engine propelling the plane through the water. Max pulled himself into the passenger seat as the plane began to ascend into the sky, and away from the killers.

Another rocket grenade exploded to the pilot's left, shaking the plane as it climbed one hundred meters.

The pilot dove towards the water. "It's an old trick I learned," he said to his dripping wet passenger. "Hold on!"

Moments later, they were far enough from the rocket grenades range.

"Max, I'm Daniel Harmon. Sara's contact from London. I imagine she was taken."

"How do you know that?"

"We intercepted a communication from one of the helicopters. They spoke about the 'girl' but weren't sure if you were on the
island with her."

"Well, they do know now."

"That's for sure."

"Did they say where they were taking her?"

"No."

***

A tall muscular figure looked out the window of a dark second floor
bedroom located in the manor home. Outside, the majority of the
guards on land responsible for securing the estate were hurrying
back to the granite home. Judging from their distance, they were
five minutes away from the house. Underneath him laid a bullet
infested dead body of a guard.

He walked downstairs, gun in hand, and recognized a loud
voice speaking on the telephone.

Nearing the caller, he heard the voice specifically state to
the person on the telephone he was speaking to the "helicopters
would land outside of Manchester, where a private plane will take
them to America."

The Scorpion grinned. The previously unknown group of
industrialists his Confessor blackmailed into subservience would
soon become his own slaves. It was evident Max Train escaped the
guards Mugant's 'Crusaders' had assembled. The scientist's disappearance, assisted by a seaplane according to the guard on the
phone, would only strengthen Mugant's desperate need for his services.

The night was not a complete loss, far from it, he thought to
himself. Though the Cross once again escaped him, the discovery
of the clandestine existence of the now vulnerable Crusaders made
up for his missed chance.

Max Train would have to be dealt with, and he intended that
without pause. Max Train could identify him. Max Train had seen
him too many times. Where the Cross bearer had traveled to for the
moment, and who assisted him were not known, but it didn't matter. That information might be attainable; after all, he was with
great resources. He had operated in the United Kingdom in the past
and never let loose his grip on the important hands who once sought

261

his services. Besides, there were six extremely influential individuals with everything to lose if Train was not found.

A plan was clearly forming in his mind that would bring him the artifacts of Jesus he desperately sought.

Hearing the guard hang up the phone, *The Scorpion* entered the small room filled with video monitors and other security equipment. The seated guard was looking at the six monitors, his back turned towards the silent intruder.

Without remorse, he lifted his gun and fired a slug into the unsuspecting man's skull.

Moving to the blood splattered desk, he inspected the desk for any papers or notes. There were none of any use. Still, the information gained tonight was significant.

Walking into the kitchen, he noticed a rear entrance used for deliveries. He exited the door and disappeared into the nearby woods.

***

Ten miles off of the coastal city of Derry, located in Northern Ireland, Max watched from the deck of an old tug boat as the Cessna sea plane purposefully sank into the deep coastal waters off the war savaged land where Christians and Protestants fought in the name of Christ and land for centuries.

He had spoken moments ago to Rabbi Kohn via a secured satellite connection and informed him of what occurred in Scotland. Max went over with him who the identifiable players were, and made special note to mention they appeared very interested in the Pope's arrival in New York where he was to speak about the issues of cloning and stem cell research.

The disheartened Rabbi, saddened by the news of his niece's capture told Max his efforts thus far to find information regarding the news leaks had come up empty. The news of Schemmizzi's involvement made great sense to him. However, the stonewalling still occurring with the American government didn't. Previn's involvement made sense, but how could he prove it?

As the boat pitched in the dark waters, he reflected on what occurred less than two hours ago. A flood of questions besieged him. Who was the Cardinal who so easily controlled the five industrialists? Why would the Holy See believe Max intended to clone

Christ? How did they find out about the discovery in Jerusalem in the first place? It was evident the one who professed the Ways of Jesus to the others attending the meeting tonight acted in manners other than what the Nazorean taught. Was this way the actual Way of the Cross? After all, unnecessary murder followed it every-where.

What was it the others in attendance spoke of when they referred to their financial exposure? Past actions of extortion, money laundering, concealed bank accounts, and mirrored financial records all with a long history were evident, but to what extent? What was the denominator that tied them all together? And who was the unidentified person who spoke with familiarity about genetics?

Where did they go, and what were they intending to do with Sara? It was evident that the Pope's highly expected arrival in America where he would speak in front of the United Nations was at the forefront of Sara's abductors' minds. But would they take her there? Anything seemed possible, including that.

Most of all how would he save the life of the soft-spoken woman who continually put her own life on the line to protect his?

"Max, we're sending someone back to Kyleleakin to pick up your items," said Daniel Harmon wearily.

"I wonder if they're still there," Max questioned.

"Probably. It's an hour drive from Kyle to where you were. They probably didn't react that quickly."

"I hope so," he replied, aware that it saved Sara's life, he needed a tangible negotiating tool: the True Cross. What he had been witness to would not be believed by anyone, especially since he was a fugitive wanted for murder on three separate continents. His only hope to save Sara was direct contact with her abductors. Max was tired of losing people he was close to. "Any idea where those helicopters went?"

"Not yet, but with a little time and some luck we might," the Mossad agent replied.

"What do you mean?"

Daniel Harmon pointed towards the sky. "Photographs."

Max realized the Israeli government had several satellites orbiting the earth, and also had access to the American satellites. "I hope it works," he said unenthusiastically.

"Me too. Sara is important to us."

Max nodded as he took a deep breath. "What's next?"

"Once we get into Derry, you and I will take a private flight over to Iceland. From there we'll travel to Toronto, and figure out the safest way to get into New York."

Max leaned over the side of the boat and peered into the dark waters. "I hope she's not hurt."

Chapter XIX

The roaring sound of the breathtaking Niagara Waterfalls cascading over the rocky edge could be heard from nearly a mile away. Mother Nature's natural border that separated part of Canada and The United States was one of the world's greatest natural sites. The approaching afternoon sun, its rays bouncing off the sparkling waters, and reflecting onto the assortment of pine trees on the nearby shores assisted in making the setting a wonder for the eye to behold. It also presented an opportunity for undetectable access into either country, even now, in a time when both nations heightened their border security.

Dressed in casual attire, knapsack in tow, and a camera dangling from his neck, Max smiled as he handed the Canadian ferry operator his sightseeing ticket. Behind him, two older women from the Midwest spoke about how impressive the casinos were on the Canadian side of the Falls, and how they actually won money playing the slot machines the other night. Judging from their loud conversation, it was obvious they were staying at the more accommodating Canadian side of the Falls. Daniel Harmon, Max's newest traveling companion, stood nearby in the crowded line of passengers eager to take the tourist boat ride under the Falls.

Taking the green poncho the ferry operator handed him, Max immediately went to the top level of the ferry, as planned, and took several pictures of the spectacular landscape. Mindful of those around him, he didn't notice anything strange, including the all too familiar face of the killer hunting him. He eyed the Mossad agent standing nearby, indicating everything appeared to be safe.

After five minutes, the crowded boat, called *The Knickerbocker*, began to move into the choppy waters towards the imposing cascading waterfalls.

The dangerous escape on the North Sea seemed as if it were only moments ago, though it had been nearly fifteen hours since the sea plane rescued Max from his enemies. From Ireland, Max traveled by private plane with the quite Mussed agent to Iceland, refueled, and then continued onto Toronto. After several hours, a private car drove them two hours to the Canadian side of the famous tourist destination, where 'Michael Landers', holding a new passport, and Daniel Harmon would embark on their sightseeing excursion.

His clandestine entrance into the States appeared to be going as planned; however, Max knew he was traveling into dangerous unknowns. Paramount to Max's concern was the fact he really wasn't sure if Sara was going to be taken to America by the mysterious Cardinal and the international capitalist who supported him. Or, if his plan to free his protector would actually work. There was no doubts in Max's mind that if he was captured by any police, those who were in attendance at the Avalon Manor would arrange for his immediate death. Sara's freedom, more than anything, depended on him staying alive.

Max looked south, at the Niagara Falls' Rainbow Bridge, and noticed the gray car he traveled in with Harman carrying the "package" retrieved earlier by one of Harman's associates heading towards the New York State border as expected.

"Okay," he mumbled to himself, before turning his focus on to the roaring waters ahead.

As the boat moved closer to the powerful falls, spraying everyone on the waking boat, Max's plan became clear. He had the Cross, and knew who some of Sara's abductors were. They were now vulnerable, and Max believed each of them knew it.

The ferry began to approach the docks on the New York border. Max walked down to the cabin deck, soon followed by Harmon. Ten minutes later, both men, accompanied by twenty other tourists, exited the boat on American grounds.

The Immigration guard looked at the passport of Michael Landers, and asked him if he was enjoying the day.

"I have a bunch of great photos," the friendly scientist told the casual official, as he was handed back his passport.

Following the previously arranged plan, Max walked towards the gray sedan waiting nearby. Harmon followed moments behind.

Once in the city of Buffalo, Max directed their driver to pull into an approaching convenience store. There, he purchased a calling card and immediately went to a pay phone located in the parking lot.

He removed a sheet of paper containing an overseas telephone number and dialed it, careful to correctly enter the pin code for the calling card.

"Schemmizzi Entertainment," a switchboard operator said

in Italian.

"Senor Schemmizzi," Max asked in English before he was placed through to the Chairman of the massive media and telecom conglomerate.

"Senor Schemmizzi's office, this is Carla Giorno speaking," a middle age woman answered.

"Yes, Guillermo Schemmizzi, please," Max answered.

"Mr. Schemmizzi is unavailable. May I help you?"

"I would like to leave a very important message for Mr. Schemmizzi. One he is urgently expecting."

"Oh?" asked the assistant. "Yes?"

"Can you please let Guillermo know his friend from the Highlands whom he missed seeing yesterday in Scotland called? Let him know I have several personal packages in my possession that he was interested in. Let him know I said it was very thoughtful for him to pick up my package, too, and I called personally to thank him. But tell him to please make sure not to drop the item he picked up of mine. You know how Guillermo is, dropping things all the time," Max said with a laugh.

"Oh, yes. I'm sorry, I didn't catch your name?"

"It's Cross . . . Cross Highlander."

"Oh, and you're a friend of Mr. Schemmizzi?"

"Of course! We go back to Edinburgh. Carla, would you please do me a favor, as I am about to catch a plane. Tell Guillermo that I'll call back in six hours. I'm sure that if you reach him by then, he'll have you patch my call to wherever he may be. But please let him know that I called. He asked me to contact him today, and I promised I would. And don't forget about the packages."

"I expect to hear from Mr. Schemmizzi in three hours, Mr. Highlander. I'll let him know."

"Please call me Cross."

"Oh, okay Cross."

"Carla, is he in Rome?"

"No, he's traveling."

"Well, thank you Carla, it was a pleasure speaking with you," Max said as he hung up the phone.

Entering the rear seat of the car, Max looked at Harmon. "Okay, let's go. We're eight hours away."

***

"What's this?"

"The papers came by courier just now, Mr. Previn."

"Fine, Lydia. Close the door on your way out."

Rising from his deep high back black leather chair, Previn walked towards the three windows to his left in his opulent cedar wood lined suite that overlooked Washington's K Street Northwest. "Power Avenue" was its name to those insiders living in the Capitol.

McGeorge Previn was the quintessential insider.

Washington was filled with agendas and clandestine operations not known to general publics worldwide. Information collected, data distorted, decisions made for optimal use were all typically relegated by a handful of faceless insiders. For years McGeorge Previn purposefully ascended the invisible ladder leading to the ultimate plateau of true national policy decision making from where he now stood, a height few reached, and none from below could see. From his privileged standpoint, Previn felt quite comfortable breathing its air.

Framed photographs of his meetings with world leaders and industrialists sat on the highly polished bookshelves where were kept leather bound volumes of various treaties the United States had signed during his years as a Washington insider.

From his privileged seat as the National Director of the recently established Office of Counter-Terrorism formed by the currently seated President, known for his collections of black cowboy hats and autographed baseballs, Previn was given the significant responsibility and power of coordinating all American law enforcement agencies' efforts in removing any national security terrorist threats, including threats abroad. This intricate role Previn was elevated to occurred due to the fatal day in its not distant past when America was devastated by the attack on her own soil. His protective role in American affairs allowed McGeorge Previn unheard of access to intelligence information by allied nations.

He *was* the invisible Washington insider.

Removing the papers just received from their soft leather folder, Previn saw a nineteen page listing of phone numbers and phone calls with dates spanning twenty years. Besides different phone numbers were handwritten notations: "Mossad" was written next to three of the numbers. "Brooklyn, Morton Kohn" next to a fourth. Four other phone numbers had the name "Max Train's Phone" written next to them, identifying the scientist's home, cell, and two office numbers at the university. Looking at the list, Previn saw that Max Train had called Morton Kohn from his Syracuse home 47 times, from his office 36 times, from his cell phone 31 times. In addition, Morton Kohn, he saw, had recently received phone calls from Tel Aviv, Milan, Zurich, Scotland, and Iceland. It was not a trail lost on the intelligence officer.

Previn immediately noticed the call from Iceland was made less than eight hours ago. *He's crossing the Atlantic.*

"Get me Keever," Previn told his secretary.

"Yes sir?"

"This list, Malcolm. You think that our subject may have connections with the *desert*?" the name Previn always used for Israeli intelligence.

"Yes, sir."

"Our subject has been using these people and I just find out about it now?"

"Sir, it's very difficult to get desert links, considering the many times their communication lines are scrambled," Keever, a former NRO staffer told his superior. "It's amazing we were able to get this data this quick."

Previn paid no attention to his subordinate's statement. "This list indicates a call was made to Morton Kohn, whom you link to our subject, from a desert phone overseas nearly two weeks ago! Why wasn't I told sooner?"

"As I said sir, the numbers are not easily secured."

Previn looked down at the piece of paper and focused on the call from a town north of the Highlanders' capitol, Aberdeen.

"So, our subject has assistance from the desert folks?"

"I would place that at a high probability, Director Previn."

"Jesus Christ," Previn responded, hanging the phone up. *My God, the Mossad is with Train? Geez, these monsters will break everything open if they have to. If they can link me to the hunt for Train they'll blackmail me to get off the trail. If I don't, they'll expose me. I cannot believe that he got the Mossad with him. For what purpose? Good God, they're helping this guy with a relic that is of no value to them.*

"Tell Keever to come to my office immediately, Lydia." Tapping his fingers on the desk, Previn waited for his aide to enter.

"Yes, Director?" Previn's trusted lieutenant and dear friend said.

"We're alone, Malcolm. You don't need to call me 'Director'," Previn said smiling, as he placed his hand on the younger man's shoulder and gently squeezed it.

"Where does this Rabbi Kohn live?"

"I have his address in my office."

"You think this Rabbi's connected to Train?"

"And the Mossad. He was a hero during the Second World War. Escaped Auschwitz and wound up destroying a bunch of German rail lines carrying ammo and supplies to the Russian Front. He also helped a bunch of Jews escape Nazi persecution. He's been here for about 40 years, running a printing company. He's supposedly now retired."

"Doesn't appear that way, does it?"

The handsome intelligence officer smiled at his close friend. "No. I think Kohn's involved."

"I want some of my close friends to pay a visit to this man. You know what has to be done?"

Malcolm nodded.

"Make sure he tells you everything before you dispose of him."

***

Anselm Mugant was looking out his Curial office, having just finished reading notes sent to him for the Pope's American visit, where he would give his much anticipated speech to the United Nations. The Swiss cuckoo clock on his office wall signaling more time had passed in his life brought his gaze back to his office desk. Suddenly the phone light flickered on the line he knew only one caller could use.

"Cardinal Mugant speaking," he said, picking the receiver up.

"Thank you *Eminenza*," the voice on the other end sneered.

"Did you get Max Train yet?" Mugant asked his caller. *What is he thanking me for?*

"Seems like he has vanished into thin *sky*, Your Eminence."

"Well you've accomplished nothing again. Every time we speak, you tell me you have not gotten this man."

"I told you the last time we spoke others were interfering

with me in this project."

"Another call is coming in. I'm putting you on hold."

Let them interfere with me. I will have my greatest treasure, the Cross of Jesus. And now you have added to my spoils. Those morons who followed you are now in my hands. Soon I shall take the Kingdom.

"Yes?" Mugant answered the line.

"It's Previn. I have some information."

"Well, what is it?"

"I'm not sure you're ready for this."

"What is it!"

"Our friend has received help from Israeli intelligence."

Mugant's hand tightened on the phone. "Mossad?"

"There's more. A Rabbi in Brooklyn seems to be helping along, too."

"Incongruous, Previn. A Rabbi? Train has the Cross and a Rabbi is helping him?"

"That's the hard data coming in."

"You're on top of this?"

"Yes."

"I'll get back to you," the enraged prelate responded.

"Get to New York City, now! Not tomorrow, now," Mugant told his first caller.

"I might have more treasures after this *Eminenza*," the caller said in a slow whisper. "I'm on my way."

"Wait for further instructions from me," Mugant replied, and hung up. Turning to his left, Mugant saw the Curial cleric, Flavio Rinaldi walking to his office door. *What was that lunatic talking about? He's in his own world.*

"Cardinal Mugant," the Curial aide began.

"Yes, I know. We have to get to the airport."

"A car is waiting to take you to da Vinci."

Anselm Mugant motioned to the Curial aide to precede him out his office, and then locked the door.

"Brother Leo will drive you, Cardinal Mugant."

"Yes, indeed, he shall," the Canadian prelate said to the Curial monsignor as he walked down the steps into the car waiting to drive him to Rome's da Vinci airport.

***

"His Holiness has asked that you sit by his side, Sister Pasquale," the Pope's personal attendant, Monsignor Sylvestro Ricci, said. The specially equipped Al Italia flight was ready to depart for the long awaited Papal visit to North America, the first stop scheduled New York, where the Pope's United Nations address on "Genetics and the Soul of Man" was to be delivered in two days.

"Thank you so much, Monsignor," the blue-eyed nun replied. Walking up the row to the seated Pope, she could see him smiling. "Sister Pasquale, sit here with me and let us go over some further revisions for my most important address. Your work has been so instrumental in aiding me to deliver what I hope can have a beneficial effect on the world. Many have been helping in this effort, Sister. Many. Sometimes we never get to thank them by name," the white robed Pope said looking at his *peritus*, his specially chosen advisor on the issue of genomics and Catholic doctrine, as the Al Italia flight began moving down the da Vinci runway. "I wish I could thank every one of them personally. Hopefully, the message I will soon share with the world will reach their ears."

Chapter XX

The George Washington Bridge, always crowded at rush hour, was moving at a tortoise pace once again. Still on the Garden State's side of the bridge, Max looked at the digital clock in the gray sedan's dashboard and instructed the driver to pull into the Mobile gas station on their right side.

Six hours had passed since he made the call to Schemmizzi.

The trip from northwestern New York to New York City was faster than expected.

Max's body was exhausted, but his mind raced, reflecting on the chaos that devoured his life. He had become very fond of Sara, though he was guarded in expressing his growing feelings. Max's heart knew his heart was opening up towards her. It had been a long time. Somehow, he sensed, her feelings might be the same. Now she was abducted by the ones who sought his death, all because he carried the Cross. He was Sara's only real hope for survival.

He looked at the gold wedding band on his finger. Memories of his wife and daughter brought a smile to his face. They were always there, in his heart, and in his mind. And he knew they wanted him to be happy. To live again.

For most of the car ride down state, Max discussed with Harmon the various individuals who were in attendance at the meeting in Skye. It was the third time the Mossad agent went through the story with Max. Though Train felt as if he was being interrogated, he knew his traveling companion was trying to make sure Max mentioned everything. The repetitive discussions did work, as Max added more detail with every conversation.

Unfortunately, the Israeli government's hands were tied. Sara and Max had been trespassing on Mühlor's property, and he had legal right's that would protect him. There was also little obtainable proof of Max's claims, though there were no doubt those that assisted him believed him. However, Max was effectively portrayed in the media as a killer with a past for stories and murder. Justice could be manipulated by those who wielded its power, and there was no reason to believe those who sought Max wielded this power.

Of great focus to Max was why anyone would have thought he had intended to clone a person — yet alone the possible body of Jesus. Yes, it was true that Max's notable research in the field of DNA sequencing was the foundation for all genetic sciences. So too, was the fact he hoped one day his research, or parts of it, would enable science to identify genetic strands carrying crippling diseases that could be extracted or treated. But to clone? His published works clearly were not supportive of it.

Nevertheless, Max knew the arguments well, both theologically and scientifically. He also knew there were people in the world who feared the science of DNA understanding. Many of whom believed this science would eventually lead to activities prohibited by their own fundamental perspectives of God's Way on creation.

Evolution is reliant on all living bodies' capabilities to continually mix and match genes sequences. Adaptation to the continually evolving environment on the planet required the natural process of genetic evolution. Without this natural process effectively leading the way, Max believed man's ability to adapt could end, and so too, could Mankind's existence.

He also knew there were concerns that in time, perhaps not in his lifetime, but in the future, men may try to raise or breed human clones. Cloning to create a superior or subservient race was not an obscene science-fiction notion: all society had to do was recall what the Nazi "Angel of Death" attempted to do during Hitler's regime.

But where were society's safeguards to protect men from the illicit actions of those who may challenge the human race's evolution? Bio-ethicists were continually challenged. The science of genetic research had great potential benefits if used for medical purposes, but the process of discovery, including harvesting, and the uses from it could be questionable. Was stem cell research and potential development that could be used to benefit those with illness only a stepping stone to gene identification, whereas, physicians could extract or treat corrupt genes which may cause the body illness? After all, medical scientists throughout history had been challenged at times by ethicists who condemned their research. The condemnation that took place several centuries ago of scientist exploring the human cadaver exemplified this challenge Was it not God's intent by creating the distinct differences between man and other living animals that Man was able to cognitively think and understand the mysteries of science in order to better humankind? Was not medical research a critical part of man's ability to care for himself?

Max got out of the car and walked to a nearby pay phone. Again using the prepaid calling card so his call would not be immediately traced, he called Mühlor Industry's New York office. A receptionist answered the phone, and informed Max that Mühlor did not work out of that office. Declining to take the number to his office in Buenos Aires, Max firmly shared with Mühlor Industries' receptionist a similar message that he left with Schemmizzi's secretary, and strongly advised that someone from her office contact Mühlor's assistant in South America in order to relay the message to the capitalist. Max would call the New York number again in five hours.

Max's next call was to Italy, where it was nearing 1:00 a.m. After three rings a woman's voice answered the phone.

"Guillermo Schemmizzi," Max said, paying attention to the time on the line. By the sound of the connection, his call was patched to another location.

"Yes." It was Schemmizzi.

"A trade."

"I'm listening."

"The woman better be alive."

"I'm listening."

"Those hounds —"

"— I'm aware who you are, Mr. Train."

"Don't interrupt me. I know too much, and my information is hard and secure. The girl gets hurt, and you're all exposed — regardless if I live or die. Got it?"

There was no response.

"Schemmizzi, do I make myself clear?"

"Yes."

"I will call back in six hours. Be ready for my instructions," Max said before hanging up the phone.

His next stop was the world's melting pot: New York City.

"Turn down this street, 16th Avenue," the front seat passenger said, referring to the main commercial strip in Brooklyn, New York's, Borough Park neighborhood. "Looks like no one believes in parking signs in this city either. So parking is going to be difficult. We may have to do some walking to get to his place."

The black Chevrolet Caprice went unnoticed by the pedestrians of this faithful Jewish community.

The Borough of Brooklyn in New York City was home for people from countries that were as diverse as Thailand and Romania, France and India. In Prospect Park, a place of recreation for many, one could find refuge from the concrete and the hustle. A tour through Brooklyn's fifty-two acre Botanical Gardens would bring one in touch with exotic Chinese and Australian foliage, a realistic experience, if one chose, of an Amazon rain forest, or the desert life recreated in its Desert Pavilion. Writers, actors, musicians, entrepreneurs young and not so young, and students attending many of New York City's centers of learning studied and lived in this fine Borough—a Borough filled with many attractive culinary spots that would make sistering Manhattan jealous. The saying that "all good things come from Brooklyn" would be shared by a majority of 2.3 million residents who called the Borough home.

"From the photographs, Morton Kohn is a thin man. Doesn't look at all as old as his birth date would indicate. Has thinning gray hair, the sideburns are unkempt, and a long beard."

"That's not too much help, Steve. Look at the men walking around here," said Ben Harris, a Previn operative living in Kew Gardens, Queens. "Each is wearing almost the same get-up. Black suit, white shirt, beard, black hat, and it looks like—"

"—it's the Hassidim attire. Make a right, Roy, on to that street—52nd Street. Let's park right there, far enough from the hydrant. Looks like his home is over there, eight houses down."

The black Caprice just fit into the parking space. Pausing, the three in the car looked at the photo they had been given of Rabbi Kohn and noticed the heavy pedestrian traffic suddenly appearing on the sidewalk. Increasing numbers of Hassidism began leaving their homes and now walking the street. Suddenly five yellow and black school buses crowded with men, young and old, wearing the Hassidim attire, chugged up the street stopping in front of Rabbi Kohn's home. The doors immediately opened and a beehive like swarm of black hats and black shoes hit the street. Several other similar school buses soon followed.

The men in the Caprice stared as the bizarre scene unfolded in front of their very eyes.

What was a small trickle of pedestrians only moments ago turned into a sea of hundreds of black-hat Hassidim men crowding the entire area in front of Rabbi Kohn's home. There, they raised their voices in song, as more friends and supporters of the Rabbi joined them. The street, becoming a festive bazaar of long black coats, wide brimmed black tops, and in essence a protective barrier for the beloved Rabbi.

The outpouring of supporters continued.

So too did the yellow and black buses.

"Is there a parade or something today?" Harris asked, a confused look crossing his face.

"I don't know," Steve Richman answered the Previn employee from northern New Jersey. "I can't believe this. Where did these guys come from?"

"How're we going to get out of here," Harris asked as the thick sea of black cloth and wool hats surrounded the car, making any departure nearly impossible.

"That's the address, there," Richman said.

"You can see it? I only see the hats."

"There's no way we're going to get to him."

"You're not going to be able to open up the car door," Harris said conscious of the laughing faces belittling them through the car window.

"Oh, Christ! We're stuck."

"Damn! We'll never find him. We've been had. All these Hassidim were meant to stop us from getting to him. Let's go," Ben Harris said to Richman. "Saunders will never believe this."

"Go? How the hell you going to drive down the street?"

***

"Let's invite the Cardinal to sit with us on this discussion," the Pope said to his Secretary of State as the Al Italia plane continued its New York journey. "Dr. Cordesco," the Pope continued, nodding towards Sister Pasquale, "and I have reviewed the important points on this address. Anselm has been our spokesman at the Radio, so I wish to inform him of what we will be saying to the United Nations."

"Excellent, Your Holiness," Cardinal de Salvoyar replied. "I agree." Rising he walked down the aisle and into a blue carpeted cabin of the plane where Anselm Mugant was sitting, reviewing papers on the table in front of him.

"His Holiness requests you sit with him to discuss the UN address, Anselm," de Salvoyar said, standing at the cabin's narrow entranceway. Mugant did not look at the Cardinal Secretary of State. Rising from his chrome framed white leather seat chair, Mugant moved towards the cabin opening as the Pope's senior advisor turned to walk back to his seat by the Pope.

"Anselm, I want to go over some of the issues I will address in New York," the Pope said to Mugant, who was standing in the aisle two rows from where the Pope was seated. "Your very knowledgeable and efficient collaborator in the Life studies, Sister Pasquale, has indicated some change of language today that I found beneficial."

"Change of language is not what we need to isolate, Your Holiness," Mugant frostily replied. "I cannot stress enough the need to demand respect for life at all stages."

"Of course, Anselm. I know your direction well and we are in agreement, basically," the Pope responded.

"I don't think so, Holiness," Mugant replied, still standing.

"Be seated, Anselm. We are all to work together in this."

"You don't appear to discuss the dangers that cloning may bring to humanity," Mugant began. "Not once can I find you mention in any of your speeches or writings what dangers loom if monstrous forms are created through genetic science playing God."

"We have stated that experimentation in this area has no place when its sole object is to provide parents with a child of certain physical characteristics."

"That does not address the issue of dangers from this science," Mugant answered. "What if suddenly there is a demand for a class of workers to handle all the menial chores. What if we clone to build an army? You have not mentioned these dangers, Holiness. Are we building a class of sub humans in this cloning? Do we engineer the production line so that only identical products, identical individuals are mass produced? Then what?"

"Anselm, these are science fiction horror stories."

"Are they Holiness? Did one ever think that man would be able to regulate fertility? Birth cycles through medicine? What is to make one think these scenarios I have just mentioned are not possible?"

"First of all, Anselm, they are not near. So we have the time to mold the culture and have it think in terms of cooperation between science and religion. It is the only solution that works."

"Holiness, what of evolutionism? Does it not tell us that the body has programmed itself over eons so as to survive? What happens with scientists who, through a mistake or misunderstanding, interfere with this survival mechanism? Science did not bring about life, your Holiness. So it must not be able to tamper with it either."

"We are in agreement, Anselm. We differ on one perspective. The Church must take the intervening time available between now and what you have said can happen—the armies of cloned beings, which is far into the future—and work to convince all that humanity must be respected. Not just the Church, but all faiths and philosophies. You were there when I originally said, at the meeting after the story of the *Paris Match* piece, that this work of bringing about harmony between science and religion is not ours alone. It is the work of all people of good intent and good hopes."

"We have worded the United Nations document exactly that way, Cardinal Mugant," Sister Pasquale Cordesco said to him. "The Church knows of the mistakes it made with Bruno and Galileo. It has to reach out to science, as the Holy Father has written."

"I am not persuaded that the faithful have been informed about the potential dangers to the degree necessary, Holiness," Mugant said, ignoring his Curial assistant.

"We run the danger of alienating more if we follow a route of condemnation and recrimination, Anselm," the Pope responded. "Who will listen to us then? We cannot show ourselves opposed to technology and the advance of science. We must be the one that promotes it through the respect for man, because he is a creature of the Almighty. That is the guiding principle of all human development."

"We are about to land, Holiness," his aide Monsignor Ricci said. "We have to all be seated."

Anselm Mugant nodded to the Pope, and returned to his cabin.

***

"Adrianna?" sounded the voice in its distinct Roman accent.

"Guillermo, this call is unexpected," said the Brazilian Crusader, Adrianna Corvoso de Sa.

"A matter needs to be addressed for the Cardinal," the Italian magnate replied, seated in his private plane as he crossed the Atlantic.

279

"What matter?"

"Bring the woman to Washington, D.C., and do it quickly. It appears that a little pressure is being applied, and we need to get ahead of it." Schemmizzi said. "We'll talk again shortly," he said, and hung up the phone.

"Previn," Corvoso de Sa said as she reached for her next phone contact.

"Yes, Adrianna?"

"We have the woman from Avalon here, and tried to work some truth out of her. She has told us very little."

"What have you gotten out of her?" Previn quietly replied.

"Only enough to confirm she's Mossad. She definitely knows all of us, but I'm not sure if she has contacted her superiors. The truth serum we gave her had little effect."

"Train may have been at the Manor, for all we know, Adrianna. If he is with the Mossad, we have a loose cannon on our hands. He is not under our control at all, and we don't know what he knows, or who he has talked to," Previn said nervously.

"You're jumping the gun. McGeorge," the Brazilian replied, taking a soft drag on her cigarette. "We're all speculating."

"Adrianna, let's get the woman up to D.C. I spoke to Guillermo. I think it's a good idea. We need some leverage to negotiate with."

"How soon?"

"Now," Previn replied. "Some of my people can chat with her, and see what we can find out," he went on. "Besides, Mugant is close by. He may have some ideas."

"All right, McGeorge," the Brazilian responded, now having heard from two of her Crusader colleagues that Sara should be brought to Washington. "You can have your people meet us at the usual runway," she said as she ended her call.

Hanging up the telephone in his home Previn began to pace nervously on the wooden floor. With the Mossad seeking information, he knew it was only a matter of time that his name was brought into the muddy waters.

***

Thousands of feet below, the still welcoming skyline of New York, its millions of distinguishable flickering lights reaching to the sky, met the dark eyes of another, whose commercial flight was approaching LaGuardia as he looked out his window on to the majestic island of Manhattan. These dark eyes immediately roamed its southern tip. Eleven red crane lights mounted above brightly lit buildings now under construction screeched to the heavens.

I still do not have the Cross.

Chapter XXI

Deep violet hues draped over the Manhattan skyline as the sun slowly set in the West.

Max felt the electrical charge generated by the pace and will power of the diverse peoples who lived in New York City. No matter how many times he came to the "City of the World," a powerful sense of personal freedom swooned through Max's body, liberating his imprisoned spirit.

Amongst endless rivers of hard concrete, reflective man-made mountains built of glass and steel, space measured vertically, all energized by the bustling sounds of life every minute of every sleepless hour, a smile swept across his face.

His roving eyes gazed at the steel manhole covers pocketing Central Park West as steam from the underground subterranean world of which few knew drifted past honking taxicabs trying to dodge the always present potholes on the West Side's prestigious roadway. In front of the Museum of Natural History, he noticed museum workers hanging a large colorful banner announcing the upcoming exhibit "The Possible Existence of Life In Our Galaxy".

It was in New York where he grew up, where he studied, and where the foundation for all he became had been forged. Though now without any family, the only son of two caring parents that had been gone a long time, Max felt good to be home. New York City was like your first house in which you lived as a child; it was always home no matter wherever else you lived.

In an odd but very real way, New York City somehow reaffirmed Max's belief in his own faith. His eyes peered out the car window as it traveled south on Central Park West, as the passing images seem to become one blissful collage. To his left, he noticed the city's magnificent playground of Central Park. There were people of all races enjoying the open greenery located in the middle of the dense metropolis. The unfolding typical New York scene caused Max to wonder, as he frequently did, if there really were national boundaries, or was globalization something that would eventually unite all peoples of the world, enabling them to live in relative peace with one another, accepting and appreciating their differences the way those who lived in New York City did.

Passing the grand residential towers bordering the park on the residential "West Side community", the gray sedan made a right turn onto a quiet beautifully tree-lined street where gorgeous million-dollar brownstones built over one hundred years ago stood. The car slowed in front of the second brownstone closest to the park. A hand carved stone stairwell on the street's south side majestically welcomed all visitors. The address read: 10 West 73rd Street.

"This is us. Let's be quick," Daniel Harmon said to Max, as the driver popped open the trunk of the car.

Trailing the agent, Max and the artifacts were standing on the ground floor with Harmon in what was obviously a "safe house."

"Follow me," the Mossad agent said, before locking the door behind him as he walked up a meticulously crafted mahogany staircase leading to a large parlor floor room of equal old world craftsmanship.

"I imagine those windows are bullet proof - probably like the rest of this place," Max noted.

"Pretty much. You could drop a bomb on this place. The whole building was gutted a few years ago and replaced with reinforced steel. It has come in handy a few times."

"I would imagine so."

"Do you want to take a shower? I'll make us something to eat," Harmon suggested.

After a quick shower, Max met Harmon in the kitchen, where the agent had prepared several turkey sandwiches. "Max, a series of records was obtained on the individuals you mentioned. They're not complete, but it's a start. Grab your sandwich and follow me."

Leading Train to the ground floor from where they had previously entered, Harmon hit two concealed switches nearby. Suddenly, a large wooden cabinet rolled away from the eastern wall. A thick small steel door, half the size of a normal door, appeared. As he placed his hand on a small steel plate, the thick door slid open. "We like having options."

"I see," he said as he followed the Mossad agent through the door.

Moments later they were standing on the third floor of the second brownstone, whose decor appeared to be stylishly similar to the first building. The large room they entered had three computer terminals and several satellite telephones, their receiving dishes carefully hidden in undetectable areas in the neighboring West Side community for security reasons.

In front of Max were six neatly stacked folders. One for each of the five industrialists. A sixth folder was marked "Lab Destructions."

"You might want to study these," Harmon suggested.

Max didn't need to be told twice.

Glancing at the files on the five individuals, Max saw summarized reports on each of their vast financial empires. Immediately, he realized each of these conglomerates began approximately seventy years ago. The media tycoon, Guillermo Schemmizzi, now in his early eighties, was the oldest of the odd group. Rupert Hawkins, the London financier, was one year younger than his college alumnus and old roommate. McGeorge Previn, the fifty-year-old heir to the mayonnaise fortune, had an interesting dossier Max of which Max was not aware. Next to the Director of the "Office of Counter-Terrorism" were the written letters *FOG*.

Harmon watched Max's expression. "A surprise, wouldn't you say?"

Max nodded, then continued viewing the remarkable files.

Adrianna Corvoso de Sa, the forty-six year old Brazilian land baroness had inherited great fortunes from her father. The report Max viewed contained the true source of the family's real income.

Next viewed was Hernando Mühlor. After the forty-five year old man's name appeared the word "*Nazi.*"

Max thought to himself how in the world these five people, their financial empires located in separate countries, became connected to one another. The two older men had started their businesses, but Previn, Mühlor, and Corvoso de Sa inherited their moneys. Each, from what he read, had different lifestyles and different interests - yet, they were somehow tied to the Church, or, maybe to the unknown Cardinal. He reflected on the events in Skye. Thoughts of Sara were soon erased by the vicious faces of the crazed bloodhounds.

The son of a notorious Nazi involved with the American Director of the Office of Counter-Terrorism, who was connected to the active daughter of a weapons monger. According to the prepared report she sold weapons to the Irish freedom fighters of Sinn

Fein, in their conflict with the patriotic Hawkins's homeland, who attended Edinburgh with Schemmizzi. He, according to the report, had an 'apolitical' history — he really didn't care who was the head of the Italian Government, as long as the politicians didn't interfere with his business affairs.

Max knew there was an obvious deep history that connected the five together, but how and why?

Studying the papers, he recalled the tone of the meeting at Avalon Manor, and how the unknown Cardinal mentioned that none of the five had any financial exposure. What that meant, and to what extent the clergyman voiced his concern were critical parts of the puzzle.

Unknown to Train was the fact that an older man, in his early eighties, wearing a jogging suit and sneakers had entered the large prewar Langham Condominium located on Central Park West, and right around the corner from the Mossad safe house. After greeting the doorman, the gentleman took the elevator to the fourth floor, before walking down the steps to the basement. Navigating his way around several turns, the older gentleman entered two adjoining musky locked rooms, making sure the dead bolts were in place before moving on.

After locking the door to the second room, the odd looking man placed his hand on a metal plate. To the unseen eye, it was impossible to know the man's hand was being scanned. A second later, the cinder block wall slid open onto another thick steel door. The man put his hand on a similar metal plate, causing that door to immediately open.

Entering into the cellar of the brownstone located on West 73rd Street, Rabbi Kohn walked towards the familiar stairs leading to the ground floor of the building. As he did, he heard the heavy doors close behind him.

Agile for his age, he darted up the stairs, and towards the third floor, where he knew Max would be. Quietly, he walked on the wooden floors, his foot gently touching the wood so not to make a sound. It was a game he always played, especially since the wooden floors were arranged so that footsteps could be heard. Twelve quiet steps, and he was standing in the doorway unnoticed by Max and Daniel Harmon.

"It's awfully quiet here," the Rabbi said, as a warm smile filled with relief at seeing Max covered his face.

Both men turned towards Marty. "Marty," Max spoke out.

"I see you're reviewing the files."

Max approached the older man, who, unknown to either man, had his beard removed an hour ago. "It's good to see you. Thanks –"

"— you can thank me when we get Sara back," he said, before kissing Max on the cheek. "How are you feeling?"

"Okay, I guess."

"You look good, considering what you've gone through."

"Thanks, Marty. Any word on Sara?"

"No, but I think we're making some progress."

"Oh?" Max voiced.

Rabbi Kohn went on to tell Max about the scene that took place in Brooklyn four hours ago. He informed Max he had every reason to think that the individuals out in front of his home were sent by Previn. Photographs taken of the three men sitting in the car were going to be scanned into a data bank the Mossad had developed. If they were intelligence officers, there was a chance they would appear in the computer.

For the next hour Max went over the events in Skye with his old friend, carefully recalling everything that was. Once done, Max leaned forwards. "Marty, can I ask you something?"

"Of course."

"How long —?"

The Rabbi smiled. "All my life. When Israel was formed in 1948, thanks, in many ways to our great nation of America."

"You've had some life," Max noted.

"You could say that. By the sounds of it though, you've had some interesting experiences, too."

Marty looked towards the file containing the growing list of genetic labs destroyed throughout the world. "It's a shame this has to happen. So many good, educated scientists dead for no reason."

"I knew many of them. They were all actively researching stem cell reproduction."

"Funny Max, isn't it. You're one of the leading genetic scholars in the world, and no one attempted to kill you in Syracuse. You had to go to Israel and Europe for that."

Max looked at his old friend, when it dawned on him. He was a leading scholar in genetic sequencing, but Max's studies were primarily conducted with mathematical programs that identified gene sequences. He seldom ever went into a lab filled with Petri dishes. "All the names on the list - they were in the labs, conducting actual test, Marty. I think that's why I'm alive. I never did any of the actual testing. I could if I wanted to, but I never did since I thought it was more important to continue my studies of gene sequences."

"Oh, I see. Speaking of scientist, neither of the two friends of yours has been found in the cave so far . . . but there's still a way to go. It's slow moving."

Max looked solemnly down at his hands, thinking about his pal Luke. "You would've liked my old partner, Marty."

"I know. You spoke highly of him."

"He was a good man. John Muir and Lynn Johnson were also good people. You know, I met them because I was giving a detailed lecture on 'random sequencing', which is critical to my work in genetic research, and these two students who had never taken any advanced classes in microbiology or micro chemistry were the two stars of my three hour lecture. We went for a beer one night, and became friends. So, when I decided to travel to Jerusalem, I invited them with me."

"I'm sorry."

"Me too. I'm sorry I got Sara involved with all of this, Marty."

"We'll get her back."

"You bet we will," Max added with a sense of great determination. "Marty, are these lines traceable?"

"Impossible. Four relay satellites each owned by a different company."

"I need to make a call."

Dialing Schemmizzi's number in Italy, Max reached the same woman as before who answered the phone, even though it was nearing 5:30 a.m. in Rome. Max's call was connected immediately to Guillermo.

"Is the girl safe?"

"Yes."

"What about her gun shot wounds?"

"I don't know about any of that. I know she's safe. I'm sure she's being attended to if she is in need of medical help."

"Something happens to her, and you're all done with. Schemmizzi, I have an idea, but I'm not willing to share it with you unless I speak with the girl. You have twelve hours to get her to the National Cathedral in Washington. I'll call you then, and I want to speak with her."

"Washington?"

"There's no negotiating."

"Mr. Train, you're in no position to negotiate with me," whispered the old voice.

"Oh, really? I bet there would be a lot of people interested in knowing you were at a very secretive meeting with the Cardinal, a Nazi, the Director of the US Office of Counter-Terrorism, a renowned international arms dealer, and your old pal Rupert Hawkins. A matter of fact, I think we might have some interesting financial data I could share with the media, as well as some newspapers, who would love nothing more to sensationalize your name," Max said, holding his breath.

There was a long pause on the phone.

"What do you want?"

"The girl," Max replied. *The bastard is petrified about some financial records.*

"That's it? You're wanted everywhere."

"I bet since you planted those stories, you can find a way to help me clear my name. In the meantime, I have several options. Don't worry about me. Just bring the girl to the National Cathedral by 11:30 tomorrow morning. If she's there, you'll be close to having those very interesting records the Cardinal failed to get for you. I guess he missed a few," Max bluffed.

"She'll be there, but not with me. You're call will be connected to her."

"Fine, but if one thing goes wrong, several of your competitors will be receiving detailed records on everyone who attended the party on Skye, including the financial records," Max reaffirmed before hanging up the phone, his heavy voice indicating his seriousness.

Max looked at the Rabbi. "I trust you have people in Washington?"

"Yes, but we have to be careful of Previn. He's a king-cobra . . . very deadly."

"Schemmizzi seems very concerned about these financial records. He bought my bluff, and thinks I have a copy of the records this mysterious Cardinal was trying to conceal. I need to call Mühlor."

"Keep it short. Let their imagination wander."

Max called the number to Mühlor Industries. His call was immediately connected to Hernando Mühlor.

"Mr. Train, I've been expecting your call. How's life as a fugitive treating you?"

"Probably no better than how your father lived, Mühlor," Max shot back. "I got no time for ideal chat, so –"

"—well, Mr. Train, I'm not interested in what you have to say. You're a killer 'wanted' by authorities everywhere. It's only a matter of hours before you're caught."

"You think so?"

"Oh, I am sure of it."

"Just as sure as you were thinking the Cardinal could protect those precious financial records he was trying to conceal? Well, Mühlor, guess what? He was sure, too," Max laughed hysterically; making sure his point was fully understood.

Hernando Mühlor's attitude changed instantly, as evidenced by the silence on the other end of the phone.

"Listen Mühlor, something happens to the girl, I promise the world will enjoy knowing the son of a Nazi who stole millions of dollars from Jews during the Holocaust is now very close with McGeorge Previn, the Director of the American Agency for Counter-Terrorism."

"What are you ?"

"— Mühlor, don't play me!"

"I'm listening," he replied.

"As I was saying, I think some of Schemmizzi's competitors would enjoy knowing of your little group. I'm sure they would love to see these financial records I have of you guys . . . wait, should I say of you guys and one bitch?" Max said carefully, not knowing the involvement of the unidentified stranger brought to the meeting by the Cardinal.

"What do you want?"

"Let your friends — the Brazilian arms dealer who supplies weapons to the Sinn Fein in Ireland who attack Hawkins' beloved England — that if the girl gets hurt, you all will hang together. I will call you back in twelve hours. And Mühlor –"

"Yes?" a shallow voice answered.

"Get a haircut."

***

The humid dense air lay heavily on the dark El Yaque Beach, on the Santa Margarita Island off the northern coast of Venezuela.

Recessed further in from the beach coastline stood a red-tiled roofed stone beach villa which served, when available, as a vacation spot for various high level Venezuelan government officials. Outside the isolated house were three guards, their firearms concealed.

"Make her talk. She has things to tell us," the woman seated in the wicker chair said, taking a drag on her cigarette. "She has information she can share with her friends, isn't that right bitch?"

A wide-shouldered dark skinned man slapped the captive across the face from the left and then the right. Blood began flowing from her nose.

Brilliant eyes of blue raged as the captive stayed silent, bound by the nylon rope restraining her.

Smack.

Smack. Blood spat from Sara's bruised mouth.

"Harder!"

Smack. The long cold hand of the thug landed on Sara's face again

"You like being hit, my lady friend?" the woman tormentor asked. "Hit her again. Do I have to tell you how to get a confession?"

Smack.

Smack. The rough hand slapped her open back.

Smack. It landed on her beaten purple shoulders.

The white shirted guard standing at the window walked towards the tightly bound prisoner. As the balled fist of his sun darkened tattooed right forearm was prepared to mete out additional punishment he heard the order "Stop!"

"There is an easier way to get a confession out of her," Adrianna said. "We can give her thiopental sodium. Just the right dosage combined with the right amount of persuasion should release her inhibitions. She's already been shot and beating her seems not to be working. Mossad bitch."

Sara inhaled the air around her, trying to keep whatever remaining strength her beaten body could. The flight over from Skye to Venezuela had not been easy. The sadistic arms dealer, Adrianna Corvoso de Sa, had wielded similar punishment to her on the private flight over. Still, Sara did not speak

The thug looked at Adrianna Corvoso de Sa. "As you wish."

"We try it first, this is a bitch that is not just a housewife," the *patrona* said sneering at her prey. "Get her arm ready, and make her talk. Or does the lady want to tell us now before we do more to her?"

The prisoner sat motionless, without a reply.

"Fix her up. If it doesn't work, we will beat her, and kill her if we have to," the raven-haired de Sa said.

"It takes a few minutes," the henchman told de Sa. "We'll keep her 'high' till she does talk."

"High or dead?" de Sa replied, making sure her female captive heard her. Walking over to her helpless prisoner, de Sa slapped Sara's bruised face again. "You've been a great inconvenience, you stupid bitch."

***

The peace and quiet of the Mossad "safe house" did very little to comfort Max's mounting concerns. His body was miraculously recovering from the bullet wounds sustained in the Holy Land better than could have been expected. But the physical drain from being chased halfway around the world was exhausting. Adding to his fatigue was the psychological scars left on his spirit caused by mans' self-destructive behavior.

He stood up from the desk where he had continued researching for information on the five known capitalists whose voices he heard at Avalon. The information he discovered appeared to be insignificant, as there was no mention of Alpha Acquisitions or Como Ventures. Neither was there any obvious connection to the genetic labs being destroyed around the world. The two unmistakable facts were each of the five had mountains of money, and were devout *believers*.

He looked at Rabbi Kohn, who had nodded off on a sofa nearby. Held in his bandaged hand was a photograph of Sara. The sound of Marty snoring caused Max to smile. "I'm going upstairs," he said to Daniel Harmon, the heroic agent who rescued him in the North Sea.

"It's late, and we've got a busy day ahead of us."

"Yeah."

"Find anything useful?" Harmon asked, referring to the Internet search.

"Not really. Just that they all have a great deal of money."

"Max, what records have you been looking at?"

"Anything public. But it's hard. Other than Hawkins, who has to file public statements because of his investment company, all the other companies are private."

"How far back were you able to go?"

"Mid-seventies."

Harmon looked at his guest. "You told me most of these companies started over seventy years ago, right?"

"I did."

"And we know each has some questionable business practices, right?"

"Without question. They said it themselves in Avalon. Money laundering, blackmail, tax fraud — all the goodies."

"Who else was at this meeting, Max?" Harmon asked.

"A Cardinal."

"Why would a Cardinal be at this meeting? And why —"

"—would a Cardinal have so much control on them? Their bank accounts, but —"

"—Vatican Bank."

"What?"

"The Holy See had its own bank until it was purchased —"

"—in a merger by one of the banks Schemmizzi has influence in," Max slowly said. "I now remember reading something about this in passing."

"I bet your unknown Cardinal was involved somehow with Vatican Bank."

"And has records he's using to blackmail them," Max said in shock. "By the tone of his voice at that meeting, he controlled them — and they knew it."

"You can say he's holding them hostage. Must be pretty bad stuff he has on them, you know."

"Must be."

"Do you think this Cardinal is working with anyone else high-up in the Vatican?" Harmon asked.

"I have no idea. But I remember him saying he had everything under control, and he alone had their records."

"Interesting, don't you think?"

"A runaway cleric."

"Using the Church of Rome's guise for his own personal agenda."

"My God," Max said, staring at Harmon.

"Do you think there are any records on the Internet?" the

agent asked.

"Worth a look."

For the next hour both men searched the Internet attempting to get information on Vatican Bank. Little information was found, since the merger had occurred nearly two decades ago.

***

A loud ring disturbed Anselm Mugant's reading as he sat in his Waldorf Astoria quarters down the hall from the Papal entourage. Annoyed already at what he considered to be the room's inadequate décor and ill-designed layout, he grabbed the receiver, waiting for a voice on the other end.

"Cardinal Mugant?"

"Yes?"

"It's McGeorge Previn, Eminence. We didn't get Train's Brooklyn man, this Rabbi Kohn."

"You also did not get anyone in Edinburgh."

"We got the woman, Cardinal."

"You didn't get her. I got her."

"We have much more information now, and have reissued the news stories about Train. We're closing in on the menace."

"You are? You just told me that Train's Brooklyn accomplice got away." Mugant took a white handkerchief from his pants pocket and began dabbing his brow. "Is this how you counter terrorism in your own country? Train has the Cross, don't you get it?"

"Your Eminence, we all know what he has, and we all know what is at stake. If the Mossad is actually working with this scientist, I can be totally compromised. There is a danger that many of our activities could be exposed if we're not careful."

"The Mossad are not that dumb. They have their own peccadilloes and cannot afford certain of their actions to be made known. There will be balances along the way."

"I have no leverage. They'll break me if they find out I'm connected to this. They also have access to this President."

"Well, I don't see how, unless there's something I don't know about. We have things on them," Mugant bated his nervous caller.

"There is nothing else," Previn said.

"Meet me at 3:00 a.m. at the Central Park weather post. I trust you'll have no problem getting a flight."

"You mean Belvedere Castle?"

"Exactly, Previn. We can discuss your concerns and the Crusade's and make additional plans."

Ending his call with Previn, Mugant made a call of his own. "Where are you?" Mugant said to the listener on the other end of the phone line?"

"Close enough, Cardinal Mugant. I am near everything."

"The fugitive has Israeli help. He has a Brooklyn contact whom the Mossad are protecting."

"I know some of the Mossad spots here in this fair city, Cardinal."

"Good, then find Train."

"I'm closer than you think."

***

"That was a good walk, no Previn?"

"Far different from being in DC, Cardinal. We have been through too much these past two weeks. For years everything went as planned. Not a hitch. Now, an individual running amok across Europe with the Cross of Christ, we can't get him, and the Israelis have been helping him all along."

"Nothing has happened that is not under control Previn," Mugant replied calmly, leaning forward on his walking stick. His long black coat moved with the wind now beginning to blow across the Park.

"I am not so sure, Your Eminence. Train's Brooklyn con-nection evaded my men yesterday."

"An absurdity, Previn. You should be embarrassed."

Mugant took a step, and continued, extending his arm out-wards. "From this Vista Rock, Previn, everything is visible to us. So also from our vantage point. We are followers of His Way, and He gives us the ability to see and prepare for everything around us."

"I am wondering, Your Eminence, if perhaps the Mossad might not also have that ability. Their intelligence network is top notch, just like mine."

The Cardinal looked slyly at the American intelligence officer who he was sure traveled alone to Central Park.

From behind a tree the two had just walked past suddenly lunged a figure with a knife. Swiftly, brutally, and without pause a long, razor sharp blade was thrust into the neck of the unsuspecting and unprepared McGeorge Previn. The knifed victim looked at the long coated Cardinal in horror as another knife thrust tore open his jugular, and blood rushed out. Wheezing sounds of a man desperately, impossibly trying to fill his lungs with fleeting air were momentarily heard until the sliced flesh stopped moving and Previn's eyelids fluttered before being overtaken by permanent stillness. Lunging his heavy frame forward on top of Previn the assailant thrust the knife into Previn's neck again, securing his death.

The leader of the Fifth Crusade silently watched, anxious to return to his suite. Another deep knife thrust brought a sneer to Mugant's gaze. *So much for exposure, McGeorge.*

The assailant thrust the knife two more times into Previn's body, twisting it hard on the last thrust before pulling it out, and then looked at Mugant. The Canadian bent over the motionless body on the ground under the dark sky. Blood was still rushing from the victim's neck.

Turning, Mugant adjusted his coat as he casually left the convulsing, mutilated body and walked down the dimly lit path to Manhattan's 79th Street, his walking stick tapping the black asphalt pavement being the only sound the Canadian prelate made.

Chapter XXII

Hard concrete and black asphalt were the assassin's lonely companions on this dark early morning in New York City. Gray somber shadows cast from the moon fingered the silent city streets as most New Yorkers slept. Unknown to them an intruder had descended upon the city, hell-bent in a race against the coming sun as he sped in his rented auto looking for the one prize that eluded him: the artifacts Train carried.

Using well-kept resources and contacts established over the years, ransom for his blackmail, he was provided information of the existence of several "safe houses" where the Mossad might keep his prey. Scattered through Manhattan, the Bronx, and Brooklyn were at least five such residences Saudi, British, and Chinese intelligence had made him aware of. A hit in Taipei some four years earlier, which he had carried out for the Ministry of Communications in Peking, gained him prized information on the layout in these "safe houses", information he would seek to exploit in the hunt for Train.

Driving on empty and dimly lit streets in Brooklyn and narrow unkempt roadways in the Bronx brought him nothing. To the hired killer's trained eye, bulletproof glass was immediately recognizable. If the Mossad were protecting someone as important as Train, he'd be in a location having such protection. That sort of window wasn't found in the outer boroughs.

Manhattan, Mugant's henchman believed, was too obvious. But was it?

Quickly leaving Brooklyn and crossing the very narrow Williamsburg Bridge, *The Scorpion* determined Manhattan was where the Mossad hid Train.

Reaching a side street off of East 33rd Street at Third Avenue, the dark shadow approached a gray uniformed doorman standing in front of an old pre-War co-op building who was smoking a cigarette. On its seventh floor *The Scorpion* knew was Mossad housing. "I haven't seen the guy," the doorman said when shown a photo to look at. "He doesn't look familiar at all."

"What time do you get off," Mugant's thug, pretending to be a city detective, asked the doorman.

"6:00 a.m., we have twelve hour shifts," came the response.

Driving toward Park Avenue and East 64th Street, *The Scorpion* found a space for his rented black Altima. Walking up to the end of the block to a building with a Mossad protected apartment inside, the henchman repeated his detective line as he showed Train's photo to the doorman of the building.

"Nope, haven't seen anyone like that, buddy," he was told.

"You sure?"

"6:00 a.m. is when I get off, been here for almost twelve hours. Haven't seen nobody," he said.

Walking back to the auto, *The Scorpion* ignored the moving cars passing him in the early hours before dawn in this busiest of cities as he crossed East 64th Street. Getting into his car, he checked the mirrors before starting out towards Manhattan's West Side, the only remaining "safe house" address he had not checked.

Parking off of Columbus Avenue at 73rd Street, he walked down the tree-lined block filled with magnificent century old brownstones and towards Central Park. The two brownstones that Chinese intelligence had revealed were Mossad owned appeared at the end of the block, adjoining an old pre-War building, the Langham that took up the first one hundred feet of West 73rd Street's southwestern corner. With each purposeful step, his dark chameleon–like eyes roamed the sleeping historic block, searching for any possible movement. There was none.

A slight breeze swept by, breaking up the night stillness.

Pausing for a moment, he searched for anyone on the rooftops above. Continuing his walk towards Central Park, he checked each parked car that he passed.

Paying little obvious attention to the memorized address given to him as bounty, the figure glided past the buildings as if he had no interest other than getting home from a late night out.

Piercing sirens erupted into the quiet night, filling his ears as he approached the park. Looking north, he noticed two police cars tearing down Central Park West. He turned left towards the nearby subway station. As he did, he heard the blaring sirens of additional police cars echoing off the tall buildings that made up the West Side skyline. He crossed the street, walking towards the gothic San Remo residential tower that majestically overlooked the wondrous park.

Suddenly the first two police cars screeched on their wheels, darting into Central Park as fast as the drivers could steer them. Another police car, paying no attention to the red traffic light, raced into the Park from West 72nd Street moments behind the other two vehicles.

A wicked smile spread across the shadow's face, before he turned on his heels and retraced his steps, keeping careful notice of the unfolding emergency apparently taking place in the Park.

Back at the corner of 73rd the lone walker made a quick left. Adrenaline raced through his body as the narcotic of killing elevated malevolent desires to torture Train in a way no human being had ever been tortured. Then, he would take the items containing the body remnants of Jesus into the bottomless world where he dwelled.

A shadow moved in the window where he believed Train was located. His muscles tightened. He could sense he was close.

If Train was harbored here by the Mossad, it wouldn't be long before he devoured his prey. The ways of the Mossad were intimately known to him. So were many other intelligence agencies whose bidding he had done.

He licked his top and then bottom lip as the red flashing lights, blue and white, of the cop cars now in Central Park bounced off the old buildings anchoring Central Park West and into his colorless eyes. Looking up towards the sky, barely a star was visible. He clinched his violent fists as his nostrils flared. *Train, you are mine! And YOU—will soon be in my hands.*

Thirty steps and he was in front of the two brownstones he sought. The townhouse closest to the park that adjoined the neoclassical pre-War residential building had its third floor lights on. There appeared to be moving shadows. The building next to it appeared silent.

The Scorpion darted in the night darkness to the ground floor window looking out to the street. Believing the window was bulletproof; he felt the glass and confirmed by touch what his eyes had suspected. *Mossad.*

A quick look at the ground floor entranceway indicated the doorknob had been wired. There were two possibilities: either the doorknob had electrical volts running through it or it had a heat sensor that would trigger off an alarm somewhere in the townhouse. *Mossad. They prepare for the anti-Zionist—but not for me.*

Crouched down, the Scorpion quickly moved towards the garbage cans at the base of the brownstone. Scrutinizing the painted numbers identifying the street address on the can, he quickly darted to the brownstone also identified as Mossad. The painting style on the cans was identical.

The sound of a noisy private sanitation truck tumbling down the street stopped to pick up the refuse cluttered on the side of the pre-War building. While the sanitation workers noisily removed the garbage on the sidewalk, *The Scorpion* quickly emerged out of his hiding spot, and approached the sanitation men. To his right he noticed an unsecured stairwell leading to the basement of the pre-War building. He turned around and walked back towards the brownstone, gazing at the adjacent walls between the two buildings. He continued walking up the dark street, satisfied.

Minutes later, *The Scorpion* descended into the musky pre-War building basement. Guided by the flame of a small lighter he began walking through the maze of underground passageways, making his way towards the building's western wall.

A fat Norwegian rat hissed at him from a nearby corner. Blank eyes stared at the two foot long gray rodent. "Hello," he said before kicking it with his steel tipped boot.

He came across a locked door. Removing a wire from his coat pocket, he soon entered the room.

The light from his butane immediately shown onto a small metal plate embedded into the building's western wall adjacent to the brownstone. He noticed the markings of another doorway. He approached its thermal metal plate used to identify fingerprints.

These asses, they think they can hide from me?

With frenetic fervor *The Scorpion* left the room and soon ascended onto the street above.

Walking back to Central Park West, he quickly turned left onto West 74th Street towards his parked car.

Heading north on Amsterdam Avenue, he drove towards the imposing gothic Cathedral of Saint John the Divine, the awe-inspiring Cathedral of the "Seven Chapels", to meet Anselm Mugant at the time previously agreed to; 5:30 a.m. Passing Columbia University, the lone dweller reached Manhattan's revered landmark and saw across the street from it a long coated figure with a walking stick. He parked the car.

"The time is drawing near *Eminenza*. I believe I have tracked down your precious desires," he snickered as he stood next to the canon lawyer. "Now tell me what his friend looks like," he continued, the gray stillness of the early dawn touching Cardinal Mugant's disturbed face.

Mugant eyed *The Scorpion* warily. "Let's walk towards the river."

The white full moon was still high in the early dawn sky as the two stood concealed by a large tree in Riverside Park, down from the Cathedral where construction, begun in 1892 is still not completed, and whose interior walkway of 601 feet is the largest of any Cathedral in the world. Three ton bronze doors, and its famed Portal of Paradise limestone carvings of biblical figures, stand out to any of its visitors whose voices at religious services can sometimes be heard in song accompanied by the famed 8,035 pipe Aeolian Skinner pipe organ.

Silently they entered the long narrow field of Riverside Park. The uncomfortable tension between them built with every passing step. To themselves, they considered how much was at stake in the hunt for Max Train: lifetimes of effort would come to naught if Train eluded them any further. Neither was blind. Each knew the other had a separate agenda, though specifics were not identified. Either way, neither could simply walk away from what they started. They were connected to one another just like the confessor had said previously, and there was no way around it.

"What friend?" Mugant asked as they entered the park.

"*Eminenza*, I know Train has help. And I know of the woman."

Mugant pushed down hard on his Gastock walking stick. "What makes you speak of a woman?"

"I know everything. I have ears and know a woman's voice. You want my steel, but you know not of truth. It means telling everything. There will never be secrets between us. You have not learned this yet. Why do you try testing me? Now I'm tripling my price for Train."

Mugant turned to look at the reflected waters of the Hudson at the end of the park grounds. *Bastard.* "Done," he replied, as he closed his lips together to moisten them.

"You've been quite busy," a sinister glare passed on the Cardinal.

"By the outcome so far of your efforts, you haven't been."

"My time spent has been useful."

Useful? "I see nothing."

"Cardinal, you have traveled often, and—"

"—how do you know of my whereabouts?" Mugant seethed as they continued walking.

"Come, Cardinal, let us walk towards Grant's Tomb."

Mugant stood his ground. "No. I don't have much time. How long is this going to take for Train?"

"Soon, Cardinal, soon."

"That tells me nothing."

"Get the woman up here as bait. I'll have Train as soon as I have her," he sneered.

He nodded. "Later today. I have other matters to which I must now attend."

Mugant's perceived penitent looked loathingly at the man who had once been his confessor as the moon's rays continued to beam brightly down upon the water below. As Mugant began to turn, he heard *The Scorpion* speak, "Upon the freedom you seek on this earth, for I do know everything, *Eminenza*, I will come to you for an item and you shall not deny me."

The Canadian continued to walk away, east, into the early dawn as his assassin disappeared.

***

Morning, filled with speeding taxis carrying New Yorkers eager to get to work, unfolded as it always did in New York City on this morning.

The news being broadcast over all the major networks spoke of the tragedy that had occurred several hours previous.

"This is Terri Ann Hochberg for 1010 WINS News reporting live: The savagely beaten body of McGeorge Previn, the National Director of the Office of Counter-Terrorism, was found dead in Central Park's Belvedere Castle area earlier this morning by a pair of unidentified joggers. New York City Police so far have been very sketchy in their remarks about the slaying, given its gruesome tone. Detective Brian Donahue of the NYPD Counter-Terrorism Special Task Force said earlier that Police do not believe this is a mugging gone wrong. Law enforcement officials on why Director Previn may have been in Central Park at that time of the night.

It is unclear at this time who may be behind the murder of Director Previn. However, sources say, it is possible that terrorists from the Middle East may be involved.

The Police have cordoned off the entire Belvedere area and brought in trained police dogs to look for any clues the killer or killers may have left behind.

Obviously people are very nervous right now down here, in Central Park."

Sitting in defiant amusement on a bench adjacent to Central Park from where he could watch any movements in and out of the West 73rd Street brownstones, *The Scorpion* sneered to himself, as he heard his walkman transmit the 8:00 a.m. news of the death of Mugant's pawn.

.

***

Rubbing his hand over his scruffy face, Max stared in amazement as he watched the early morning CNN broadcast reporting the murder of McGeorge Previn. Not lost on him was the fact the chaos chasing him halfway around the world had now descended onto New York City. He knew where Belvedere Castle was—only a few blocks north from where he was hiding. *This wasn't a random act. Why would they kill Previn?*

Max stood up and walked to the bedroom where he kept the artifacts. Retrieving them, he placed them on the bed and opened the box. Carefully, he removed each wooden piece.

What was it about this Cross that made men act so violently? A person's faith could sway at times, especially when holding onto your faith is the one thing that seems most ridiculous. But that is when faith appears and comforts us. To believe in one another, to believe in God, and to believe in yourself meant holding onto your faith, and whenever possible, sharing your belief in one another to others.

Max looked at the *titulus*. The inscribed words condemning Jesus darted right to his heart, filling him with the deep sorrow that was contrasted with remarkable waves of hope. "I'm not sure if you were a man, or the Son of God," Max whispered as he stared at the remnants on the Cross. "But I believe in what you represent. I believe in your Way. I doubt we will ever really know for sure based on these items left behind. But I do know you were a very special person . . . a person who cared about others. You spoke of loving others, and for each person to respect life. I'm not sure if all the stories told about you are true, but I believe in the messages you shared. I want to believe there was a greater reason for the deaths of my family and friends. But it feels like I'm free falling into a powerful dark void and I'm afraid that once it ends, this journey is going to only get worse — if that' at all possible. I want everything to stop, but I know that's not going to happen until others know of your existence, but if I do that now Sara will probably die. And Sara — I have to get her back. I can't take having more people dying, especially her.

***

"We are grateful to you for attending this most important meeting His Holiness has called and to whom he has extended his most heartfelt invitation on behalf of persons of good will everywhere," the Vatican Secretary of State began. "We wish to thank the Cardinal Archbishop of New York," the Pope's aide continued, looking at the New York Archbishop and the religious leaders sitting around the mahogany conference table in the rectory conference room, "for the generous use of his rectory facilities here at Saint Patrick's on such short notice. Ours is a meeting of moment," the Pope's aide went on. "Christendom is being blamed for the absolute evil perpetrated by unknown forces against genetic scientists throughout the world. We have each separately condemned these actions in print and in speech. The Holy Father, as well as his Prefect for the Office of Human Life in the Curia, Anselm Cardinal Mugant, have denounced these actions. Cardinal Mugant," the Pope's chief aide went on, looking at the Canadian seated at the opposite end of the long table, "has from our own Vatican Radio, at the Holy Father's instructions, spoken to its listeners throughout the world against the killing and bombings of innocent people. The Holy Father, and only the Holy Father, speaks for the Church. We, his Cardinals, in unison with his voice, condemn the actions that have brought us here today."

"Thank you Cardinal de Salvoyar," the leader of the Church of Rome began. "The Cardinal Secretary has welcomed all of you here, on behalf of believers worldwide. I am grateful all of you have come today to join me in solidarity on such an urgent matter."

The Church leader stood and continued. "The Lutheran Synod has met with us in Rome, and we are grateful you are here so early this morning. And I see the Patriarch of the American Greek Orthodox community has graced this meeting," the Pope went on as the bearded Primate acknowledged the Pope's mention. "The President of the Southern Baptist Leadership Conference and I have discussed the issue of the respect for all life, and we are in the Conference's debt for your agreeing to join with us, Reverend, in our mission to end the violence that has hit the civilized world. I see our friend from Trinity Church in Manhattan is with us, and we extend our deepest gratitude to you and to all those faithful your Church represents throughout this land. The President of the Methodist Council of Bishops we are pleased to acknowledge here, as also the Elder from the Presbyterian General Assembly Council.

"Tomorrow," the Pope went on, "I will be addressing the United Nations on this issue of bettering the human condition through medicine and the respect science needs to show for human life. The two statements are in nowise opposed. Science and the Church have now been given notice, through the violence that is killing innocent researchers worldwide, to come together and set aside past differences and work together. Our ethics need not be at odds. Medical science, in its role to promote human health, already has shown its objective is the respect for human life. We do not seek to inhibit medical science in our call for the respect of this very same life. Our goal and that of science is one: the respect for life is totally integrated and complete when both religion and the researcher acknowledge that one promotes life by ensuring all life is protected and at the same time healed of whatever ills this earthly existence has brought the children of God.

"It is our tragedy that perhaps there are those in our flock that believe His Way is to raise the sword. As I know we all believe this is not His Way. We the leaders of Christendom need to stand together and share a healing voice with those carrying the sword to end their killing. We must unilaterally condemn these practices."

The Pope paused and looked at the leaders of the various Christian denominations in the room. "May I ask each of you to attend the address at the UN tomorrow as a sign of solidarity?" he asked.

"We share your belief in the need to make a declarative

statement on the issue of genetic science and human life," the silver hair leader of the American Unitarian Church responded.

"I agree with that," the tall, bespectacled leader of the American Dutch Reformed Church said in his deep baritone. "I will speak to our concerns here today on my next television broadcast and engage all our viewers to reflect on ways to stop this bloodshed."

"While we have variations on how we think the respect of life should be addressed, we are in agreement with the principle of our Faith that we are called to aid one another, just like in the parable of the Good Samaritan of the Gospels," the leader of the Southern Christian Leadership Conference responded. "We should all agree here that our presence is essential to showing that Christianity across all its denominations condemns killing of whatever kind in the name of God. Like the Good Samaritan, medicine is called to heal the wounded. We are called to encourage that science do this with all the respect life commands."

Cardinal Fernando de Salvoyar looked at Anselm Mugant, as if prompting him to make a comment, now that other religious leaders had spoken. Mugant, however, was rising from his chair with the others now preparing to leave who had just heard the Pope and their co-leaders of Christendom. Turning to exit the conference room without acknowledging de Salvoyar, he took his coat and walking stick from a rectory attendant, and continued down the carpeted corridor to the floor below.

***

The city streets of the residential upper West Side community were abuzz with angry local and Federal law enforcement officers patrolling the area. The news of McGeorge Previn's assassination, and there was now no doubt the Director was pointedly murdered, began to reverberate across the already shaken nation. With no possible reasons other than Previn's critical role with the U.S. Government to blame, there appeared no other reasons why he would have been butchered the way he was.

A brown hair middle age man, dark glasses shielding his weary bloodshot eyes from the bright morning sun, and wearing a long olive green trench coat over his crumpled clothing, stretched his long neck. Black leather steel tipped boots, cushioned by thick rubber soles, were easy on his well-traveled feet. An identifiable gold NYPD detective badge hung on a thin stainless steel chain around his long, powerful neck. He purposefully approached the brownstone on the north side of West 73rd Street and rang the bell to the main residence. He was in no mood to begin knocking on doors, but it had to be done. Moments later, an older woman came to its heavy door, saw the police badge, and opened it. "Yes. Hi, officer."

"Sorry to disturb you this morning, se—ma'am. I'm Detective Bhoj. I trust you heard about the incident in the Park?"

Moments later Detective Bhoj slowly left the woman's brownstone steps; satisfied his presence was visible to any observing eyes on the city street.

Moving west, to the next elegant townhouse, he rang its doorbell and soon was greeted by a middle age male. Introducing himself, Detective Bhoj asked the man if he had noticed anything peculiar the prior evening, informing the resident of Director Previn's death. Satisfied with the man's negative response, he turned and walked down the steps and then removed a torn lined sheet of white paper from his trench coat. Staring at it for a full minute, he then proceeded to the next building.

This process of local questioning was repeated for the next thirty minutes. Crossing the street, and now standing on the same side of the hidden Mossad "safe house," the detective began repeating the same procedure. It was nearing 11:30 a.m. when he looked at the address numbers of a beautiful brownstone on the southeastern tip of the block. His eyes looked up to the second floor window where another's met them. Behind him a local police car passed by. He turned and gave a nod. Then returning to the gazing eyes in the brownstone he walked up the steps and rang the bell.

A blond haired man with the build of a fire hydrant approached the protected doorway where the detective waited. Noticing the authenticity of the shield, the Mossad agent carefully opened the door. "Can I help you?" he asked, ready for anything.

"Yeah, I don't know if you heard but there was a problem in the park last night. I've been asking folks in the neighborhood if they saw anything odd last night."

"I heard on the news about Director Previn's murder."

"You wouldn't've noticed anything suspicious, would ya'?"

"Sorry, I just got here," the Israeli said while beginning to close the door.

"Wait a moment, do you know this photo?" the detective asked as he quickly lifted the small picture he had in his hand towards the man's gazing eyes.

Instinctively, the blue-eyed man glanced at the picture.

His eyes then opened wide in horror as a long poison tipped stiletto emerged from nowhere and slashed deep into his gut. As he felt the twisting deadly blade churn deeper into his stomach, his warm blood gushed out as he instantly lost all body sensations. The powerful free hand of the assassin reached for his throat while the blade violently tore deeper into his body's organs. As he gasped for air that would never come, the last thing he saw were the eyes of Max Train.

Shoving the Mossad agent's thick neck backwards, *The Scorpion* pushed the dying man into the doorway before closing the wooden door behind him.

His heart pumped in excitement over the kill. Dark shadows clouded his mind blocking the lightness of life, the way it always did when he was killing. He licked his upper lip and then his lower as he gazed upon the hallway.

Before *The Scorpion* was a staircase. The door to the brownstone's main parlor room on the first floor was partly open. Down the end of the hall Mugant's assassin saw a room with green walls: the kitchen. Clearly audible from it were the sounds of a person moving. He listened carefully.

It sounded as if only one person was in the kitchen.

A young dark suited brown hair man walked by the room's entranceway. As if that were a cue, *The Scorpion* raced to the room and, lunging at him, brought a powerful fist to the back of his prey's neck.

The struck man, falling forward, grabbed for his gun as *The Scorpion* lifted his foot and savagely kicked agent Harmon in the face. As his head flew back, *The Scorpion* lunged towards him again and brought his fist against the victim's nose, breaking it in two. Not satisfied at his damage, Mugant's assassin quickly drew the stiletto from his pocket and drove it through the prone victim's Adam's apple, puncturing his throat. The blade entered Harmon's body repeatedly. Harmon slumped to the floor, gurgling as blood gushed out of his neck and formed a pool around his body.

The killer looked cruelly at Harmon. "That's what you get for helping the key bearer," he whispered as the long blade slit down into the Mossad's throat.

Agent Daniel Harmon was dead.

Mad dog eyes prowled the parlor floor searching for the precious treasures. Noticing nothing, the assassin knew his treasure hunt would have to wait. There was something else on his mind.

Max Train, the elusive holder of the believed artifacts of Jesus, was close by. He had no intent of allowing Train to escape him this time.

Turning out of the room and stealthily going up to the second floor, he saw shadows slowly walking about in one of the rooms. There were two voices distinguishable in age heard in a large room, its door ajar. He listened carefully: one voice was Train's. A broad smile of hate covered his face as he looked at the bloodstained blade he clutched in his hand. "It's time to die, key bearer."

He moved to the top of the landing, carefully listening.

His dark eyes roamed the stairwell above, searching for any other sign of Mossad. The voice of the one who escaped him along with that of an old man echoed over a news broadcast. He inched his way towards the open door of the long room at the right of the stairwell where the voices came from, mindful of any other sounds.

The artifacts would soon be in his possession.

The stiletto was ready as he peered into the room.

Max Train and Rabbi Kohn were sitting in front of a computer terminal that was situated midway into the room, where the two appeared searching the Internet for information.

"Marty, do you think it's possible to connect these bastards?" Max asked.

"I'm not sure, Max. We know they're connected, but proving it is going to be hard."

"If we can only get the records from the Church."

"Good luck. They're probably destroyed."

"Someone must have great access."

"No crime is perfect, Max. Remember, those with staying power will prevail. You have that."

From the corner of his eye Max noticed a shadow move in the hallway. His muscles tensed as he began to stand.

With lightning speed, *The Scorpion* raced into the room, leaping at Max. The reddened knife extended towards Max as Train heard the sound of death.

Moving to his side, Max caught the glimmer of the knife. Instinctively extending his right arm, Max deflected the assassin's deadly charge as both bodies crashed into the wall nearby, the killer on top of Max.

The Scorpion clawed at Max's face, trying to put his fingers into Train's eye sockets.

Max tried to move the killer's hands away from his face, but they were too powerful.

"You're mine," *The Scorpion* hissed, his fingers gashing at Max's eyes as his prey twisted his head in desperation. "You'll know darkness!"

Max reached up, trying to push the killer off of him, as Rabbi Kohn stood from his chair.

Max had no leverage: the lunatic clawed deeply at his face.

Interlocking his hands onto the assassin's tearing hands, Max pulled down and bit the killer's right hand, causing *The Scorpion* to retract in overwhelming pain.

The Scorpion immediately uprighted himself. "You bastard!" he roared, removing the stiletto.

The blade slashed at Max, missing Train by inches.

Rabbi Kohn, moving towards the door, reached into his waist belt. Kohn's movement was caught by the killer, who instantly sliced at the old man's arm. The blade came down deep in his wrist. Kohn looked down at his gashed hand, and screamed in pain as blood poured from its severed veins onto the room's light beige tone carpeting. The gun lay on the floor.

Max charged at the killer. His shoulder crushed into the hardened back of the assassin, throwing the lunatic into a heavy wooden bookcase. *The Scorpion* turned to Max as Train lunged for the gun the Rabbi had dropped by the door when *The Scorpion* cut him.

The black steel tipped boot of the lunatic crashed into his face, throwing him backwards as he clung onto the gun. The killer lunged at him again. Cold steel pressed down at Max as he desperately tried to fight off the killer's deadly knife inches away from his chest.

"Die, bastard!" the killer screamed as he pushed down violently at Max.

"Go to Hell!" Max screamed, fighting off the blade.

"I am Hell!" he bellowed back as the poisonous knife inched closer.

"You're—"

"—die, you—" he gasped as the wounded Rabbi kicked *The Scorpion* in the face, breaking *The Scorpion's* hold on Max.

Max rolled to his side and reached for the revolver near the door.

The Scorpion charged after him, the blood drenched stiletto still clutched in his unforgiving hand. As he stood, *The Scorpion* rammed Max. knocking him backwards through the doorway and out of the room towards the top of the stairs. Max's shoulder hit the stair banister. The Scorpion raised his knife expecting to plunge it into the prone body of his prey.

Revolver in hand, Max's tense index finger moved towards the trigger when the Scorpion, losing his footing, tripped forward over Train's body. Grabbing Max's gun-totting arm as he started hurtling down the stairs, he brought Max with him.

The two grabbed at one another as their bodies free fell down the stairs.

Their bodies were locked against each other as ferocious hands of brutal strength unrelentingly clawed at one another in each of their attempts to yield off the powerful violent grasp reaching for them. Tumbling downward, an infinity of time passed by in surreal motion. Their bodies continued to twist as a fierce battle of wills and purpose raged, each humanly form wielding every piece of energy it possessed.

Grunts and agonizing screams were heard from the two unimaginable figures as the blur of their free fall continued.

Suddenly the gun, lodged between the two falling bodies, went off.

Two motionless bodies lay at the bottom of the brownstone stairs.

Rabbi Kohn raced to the scene.

Slowly the bodies below began to move.

It was Max.

Looking at the body under him, Max saw *The Scorpion's* knife stuck deep into the killer's heart. Warm blood spurted from the dead body's chest covering Max's torso. Flowing from the dead body's arm was blood from a bullet wound.

The Scorpion was dead.

***

"This is Max Train."

Immediately the phone operator, hearing the name, rerouted the call.

"I see you got to Previn," the speaker on the other end of the phone said.

"What do you mean, 'got to Previn'?" Train responded.

"News reports in New York today stated McGeorge Previn was killed in Central Park."

"It wasn't me, you bastard. I told you to keep your dog off me. Now he's dead. If anything has happened to Sara you'll be next."

"Mr. Train, I don't know what you're talking about. I sent no one after you. You asked me about the woman and I have delivered."

"Where is she?"

"Right where you asked."

"Put her through."

Moments later Max heard the voice of Sara.

"Are you okay?" he anxiously asked.

"Yes," she weakly replied, feeling the effects of the beating and the drugs.

"Are you in Washington?"

"By the Cathedral," Sara replied before her connection was lost.

"Mr. Train, I suggest we meet today."

"So do I. If you try anything the world will know your escapades. Remember my data is hard."

A pause followed on the receiver end.

"Are you there?" Train asked.

"I'm here."

"How soon can you meet me in New York?"

"An hour."

"You're to meet me alone in the Rose Center, at the Museum of Natural History. Go to the exhibit on the Black Hole. If anyone else shows up, my guys will have a field day with the press. Anything happens to me—"

"—there's no need to be hasty. I'll have a long yellow legal pad and white ribbon both in my left hand. So I should not be hard to pick out."

"I know what you look like."

***

As he walked into the Museum of Natural History's world renowned Rose Center for space exploration and astronomy from the West 81st Street entrance, Max Train proceeded to their agreed upon site. Passing a Jumbotron showing live images of space from the Hubble telescope, Max looked carefully for any suspicious faces. Noticing hundreds of tourists interacting with the spectacular exhibits, he walked towards the exhibit on the Black Hole.

Seeing his contact alone sitting on a bench in the dark room projecting a film on the universe's creation, Train slowly walked towards him.

Train's phone contact nodded as Train sat next to him, and began to speak, his eyes looking straight ahead. "Mr. Train, we can be collaborators and work together to meet both our needs. You fear for the safety of a woman in Washington, and I have reason to have similar concerns, but not about a woman."

The speaker paused to let his words sink in. "Without going into details of my concerns, I want to make a deal with you."

Train looked hard at the speaker, and then around them to see if there was anyone close by.

"What's the proposal?"

Chapter XXIII

"Your Eminence, it is imperative we meet now that Previn has been killed. Rupert will be arriving in the city in an hour. Hernando is the only one out of reach right now. Adrianna is dealing with the Mossad woman, but it is important we meet now," Guillermo Schemmizzi said from the confines of his New York City apartment on Fifth Avenue overlooking the world famous Metropolitan Museum of Art.

"Previn's death is a strange happening, Guillermo. He had other leanings, which I never discussed with any of you, and I believe this is what led to his calamity. He could not bring anyone with him to where he went last night for fear that others may find out something about him that could compromise him."

"You are saying what, Cardinal?"

"Let us not discuss this on the phone. Let's you, I, and Hawkins meet at the Saint Regis, make it 4:00 p.m."

"That will be convenient. Hawkins keeps a room there," Schemmizzi cautiously answered the Canadian.

"I am agreeable to such a meeting, Guillermo. I shall see the two of you in Hawkins' suite at 4:00 p.m."

"Cardinal, has there been any news of the fugitive?"

"Yes. My sources are close. We may even be rid of him as we speak."

"We're concerned, Cardinal."

"Nonsense. Man, where is your backbone? Remember, we have the woman, too. Train's no fool, an idiot, yes, but not a fool," Mugant said from his room at the Waldorf.

***

"The situation seems to still be very fluid, Cardinal Mugant," the English Crusader told the Canadian prelate with some concern as he sat next to Schemmizzi. "We're here now in New York, McGeorge Previn is murdered in Central Park, and we're nowhere near a solution to finding this scientist."

Mugant looked at Hawkins warily. "You are not correct. Matters are being dealt with."

"At the Rome meeting, and the two subsequent ones, you assured us matters were under control. Now the Mossad may have killed Previn—"

"—the Mossad would not kill a man like Previn," Mugant answered back. "Previn had tendencies." Mugant paused to let the words sink in.

"Yes, Rupert, that is why he is not here. He fell victim to a leaning that did him in."

"A 'leaning', Cardinal? Can a 'leaning' as you call it not ever be called 'love'? Or do we always use words that never really say what is supposed to be meant?" Rupert Hawkins asked Mugant.

Both men looked warily at the cleric.

"The Police report said that they did not believe it was some sort of traditional mugging," Hawkins responded, looking at his Italian counterpart. "My sources tell me he was hacked," he continued skeptically.

"Of course the police are not going to say anything that would jeopardize the Previn name, Rupert," the Canadian quietly said. "They will say the usual boilerplate, and that is all," Mugant answered, looking at both men. "And believe me when I tell you no one is going to tell you or me exactly what went on. I even asked McGeorge to join me last night for dinner, but he had other commitments—commitments of the flesh. What I don't understand is that he was in Washington according to Adrianna last night. When I spoke to him he was in Washington. But he had tendencies of the flesh that were different than yours, Rupert. It was something he struggled with."

Satisfied that his listeners believed him, Mugant continued. "Things in our effort to find Train are under control, Rupert," the Canadian Cardinal said, as he moved in the deep overstuffed sofa across from where Hawkins was seated. "Trust me. We know he's in New York."

"So far, we haven't the slightest notion of where this scientist is, or where the Cross is that he is supposed to have. And however it is that Previn died, we still have to deal with that as a current unknown."

"Previn, I've already explained," Mugant shot back. "You say, 'Supposed to have', when talking about Train and the Cross.

What do you mean, 'is supposed to have' the Cross? You are not doubting what I've said, are you?"

"Cardinal Mugant," Guillermo Schemmizzi interjected, "Rupert has in mind, I am sure, the incident at Avalon. Neither of us can see why the Mossad is helping one who has a Christian relic."

"We know the woman is Mossad," Mugant answered Schemmizzi, now rising from his chair. "The question is, why is a Mossad agent helping a genetic scientist, not why is the Mossad helping someone who has the Cross? isn't it gentlemen?" Mugant paused, and then said with a sneer, "Perhaps he is in love with the woman, and this explains his Mossad help."

"Not necessarily in that order," Hawkins responded. "The Mossad started helping him for some reason and then she, a Mossad, fell in love with him. The Mossad help may have come first, and that is what I don't understand. Adrianna hasn't been able to get much out of her, but she said it appeared the woman may have feelings for him."

"A trite story line about love, Rupert. This Train has the Cross of Christ as I stand here. We have committed ourselves and whatever it takes to stopping him. Besides, I too spoke with Adrianna and it appears that the woman never contacted any of her superiors. Most likely, Train is the only one not in our grasp who may know of our existence. Also, we're not even sure what he may have heard in Avalon. You all forget this."

"Where is Train, Cardinal Mugant? How do we know the Mossad are not ready to use him as a pawn in a way that leaves us exposed?"

"The Mossad know nothing about us. Remember, Train's a wanted man—a confirmed killer. Your concerns have no legitimacy," Mugant responded. "Years we have been together in this fight, and as it escalates we are more prepared than ever to do battle with the foe—now it appears you two have weakened. Is this true?"

"No." Schemmizzi firmly remarked.

"Cardinal Mugant, while you may encourage us to believe the Mossad is without knowledge of us, their organization is certainly sophisticated enough to gather information that could lead to us. After all, the woman got to Avalon," Hawkins added. "We need to weed them out. That's all we're implying."

The cleric nodded. "It will come to be. Previn's passing is only added motive to recover the Cross of Our Lord from this madman," Mugant answered, concerned that his control of the Crusade was in jeopardy. "We are all in this battle, and there is no turning back. Anyone who leaves the mission now puts his own past in danger of being exposed," Mugant went on. "We are renewed in our commitment, else the past we have all lived will rise up against us and destroy us."

Rising to exit the suite in the Saint Regis, Mugant took his walking stick and long coat in hand. "We will chat soon, gentlemen," the canon lawyer said. Closing the door behind him, and starting down the thickly carpeted hallway the prelate took out a white handkerchief to wipe his moist brow.

***

Later that afternoon a ground breaking news report was announced all over the world:

A team of unidentified New York geneticists, working for the little known Genetic Molecular, announced today that they have successfully cloned a human body. The surprising news comes after twelve prior attempts at cloning by this team, according to the company's press release, and appears to place Genetic Molecular at the forefront now of this field in genetics. Genetic Molecular will host a press conference at its headquarters, at 38 Prince Street in New York City at 9:00 a.m. tomorrow. Special police presence is expected outside the building tomorrow, given the recent spate of violence against genetics research facilities over the past year.

Rumors are circulating as to what the press conference will announce, and whether the scientists will claim that they have unlocked the mystery of cell cloning. It is not sure if Genetic Molecular will unveil the first cloned human being tomorrow, but rumors persist that this may occur. Skeptics already have remarked that the cloning is by a freak accident in the procedure the scientists performed, and cannot be duplicated. Others believe this is the first of many such clonings that will take place, and have praised this news "as the announcement of a new dawn."

***

"This is remarkable news, Dr. Cordesco," the Vatican's chief diplomat stoically said. "As soon as His Holiness finishes his breviary, I shall notify him of this."

The *peritus* nodded with concern to Cardinal de Salvoyar. "I am surprised the announcement comes out today," the Ursuline nun said."

"It obviously is timed for the Pope's address tomorrow, I am sure, Sister Pasquale. Probably to counter His Holiness' statement. Ah, here comes the Pontiff now."

"Your Holiness," the Vatican Secretary of State began, "CNN has just broadcast news that New York scientists claim to have cloned a human body."

The Pope, appearing taken aback, looked at his chief aide. "This is announced the day before my address at the United Nations?"

"Timed, Your Holiness, for maximum impact, for sure. There will be a 9:00 a.m. press conference tomorrow, according to the report, right here in Manhattan. Genetic Molecular is the name of the company. We will have an observer there, of course."

"We must share the press conference details with the religious leaders who met with us today, Fernando," the Pope said to his advisor.

"Anything they do not themselves obtain from the press conference we will of course share with them, Holiness," de Salvoyar responded.

"Of course, Cardinal Mugant will want that information, also."

"That will be taken care of, likewise, Your Holiness."

***

"You may now leave now, Monsignor Ford. I have to prepare some work for tomorrow," Anselm Mugant told his clerical attendant.

"Close the door as you leave, also."

The cleric did what he was asked, and left the room.

"There has just been issued a news report about a cloning breakthrough," Mugant began, reaching his contact at the other end of the phone call he had just made.

"I saw it myself, Cardinal," the listener replied.

"I want you to be there. This news sounds like the scientist went too far after all," Mugant voiced in palpable disgust. "He may tell all tomorrow that he in fact has the cross, for all we know."

"Train is not that stupid, Eminence. Who was the company making the announcement?"

"I never heard of them. They're called Genetic Molecular."

"Odd. It must be him."

"Train must be handled."

"I know. He may want the news of the Cross to get out since he knows he is a wanted man."

"He is not so reckless to show up at a press conference when he knows there is a nationwide manhunt out for him, Cardinal Mugant, don't you agree?"

"I want you to get to the press conference tomorrow. Get there early. You will have to be in disguise of course. There will be many there who will distract Train from you. Do what is necessary."

"9:00 a.m. tomorrow is the press conference, Cardinal. Maybe this will be Train's last press conference."

"If he does not make it through the conference, it will make retrieving the relic that much harder," Mugant answered his listener at the other end of the phone. "However, we cannot chance letting him through our hands when he will be a patsy for us at the press conference. Besides, I have someone on that."

"Obviously, Your Eminence. I will do what is necessary," he replied.

***

The crowded line of reporters trying to pass through the police barriers that were placed in front of the old industrial building in Soho were finding it increasingly difficult to make their way into the building. Conscious of any fanatics who may attempt to ambush the press conference, New York City's Finest were not taking any chances; bomb dogs and crowd control teams were out in numbers. A pre-confirmed list of reporters' names was the only way a person could enter the conference.

Along the concrete sidewalk and on the black asphalt streets nearby were scores of protesters carrying signs and voicing their right to protest. It was like a loud carnival.

The large open loft on the building's fourth floor was buzzing with journalists lucky enough to make it into the building. They were from every major media outlet that had a New York presence, talking about the scientific ramifications that the newly announced science would have on society. The conversations and debates pertaining to the ethical issues became as intense as an aroused hornet's nest not wanting to be disturbed. Reporters representing the extreme far right clashed with those journalists who took a more ideal approach towards the science of genetics research. According to press releases there was the startling announcement of a major breakthrough in the field of human cloning and this news had appeared out of nowhere in the newsrooms.

Television cameras were lined up in the front of the podium placed in the center of the room, as reporters vied for space closest to the podium.

"Who are these scientists?" was a common question asked, though well-established reports stated the identities of the scientist would not be announced until they took the stage, citing fears that their life, like that of many geneticists before them, would be endangered. The mysterious identity of these scientists brought to new light the unfortunate tragedies that plagued the genetic industry over this past last year.

Seated in the back corner of the large crowded room was a man with long blond hair sporting a goatee holding a note pad and a microphone. He watched carefully as the room continued to fill with newspersons there to cover the groundbreaking story.

The time was approaching 9:00 a.m., when a middle-aged woman who represented herself as being from Genetic Molecular said the news conference would begin shortly, and asked everyone to please take a seat.

Like clockwork, those who were standing found whatever nearby empty seats remained in the room. About fifteen people were left standing.

The anticipation of the news conference was growing, as

several more news crews entered the room, carrying their own set of cameras and lights.

Standing against the wall of the room was a bearded man of average weight and height wearing a baseball cap over his brown hair and sipping coffee. His eyes darted around the room in search of any familiar faces.

Light chatter resumed as the wait for the scientist continued.

It was now ten minutes past the hour, and most reporters were becoming anxious. After all, there was another major news story to cover in less than three hours: The Pope's speech on Life at the United Nations.

Heads began to turn towards the doorway, as people began to wonder where the scientists were. Minutes later, the same spokeswoman for Genetic Molecular took the podium and announced that the scientist would soon arrive with the news of their amazing scientific announcement, before she departed from the stage.

The commotion on the possibilities of human cloning began to grow once again in anticipation of the unidentified scientist pending arrival.

The blonde hair man turned in his chair, pensively wondering where the guest speakers were. His eyes noticed the familiar gaze of the fellow sporting the baseball cap nearby.

Their eyes locked on one another.

The clattering noise of the room was lost on both of them.

The standing man's eyes squinted, then he quickly moved passed the standing crowd and out of the room.

The seated blond hair reporter immediately rose from his seat. *Bastard!*

Racing down the building's emergency stairwell, the hat-wearing man turned and noticed the bizarre face chasing after him. "Train!"

Reaching the ground floor exit door, Max pushed the door open. It was locked. His heart surged, as clouds of the unthinkable exploded in his mind.

The pounding footsteps chasing him were closing. It appeared as if the lunatic was only a landing away.

He looked at the door to the basement, and then up to the stalker, who was carrying a long knife in his hand.

Opening the door to the basement, Max quickly descended into the musky darkness.

Moments behind him, the assassin followed. The creaking sound of the heavy man's foot moving on the wooden stairwell was threatening.

"Where are you?" screamed the voice as it moved in the darkness.

"Train, you'll never leave here alive!" he said as the door to the basement closed behind him.

Max moved into the cluttered basement searching for a place to hide. There were stacks of old furniture and boxes everywhere. He leaned up against a cold brick wall, his heart pounding in horror over whom he had scene. It was all coming back to him now—mutilated bodies, the explosion at the bridge in Rome, the Zurich mountains—everything.

The footsteps of the stalker moved closer. "You'll never leave here."

Max tightened his fists as he noticed the nearby shadow moving nearer.

The reflection of the blade caught his eye.

The full shadow of the lunatic was now less than five feet away.

"Train, you should have —"

Max sprang out of the darkness, and onto the heavyset killer, knocking him into a steel pole.

The powerful blow had little effect.

"You're dead, fool."

"How could you have —?"

"— shut up!" Luke Gartner screamed as he charged towards Max in the darkness.

Max dropped to the floor, as the knife fell towards him. Using his wounded leg, he kicked at Gartner's unbalanced legs, dropping him to the floor.

Max rolled on top of him, reaching for the knife.

Gartner's knee hit Max in his groin, causing great pain. He held Gartner's knife-wielding arm tight. "How could you do this?"

Gartner thrust the knife down towards Max. "You were the one who did this to yourself."

"You killed my wife!" he yelled back, his grip on Gartner's arm not moving.

Their faces were less than a foot apart.

"And your daughter!" Gartner snarled. "You're next," he said as he pushed down harder on the deadly blade that was inches away from Max's heart.

With his left hand, Max shoved his fingers deep into Gartner's nostrils, forcing his head backwards. Luke's hold on him was instantly compromised.

Pulling Gartner's hair away from him, Max broke free from the assailant's hold and immediately stood up. "What's wrong with you?" he said, paying careful attention to the knife still held in Gartner's hand.

The long blade reflected on the shadow filled light of the cavernous cellar. It was pointed at him.

"Me? You have no respect for life," came a wicked reply as Luke stood, ready to charge again.

"What are you talking about? Have you gone mad?"

"You're the one responsible."

"What are you talking about?"

"The sequencing—look where it led," Luke loathed.

"The sequencing?"

Luke slashed at Max, easily missing him.

"Without the DNA codes, there'd be no cloning. You allowed for so many innocent lives to die."

"You're out of your mind."

"It was you —" Luke screamed as he rushed towards Max again.

Max charged towards Luke.

Like two raging elephants their bodies brutally collided, as the knife wielded in Luke's hand began to descend towards Max. As it did, Max's left arm was raised towards Gartner's chest.

Upon impact, Max's arm glided up to Luke's neck, smashing into it with all of Max's body weight behind him.

The unexpected powerful blow wielded by Max hit Gartner's windpipe perfectly, causing him to fall backwards as the descending arch of the blade fell short.

Without hesitation, Max raced over to Luke and resoundly kicked him in the face repeatedly, causing Gartner to drop the knife.

Max instantly kicked the knife away, before hitting him again. "How could you have done this, you son-of-a-bitch? We were your friends!"

Curled up in a ball trying to protect himself from Max's continual pounding, Luke reached into his waistband and removed a small gun.

Turning on his side towards Train, the distinguishable *click* of the gun froze Max.

Max looked at the snub-nose barrel of the gun. "Why, Luke?" he asked defiantly.

"You will never understand, Max. Never," he whispered.

Max's eyes were riveted on the gun barrel. "And now you're going to kill me? You were like my brother, Luke. I loved you."

Luke glared at Max.

"Don't do it," Max pleaded.

"You don't understand, Max."

"Understand? You killed my family. You killed—"

"—stop it! Shut the hell up!"

"You were my friend."

"I know."

"Friends don't do what you did!"

"Stop!"

"Now you're going to kill me, too. Go ahead then – you've taken everything I ever lived for anyway."

"Go ahead."

"You think I wanted to do this?"

"Killing? Yeah – you have choices and decisions you must make regardless of how much life has you backed in a corner. You made your choices, Luke."

Luke's body trembled. "I no we were—"

"—friends – no, best friends, so I thought."

Luke raised the gun towards Max's chest.

"The bastard, Anselm Cardinal Mugant, he had me trapped. Max, I'm sorry," Luke said, as he quickly made the sign of the Cross, then placed the gun into his mouth, and pulled the trigger.

Sitting across from Rabbi Kohn in the safe house located on West 73rd Street, Max, trying to recover from Luke's betrayal and suicide, excused himself from the main parlor seating area and walked into the dining room. On the table were the ancient artifacts carefully laid out.

Max closed the large wooden partition doors behind him, and looked at the Holy remnants on the Cross. As the magnitude of Max's understanding that before him was the possible remains of Jesus – Max's Christ — a tear fell down his eye as he thought about his friend Luke, and the betrayal that was inflicted upon him grew. "He could have killed me, but you prevented that," he said aloud as he read the words etched on the *titulus*. He placed his fingers on his golden wedding band. "I'm not sure what I do next, but I know they are with you in Heaven. And I know you have protected me," he continued in a low, respectful voice.

Max was soon overcome with exhaustive waves of peaceful understanding. For him, Max, he believed he was touched by God, and perhaps there was a purpose after all to all he had to endure. Why else would Max have been selected to discover the apparent True Cross of Jesus?

The sound of the door's opening interrupted his thoughts. "Max, we need to leave."

"When will the insanity stop, Marty?"

"I wish I could tell you. One day we will find an answer, or a way to find peace. It's called faith, Max."

Max nodded. "I know."

***

EPILOGUE

***

Epilogue

His Holiness sat solemnly in a chair at the far end of a long wooden conference table deep in thought. Next to him in the United Nation's press room quietly sat the Secretary of State, along with the Mauritanian Cardinal Laurian Lisawara, Dean of the College of Cardinals, the Cardinal Prefect for the Evangelization of Nations, Gabriel Jayant, and Sister Pasquale Cordesco. Also seated in the room were the four surviving members of Anselm Mugant's Fifth Crusade.

Distinctly missing from the meeting was Cardinal Mugant, whose whereabouts were unknown.

It was nearing noon, and the world was expecting to see the live broadcast of the Pope's speech on Life.

Suddenly the door to the room opened, and in stepped Max Train, accompanied by Rabbi Kohn and two Federal Agents, there to escort the 'free' scientist. One of the Agents carried a battered cardboard box.

The Pope immediately stood as his solemn eyes looked at the beaten scientist. "My son, you have endured more than any man should," His Holiness said as he approached Max. "Rabbi, we are grateful to you and all of our brothers and sisters who have helped during this awful time," the Pontiff added as he looked at Rabbi Kohn.

Rabbi Marty Kohn nodded his head respectfully. "The time is amongst us Your Holiness for continued cooperation. Max Train represents this to all of us. His caring of people is universal."

The Pope moved closer to Max, his warm smile easing the tension in the room. "How are you feeling, Max?" he asked, as he placed his warm hand on Max's arm.

"Overwhelmed, Your Holiness," Max replied as he accepted the Popes extended greeting of friendship. "There have been many tests."

"I would be too, if I went through all you have these last two weeks."

"I have had a lot of fortuitous help, Your Holiness. Someone was looking out for me," Max replied, the touch of the gentle Pontiff's hand soothing his wounded heart. "Actually, there have been many wonderful people that have helped me."

"I am aware of this," he replied as he slowly let go of Max's hand. "We are tested many times in our life. Most of the time, we are not sure why He possess the challenges we must face, but I think we will all agree that there is reason for everything," The Pope softly spoke as he turned to the standing members of the Fifth Crusade. "It takes a great deal of courage to stand up to the mistakes one makes, Max. Our friends here are showing this courage by being here today with us," The Pope remarked, acknowledging the fact that each of the four industrialist had previously confessed their involvement with Anselm Mugant, who was no where to be found.

"I see."

"Max, you have been tested in ways I still cannot grasp. Each of us in our own way face daily challenges, regardless of our position in life. Sometimes the pain we must endure leaves us wondering what our own purpose in life is, and why His purpose subjects us to events or actions we would not choose. The suffering we must endure at times may allow each of us to question or deny our faith. This is understandable, for we are pragmatic, are we not?"

"I think so," Max replied.

"And so, our pragmatism tells us that we are responsible for many of our actions. We have choices in almost everything we do. Most of our choices are based upon the perspectives we hold. Our faith, in Him and each other is a critical aspect of how we make our decisions and choices."

Suddenly, the door opened again. A large burly man entered. Behind him Sara, with her long silken black hair, entered into the room.

Max's heart soared as he turned towards his protector. "Sara," he cried as he rushed towards her, wrapping his arms around the woman who never intentionally left his side. Tears of joy fell from his cheeks. "I was so worried."

She held him back with all the energy and love she had. "I thought I would never see you again," she cried.

"I love you," Max whispered.

"I love you, too," she said holding him tighter. "Don't ever disappear on me again."

"I never will. Never."

Soon turning to The Pope, Max looked into the Pontiff's gentle blue eyes. "These are the items I discovered, Your Holiness.

They do not belong to me."

The Pope nodded as he looked at the box. "If they are part of the True Cross He died on, then they belong to the world."

"Is there a way to know?" Cardinal Lisawara asked.

"Max?" the Pope asked, turning from the Dean of the College of Cardinals. "Is there a way to know?"

Max Train, thirteen years removed from discovering the mysterious blueprint of Man's bodily structure, the DNA sequencing codes, of which all people were composed, looked at each person carefully in the room.

Each person there looked at him with bated breath, as they each individually wondered if the remains could be identified as those of Jesus.

"Well?" asked Marty.

"More tests should be done to determine the age of the remnants; however, I have no reason to believe they're not from the time of Jesus."

Everyone stayed quiet.

"The markings—the bloodstains and the hair strands, I suspect are human. They too should be tested to determine their age and if indeed they are human."

Max looked quickly at everyone once again before continuing.

"But there is nothing that I am aware of that we can compare these items with. I think it is up to each person to determine in their heart who died on this Cross, and in their own faith, determine what that means to them."

"Max?" voiced the Pope.

"I believe it is a matter of faith," Max replied as he smiled warmly to the Pontiff, and then to the Rabbi. "Like all things, our perceptions and understandings are really a matter of faith."

The room remained silent as the Pope put his gentle hand on Max before turning his attention to Sara. "Sara, I believe you're anxious to say hello to another," the Pontiff said, as his eyes glimmered.

Sara looked at him warmly, as she began to smile.

"Go ahead," he nodded.

Sara hesitated.

"Go ahead."

Sara turned to the table and noticed Adrianna Corvoso de Sa. She nodded indifferently. Then with open arms she rushed towards the Pope's special advisor.

"Sister," the two blue-eyed siblings said hugging each other tightly to the amazement of everyone in the room but The Pope and Rabbi Kohn.

The Pope shook the Rabbi's hand, and then turned towards the doorway to the podium where he was to deliver his address.

The leaders of Christianity joined him as he walked towards the stage. Those that were in attendance in the pressroom followed nearby. Max held Sara's hand as Rabbi Kohn escorted his niece Sister Pasquale.

Silence fell on the UN members as the leader of the Catholic Church slowly walked into the auditorium and stood behind the podium. The green lights above the television camera broadcasting this historic address were lit. Reaching the podium, behind which was the large logo of the United Nations, the Pope began his address.

"Too long and too often conflict and hate among religions and cultures have been the weapons used to resolve disputes among believers and non-believers in the world. Sometimes the conflict has been within one religion, at other moments religion has brought arms against another people."

The Pope looked at those seated before him.

"The conflict," he went on "has resolved nothing.

"Religion and science have fought in the past, the fruit bitter, the ends never reached, the condition of humanity never bettered by the battles waged.

"Let today be a new day for man. Let the conflict end."

The members seated in their chairs, representing hundreds of differing and converging interests, skilled in negotiation and in persuasion, spontaneously applauded the Pope's call.

"We have before us," he continued once the applause ceased, "the solemn imperative to better man both spiritually and physically. Rather than be in conflict with each other, science and religion should co-operate in this endeavor to which man has been called. As Truth is one, so too can science and religion reach unity and singleness of understanding. Improving the physical condition of the person is the goal of medical science. But it cannot come about without respecting the person. But respect for the person, which religion preaches, involves of its very self-bettering the physical condition of man. Healing the body is part of preparing the soul for the Vision that brings every restless heart to final peace.

"We support research on stem cells of post natal origin as a sound and ethical approach to achieve tissue transplantation and cell therapy that may benefit humanity. Science has led the way where forms of therapeutic cell intervention would not involve the use of cloning or embryonic cells, but would cultivate stem cells taken from adults. We believe scientists should direct their concentration in this area, and by doing so, continue to respect the dignity of each person regardless of the age of the individual. This is in accordance with the ethical oaths that physicians undertake when they promise to serve mankind."

The attendants in the large auditorium stood in applause.

The Pope paused before he went on, looking, it appeared at each member before him one by one.

"The world has been through much this past year as scientists seeking the new and bold road of genetics to human healing have been killed, all, it appears, in the name of a god that religion neither confesses nor knows.

"The human body is not a collection of materials with which science can indiscriminately experiment to promote the body's longevity or its well-being. The civilized world has accepted safeguards in the laboratory to ensure that the body is not abused, nor exploited. It has also said that you must not kill.

"One scientist with whom I have just met has suffered dearly and incalculably from the raw misunderstanding of his intent and motives. Faced with a remarkable discovery in the hills near where Jesus of Nazareth we believe was crucified, this scientist became the sudden object of a chase that went from Jerusalem to Rome, through Italy, across the continent to England and finally here to the United States. He had with him what may be the True Cross of Christ.

A loud commotion in the auditorium was silenced as the Pope soon continued.

"But he was a geneticist. So, would this scientist take this relic he found and would he, horror of all, seek to bring Christ back by cloning physical remnants on the Cross?

"No one knows if what is on this Cross is any part of the Body of God," the Pontiff paused. Turning to his right, he nodded towards Max.

Max Train, the no longer wanted "fugitive", walked onto the stage accompanied by Sara. In his hand he carried the carefully wrapped ancient relics he discovered in Jerusalem. Unfolding

them on a nearby table, he removed the items and lifted the *titulus*.
Sara lifted the *patibulum* for all to see.

The audience of Ambassadors from every nation in the
world was silent. In the crowd a black suited figure sat watching
Train, as his long index finger traced a never forgotten facial scar.

The Pope looked at the two and then to his fellow Christian
leaders who now stood nearby on the stage. "No one knows if the
Cross found is the Cross on which Christ died. The Church has a
tradition that the Cross was found long ago.

"Christ, however, does not come back by cloning His bodily remains, if they do exist, and if they were ever recovered from a
two thousand year old instrument of murder and brutality. We do
not know if science could effect such a return so many centuries
later. Of equal importance is that though there appears to be human
markings on these items we will never know for sure who they
belong to. It is a matter of faith each person must resolve on their
own. Belief in Jesus, and belief in God, is not only a matter of Faith
but also a matter of tradition in our Faith.

"What we do believe, however, is that Christ comes back to
the world by each person living out His teachings in the way understood and believed by each heart in its own way. It is the universal acceptance of each of us living on this earth in a respectful and
caring way that His teachings, along with the great teachings of all
through the years that profess peace and human dignity, that universal faith and trust in one another will flourish and grow. In doing
so, this world which we all share will become one in peace.

"Science and religion, man and all the religions of mankind,
in cooperation with each other towards the understanding that raises both science and religion to a higher plane in the service of man
towards his ultimate calling: this is the new day of man in the twen-
ty-first century. It is a day closer to man's ultimate destiny. It is
this day.

"As for this discovery there is little against which to compare the findings left behind on it. From what I have been told, the
artifacts are from the time of Jesus. The leaders of the Christian
faith along with our dear friends in Israel," the Pope continued,
nodding to the two Ambassadors seated in the auditorium from
Israel, "will soon develop a team of scientists who will study the
age of the artifacts in front of the world to see. However, it is up to
each and every person to hold onto their faith—for the essence of
faith is believing in Him and each other. The essence of life is to

respect life, which I may point out, is part of faith. It is through the acceptance of the faith we may each hold, as I said earlier, that we may accept who may have died on this Cross."

After the well-received address at the United Nations, the Pope reconvened with leaders of various faiths, including a congregation of Jewish leaders, to continue discussing the issues of stem cell research.

Hernando Mühlor, Guillermo Schemmizzi, Rupert Hawkins, and Adrian Corvoso de Sa were meeting with the Ambassadors from their respective nations discussing most of their hidden secrets and determining how best to use their resources to benefit mankind. None of the Crusaders mentioned how deep their knowledge of Mugant's intentions to destroy genetic labs ran, though they each cited Mugant's adamant position on genetic research. Penalties would be paid by the Crusaders to those who their families had taken from, especially Mühlor Industries, whose family's World War Two activities were obvious. Attending this large meeting was the Holy See's Secretary of State who oversaw the peaceful negotiations.

Anselm Mugant's disappearance would have to be dealt with another day.

The identity of the killer found in the Mossad house, *The Scorpion*, was never made public. Several government officials representing separate nations kept to themselves who he actually was and their intimate knowledge of him.

Luke Gartner would be buried in upstate New York, alongside the body of his wife Eileen, whose remains would be flown into New York shortly. The body of John Muir had been discovered just hours earlier in Jerusalem. Syracuse University was intending to hold a special memorial for both lost students Lynn Johnson and John Muir.

"Well, what would you like to do?" asked the free man.

Brilliant blue eyes, now rested after the long day, looked at Max as they walked in Sheep's Meadow in Central Park. "All I know is I want to spend these days with you."

Max looked at Sara; a broad smile filled his glowing face as his heart opened. "So do I."

***

PLEASE VISIT THE CLONING CHRIST WEBSITE AT

WWW.CLONINGCHRIST.COM

AND FEEL FREE TO LEAVE YOUR COMMENTS FOR

AUTHOR'S PETER SENESE AND ROBERT GEIS.

F SEN
Senese, Peter
Cloning Christ : a
challenge of science and
LIB Free text.

Boyd County Public Library